Those Close Beside Me

Bruce Parkinson Spang

Eliot, T.S. "Four Quartets." *The Complete Poems and Plays: 1909-1950*, New York: Harcourt, Brace and Company, 1958.

Published by Piscataqua Press
an imprint of RiverRun Bookstore
32 Daniel Street
Portsmouth NH 03801

ISBN: 978-1-944393-89-2

Dedication

To my husband Myles Rightmire for the life we live together; to Erling Duus for his vision of America as a place where people value democracy, where the have-nots can be heard and seen; and to Don Beisswenger for his right words at the right time. To many other real-life figures such as Reverend James Lawson, Baxter Bryant, Dean Walter Harrelson, Father Flye, and Marie Cirillo, I owe a great deal for their wise and compassionate counsel. I hope that, as much as I can, I was faithful to their spirit. Much of this novel is fictionalized. But it reflects, as best as I could, the spirit of the times and those I knew. The people in Cross Creek aren't meant to reflect any one family or person, but rather to represent the abiding and courageous spirit of the people whom I admired and who taught me much more about religion, faith, and trust than I ever learned in a textbook. But I would be remiss in not mentioning two families in Rose's Creek who changed my life: the Metzlers and Kings. In particular, I'm forever grateful to Dorothy, her daughter Lois and her son Bobby, who I loved as a second family. And Bonny King and her children who welcomed me as part of their family. I'm indebted to Nancy McDaniel, Steve Putnam, John Michael Albert, Alice Persons, Dick Schmidt, and John Himmelheber for their counsel, suggestions, and wise editing. I'm grateful to Kellsey Metzger for her editorial suggestions and dedication to making this book what it is.

The Waking

I wake to sleep, and take my waking slow.
I feel my fate in what I cannot fear.
I learn by going where I have to go.

We think by feeling. What is there to know?
I hear my being dance from ear to ear.
I wake to sleep, and take my waking slow.

Of those so close beside me, which are you?
God bless the Ground! I shall walk softly there,
And learn by going where I have to go.

Light takes the Tree; but who can tell us how?
The lowly worm climbs up a winding stair;
I wake to sleep, and take my waking slow.

Great Nature has another thing to do
To you and me, so take the lively air,
And, lovely, learn by going where to go.

This shaking keeps me steady. I should know.
What falls away is always. And is near.
I wake to sleep, and take my waking slow.

Theodore Roethke

PART I

I. In order to possess what you do not possess
   You must go by the way of dispossession.
   T.S. Eliot, "Four Quartets"

PART II

Although the word is common to all, most men live
   as if each had a private wisdom.
   T.S. Eliot, "Four Quartets"

PART III

What might have been and what has been
Point to one end, which is always present.
T.S. Eliot, "Four Quartets"

Part IV

Neither flesh nor fleshless;
Neither from nor towards; at the still point, there the dance is.
T.S. Eliot, "Four Quartets"

Part V

Footfalls each in the memory
Down the passage which did not take
Toward the door we never opened...
T.S. Eliot, "Four Quartets,"

Part VI

What might have been and what has been
Point to one end, which is always present.
T.S. Eliot, "Four Quartets"

PART I

In order to possess what you do not possess

You must go by the way of dispossession.

T.S. Eliot, "Four Quartets"

Taking Leave

My father wanted a winding staircase in his house. He must have considered it a statement of elegance from a bygone era when ladies walked down them in a grand manner and gentlemen took them by the arm and led them into a ballroom. Trouble was there were no ladies on the second floor. Only me. My bedroom, first on the left, was at the top of the stairs, tucked away from my parents on the first floor.

I woke late, nearly nine o'clock, sat on the edge of my bed, and stared at a gray squirrel in the oak tree. Quite acrobatic, he leapt from one branch to another. Most likely it never occurred to him that he might fall. He perched on one branch and looked at me. He sat upright, his front paws in front of him, almost as if he was coaching me to applaud. He had a right to be pleased with himself. He knew what he was doing. I wished I had his assurance. I had many doubts. Maybe everyone did. But in my case, it was a preoccupation. I'd spend hours second guessing what I'd done. "Should I have," "if I only was," and "what if I'd" were regularly scheduled in my brain.

The squirrel scampered off. I rubbed my face. Time to get moving.

After a shower, I combed my hair. At the hairline on the left side, a cowlick would rise, untamed, and point in the opposite direction. Dab it with water, smack it down—nothing worked. It had a mind of its own. That's how my sex life had been. Other guys had told me I was attractive. "Geez, you could have *any* girl." In the mirror, I'd see a regular guy, clean shaven, nice features. I'd tell him, "Hey, go for it. Ask her out." But I wasn't interested in girls. They scared me. I was more attracted to guys. It's not something I wanted to admit to anyone, least of all myself. My body didn't behave as it should. When I'd least expect it, I'd get aroused—the young clerk measuring the inseam of my pants, a buddy's knee pressing against mine at a pep rally, the lone boy stripping off his swim suit in the changing room—and have to hide my erection. Sometimes the veneer of who I appeared to be and wanted to be was so thick it was impossible to peel it off and expose the truth that lay inside. I was like those insects encased in amber. I could see out at the world around me but always felt trapped in a body that wasn't my own.

I couldn't get away from that trapped feeling. It just was. But I could get

1

away from my parents' house. That was a start. I was leaving for graduate school.

Who knew where that would take me? I had my apprehensions, suitcases full of them. Reading was a chore for me. In third grade, Mrs. Dowling noticed I read right to left. Sentences started with objects and like a car backing up, bumped into the predicate, and then crashed into the subject. Even now, if I hurried, my eyes went in reverse and I'd slam into the wrong word. I'd taken four speed-reading courses, two the previous summer. I learned how to skim and to preview a text. But the truth was I liked reading in the slow lane and rolling the words over my tongue. At Vanderbilt, I'd have to read in the fast lane.

But at least I wasn't in a body bag on a tarmac in Saigon—not like Tom Duffner, my high school classmate and the best, quickest running back on our football team who'd been in a hurry to serve his country and was the first in our class to die in Vietnam. His head was blown off by a sniper.

By luck, and the recommendation of a college professor, I applied to Vanderbilt Divinity School, was accepted, got my 4-D deferment, and, for at least two years, put off military service. I didn't question that decision. I bade the squirrel goodbye, dressed, and gobbled a bowl of Raisin Bran—only five raisins, hard as rocks, in it.

My mom was out in the back-garden picking roses to set in a bowl by the kitchen window. I piled my dishes in the sink, brought my suitcase downstairs and set it by the front door where the scent would fill the foyer.

I walked through the living room, slid open the sliding glass doors, and stood on the back porch. I gazed at the garden, the last of the Shasta daisies, their white faces straining up to catch the early sun. My mother waved at me.

"Lovely day," she called out.

"Good day to drive," I said.

I'd already packed—my records, Motorola record player, clothes, and books in the trunk of the new Volvo. It was a graduation gift from my father, a practical car, one that would last or, at least, that's what I thought. Dad preferred an American car, a Mustang. Too flashy for me, but money was no object for him. "Get a classy car," he said.

I drove one. "See, it's powerful. And a girl magnet," he said.

"Sure," I thought. "That's all I need." I settled on the Volvo sedan, four-door with a trunk that could hold an elephant.

Dad was off to work. As the Vice-President of the Motorola Corporation, he was always at work when he wasn't playing golf. That made it easy to leave. No lectures about "work before pleasure." No pressure to date more, find a good girl, one with money. "If you have a choice," he'd admonish me. "Find one with money, lots of it."

All I needed to do was say goodbye to my mom. When she came back from the garden, she fussed in the kitchen and put dishes away. They clanked angrily as if they didn't want to be where she wanted them to be.

She was worried I'd never come back. She was right to worry. Home no longer felt like home to me. I had no other home, no place I could say, "I belong here." I was a nomad about to head off with no compass, no map, and that trunk full of "what ifs." I had at least a year, maybe two, at graduate school to figure myself out. Something was bound to happen.

"Mom," I called out after checking my room one more time, picking up a journal, and a golf cap, "I'm going."

She stepped out of the kitchen, drying her hands on a dish towel, her face drawn, the crow's-feet at her eyes distinct.

"Oh, honey," she said, reaching out to hug me, "Are you *sure* this is right for you?"

Sure, I thought, how could I be sure? I was never sure of anything.

I hugged her. Her hair, frosted but not overdone, quite understated with a few waves of light blond hair in her natural brunette color—a plain style that easily shook back into shape after a swim or round of golf— smelled clean as if it had just been washed. She looked up at me, the squint in her eyes giving away her fear. She'd been crying but managed to wipe the tears away.

"It's fine. I gotta do what I gotta do," I said, smiling. I picked up the suitcase, gripping it tightly in my hand.

She shook her head and smiled weakly.

"Say goodbye to Dad," I said.

"Your dad is proud of you," she said, stepping back. "You know that."

I suppose he was, but that wasn't what I felt. I wanted to get as far away from his expectations as I could. Five hundred miles seemed right. No more his insistence I find a job with his corporate friends. No more his queries about my friends who had been protesting the Chicago Democratic Convention: Why *are* they protesting? Who *do* they think they are? Do they *realize* Communists support these protests? Are *you* in contact with them? It was as if J. Edgar Hoover were scrutinizing me. Besides giving me the third degree, he was nosy. When I was at work one day, he paged through my journal. I could tell because I left it in a certain place on my dresser with a pen on a page. When I returned, the pen was on the wrong page. The journal had been moved to the opposite side. The journal had my thoughts about the war that I opposed, and about the social injustice that I saw among my father's friends. At the club, "Negro staff" (as he called them) only worked in the kitchen, never as waiters in the dining room. I hid the journal under my bed, buried in underwear. I'd had enough of him. I suspected he'd had enough of me.

My mother acted as if everything was fine between us. That was her role. Our being happy was a religion to her.

"Yeah, mom, I know," I said. "It's just he has strange ways of showing it."

"But he is, you know he is."

"Sure."

She sighed and brushed something off my sweater. "I'm off," I said. She nodded and walked out with me and stood by the front door, the towel knotted in her hands. When I pulled out of the driveway, past the chokecherries and hawthorn and oak, I let up on the accelerator. A squirrel scampered across the driveway and leapt into a tree. He looked over his shoulder as if to say, "This is fun. Give it a try." Another time, I thought. My mother waved. I honked the horn and waved back. I turned onto Swan Lake Drive, drove down Butterfield Road to the East-West Tollway and, from there, on Interstate 65, headed south to Nashville, Tennessee.

The Wounded

I drove south, past Gary, Indiana. The steel mills had a foul, acrid odor like burnt tires. My father's friends called it "the smell of money." If it was the smell of money, it was dirty money. I closed the windows and sped by the belching smokestacks.

The road turned south and inland toward quaint villages, yellow cornfields of southern Indiana, and fresh air.

I drove by Greenview where I had gone to Ashbury University. Three months ago, my friends, one after another, said their goodbyes and headed off into their new lives. In 1968, some went on the campaign trail with their respective candidates—Kennedy, McCarthy or Rockefeller—and some, later in the summer, drove to Chicago, to protest the war at the Democratic convention.

Paul, the most politically active of my friends, had been beaten and arrested in Chicago. My father suspected he was a communist. "How come your friend," he'd ask, "is involved with those radicals?" I didn't explain because to do so I'd have to admit I wished I was with him. Another "what if." I wanted to be on the streets with Paul. But if I had, my father would have cut me off. I couldn't do that.

After the convention, Paul and I had sat at the terminal at O'Hare to wait for his plane. His eyes, both blackened like he'd been pounded for fifteen rounds, scared me. It wasn't their yellowish-purple hue. It was the look *in* them. They appeared wild, dangerous as if he might attack at any moment.

While we were waiting for his flight back to New York, he kept folding and unfolding his hands and glancing in front and back of him as if he expected someone to accost him and take him away.

"You don't know what it was like," he said. "The cops came at us, a phalanx of them, moving without a word—all you could hear was their boots—so at first we didn't know what to think. They kept marching at us. No expression on their faces. Just doing their job. Maybe they were just going to herd us down the street, we thought, block us off, keep us from the convention."

At first, he spoke in a whisper. He glanced around him, making sure no one overheard him. He tapped me on the arm. His voice became, more strident, frightened.

"But without warning, they charged and their boots—steel-toed—and clubs, they were on us, hitting, kicking, bashing at us. There was no getting away. I kept thinking, 'Is this America?' and it didn't stop. It's like they wanted to *kill* us. It's like *we were* the enemy. Like we were Vietcong. An arm rose. I ducked my head—you know duck and cover—but it was no use. He slammed his baton at me. I thought I was gonna die."

I put my hand on his shoulder, but he pulled it back, wincing.

"Don't. It hurts."

"I'm sorry," I said.

"Sorry," he laughed. "Sorry? Hey. Fuck that, man. *Get mad.*"

"Mad?" I said.

"Damn right. This *is* a fuckin' revolution. We *need* to fight back. They don't care. No one cares. It's fucked up. Totally fucked."

His face flushed, his fists clenched, and his jaw gripped tightly; he seemed as if at any moment, he might explode.

"Paul, it's not that bad," I said. "It's *really* not that bad."

I knew I'd said the wrong thing the minute the words came out of my mouth. They were words my mother would say to mollify me when I'd get banged up at football practice. He winced as if he'd been slapped, stood up and shouted, "Bullshit! You don't know. How can you say that when you sat in your daddy's plush house watching TV? It's not the same. You *don't* understand how it is."

"Maybe I..."

"I met Black Panthers—you know who they are?"

"Of course, Huey Newton and..."

"Not really, but anyway, the Chicago police are harassing them. Fred Hampton, their chairman, wants to form a Rainbow Coalition to support the revolution. He's a good man. Really good man. Charismatic. Wants food and education for the poor. And the pigs beat them. Death threats. It's madness. You don't know," he said, staring at me.

"Maybe I don't."

"You don't. Trust me. You don't have a clue." His voice pitched higher. "It's so FUCKED UP." He slammed his fist into a pillar.

A couple sitting near us frowned and pulled back. The husband shielded his wife from Paul who glared at them.

"Dumb fuckin' bastards," he muttered.

I grabbed his arm. "Let's take a walk."

"Get your fuckin' hands off me," he sneered between his teeth and lurched back, nearly falling down. I had no idea what to say and gazed at the couple apologetically. The man leaned over the woman, who clutched her purse to her chest. He whispered to her, patting her hand. An attendant at the airline gate came toward us.

"I better go," I said, stepping a few feet from him. I had to admit, he frightened me too.

He wiped his hand across his face and gently pummeled his mouth with a loose fist. "Fuck, fuck, fuck." His eyes, lowered but focused on me, glistened. "Don't go!" he said. He reached out to me and pulled me close to him. "Oh, fuck man...I'm ..."

"Is there something wrong here?" a petite attendant in a blue uniform asked. Wordless, we ogled her. With a bright agreeable face and sensuous lips, she was quite attractive in the conventional way airlines want employees to look: every hair in place and cherry lipstick glistening on her lips. I couldn't tell if Paul was taken or appalled by her. With her tiny blue cap, perched and pinned atop her puffed-up hair, she looked absurd.

I burst out laughing.

"Excuse me?" she said, tilting her head sideways.

"Nothing," I said, putting my hand to my mouth. "No, we're fine," I responded. She stood for a moment, her hands clasped in front of her. "Fine," I repeated, more severely. She smiled back at me, gave a quick glance at Paul, who also grinned and, in reaction to her querulous look, ducked his head and shuffled behind the pillar. She strode back to the gate, glancing over her shoulder at us several times.

Leaning against me, his arm around my shoulder, Paul said, "Did you see the hat?"

"Miss Potato Head," I said. He laughed and for a moment it seemed the ghastly spell had been broken. His eyes lightened as if someone had flipped on a switch. The pall that had been draped over him lifted. He was back to his old self. Then, he squeezed me by the arm so hard it hurt. His face drooped. A mask of terror came across him so suddenly it felt as if he'd become another person. His eyes winced, his mouth drew in a thin, taut line. "Shit, man, I'm scared, really scared. I thought they'd kill me and there was nothing, *nothing* I could do." His eyes were glassy. Tears welled up and leaked over his cheeks. I held him and felt like crying too, crying for not being there with him, crying for not understanding what was happening in Chicago, crying for all the "what ifs" that got in my way, crying for not having enough courage to defy my dad, for being a wimp, for being the good, obedient son.

The attendant announced the boarding of his plane. He sighed and put his arms around me. He hugged me tight against his body, the whole of me against him. We embraced for what seemed like minutes. The attendant called for those who were in need of help to go first. Paul should be, I thought, among them. The couple by us whispered to one another and shook their heads. I didn't care. I wanted to be there in whatever way I could for him. If that meant holding onto him for as long as he needed me to, that was fine. They could think what they wanted to think. Fags. Queers. To hell with them.

"I'll be in touch," he said. His hand loosely trailed down my arm. "I'll be all right. Don't worry."

"Call," I said. He nodded and walked down the corridor toward his plane and waved, his arm barely reaching waist high, a grimace gripping his face.

I haven't heard from him since then. Not a word.

And the other classmates? They slipped into the folds of their families, demands of work, or rigors of military service. Some left their families just as I was going to go to a place they'd never lived. It seemed as if all of us who had lived through the spring and summer of 1968, with the assassination of Dr. Martin Luther King and Senator Robert Kennedy and who'd seen the country being ripped apart, wanted to slip out of history and retreat into unassailable niches. We burrowed into them as squirrels in the winter hid away from the cold until the worst was over.

Crossing Over

A student orientation for new Vanderbilt Divinity School students was on Wednesday. Right after it, I had to attend training for dorm advisors. It was on Thursday. Except for stopping for gas and a coffee, I drove straight to Nashville. Midday, I crossed into Kentucky, over the bridge that spanned the Ohio River. I'd read how slaves tried to cross it during the era of slavery to get to free states. I was entering enemy territory. I'd seen images of students hosed against cement buildings in Birmingham. Freedom riders' buses were burned with them on it. Voting rights advocates were murdered and buried in an earthen dam.

My only real experience in the South had been a road trip I'd taken with my mom in 1954. We drove to St. Petersburg, Florida where we spent half a year on a vacation paid for by my dad's company. While my father got an abbreviated MBA, we drove our red Ford station wagon south. In the same small roads in Illinois and Indiana as I had driven—well before the interstate highway system was completed—we crossed over the Ohio River into Kentucky and into the deep South. A flood that year gutted many of the main roads in Georgia and Alabama. We made detours, taking country roads, often unpaved. The rundown shacks, the children, half-naked in the dirt yards, and the chickens in the front yard fascinated me. The Spanish moss's grey beards hung from mammoth oaks. I'd never been outside the suburbs. Rusted-out jalopies were heaped under trees; houses bent over with the weight of years; windows gaped with white curtains flapping out. People lounging on porches, fanned themselves. Red clouds of dust from our car settled on shrubs, chickens, and people on the porch. Mother told me to sleep, but I couldn't. This strange world with yards so different from mine fascinated me. In our neighborhood, lawns were mowed, every one of them. Gardens were well kept. People stayed inside air-conditioned homes. Nothing seemed out of place. And nothing was.

Mother stopped only at gas stations. Even there, she rushed me to the bathrooms. She showed me which to use: 'White only.' Not the one marked 'Colored.' She didn't talk with anyone. That was entirely unlike her: she loved to make small talk with anyone—clerks, waitresses, car attendants. She seemed, looking back on it, frightened, worried that she (or my brother and I)

9

might make a wrong move, might violate some prohibition. The attendants in bib overalls eyed us warily. I also felt afraid. There were so many choices about where to go. Even the drinking fountains had signs over them—"Colored," "White"—not five feet from one another.

When I asked why we couldn't go in a "Colored" bathroom, she snapped, "It's unsanitary," shooed us to the car, and sped on as if she were fleeing. I guess she was—fleeing from a way of life that she wanted no part of. For a woman who'd grown up in a small town on Long Island, New York, there were few, if any blacks. Prejudice, if there was any, was never part of her upbringing. "Colored people" lived far from her. Her fears of the south were greater than I knew, and probably led her to ask me before I left, "Are you *sure* this is right?"

Since that was my last time I'd been in the south, I wasn't sure myself. But I kept on driving.

By late afternoon, I'd crossed the Tennessee state line. From the ridge above Nashville, its skyline was visible in the river valley. The interstate was built like a rollercoaster into the hillside. For several miles, the highway tilted sideways toward the Cumberland River and obscured the view of the city. After a long curve, several buildings like tips of fingers came into view. Below them, on either side of the hill, there were other buildings and shabby houses that lined the river bank. At the bottom, one bridge spanned the river.

I drove across it onto Gay Street and from there, followed Commercial Street to Route 70 and Broadway. On either side of it, lining the street, were country music and adult bookstores. Broadway headed up a hill. The further it was from downtown, the more upscale the buildings became. The verdant campus of Vanderbilt University sprawled across a hillside.

Once parked, I raced to the admission building before it closed for the day. It was brutally hot. Sweat drenched my shirt.

The looming façade of the Divinity School, the campus with its brick dorms and classroom buildings, as well as the statue of whiskered Cornelius Vanderbilt hit me with a realization: this was my new life.

A kind lady with a distinct southern accent helped me. "Here you are, my dear," she said. "My, get yourself a bottle of water. It's horrid out there." I thanked her for the packet and gazed up at the paintings of deans in their ministerial robes. I had no intention of being a minister. Religion in my family happened on special occasions: Easter and the Christmas Eve candlelight service. Mom loved the candles. As a rule, if the call of golf was weighed against the call of God on a Sunday morning, we'd be on the first tee. I had no religion, no interest in the church, and no real faith in God.

I worried about my lack of faith. What if some believer—or professors— exposed me for a fake? Or, even worse, they wanted to convert me? Sure, I could say I was an atheist. That would give them pause. And it was true. God never interested me. I couldn't get my head around the idea of God, a being who's out there, hovering, invisible, hearing everything we say, knowing everything we do. I wanted to ask people who believed in Him, "What's He like?" Maybe they could tell me.

But, maybe, as a divinity student, you weren't expected to believe in God. It wasn't like signing a loyalty pledge as you had to do when enlisting in the army. Besides, there might be others like me—ones who came to graduate school to avoid the draft and not bent on making a career out of it.

My other "what if" hit me as I looked at the book lists for my classes. What if the workload crushed me? I'd have to head back to Illinois, my tail between my legs, to face enlistment and serve in a war I opposed.

With packet and keys in hand, I headed to the Bishop dorm complex. The walkway to the dorm had magnolia trees with blossoms the size of soccer balls. I lugged my books, record player, and clothing up to a small third floor dorm room.

I unlocked the door—thick, blond, heavy. It swung open. Three feet from it, a bed jutted out into the room. A couch during the day. Across from it, a closet with three wire hangers. Next to it, inserted in the wall, a desk. By it, a cabinet with five drawers. It, too, built into the wall. Above it, a counter with a mirror. Facing the door, a window that revealed an expansive lawn and, beyond it, the law school. Two hundred yards from it, the Divinity School.

The books on shelves, clothes in drawers, jackets on hangers, this space was now mine.

I played Simon and Garfunkel's new album "Bridge over Troubled Water." Dizzy from the long drive, I sipped a Coke.

When you're weary
Feeling small
When tears are in your eyes
I will dry them all

I'm on your side
When times get rough
And friends just can't be found
Like a bridge over troubled water

I'd crossed two rivers into a new life. I had no friends. The room was small. I'd left my old self, or parts of it, behind. My whole body, from my neck to my feet, felt sad.

I thought of Tom, a fraternity buddy, who along with his boyfriend Tim was working with the Rockefeller campaign. They'd moved to Greenwich Village. Tom had told me he was homosexual. It scared the hell out of me. For all the years I'd known him, I thought I was the weird one. I never told him, not even when he told me about his boyfriend, how I felt attracted to him. I wasn't about to let on. I had an image and it was the only one I knew: the straight guy. And maybe I was straight. The more I thought about it, the longer I pretended to be what I wanted to be, the more it seemed to be true. Or, if not true, at least something I could accept in myself.

Tom told me Paul had joined an antiwar group—not sure of its name—and organized protests at Nixon's and Humphrey's rallies. True to his word, a revolutionary.

My room was the size of my mother's walk-in closet. Yet here I was. My days of ease at Ashbury with my old friends when I could rise when I chose and stay up as late as I wanted were gone. The record played on. The window was open. A breeze invited itself in.

Orientation

The retreat for new students was housed at a church camp in the woods. New arrivals registered at a lodge. When we entered, a stout woman at a table asked our name; we gave it, and she smiled and said in a thick southern accent, *Mr. Follett, yes, here it is, honey.* We were handed a packet and told to fill out a name tag. We milled around. Some headed to a table with sodas on ice. Some sat in folding chairs, packet in hand, perusing it. Some greeted faculty who mingled among us, asking our names, where we were from, *Illinois, yes, I know it well.*

Soon, as more arrived, the volubility in the room increased. People joined in groups of two or three that broke apart and came together and talked of nothing of substance, nothing of interest, nothing at all. I met a guy from Tennessee, a Baptist, *Southern Baptist,* he pointed out, and a guy from California, a hippie, who seemed to be stoned, and a girl from New Jersey, a revolutionary. Groups gathered and dispersed, *Excuse me, I need to talk with...* or *I think I'll get a soda...*I withdrew to a chair by a window to watch them mix, doing what I should be doing, but, happily, what I gave up doing. I waited for someone to tell us to stop, to be seated, and for the program to begin.

The trees had the faintest yellow tinge, well behind the maples in Illinois.

Several long-haired hippies with beads in their hair, purple vests and sandals, looked remarkably like Jesus. They appraised me warily. I'd dressed in Docker slacks with an orange golf shirt and blue sweater and looked as if I were about to tee off for a round of golf. One hippie asked if I needed a caddy. I said, "Our tee off time is in fifteen minutes. Hope you can join us."

Professors wore turtlenecks and brown sports jackets. Most had pipes that they puffed on with an air of sophistication. Students gathered around the smoke.

Would-be preachers were in suits and ties. They acted as if they were on a political campaign, shaking everyone's hand. Several noticed me in the back and came over. One grabbed my hand and asked what church I belonged to. I said, "None. I'm an atheist." He smiled harder. His teeth showed. He said, "Oh." He made small talk, wanting, I suspected, to investigate what an atheist was like. Then, he saw someone else in a suit and tie and excused himself.

Ivy Leaguers with buttoned-down Oxford shirts, fancy slacks, sweaters tied around their necks, and loafers (no socks) circled together. They hung around with the professors. They even smoked the same types of pipes.

One guy, handsome, whose long brown hair kept falling over his eyes so he had to brush it back, was talking with a professor. A pipe was cupped in his palm. He looked at me and smiled. He had an ease about him that was attractive. His eyes were a marble blue. He came over to me.

"I'm Bob so you can't be Bob, too," he said.

I laughed. "Oh, yes, I'm Bob Two. That's my name."

His brow furrowed. "Really?"

"No, not even close. Name's Jason," I said.

"Oh, the one who's after the golden fleece," he said, appraising me from head to toe.

"I prefer brunettes," I said. He laughed.

"I think we'll get along, Jason. I *must* find out where you are living."

"Bishop Hall, third floor."

"A dormy. That's cool," he said. Taking me by the arm, he pulled me aside, away from the crowd. "Most of these guys are so damn serious about religion. I mean, have you met any of them? It's like they believe all that bunk in the Bible and I…"

I interrupted him, "We *are* going to get along. This whole thing grosses me out."

"Hey, wait. It's not all bad. There are a few cool dudes here. Very cool. Wait until you hear James Lawson. He'll shake up some of these religious types."

A professor tapped him on the shoulder and whispered something in his ear.

"Gotta go," he said. "Master of ceremony thing."

He conferred with several professors and the Dean of the Divinity School.

The few women students kept to themselves. One had plain brown hair and big black glasses and dressed in black slacks, quite wrinkled as if appearance was incidental to her. She seemed to be the one person who was wholly herself. She looked bored. Her jaw moved back and forth. She squinted at the crowd as if appraising whether any of them was worth a minute of her time. I smiled at her, but she turned away and walked to a seat on the other side of the room. She opened a book and couldn't be bothered with the goings-on.

I could identify with her. I wasn't sure I belonged or wanted to belong. Whatever self I was slipped away from me in these gatherings. Maybe academe wasn't for me. Maybe mom's apprehensions were right. Maybe the Divinity School was a bad idea.

Characters

The Dean welcomed us. Bob talked about the importance for the class of 1968 to keep the civil rights movement in the forefront of whatever we did. Reverend James Lawson spoke in a gentle, deliberate manner about the Divinity Schools' involvement in the 1960s sit-ins at Woolworth, S.H. Kress, and McLellan Department Stores. Students at lunch counters were beaten and bloodied, but prevailed. Christians, he contended, were called to reach out to those who were oppressed. It remained the central tenet of the tradition. He peppered his comments with good humor and wit.

Next, Don Biesswenger, a professor in charge of community outreach and field experience, told us that each of us would be involved in "The Plunge." Its purpose was to teach us about the underprivileged in Nashville and to understand, briefly, about poverty and disenfranchisement. "The Plunge" was what Reverend Lawson has spoken about: a way to be engaged, to reach out to the oppressed.

Biesswenger, a short stocky man with salt and pepper hair, asked if we had any questions or comments. Several students stood up and applauded this idea. But one objected.

"I don't think we need to be on the streets to understand poverty," a tall, red-haired student said. "I've come from poverty and I tell you this: I'm *not* going back." His voice had a snarly edge to it like a chainsaw, the voice I heard in high school classrooms that stopped a student in his tracks. Dressed in a blue suit with a red tie, he boasted that he'd earned a Ph.D. in anthropology. He scanned the room to see if anyone would defy him. He'd caught the instructor off guard and liked doing it.

I took an instant to dislike to him, but I didn't challenge him. The frumpy girl I'd seen earlier jumped right in. "Hey, mister Ph.D., why don't you just sit down and listen to what the man has to say? Stop bemoaning what's going on before you even know what's going on."

The redhead turned sharply and barked, "Why don't you learn how to dress?"

There was a smattering of chuckles.

She didn't miss a beat, "I'll do that, carrot head, when you learn to shut your mouth."

A hush settled over the room. Professor Beisswenger hesitated, bit his lower lip, and took a slow inhalation before pointing right at carrot head and calling him by name, "Jack, I understand your resistance," he said. "But this isn't about going back. It's about delving into Nashville *right now* and seeing how it is on the streets when you have only your own resourcefulness to get you by. It's not about your past. It's about September 1968."

Not about to let up, Jack clearly enjoyed being center stage. After arguing that indeed, it *was* about his past and *was* an insult to him and to how far he had come, he finally relented and said that he would give it a try, but was not happy about it.

Professor Beisswenger said, "Good. You don't need to like it," and the meeting ended.

Jack grumbled about it throughout dinner, complaining so everyone could hear him (and most people could).

After dinner, I took a chair on one end of the porch. At the other end, Jack continued his argument, drew it out, pulled at it, kneaded it, and spread it until it took over every other conversation and left him and his disgruntlement as the sole topic of conversation. I sat with Professor James Herd, who introduced himself and, much to my surprise, told me that he was my advisor. We sat with the woman in the wrinkled clothes and with second-year transfer student Rick Smith.

From where we sat, we saw dense woods lined a lake. A narrow path led to it.

Rick muttered, "I could use a drink." Dr. Herd echoed his sentiments. I agreed. To my surprise, the woman, who introduced herself as Evie, said, "There's a good bar several miles back." We plotted how to disguise the liquor; the retreat was supposed to be chemical-free. Evie said that she could buy some Coke, empty most of it and mix in the bourbon. Did we mind Jack Daniels? "Anyone want to ride along?" she asked.

I volunteered. She drove an old Volkswagen Beetle, faded blue, the back seat stuffed with books and clothing.

"Where you from?" she asked.

I told her and asked her where she came from. "Oh, shit, from all over. My dad was career military. Army brat. I can't call anywhere home."

She drove down a road that wove like the laces in a shoe and finally unraveled on a ridge. She took curves like a driver at the Indianapolis 500, downshifting as she came in and shoving it into high gear as she came out. The car slid. I held onto the door. She laughed. "Not to worry, I know this road."

She slammed on the brakes, shoved open her door, and strode purposefully to the bar. This was familiar territory for her. She pulled a six pack of Coke from the cooler and went up to the bar. "Hey, Rocco, give me black," she said, slapping a twenty on the bar.

"Sure, Evie," the bartender said and reached under the counter.

She was no nonsense. Her face didn't at all look feminine, but didn't look masculine either. It had a pudgy quality. Her hair fell over her head as if it was poured from a bucket; she walked like a man with a long stride, her arms thrust out in front of her. On the way back, she told me she wasn't a fan of the military nor, for that matter, religion. Her father was mostly a drunk. She came to Vanderbilt because of the commitment by the faculty to activism. She wanted to be a journalist, but also liked theology and believed in the civil rights movement. Faculty at Vanderbilt invited students to call them by their first names and were involved in organizing civil rights protests.

My undergraduate professors kept their professional distance and played by the academic rules. They saw themselves as experts, the students as novices. Professor Herd blatantly violated these old rules, wanting to drink with us when drinking was prohibited. I told her I was surprised by his willingness to break the rules.

"Oh, come off it," she said. "Look at him. He's only maybe 4 or 5 years older than we are. He's a puppy. With that long stringy hair to his shoulders and wire-rimmed glasses, he's more interested in looking like John Lennon than a university professor. He wants to enjoy life. Fuck authority. He's more like us than those older codgers who are supposed to be his peers."

When we came back with the liquor, we all sat on the porch swigging our bourbon and Cokes, our feet on the railing and our drinks rapidly unscrewing our heads. The atmosphere had a sour mash tint to it. Evie grew quiet and slugged down one can, then another. She could hold her liquor.

I asked professor Herd what he studied. "Call me Jim," he said. He worked with the Lakota Indians, researched their rituals, their connection to the earth. He expounded on some of their practices. He went on and on.

My mind drifted.

A silver haired gentleman came over to him and whispered in his ear. Disappointment spread across Jim's face. A meeting of the faculty. He pulled out a little aerosol container and sprayed it twice in his mouth, his Coke left on the railing.

"Save it for later." He straightened himself up and shook out his hair.

Evie scrutinized him. "He's a pompous ass," she said after he left.

"I think he's nice," I countered.

"You would," she said and took another can, opened it, poured out some of its contents, and filled it back up with Jack Daniels. "To the good life," she said and took a swig. "I'm going for a walk," she said and went into the woods, following a path that quickly swallowed her in the dark.

Rick and I were left on the porch.

"She's quite a character," he said.

"Yeah, but I like her."

"Don't get me wrong, so do I."

He informed me that he was an Episcopalian and came from Louisville and, just this last year, was married. His words were honey coated. He drew out his O's and A's in a lovely southern accent. His mind was sharp, his wit quick. He scoffed at Jack and his pretension.

"Jack has an attitude a mile long," he said. "Being close to God for him is proportionally correlated to level of income. Salvation has more to do with a triple digit income than God. I suspect that for God, if He values income, it's not the dollar and cents worth, but the sense worth."

"Jack got shortchanged when it came to sense," I said.

Rick told me that he'd like to have me over for dinner. His wife made a mean roast beef. I got his telephone number.

Later, Evie was sitting on the back step looking at the moon that was perched on top of the pines.

"Pretty," I said.

"Yeah. But I'm not the romantic type. It's just the moon. It's there almost every night and is going to continue to be there no matter what we do," she said, shrugging her shoulders.

"I suppose. But it's still pretty."

"'Pretty'—that's a word I hate."

"Why?"

"Do you pay attention to anything?"

"Yep, I think I do."

"Well, buddy, take a good look at me."

I didn't know what to say and shook my Coke to see how much was left in it.

"No need to respond," she said. "I'm used to being who I am."

"I like that," I said.

"Good," she chuckled. "Are you sure? 'cause that's all you're going to get."

"I'm sure."

"Well, handsome, that's a surprise. But I'll take it." She reached over and shook my hand. "It's not often a guy like you just takes me at face value, especially with a face like mine!"

I laughed. She did too. She gave me her telephone number. "Call sometime," she said. "Friends is all. A deal?"

"Sure," I said. She leaned forward, snugged her chest into her knees, pressing her head between her knees, sighed, and stood up. "See ya." She clinked her Coke against mine and headed to her room.

A deep darkness drew over the porch. Crickets chirped. I sipped on my drink. I wasn't good at sleeping in dorms. If another guy moaned, I woke. I leaned back in the chair, curled up, and dozed.

"What're you doing?"

"Huh?" I said, startled from sleep.

"What're you doing out here?" Bob, the preppy guy I'd met earlier, asked. He sat next to me.

"Thinking."

"This time of night?"

"Not really. Little drunk is all."

"Really!?" he said, leaning toward me. "Have any left?"

"Sure," I said and sat up. I offered him Herd's leftover can. "Here."

Bob sipped from it. "Nice. Perfect. I could get to like a guy like you." He patted me on the shoulder. We talked as he finished the can. He came from the east coast for the same reason as Evie: to be where the action was. He'd been involved in Eugene McCarthy's campaign right up to the Democratic Convention. He asked about me and I told him that I, too, had been involved with campaign.

The moon, veiled behind the mist, rose over the pines and cast a milky glow across the porch.

The soft features of Bob's face, his heavy eyebrows and strong jaw, his squinty eyes and long wavy hair reminded me of that wayward look of James Dean. He leaned close to me as we spoke. His voice, calm and assured, made me feel at ease. He scribbled his phone number on a card. "Once classes get started," he said, "call me."

We found separate bunks at the dorm, shed our clothes, and curled under the sheets.

The moon had the rest of the night to itself.

The Plunge

On Thursday the orientation for dorm advisors spelled out my job: monitor activity in the halls, report disruptive behavior, support students with personal or academic issues, and be on duty at certain hours.

Friday morning, Dr. Beisswenger, who asked us to call him "Don," explained the logistics of "The Plunge." It would last three days and two nights. We returned at noon on Sunday for debriefing.

Jack scowled through most of the session. It didn't deter Don. "Most of our lives," he said, "we have props that we rely on to give us a sense of who we are. Just look at your wallet or purse. You have identification cards with a street address and photographs. That's one kind of identification. But we have others. The clothes we wear tell others a lot about our status. Look around the room at the other students. Some have coats and ties and shiny shoes. Some"—he laughed— "already look as if they'd been on the street for days, and some look as if they're about to play a round of golf." He smiled at me. His eyes glanced over to Jack. He wore a new dark blue blazer, white shirt and matching blue and red tie. "Well, what if you didn't have those props? What if you had no place for a few nights to call your own? No place where you really belonged? How would you find your way? Would you lose your identity? Many people, not by any fault of their own, live such lives. Many people live hand to mouth right here in Nashville. They are called the dispossessed. We want you in a small way to experience what it may be like for them and see how such an experience, however short, might change your way of thinking about your ministry and who you minister to. Do you focus on the well-to-do or do you reach out to those who, because of racism, family violence, alcoholism, or poverty, have been cast aside?"

Jack raised his hand, "Are you saying these clothes,"—he pulled on his blue blazer— "are props?"

"Yes, to some extent, yes, they are. They're what we wear to signal that we're of a certain class and have a certain social standing."

"I don't see it that way. To me, they are more a sign of who I really am and part of who I am."

21

"That's the point, Jack," Don said. "We're asking you to consider what it's like *not* being as you are and seeing what it's like to be like someone else."

"I don't want to be like anyone else. I'm happy with who I am."

"Fine."

"It's not fine," Jack continued. His voice rose. "Are you saying we have to *wear* street clothes?"

"No, Jack. You can wear your suit and tie, if that's what you want to do. But it might get uncomfortable for you. You might want to dress more comfortably."

"I'm perfectly comfortable in a suit."

"Then wear it."

"I'm sure you will," Evie observed. "And you'll probably have it pressed and cleaned every day."

"And I'm sure, by the way you dress, you'll be quite at home on the streets," he sneered.

"At least I'll be at home somewhere."

"Bitch!" Jack snarled and rose out of his seat.

Don took four quick steps across the room, took Jack by the arm, and said, "That's enough! Have a seat, Jack. We'll discuss your concerns in private later." He patted his arm and whispered something in his ear. Jack nodded, gave a glance at Evie, and, bowed his head, staring at the books piled on his desk.

With Jack quieted, Don told us next to dress in warm clothing. We would be given $5.00 and our driver's license along with a phone number to call if there was an emergency. We would each have a small journal—he passed them out — to record our thoughts and observations. For two nights, we'd roam Nashville, find out what makes the city tick, and learn what it's like when we didn't have money, when you have to make do, and when you have to live off the streets.

Jack asked, "Is the $5.00 all we have to subsist on for those two nights?"

"That's right."

"What if we want to earn more?"

"Your choice, Jack. Whatever you need to do. But, as I said, that's not the purpose of 'The Plunge.' It's for you to allow yourself to experience what it is like to be one of the have-nots."

Jack grimaced and was about to say something else, but, glanced around the room at the faces of the other students and caught the fact that Evie, eyes narrowed, was ready to take him on. He'd played his "I've-been-there" card as much as he dared to play. He pulled out a pen and jotted several notes in his journal.

"Can we go now?" Jack asked.

"No, not now," Don said. "You'll be dropped off in different parts of the city. That's part of the project: to see how your experience differs based on who you met and where you were and, before you go on the street, to make sure you're not in any unsafe areas, but you know where they are and keep away from them. So, get some warm clothing, decide how you want to dress, and be here at noon. We'll have a meal together and you'll be off."

I put the $5.00 in my front right pocket, headed back to the dorm, changed out of my golf shirt and put on a more casual pullover and jeans. I grabbed a heavy jacket and a wool hat. The news had predicted a cold night.

Lunch felt eerily like we were soldiers about to march to a battlefield.

First Nights

Two upperclassmen, one an African American, introduced themselves to me and drove me around the city. They told me to stay away from the lower south end of the city at night. "That's no place for a white guy after dark," the black man said. "Believe me. It's rough. I wouldn't be caught dead there."

"Dead," I joked. "Not a good word."

"It's not funny." He turned in his seat to look at me. "I'm serious. Be safe, man. Stay as far from here as you can."

They pulled next to a curb. "This is the historic district. But don't be fooled," the white guy said. "It can be rough. A student from my class got confronted here by some guy and had to run for it. But during the day, it's fine and it'll give you a chance to check out the music district and the Ole Opry"—he pointed across the street— "and if you get in trouble, get to a phone booth and call. We'll be on call to help out if necessary."

I crossed the street to explore The Grand Ole Opry, the Carnegie Hall of country music. For such an historic building, it wasn't elegant at all. It was a brick structure that came to a peak three stories up, giving the appearance of a church without a steeple. I wandered around it and pulled on its imposing wooden front door. It was locked. I browsed in several country music stores down the street, not really knowing what I was doing since I never listened to country music. I peeked into the adult bookstores that looked like the ones in Chicago. Same dimly lit rooms with shelves of magazines and an entrance to peep shows for twenty-five cents. I wasn't going to risk getting caught in there, not my third night in Nashville. I went up a steep hill to the state capitol, a white building with a circular dome surrounded by a marble tiered promenade with gardens, its late fall mums in bloom.

This apex of the city was quite lovely. It had a view in all four directions: across the valley to the other side of the river to the interstate strung along the river south, to the black district snug by the river, to the university up on a ridge, and to barn-like structures near a railroad yard by the tracks that crossed the river by another bridge.

The bridge over the Cumberland River was a good location to see the city from below. I'd never stood on such a large bridge over a wide river. I strolled through a park by the capitol and down a street toward the river.

The murky Cumberland River surged under the stanchions of the Woodland Street Bridge. Cars roared by me. The deck beneath my feet shuddered. A gust of wind lashed me. Cars were headed somewhere: to work, to home, to dinner. The river, too, had a destination. It meandered westerly through forest and fields, in and out of valleys, to the Ohio River and, eventually, to the Mississippi River and south to the Gulf. I had nowhere to go and nothing to do. Several massive trucks rushed by. The bridge groaned. I grasped the railing tightly. A cold wind swept under the girders. I steadied myself and held the railing with two hands. I needed to go back to my room, put on a record, and relax. Being out here alone was no fun.

That's when it struck me: I couldn't go back to my room. I stared at the river; its current roiled and twisted far below me. "Plunge" came to mind. How many people had stood where I stood and jumped? Perhaps they'd given up, had no place to go, lost love, been forsaken. From such a height, they'd never survive.

This wasn't a place I wanted to be. With my hands on the railing, I sidestepped, until I got to the end and sprinted toward downtown, putting as much distance between me and the bridge as I could.

It was getting toward dusk. I had no idea what to do. If I were home, I'd turn on the TV. If hungry, I'd open the fridge. No asking. If sleepy, go to bed. Everything was there. This was different. What would I eat? I had money for one meal, at best. Maybe even a candy bar or soft drink. After that, I'd have to fend for myself. Where to go? What to do? Where to sleep? No car to drive. The words of my mother came back to me, "Are you *sure* this is right for you?" If she were here, parked by the curb in her Lincoln, I'd have said. "No, it's not right." I'd slip into the front seat and we'd drive away. We'd stay in the Best Western. Everything would be all right.

The heavy lid of night was closing more quickly than I had anticipated. I needed to find a place to eat. But I'd had a good lunch. I could wait until the next day to get a meal. On Sunday, I would eat when I returned to school.

For several hours, people went by me as if I were invisible. They were assured of where they were headed, their eyes intently focused ahead of them. Other people who seemed lost, muddled along, hands in pockets, caught in the grip of the night.

I, too, was caught up in forces beyond my control. Scraps of headlines from the Nashville Tennessean hailed the rising national polls for Richard Nixon. I thought about Bobby Kennedy, the morning after he was shot, how I'd heard it on the radio and briefly wondered if it was a repeat of the announcement of John F. Kennedy's assassination. They kept saying "Kennedy was shot." Then, I heard his first name, "Robert." I pulled off the road and cried. Something was terribly wrong with our country.

A man in a frayed suit and scuffed-up shoes interrupted my reverie. "Got any change?" he asked. I looked up at him. Any change? I reached into my pocket. "No," I said. "I'm short, too."

"God bless," he said and passed on. He headed toward the railroad tracks.

I followed him, past the commercial district, toward the buildings by the tracks.

On one side street, off an alley, a barn with cows and horses in stalls smelled of manure. Warmth radiated through the slats. From the stalls, the eyes of horses, large and translucent, glared at me. In an empty stall, there was straw to bed down in.

I slipped through a slat, pushed the straw into a pile, nestled in it, and dozed. I woke to voices. Twenty feet away, several men crept into a stall. I froze and listened to their muttering. A police car passed by slowly and stopped, flashing a spotlight. Its long light licked against the boards over my head. Too many people were too close to me. My hands shook. I traced my fingers over my face. My skin was drawn taut against my cheek bones.

I crawled back to the opening. My right hand sank into something soft and sticky like Elmer's glue. As I pulled it out, something oozed through my fingers. Horse manure. I rubbed my hand on the straw, turned it right and left, splayed out my fingers to wipe it off. I sat back on my heels. I smelled like shit. Perfect.

The police car passed by again. The light darted back and forth. I ducked.

I hurried up the alley to a street and walked toward the Grand Ole Opry. I searched for a piece of paper to get the manure from my fingers. Nothing seemed to be going right. I was in an unfamiliar city with no sense of what to do next. I wanted someone I could talk to, to ask them if there was a shelter, some place to go.

Few people were on the street. Once the bustle of people on the street stopped, the city closed down. The few lights that there were came from offices in the tall buildings. Night workers were cleaning up the day's mess. A few taverns were open.

Cold, as if poured from a funnel, descended into the river valley.

I shivered and rubbed my hands back and forth. I didn't bring gloves. Stupid. Stupid. I couldn't put my hands in my pockets. I found a castoff Opry program and used it to scrape off the manure. I spit on one corner to wipe the palm of my hand clean. The smell, however, didn't go away.

Past the Opry, a brick building down an alley had a metal fire escape danging from the first tier. I jumped, pulled myself up, and climbed the six stories to the top.

From the edge of the flat roof, I could look down on the city: Broadway ran up toward Vanderbilt, and, in the other direction, the Cumberland River wound around the city; beyond the city lights, the hills flickered with suburban homes. I nestled against the interior wall, pulled my coat over my head, folded my knees into my chest and tried to sleep. The roof was uneven. The tarred surface rippled like ridges of hardened lava. I nestled my arms under my head. My shoulder soon became sore, so I turned over, scrunched my knees up, and put my head in my hand.

A few clouds slipped by another building. Above it, dim stars blinked at me. I'd never just looked at a night sky, how serene and contained it was, its blackness as impassive and inviting as a pool of dark water. It seemed unhurried. Cold seeped into my body; my legs shivered uncontrollably, my face was nipped with spurts of chilly air. I tossed one way, then another, and waited for a hint of dawn.

The next morning, I wandered up and down seven streets (I counted them to occupy my mind). I came to a desolate neighborhood. Many homes were abandoned, the windows shattered, as if the families had left a bomb behind. On the crest of one hill there was a small grocery, Loretta's Place, with a deli and a picnic table outside. With five dollars and another twenty-eight hours on the street, I wanted to get something to eat. I ordered a tuna sub and a carton of orange juice and went outside to the picnic table to eat. An older African American man, lean, with a partially graying beard, sat at the far end of the table. He wore a grey jacket with torn sleeves and woolen trousers. A winter cap, pulled down over his forehead at a rakish angle, gave him the appearance of a hustler. He didn't make eye contact. I asked, "Could I join you?"

"Fine," he said and scooted to one side of the table.

"How you doing?" I asked.

"Me? I'm fine. You?" He looked at my sub.

I offered him part of it.

"No, no. That's for you," he said. "Eminent domain." He raised his large hand in a circle like a preacher blessing his congregation. The skin on the underside of his hand was chalky white.

I insisted and ripped the sub in half, passing him half.

He ate it and asked where I was from. Not wanting to disclose that I was in the Divinity School, I made up a story about how I'd been against the war and my dad had thrown me out and I'd come to Nashville hunting for work.

He nodded his head in sympathy and admitted that he was also out of work. "Rough times, these are," he said. "I used to have a good job. I worked in a parts factory here in town. But it closed several months back, and I'm still looking, still looking." His eyes drifted down to the city below us. We talked for some time. He told me how he grew up in Nashville, his dad worked in the stockyards, and how they owned a good house above the river. But when they built the new interstate, they took the house, "eminent domain" they called it, but he thought it was stealing. Just outright stealing. His dad, who'd built the house, never recovered from losing it. He died and left his mother on her own. She got cancer, "the liver, bad case." She died a year later.

He offered me a cigarette, but I said no. I had to move on, check on some jobs. He stood, thanked me for the sandwich, and shook my hand with a firm grip that swallowed mine. He held onto my hand and said, "You take care, ya hear? And don't let your daddy get you down. A kid like you is gonna do fine. No doubt about it. You'll end up fine. Trust me."

I knew he was right. I may have not liked being on The Plunge, but I had it made. Being on the street was not my fate.

He was only the fourth black man that I'd met. I lived in a bubble of white people. I never thought about race. Never had to. No one called me "cracker." No one mentioned my color. Race was a subject we discussed when we talked about other people. For the man who'd lost his job, race—the color of his skin—was not incidental to who he was, but something that led some people to hate him, to fire him from a job, and possibly to assassinate him. He had to pay attention to it because his life depended on it.

All morning and well into the afternoon, I wandered the streets like a somnambulist. My shoes felt as if they were caked in cement.

Shoppers revolved in and out of stores. Consumers did what they were supposed to do: spend money on the luncheon specials, on the latest LP, and on the specials at the department stores.

I'd always had cash in my pocket. If I wanted something, I could get it. But I was cut off, irrelevant. Ostracized. I saw what distressed Jack: I was no longer who I thought I was. He was telling the truth in a way. He already knew something I was just finding out: that self-worth and identity could be based on the ability to consume. That's how he belonged: a capable cog in the wheel, one who could do what he wanted, buy what he liked when he wanted to.

I spent the day like a man waiting for his paycheck. I noted the department stores, restaurants, bookstores, and movie theaters where I could patronize once my wallet was back in my pocket. A crowded department store with clothing on racks and a cafeteria with the smells of hamburgers and fries made me remember the life I was used to living.

By late afternoon, I meandered up Broadway toward Vanderbilt, filling in time, making due. I had time to think. I realized that much of my life I was bent on becoming someone—making grades, competing on a team, getting a degree, finding a job, becoming successful, proving myself, and being liked. Without something to do, I was lost. I sat on the curb and counted the cars. Two hundred came by in an hour, more leaving than coming into town.

"What you doing?" a voice asked.

I looked up. Rick, a divinity student I'd met at the retreat, stood over me.

"Counting cars."

"That sounds like fun."

"Don't bet on it. I'm bored, really bored."

He sat next to me and pulled out his pockets. He'd run out of money too. Broke. Twenty-two hours left on The Plunge.

"What you planning to do tonight?" he asked.

"Go back to where I was last night," I said.

"Any good?"

"Froze my ass off. You have a decent place?"

"It smelled but was warm," he said and, taking a whiff of me, added, "You smell like you've been in the same place." I told him about the horse manure.

We strolled back into town, and noticed a small liquor store on a side street.

"Be nice to have a drink right now," he said.

"Let's do it," I said.

"Do what?"

"Pick some up."

"I have no money," he said.

"So?"

We sat on a bus bench to plan our strategy.

—

I went in the front door and asked whether they had a type of gin—Gordon's London Dry, the one my parents preferred. Rick went to the back and acted as if he dropped something, swiped a pint, and started to walk out. The clerk, a stout man with a double chin, noticed Rick.

He called out, "Hey, bud, can I help you?" Rick fumbled under his jacket. A pint bottle fell and shattered. Rick sprinted out of the store. The clerk, more than twenty pounds overweight, came after him. He was no match for Rick. I ran alongside the clerk. When he pulled up short and bent over to catch his breath, I said, "That's too bad."

"Bastard," the clerk said.

"I'll see if I can catch him," I volunteered.

"Don't bother. Happens all the time. No use putting yourself at risk. A friend of mine got knifed trying to be a hero," he said. "But thanks." I shook his hand and walked off in another direction.

When he'd walked fifty paces, he turned and called out. "Hey, buddy, tell your friend to watch it. Police patrol these streets."

I started to reply. Instead, I raised my hand, waved, and jogged as quickly as I could to our meeting place. I changed directions in case the cops were already on my trail and took a detour through the campus.

Rick greeted me with a frown. "Close call," he said.

"Hurry." I grabbed him by the arm. "The clerk knows." We trotted for several blocks to get as far as we could from the liquor store.

Safely downtown, Rick asked, "How'd he find out?"

"Beats me. Must have put two and two together. Customers probably don't chase thieves," I said.

"Never thought I'd ever do that." He was upset with himself.

"Hey, desperate times," I said. "Come on, we better get off the streets in case he called the cops. All we have is a broken bottle for the trouble."

"Don't be so sure." He pulled out a pint of bourbon.

That night we huddled in a stall Rick had found between the stalls of two huge heifers. Their body heat warmed us as we passed the bottle back and forth. The liquor worked its magic. He put his arm around me—being taller than I was—and told me to get comfortable, to use our body heat to keep warm.

"That's okay," I said. "I'm all right."

"What's wrong? Afraid of a little contact?"

"No, it's just..."

"Just what?" His hand was on my shoulder, gentle, tentative.

"It's weird," I admitted. "Snuggling, you know."

"Better than freezing," he offered.

I snuggled against him, my head on his shoulder, my arms curled up next to my body, my hands between my legs. It felt warmer. The alcohol left me lightheaded, content like a boy under his daddy's arm.

A cow belched. Farted. A police spotlight swept the stalls every few hours. Other men, incoherently drunk, woke us.

But I felt close to someone. And that felt good.

The next day, we wandered, as if caught in a labyrinth, down the same streets by stores with the same lettering on their windows: a jewelry store, a department store, a shoe store, a movie theater. We'd call them out as we walked by them.

We raced up the steep hill to the capitol, explored the complex of Roman colonnades, checked out the portico with its view of the park. We rolled down the grassy slopes of the hill, staggered to our feet like drunkards. We noted the different films we wanted to see. *Charly* with Cliff Robertson was supposed to be a good film.

Mid-morning, before we were to report back to the school, Rick invited me to meet his wife, Jane. She took one whiff of us. "You're pretty ripe," she said. "Wash up."

She served us hash browns and a bacon and cheese omelet.

"Slow down, boys. The food won't run away," she said.

By the time we finished, the clock on their mantel read eleven-thirty.

Thirty of us were served a delicious meal by the upperclassmen—fish in almond sauce, heaping mashed potatoes, green beans, and salad. A second hunger overtook Rick and me. We ate as if we'd been starved.

Afterward, Don asked us to discuss what happened on our nights on the streets. Several admitted that they refused to do it—too afraid—and went back to their dorms. Five guys—including Jack— found work and were able to rent a room. Most actually stayed on the streets. Rick and I told about sleeping in odd places—the roof of a building and the barn. We spoke of our loneliness and fear. We'd lost our identity. That was a common theme.

"What was it like," Don asked, "not having your props like a wallet with money?"

Jack pounced on the question. "It was stupid," he said. "One damn weekend doesn't amount to anything. People need to live as I did—"

31

"You're right, Jack." Don interrupted. "But some may have learned something. Let's hear from them."

"But I, for one, don't think they're props," Jack asserted. "We *earned* them. We have a right to them. I'm not giving them up, not for a minute."

"I don't imagine you would," Evie chimed in.

"As if you would know," Jack shot back.

"Evie, please," Don said. "Let Jack finish what he has to say." He swiveled in his chair to face Jack. "For you, they are essential to your definition of who you are?"

"Of course!"

"You've made your point. How about others? Anyone find it liberating?"

"I did," I said. "I realized that I don't have a clue about being a have-not. I never thought how I've been given a passport to success. Without the props—money in the wallet, a car at my command—I was lost. In a strange way, I agree with Jack. I count on them to feel worthy. I've always lived with a purpose, with goals, with things to do, with places to go. It's sad to say—and that's where I disagree with him because I wish I didn't feel that way—but I do."

"That's because you're some rich kid," Jack interjected.

"No," I countered. "It's not because I'm rich. But I do know I have never wanted for things. I bet others in this room can say the same thing."

Others agreed with me. Bob said that he'd not expected much from The Plunge but, once he couldn't just reach in his wallet to pull out a bill, he panicked. He felt embarrassed, or, worse, ashamed. He looked over at me. "Follett has it right. Our identities *are* tied to our ability to spend, to know we have the cash on hand. Without it, we're outsiders. It was no fun. It sucked."

Several black students joined in, told how they were familiar with the streets, they'd been there, but found the loss of cash distressing. Don talked about possessions and being dispossessed as many of the people on the street were day in and day out. Ours was only an inkling of what it was like for them. He encouraged us to consider how the ministry could reach out to them. Everyone was tired and needed to prepare for classes the next day. Don thanked us for participating.

I walked to my room, cast my clothes in a corner, showered, dried off, pulled back the sheets, slipped into bed, and drifted into a deep sleep.

Parties

Undergraduate students arrived on Monday. I milled around the halls introducing myself. My job was to watch over my floor, keep track of students who were chronically out late or seemed out of control and to provide them with support or, if need be, reprimands.

Bob and I often had lunch at the cafeteria together. My height yet with a slighter build, he exuded confidence and invited me to a party on a night I had off as dorm advisor. He told me to bring a date and suggested I give Ann Stone a call. A friend of his girlfriend, a third-year student majoring in philosophy. She liked older guys. I called her and she agreed to go.

Bob lived in an older house with one side redone to make a two-bedroom apartment with a kitchen and a large living room. At the party, I was surprised that students and professors and their wives were there. Many of them were involved in the civil rights movement. Dr. Herd came with his wife, a tall woman with a runner's build. He brought a keg of beer.

We sat on couches and chairs and sprawled on the floor. We engaged in debates about the war. Nixon's rhetoric incensed President Johnson whose Operation Rolling Thunder, a wholesale bombing of the North Vietnam, only seemed to strengthen the resolve of the country. The bombing of Hanoi had supposedly killed 185,000 civilians, but had cost Americans 900 downed aircraft. Johnson believed such assaults would hasten the end of the war. Herd was skeptical. Bob defended the president. Bob loved the argumentative atmosphere of academia. After drinking four or more mugs, rational men became agitated. There were shouts back and forth. But Bob kept his poise.

At some point, he turned up the music and pulled the chairs and couches back. The room became a wild dance extravaganza, with couples doing the tango and rumba, hopping and jumping across couches and over chairs with complete abandon. Bob was a terrific dancer. His date, lithe as she was, stuck close to him: her leg, his leg, her body, his body velcroed together. His parties went on every weekend and the professors, most of them young, had no compunction about fraternizing with students. When the party wound down, professors stumbled out carrying cups of beer, their wives often as drunk as they were. Bob and I carried several to their cars. "It was a great party, one of the all-time best," Herd said. "I'd stay all night, but my damn wife has to teach in the morning."

Once the crowd was gone, Bob turned down the music, putting on Frank Zappa's Mothers of Invention. His free-form improvisations sounded like old times to us. Bob curled up with his woman and I nestled next to Ann. Later, we split to separate bedrooms where I got to know her better.

She was quite a woman—bright, taking philosophy courses in metaphysics. And pretty, a girl my parents would approve of. She had long brown hair, parted down the middle, and wore short one-piece dresses. Like silk, the dress felt smooth as a lubricant against my skin. The first night she shed her dress like an afterthought. With no compunction about making love, already out of her dress, she unbuckled my pants. We discarded our clothes. We held onto to one another with no pressing need to make love because we were pleasantly inebriated. We chatted about our childhood, her horseback riding (she competed in show jumping events on the West coast), our fathers and mothers, before giving ourselves over to caresses and making long, uninhibited love, which seemed quite natural to me in ways I'd never expected.

Over the next weeks, I discovered that Ann, a daughter of a pharmacist in Seattle, wanted to get involved in civil rights activities and, as she put it, "to do something with her life." As we lay together one night, I told her about an event that Bob had organized along with the help of Reverend James Lawson, a march against segregation in a Mississippi town that, despite the Supreme Court's rulings, refused to let blacks shop or be in the main part of town. She wanted to go with me.

"It might be dangerous," I said.

"That's fine."

Racism

Although much of Mississippi had begrudgingly integrated, small pockets remained adamantly segregated. Reverend Lawson selected one of them to see whether, with a large contingency to demonstrate and garner more publicity, he could force the town to integrate. Protesters came from Nashville in the north, Little Rock in the west, Knoxville in the east and Jackson in the south—to converge on a small Mississippi town not far from Oxford. African Americans who went downtown there were arrested, and even worse, quietly disappeared. Bob told us to meet at the Divinity School on Saturday at five AM. I picked Ann up at her dorm and we arrived to find two buses pulled over by the curb.

Reverend Jim Warren, a white man who served at the Edgeville Methodist Church in the middle of the black community and who was the right-hand man for Lawson, and 67 students were gathered outside the buses. We were told what we needed to do: if someone tried to kick or hit us, cover our heads and pull our knees up to protect our internal organs. On our part, no violence. No name calling. Stick together, arm in arm. Keep marching from the drop-off area to the town hall.

"Hey, handsome," I heard someone say. It was Evie. She had on a blue baseball cap, her hair pulled back in a ponytail. She wore bib overalls with a white dress shirt. She grabbed by the arm. "Did you see who's here?"

"No."

"Mr. Coat-and-tie. Jack himself."

"Really?"

"He just got on the bus."

"I hope he wore deodorant."

Evie laughed. "He probably has a change of clothes." She eyed Ann. "Who's the girl?"

"It's my friend," I told her. I introduced Ann to her.

Evie leaned into me as she was getting on the bus. "Not bad, handsome.

35

You're a quick mover." She swung herself into the aisle, called back, "Later," and slipped into a seat by a nun.

Once we got on the bus, I noticed Jack in his suit and tie sitting in the back of the bus. "What's *he* doing here?" I asked Bob.

"Don't let him fool you," Bob said. "He's an activist. Has been for a long time."

"You're kidding."

"No, I'm not. He's been active in the civil rights movement for years. He knows Lawson and even marched with King. He seems to know everyone of importance."

"Damn. I find that hard to believe."

"I did too. But he's authentic."

Ann and I sat in front, our posters up against the window. "Open the Doors to Freedom." "End Discrimination."

Emerson, a handsome black student whom I had befriended in an Old Testament class, sat in front of us. Ann asked Emerson about himself. Raised in a suburb outside New York City, he aspired to teach black theology, which, he believed, would soon become the "in" topic. An admirer of Reverend Lawson, he wanted to follow in his footsteps, but he also admired Fred Hampton, the Black Panther, and his coalition in Chicago.

I asked if he had met Hampton.

"No, but I have brothers who drove there and who work in his office. It's tense. They're worried about Nixon. His law and order shit is fueling backlash in the city," he said.

"What's Reverend Lawson like?" Ann asked.

Emerson told an interesting story. He'd had dinner the night before with Lawson. Three other divinity students joined them. Lawson asked them what experience they'd had with racism and how it related to the Bible. A Southern Baptist guy believed in a strict interpretation of the Bible. What God said was true. The Bible didn't mention civil rights. That was outside the church, more a political issue. Lawson heard him out. Another student had heard God's calling. Newly married, he believed that his mission was to find a good church, raise his family, and preach the love of Christ. Emerson suspected that he was not "called" by God as much as by a nice income. The last one, a hippie, had no use for religion. He was in school to avoid the war and planned to go out west and act—movies, he hoped.

Lawson asked them what were the harmful effects of racism in their lives. The Baptist had never seen any. Several friends were "colored" and they seemed happy. "Always a smile on their face," he said. Lawson asked if any black people were close friends. The Baptist said, "Why yes, one when I was a kid, before school age. After that, he went his way, I went mine."

Lawson continued his probe of the other students' experience with race. The newly married one said that he'd never encountered any blacks but had nothing against them. The aspiring actor bragged that he'd played in a rock band with a couple of black guys. Lawson asked if he'd been to their house. The actor said, "Well, no," he hadn't.

"Had they been to his house?"

"Well, no. Never thought of it."

Emerson said that he grew up in an integrated community, although mostly white. He had several white friends, not close. They never came over to his house; he frequented theirs. In fact, he never felt comfortable asking whites over. It just didn't feel right.

Lawson asked what caused people to be bigoted, hateful, and violent toward blacks. Most said upbringing. Some said it was unconscious—inbred in society.

Lawson shook his head and said no. He didn't agree. It's too easy to blame "society." It's a convenient excuse for not acting. "Society" can't do anything about it.

Then he told a story about a white boy and a black boy who grew up down the street from one another and who became best friends. As little boys, they fished, wrestled, and played hide and seek together. They went in each other's yards and swung on each other's swings. They told each other their secrets, came and went in and out of their homes.

Then one day before the boys entered elementary school, the white father told his son that he couldn't play with the black boy and shouldn't be seen with him.

The white boy asked why. The father said that it could cause trouble. That was how it was. His son must not be seen with his friend. Period.

Lawson asked, "What do you think happens to the white boy?"

The students said that he might feel sad.

"True," he said. "But often he feels confused, even angry that his best friend can, for no good reason, be cut off from him. The white boy has no release for his anger. You know what happens to it?"

Emerson suggested it became internalized, but Lawson added to his point, "Yes, that's true at first, because the boy thinks something is wrong with *him*—that *he* may have done something wrong or that he may *be* wrong. He feels ashamed. Shame is nameless since no one tells him why he feels as he does. Shame gnaws at you inside. But instead of coming to understand it, the white boy, along with other white boys, lashes out at the black boy, the one who caused him to feel as he does. The broken relationship foments rage and anger. That is how hatred and racism starts."

Emerson asked him what to do about it, if it's so insidious. No one knew. Lawson slapped his hand on the table and told us, "That's *your* job, your work as ministers if you believe in anything the Bible says. All people belong to the Kingdom of God. Race is central to *you* and *your* ministry if this nation is to heal."

After Emerson told his story, I looked at Lawson. He sat by Reverend Warren. I remembered what Lawson said at the orientation about keeping civil rights at the center of our ministry. Here he was not only talking the talk but walking it too. He and Reverend Warren laughed together.

We arrived at the church in the Mississippi town and assembled along with those from the other schools, 300 hundred of us in lines of five. Lawson was in the lead row; Warren at the end. Jack walked alongside Warren, chatting with him as if they were best friends. Several other preachers mixed through the lines. Bob and Emerson, right by Lawson, led us down the street toward town.

On either side of the street, young men in T-shirts sat in open convertibles with shotguns resting in their arms. Other men and women called out, "Nigger lovers!," and "Yankee, Go Home!" We sang "We Shall Overcome." We joined arms and took assurance from the physical contact. Ann held onto my arm and whispered. "Geez, this *is* scary."

I said, "I know." I couldn't imagine how Dr. King had done this over and over. I looked at the eyes of the men in the cars and thought about Lawson's story. Ann held on tighter as some men with enormous beer bellies came up to us and spat at us. "Niggers!" "Faggots!" "Jews!"

Two young men in white t-shirts noticed Evie who was walking alongside us and yelled, "Look at the dyke! They even got fuckin' queers in this march."

His buddy added, "Hey, lesbo, you like it with girls?" and stuck his tongue in and out.

Evie shouted back, "I bet you couldn't get a piece of ass if you paid for it."

One man, short and stocky, lifted a baseball bat and charged at Evie. Before he reached her, Jack stepped in front of her and raised his hand. The stocky fellow stopped in his tracks. "This is a peaceful march," Jack said. "Your comments aren't appreciated." The man lifted the bat. The march halted. The two sides watched the encounter. Jack was a foot taller than the other man. His suit and tie gave him a professional authority. He stared at the man with the bat. "You don't want to do that," he said.

The friend of the stocky man came up and said, "Let the bastards be. He's probably a fag." He took the baseball bat. "Come on." They backed up and sat on the bumper of a car.

Jack nodded and gave them a thumbs-up. "Thanks." He turned to Evie. "You okay?" he asked.

"Fine. Sorry. They got to me," she said.

"They get to all of us," he said. He joined the front of the line. The march continued up the street.

Ann pulled on my arm. "Who is that?"

"It's Jack."

"Amazing guy."

"Some might disagree."

"Why?"

"It's nothing. He's odd, that's all."

Emerson called back to us, "Can you imagine growing up here?"

After a two-mile trek in the blazing sun, the group coalesced at Town Hall. The doors were locked. But white faces peered out the windows. We stood in a semi-circle around the steps. Behind us, across the street, white people stood shoulder to shoulder watching us. Down the street from us, the town square with shops, a movie theater, and restaurants, looked like any southern town.

Several students spoke, including Bob, about the Biblical injunction to act in the face of racism. Reverend Lawson spoke about Dr. King's legacy. He asked to speak to the mayor. But doors remained locked.

We marched into town, in pairs, black and white, tried to enter a Stonewall Five and Dime and a nearby restaurant with "White Only" signs on the windows. Doors were closed. Locked. Shades pulled. One proprietor gave us the finger and yelled, "Get out of here, nigger."

Emerson said, "They're ready for us."

Lawson and Warren conferred. We marched back to the buses and drove back.

Bob asked Ann and me over to stay the night. Exhausted, Bob had one drink, excused himself, and went to bed. Ann and I talked about the eyes that glared at us with such vitriol. I stroked her long brown hair. She rubbed my neck. We wanted to make love to obliterate being reviled. We made love slowly, letting go of the day, until we fell asleep.

The Turn

From October to early November, I paid little attention to the presidential election. After a slow start, Hubert Humphrey had tightened up the race. On election night, the polls looked bad for Democrats. Nixon finally snatched the job he'd always wanted. At Bob's apartment, we watched a smiling Nixon, arms extended, turn one way and another, his fingers in a "V" for victory.

Bob muttered, "What a jerk."

"Can't believe it." I took another sip of beer. "No one sees he's a fraud."

"Americans like fairy tales," Bob said. "They want someone to patch up divisions and put it back to the way it was. They believe 'It's the new Nixon.' They don't get that it's the same old thing and even more divisiveness."

Back at my dorm room, I opened a book by Moltmann on the theology of hope. I thought it might make me feel better. It didn't.

Nixon would later made grandiose statements at his inauguration that I desperately wanted to believe—

The greatest honor history can bestow is the title of peacemaker. This honor now beckons America—the chance to help lead the world at last out of the valley of turmoil, and onto that high ground of peace that man has dreamed of since the dawn of civilization.

Good idea. One I agreed with. But I didn't trust him. He knew people wanted to hear about peace. He gave people what they wanted. Time would tell if he meant it.

Advisor

The first months of classes were much more taxing than I expected. I locked myself in my room and read about religion and sociology, New Testament interpretation, systematic theology and ethics. My job as a residential advisor in the freshman dorm demanded more attention, too. Several boys came to see me for advice. A mop-haired boy, Michael, extremely shy and interested in the ministry, became a friend. He'd rifle through my books on theology.

"What does the Good Samaritan story mean?" he asked one night.

I told him that the parables were as straightforward as they seem. The Good Samaritan wasn't about how a "good" Christian should help the poor or downtrodden. If looked at from the point of view of the injured man, for example, it was more about how a person who is helpless must rely on someone to help him, how he must accept help from someone with whom they'd *never* associate. It would be like a racist having to accept help from a black man. Once a person admits they're helpless, they become open to the possibility that the source of strength and spiritual nurture may come from one's enemy. Parables, I told him, twisted conventional thinking.

"That's not what my mom says," he said. "She's a minister."

"Maybe your mom doesn't have all the answers," I replied.

"Maybe you don't," he said.

"Maybe none of us do," I admitted.

I had no idea why I had become father confessor to many boys, but the boys came in to talk. One boy, Steven, told about his father, an alcoholic, who beat up his mother and, when he tried to intercede, would go after him. He often fled, to stay at a friend's house until his dad sobered up. Another boy struggled with the pressure to be like his father, magna cum laude at Vanderbilt. The boy hated to study and liked to party. Eventually his dad and he would come to blows. His dad had already beaten him once so hard he passed out.

I listened to them and worked long hours to keep up with the reading and the assignments. Thanksgiving break, I drove home, caught up with my reading, and wrote several overdue papers. I envied Bob who dashed off papers, ten pages in an evening. I called Ann several times over break. I missed her. Maybe I could sustain a relationship with her. My first real love of a woman surprised and pleased me.

Manhood

Back at the dorm, I waited for the freshmen to return, checking them off as they came back from break. That was my job. Before I could unpack my clothes and books and settle down to do some intensive reading, several students came in and said that they were worried about Michael, the boy who had spent so much time with me. He hadn't come back from Thanksgiving break. I told them not to worry. Hours later, they came back, still worried. They sprawled on the bed. Did he have family problems? His parents were strict, born-again Christians. I assured the boys his family probably had guests. Things ran late. That's all. Not to worry.

But I was worried, too.

Michael lived only three hours from campus. His mother, as the minister, worked on Sundays and holidays. He often hitchhiked rides back to school. On one trip, a man who picked him up found out it was his birthday. As Michael hopped out of the car, the man passed him a bill. "Hey, kid, it's your birthday," he called out. "Have a good day!" Michael stuffed it in his pocket. Later he looked: a hundred-dollar bill. He showed it to me. "My parents," he said, "forgot. Big crusade."

Past midnight, his friends informed me that he had he arrived. But, even when they knocked, he refused to let them in.

I went to his room—I had a master key—and told him I was coming in.

"No, no," his voice whined.

I pushed on the door; he blocked me from entering with his foot.

I cleared the hallway, told the other boys to allow me to handle it. He needed privacy.

I told him that I only wanted to come in and sit. That was all. He needn't say anything.

He flipped the lock open.

I waited a minute to give him time and entered.

He was curled up in the bed, the blanket pulled over his head, his knees tucked up under him, sobbing convulsively.

I sat in his desk chair and spoke softly. "It's all right, all right." I sat for hours. "It's all right," time and again I told him. And waited.

Eventually, he peeked out of the blanket. He leaned against the wall. The skin on his face, drawn and pale, looked stretched like a canvas across its frame. There were contusions on his right cheek and a bump on his forehead, right below his hairline. He stared at his hands.

The words came out haltingly with intermittent sobs.

He had trouble getting a ride. It was a cold, raw day. Four guys in a van, jocks, loud, drunk, but friendly, offer him a ride. A drive to Nashville, no big deal. They seemed pleasant enough. They passed him a Mason jar of moonshine. He drank some. He told them he was a student—Vanderbilt. They said he was "pretty." He drank more. They asked if he was a "fairy boy." They mocked his lisp. The driver turned onto a side road. The driver told him not to worry. "A short cut." Michael pulled at the door handle. Two guys grabbed him. They told him, "To get out, you need to put out." Fairy boys did that. They parked. They pulled down his pants. After they were done, they left him there—him and his duffle bag.

He walked fifteen miles, not stopping until he got to his room.

I told him that it was a criminal act. I had to report it. He should get medical attention. I took him to the emergency room. He spoke with the police. His face was ashen. I bought him a hamburger and fries and soda. I arranged for his best friend, Sam, to stay with him, on a mattress on the floor beside his bed overnight.

The next day he went to a counselor. He told me that he was worried that he really was a "sissy boy"—that he'd never be the same. I said that just because they said that it didn't make it true. All he needed to know was that he was a good person and he'd done nothing wrong.

His parents, once they found out, were alarmed. They paid a visit, took him out to dinner, talked with the counselor and with me, and, once assured he would be all right, left. The father had the same lisp Michael did. His mother, a slight woman with an athletic build, ruled the family. She liked it that I was a divinity student. If I had any concerns, I was to call. "Here's my card," she said. She ran her family like a business: if there was a crisis, deal with it, then move on. She called frequently for several weeks to check on him, then moved on.

Mushrooms

Later that winter, after Christmas break, Michael seemed better. He laughed more, dated again, and seemed more secure.

I asked him what caused the change. Sheepish at first, he said, "The therapy and..."

"What?"

"Drugs."

"Really?" I asked.

"Yeah. You'd like 'em."

Taking psilocybin mushrooms, he believed, kept him sane, he added, "You know, reality is relative." Violence, he went on to explain, could step into your life just as easily as grace. Sometimes it's hard to know the difference: the guy with a hundred bucks and those guys with moonshine. He couldn't change it. He was grateful to be alive. A few nights later, he brought me several tablets—psilocybin—and told me to take them.

"No, I can't be doing that," I said.

His doleful eyes melted my reserve. "Hey, they're good"—the two tablets sat in the palm of his hand — "They *really* give you a different perspective!"

The psilocybin did send me into a new world. Disoriented, I stumbled into my chair, fell over, and stared at the things around me. A chair on its four legs came to life. It wanted to walk. The bookcase with the shining spines smiled at me.

Michael laughed.

"Told you so."

He escorted me around campus, his arm tucked into mine. He had me sit under a magnolia. The soft round leaves quivered above me, each a separate entity. They caressed the air, a startling green. I stood under a 14-story student housing complex. *Up* as a word came alive. The flat brick went up and up and up. It blotted out the horizon. A building I'd passed hundreds of times became a Stonehenge monolith: huge and otherworldly.

With the drug, I was *in* the world, *a part* of it, not just an observer *of* it. I felt the *under*-ness of a tree, its looming *over* me. I was thrown, as the philosopher Martin Heidegger called it, into the world. I dwelt in it—the sky *above*, the earth *below*, the trees *around*, the wind *through*, the heat *up*, the water *in*.

A few days later when I was on it, a car accident happened right in front of me, beautifully orchestrated. One car, a blue sedan, collided with another. Each sequence—the screeching of brakes, the sliding of vehicles, the smoking of tires, the darting of pedestrians to avoid being hit—seemed in slow motion. I viewed it all: the front fender bent, the headlight shattered, the glass splattered, the arms of man behind the wheel thrown up. I stood, calm and assured, mesmerized as it unfolded. It seemed prearranged. Two lost lovers being united: the one fused for a moment with the other, then ricocheted to the side, and twirled until it stopped ten feet from me. I never flinched. I sensed how the speed of the one car would propel it to a certain spot. Two middle-aged men emerged from their cars, faces flushed, and screamed at one another. Like dancers, they strutted, chests out, and stepped back and forth with fingers pointing. Someone called to me for help.

The dancers were bleeding.

I couldn't help. I could only observe.

I scampered to a parking lot and retreated to my dorm.

Over several weeks, I enjoyed the mushrooms—being in the world and not of it. One afternoon I went to my New Testament class while on psilocybin. I couldn't follow the discussion. Words made no sense. The breasts of a girl who tried to adjust her bra without letting on, the finger of the professor who pushed his glasses up on his nose every few minutes, and the hand of a student who cupped his crotch all caught my attention. I heard the fabric of his jeans move and the slight moan in his throat. A boy picked up a pencil, sucked on it, and I got an erection.

The evening was my favorite time to take it. I liked to peer up at the pretzel-like bend of branches and notice the vines like snakes crawling up the side of a dorm.

But one evening, someone was watching me. I could feel his gaze on my back. A campus police officer, not twenty feet away, was studying me.

If he inquired what I was doing, I would have been incoherent. I stuffed my hands in my pockets, looked straight down the path, and walked away in a direction (although I had no idea where I was going) and invented an aphorism: "Always look as if you know where you are going, even if you don't, and people will leave you alone." I kept going in a direction and others thought I knew where I was going. It certainly worked that night.

Michael came into my room often to talk. His new friend came along too. Sam, a boy whose dark hair obscured his eyes, told how his mother went into rages and chased him around the dinner table with a carving knife. Quick and nimble, he'd outrun her. Both got exhausted. He suggested they stop to smoke. She put the knife down. He took out his cigarettes. While she puffed on her cigarette, he hid the knives. The next day it was school as usual. She had a reputable job in town as a secretary in a big law firm. No one believed she had rages—such a sweet, loving lady. He bided his time until he was free from her.

I learned an incredible amount about the New and Old Testaments, about ethics, and the sociology of religion. But the dorm opened me up to something far more real than anything that I read and studied in class.

Obligations

Bob called and asked if I could come over to his apartment. His voice sounded odd. I asked if there was anything wrong. "No," he said, "but I need to talk." It was early afternoon, not a time we usually met.

He had made lunch, some salmon, beans, and a baked potato. He poured us wine and told me it was a special meal for a special friend.

"What's the occasion?" I asked.

"You're the one person whom I can talk to about anything. Do you mind listening?"

"That depends," I said, sipping on the wine.

"Depends on what?"

"What type of wine you have."

"Asshole!"

"Well, what type?"

"A merlot, French; it's different. You'll like it."

He tightened his lips. "It goes like this," he explained. "I really love it here. I've never felt more at home than with you and Ann. The girls here, they're hot. I love the faculty. We can be ourselves with no game playing. We marched in Mississippi. We protested the war. We have the most amazing classes with the most amazing minds." He took a sip of wine. "Good, isn't it?"

"Bitter, but tasty," I said.

"Want another glass?"

"Sure," I said. "And what were you saying?"

"The more I think about the other guys, the ones who were drafted and who are dying over in Nam, the more I wonder, 'What am I doing here?' I'm on Easy Street. If I'm against war, if I'm for peaceful resolution to conflict, I should be laying it on the line—you see what I mean?"

"No, not really."

"I should be a conscientious objector, not have a 4-D deferment."

"But what's the difference?"

"If I'm 4-D, that means I want to serve the church, to go into the ministry, right?"

"No. I don't plan to..."

"Exactly," he interrupted. "You don't plan to. If that's the case, then you're really using the status quo to avoid recruitment."

"You got it!"

"But that's not right. If you oppose war, especially this war, you should be making a stand and say, 'I will not abide this war, not serve in the military to advance the immoral war efforts,' and not just sit silent and get by," he said, cocking his head to the side.

I cupped my wineglass in my hands. I had to hold onto something. I felt unmoored. He was my anchor. The currents of his moral code were pulling him away. Certainly, he had a point: doing nothing was not right.

I told him that if I was doing something productive to help others that, as a soldier, I could not do, then I was using the 4-D status to do good work.

"What *are* you doing?" he asked.

"Nothing, but maybe we could find some work in Edgeville, the black area. Reverend Warren needs help with his summer programs. I've seen notices..."

"No," he said. "I need to make a stand."

"A one-night stand?" I said sarcastically.

He slapped his knee and laughed convulsively.

"You all right?"

"Sure, but let me tell you what happened last weekend. You know that older girl, the blonde with that amazing face? Well, you reminded me of my one-night stand. You wanna hear?"

He dated an older woman, in her late twenties whom he'd met at a party. Tall, with the looks of a fashion model, she infatuated him. She biked; they'd gone on day trips. She asked him over and one thing led to another. They made love. He pulled out before he came and ejaculated on her belly.

"You'll not believe what happened," he said.

"Tell me," I said. I imagined him doing it with me, not with her.

"She screamed and jumped back in bed, waving her hands and asking, 'What's *that*? What's *that*?' pointing frantically at my cum," he said, laughing.

"Why'd she ask?"

"You will *not* believe this," he said. He could barely stop laughing. "She had never seen cum before and didn't know—this is even more unbelievable—what it was and why it came out of my penis."

"What did you do?"

"I calmed her down, held her, and wiped it up. Then I explained the birds and the bees and how semen played a pretty big role in it all," he said, giggling.

"Did she understand?"

"Sort of. She thought it was gross. She didn't like its smell. Nor how sticky it was."

"Have you seen her since?"

"No, she called me a few days later. Was leaving town—a business trip—and said she would call, but never has."

He served pecan pie, poured us more wine. We finished half the pie. He talked about where he would go, what might happen.

I admitted how hard it would be for me to go on without him.

Time got the best of us. It was nearly 11 PM. I went to the front door. He put his hand on the door. He didn't want me to drive. I had to stay. I could sleep in his double bed.

We undressed and got into bed, each on our separate sides. Before he fell asleep, he reached over, tapped me on the shoulder. I turned over and he hugged me, his slender body pressing against mine with a tenderness I'd never felt from a man.

"Thanks," he whispered.

"For what?"

"For being my friend." His voice choked back a grief I knew too well. He patted my face and let his hand rest on my cheek. He stared at me; I think he knew how I felt and loved me just the same.

"It'll cost you," I said, trying to make light of the moment.

"Now what?"

"Fifth of Jack."

"Go to sleep."

I turned over and listened to him breathe. "Yes," I thought, "friendship is like this: being together without expecting anything else." His breathing grew still. I fell asleep.

The next morning, we woke early. He had to work on his Phenomenology of Religion paper, and I needed to get back to the dorm.

Star Light

Istudied my sociology books most of the day. By evening, I was tired and planned to be in bed early. Michael and his friend Sam came in. They asked if I wanted to smoke some good weed.

"No, not tonight," I said.

Sam said, "It's better than weed."

"Don't tempt me," I said.

"It's hash."

Several blocks from campus was an old Victorian house with a wraparound porch. Sam opened the stained-glass front door. He took us into a study. Floor to ceiling bookcases covered the walls. Only one or two books were on the shelves. A small coffee table with two candles sat in front of the couch. Incense burned.

Sam patted the couch. We sat down. He put his finger to his lips, motioning us to be quiet.

Several other people came in—long-haired kids dressed in psychedelic vests and jeans with peace patches on them. A stout man who wore a gold vest and black leather boots sat with a short-haired girl who could have passed for his daughter. One at a time, others came in as we had. Several sat down on the floor. No one spoke. No one seemed to know anyone. Everyone was as quiet as guests at a funeral.

After fifteen minutes, the door swung open. A tall, skinny black man with a red bandana around his afro, entered the room and bowed to us, his hands clasped in front of him.

"Good evening, my children," he said in deep voice.

He wore skin tight bellbottoms that outlined his ample anatomy. His shirt, open at the top, revealed strings of beads. He wore bracelets and had three rings on each hand, one with an emerald. He bent down and, going from one to another, asked who we were. His quiet, gentle manner reminded me of a dentist who was sizing you up before extracting a tooth. He smiled when we gave him our names and made comments—"Oh, aren't you a cute one," and "An elder has joined us."

He sat in a lotus posture. He closed his eyes and breathed for several minutes. He sang something in another language. It was not French, Spanish, or Latin. He opened his eyes.

"I'm Star Light. You've come here for what I have to offer. It's a chance for you to explore the invisible world. It's there all the time, right in front of you. You'll feel sensations you've never experienced before. I'll take care of you. Just let yourself open up." He tapped his chest. "The key is here to unlock your soul."

He fetched a small gold pipe out of a cloth bag that was slung over his shoulder. He pinched some greenish herb out of a small pouch and placed it carefully in the bowl of the pipe.

"Are you ready, my children?" he asked.

I felt skeptical. Here was some crank who bamboozled Sam. But I nodded and decided to go along. He lit the pipe and took a toke and passed it to Sam who passed it to me. I passed it to Michael, who passed it to a blond girl with sunglasses, she passed it to a boy with war paint on his cheeks. He passed it to the boy in shorts and a torn t-shirt who passed it to the gold vest and his girlfriend, then the pipe came back. It went back around until nothing was left.

My body tingled as if Tinkerbell had cast her fairy dust on me and I could fly. My skin was titillated by any sensation—a wisp of air on my face, the tug of my sleeve on my wrist—anything sent shivers down my body. My hips lifted involuntarily as they did with an orgasm.

Sam leaned, put his face next to mine. It startled me out of my skin.

"Wild, isn't it?" he said. His hand was on my leg.

I felt as if it had been caressed by the hand of God. I put my hand on his leg. Our two bodies became one. This *was* wild. Sam saw that I was aroused; I saw he was too.

I felt a moment of dread. This wasn't what I should be doing. I needed to get out of here.

Sam whispered, "It's all right. That's what happens."

The hippie girl next to me leaned over to kiss Michael. He kissed her back.

Star Light sat in front of each of us, took us by the back of our head, and kissed us gently. It didn't feel intrusive. It felt almost liturgical.

His lips were soft and yielding. He traced his tongue on our lips, let us feel the magnificent pleasure of the tongue. After the kiss, he drew his hand down our face onto our chest and belly and into our lap. He caressed our thighs and genitals. There were groans. He didn't want to have sex with us. He wanted us to feel as much sensation as we could feel. Then he slipped away and let us bask in the afterglow radiating over our bodies.

I found myself watching myself watch myself. The two books tilted against one another on the shelf. The candles cast a muted yellow glow on the paneling. The streaks in the windowpanes shivered with passing car lights. I wanted to rub my hand on every thing. I wished Bob was here to experience it and to let me touch him in a way so that he knew how deeply I felt about him.

Star Light lit another pipe and we passed it around. He continued with his ministrations. He methodically edged us to the point of an orgasm and then let us slide back.

I don't know how much time passed. One of the candles went out. Star Light was standing in the middle of the room. He bowed and put his hands together. "Good night, my darlings." The door closed behind him.

The blonde kissed Michael. He pushed her away and pulled his legs up close to him. She turned to the painted boy and they toppled to the floor and started to make love. The old man curled up with his young one to make out. Taboos melted away. Sam began to kiss me. I'd never kissed a man as passionately as I did him. My hand caressed his cheek, I felt the stubble of his beard. The simple touch on a lip, a cheek, an arm, or leg sent off fireworks. I wondered if other men became soft and gentle when they kissed.

Gradually I came to my senses. I panicked and pulled away from Sam. Michael was still wrapped in a tight ball. He winced as if he were in pain.

"Something's wrong." I pointed to Michael. I sat up, tucked in my shirt, and crawled across the floor to the divan by the window.

Sam took Michael in his arms. They pressed together, not kissing at first, just exploring. Eventually, they kissed and seemed content in each other's arms. The other couple on the floor had exhausted themselves and were passed out. The old man had left. His girlfriend had curled up in a fetal position. Other members of the group had fallen asleep, too.

The last candle went out. Gently, I nudged Michael and Sam and said, "We should get back." Arm in arm, the three of us floated on our respective clouds to the dorm.

The next day, Sam asked what I thought of Star Light.

"He was amazing," I said.

"Good," he said.

"But, I'm sorry I did..."

"It was fine."

"No, it wasn't."

He started to apologize. "I didn't…"

"No, no," I assured him, "what we did was nice, real nice. But I'm not sure, you know, I'd do that if…"

"I know what you mean," Sam said. "You're okay with me, though. Right?"

"Sure, sure," I said and tousled his hair.

I asked, "How's Michael?"

Sam's face lit up.

"He's great. Something happened to him. We, you know, we're doing great!" he exclaimed.

"Good," I said. But I wasn't so sure. Maybe I'd encouraged them to get sexually involved. If Michael's parents found out, he'd pay a price.

Sam and Michael continued to hang around and talk, but we never mentioned the night with Star Light again. I pushed it out of my mind. I'd slipped and had just barely gotten hold of myself before I fell over the edge. I thought of that squirrel outside my room at home and how he could leap with an assurance that he'd land where he should. I wish I had such an assurance. I focused my energy on my classwork, my relationship with Ann, and my concern about what Bob might do. I also had to figure out what I would do during the summer. I had to get as far from my dad's inquisitive eye as I could.

Quivering Essence

Tired by two long nights yet troubled about Bob's moral stand against the war, I'd checked out the jobs at Edgeville Methodist Church. But they were all taken. I knew I had to do something to justify my own 4-D status. Bob was right. I couldn't have a free pass while others were blown to bits in Nam.

I didn't want to spend another summer at the Glen Brooke Country Club, being a part of that set—the people who thrived on cocktail parties, clandestine affairs, and scramble golf matches. I kvetched about my lack of options with Jack Kirk, the loudmouth I'd initially detested at The Plunge but who'd been active at the civil rights march and seemed to have compassion for the down-and-out. When he wasn't grandstanding, he was engaging and liked to discuss the arts. He lived in a swank apartment off campus and told me that he knew someone who was starting a summer program in Appalachia. He'd let me know if there were openings.

His apartment fronted 16th Street, a two-lane residential neighborhood lighted by round white globes like oversized Christmas ornaments. Jack loved to drink and talk. Mostly talk. He never lost his passion for anthropology. Every argument came down to one ineluctable fact: it had an anthropological explanation. I enjoyed conversations with him about God since we were both taking Systematic Theology. My intellectual battles with him helped me hone my own arguments in class and write papers that were often polemics against his ideas.

Jack had noticed that I'd published a short poem in the Divinity School's student journal and admired it. I'd written poems for several years, mostly dabbling with form, learning the tricks of metrics. Jack read me one of his poems.

"Not bad. Where did you write that?" The poem had no set meter.

Jack leaned back in his chair, put his arms behind his head, and prepared for me to gush over his wondrous creation.

"Not bad," I said again.

"Not bad? Let me tell you, a few years ago I had it published in Cincinnati, in a religious journal. You like the idea?"

"Yeah, I think so."

"Think so?"

"I'm not sure I get it."

Jack slammed his chair down. "The idea is that a hunter," he said, "is able to give or take life like a God."

"Sure, I get that. But I'm not sure I agree."

"Why?"

"I don't think God hunts, does he?"

"No, but we're hunters and gatherers—that's how mankind started. All our early gods were nature gods: they were associated with the hunt."

"Yes, yes, I see. Good poem, nice, short and to the point."

"Thanks, you want to read another poem?"

"No, not now. Can I have a beer instead?"

"Sure."

Most of our discussions led to arguments. Jack hated to lose. If his argument scraped bottom, he said, "Yeah, but," and raised his voice. One night, he was contending that God was a "quivering essence" that surrounded us like an ether in outer space.

I asked him to clarify what he meant.

He said, "There you go, trying to name it, to fit it in a category, to describe it. That's what I refuse to do. It's a quivering essence. It defies any rational explanation."

"That may be good for you, Jack, but for me, if there is a God, I want some clarity about who or what it is."

"That's not for you to say."

"Why?"

"Because God's essence is ubiquitous, everywhere, all around us! It's quivering! Don't you get it?" He raised his hands up in the air and swung them around his head to give me a clear visual image of the quivering essence.

I jammed my hand over my mouth to stop from laughing.

He was serious. He had me, or at least he thought so. But I was not willing to cave and embrace his vague generality.

"Listen, you may think that. But I don't buy it. You seem to think that I should give up trying to figure out what this term 'God' is. But I don't want to. I think that's part of developing as a religious thinker: being able to question, not consigning God to some 'quivering essence,' which, to be honest, sounds like more like a description of Jell-O than God."

Jack's ears turned red; he scowled and jabbed his finger at me. "Don't insult me," he blared.

"I'm not. But it's all relative, Jack. You think what you think. I think what I think. If it works for you, fine. Relativity doesn't just apply to motion and space, but to God, and to ethics too."

"You think everything is relative?"

"I didn't say that."

"Yes you did!"

I threw up my hands, exasperated. "Fine, I did. Let's call it quits. I need to study."

I took the beer and headed out of his apartment.

"Hey, wait," he called after me.

"What?"

"Forget it," he said.

And I did. I strolled across the block by the campus woods that months ago had loomed in my altered state and stopped to gaze up into the trees, the intricate weave of their branches.

PART II

Although the word is common to all, most men live

As if each had a private wisdom.

"Four Quartets," T.S. Eliot

It is impossible to be an American in any deep sense without being a visionary and a mystic, without feeling the whole of human history as a mystic presence, and without having a mystic vision of the future.

Erling Duus, *Danish-American Journey*, Gauntlet Books, Franklin, Mass., 1971

Encounter

Jack informed me that he had landed a summer job as an interim minister with full pay and benefits. He asked what my plans were. I told him my dilemma again: I had work that I didn't want to do. My dad wanted me back in his orbit. Jack offered to introduce me to another student, Erling Duus whom he knew from taking several classes with him. He had a project in eastern Tennessee.

"What's he doing?" I asked.

"He plans to start a school up there, studying Whitman, Emerson, Wolfe, and other American writers—Sandburg and Cather—and learning about the folk traditions in that area. It's where the Hatfields actually live. I was going to be his assistant director until I landed a real job. You interested?" he said.

"Sure," I replied.

A week later, he barged into my room and called out, "Let's go. I told Erling about you. He wants to meet today!"

We hurried down 16ᵗʰ Street to a house set back among magnolias and overarching oaks. At the front steps, Jack held up a finger and said, "Listen, Jason, let me take the lead here. I know him well. Good friend. You know, bright. He respects me. We have two classes together. I have his trust, if you know what I mean."

"Sure," I said and stepped back to let him proceed up the stairs.

A screened-in porch ran the length of the building. The screen had several long scars on it. Its door hung on one hinge. The front door, oak laced with filigrees of glass, opened into a hallway. On the other side of it were two parlors. They had enormous bookcases with only a few books, covered with dust. The house seemed like a faded Southern mansion hinting at lost glory.

Seated in a chair at the end of the living room, Erling motioned us to come sit by him.

A copper lamp illuminated his face. The room was dark, and it was hard to make out his features. He looked familiar. I'd seen him in the hallways. Or in some class. I wasn't sure. He held a thick book in his long delicate fingers.

My initial impression was of a man totally self-absorbed and rude.

Jack tugged on my shirt sleeve. He whispered, "Come along," and stepped in front of me. "I'll take care of this."

Jack's cowboy boots clomped across the floor. His hand held out, he said, "Erling, it's so *good* to see you!"

Erling finished the paragraph that he was reading, inserted a scrap of paper to mark his page, and closed the book. He looked like a watch dog trained to keep still before barking at an intruder. He lifted his eyes didn't look at Jack but beyond him toward me. The right side of his mouth lifted slightly, and he winked.

I was not sure what the wink meant. He was dressed in wrinkled pants, an un-ironed white shirt, sleeves rolled up, and open at the collar, and unpolished shoes with the leather scraped and frayed. This slight figure looked like a young D.H. Lawrence: the narrow face and gaunt, haunted look of an artist who'd seen too much of the world and wanted to speak of its grave truths.

Jack had talked of him: a poet, writer, and mystic, of Danish heritage, yet raised in Kansas. He was an expert on the Transcendentalists and loved Walt Whitman and Thomas Wolfe.

Jack had told me about the school Erling wanted to start in the Cumberland Mountains and Jack bragged that he was to be the assistant director, but soured on the idea because it didn't pay at all.

"Hello, Jack," Erling shook his hand, "I see that you have brought the first-year student."

I was not sure how to take his calling me "the first-year student." For a moment, I was offended and put off. But that quickly passed. Maybe it was the wink that put me at ease. I sensed there was something more to him than met the eye.

Erling extended his hand to me and said, "I hear you're a poet."

"Well, yes, I write some."

"You might be interested in being part of my folk school?"

I blanched slightly, not willing to commit to something of which I knew very little. But not wanting to act uninterested, I nodded.

His blue eyes behind the wire-rimmed glasses were intense.

"Good, have a seat; let's talk."

Jack glowered at me, signaling me to keep back, and pulled up a chair in front and to the side of me.

Erling pulled up a chair.

Jack pulled his chair right next to Erling, his feet extended between us.

He interposed, "Erling, remember what I said earlier. Don't jump too quickly. Jason here is a fine fellow, but I'm sure you need to consider his views on..."

Erling waved Jack off. "I know, I know—come on, sit down—let's get to business." He scooted his chair closer to mine.

His brow furrowed deeply, Erling looked at me as if he could see right into my soul.

"What makes you interested?" he asked. "We need those who are willing to take serious risks, life threatening. We need people who can let go of their damn egos and get involved with people who live very different lives than most Americans live."

"Risks," I thought. "That is what I want to do." For my whole life—years of living in the suburbs, playing football, basketball, and golf, years of never worrying about walking the roads at night, never doubting my direction or my fate, because, no matter what I did, my dad had connections and I was always safe—I wanted to break away, to do something bold.

He put his hands together and held them prayer-like next to his lips. He stared at me.

Jack started to say something, but Erling deflected him.

I fumbled out, "I think I'm..."

"You're what?"

I spoke about how I wanted to change my life. Every word I said, every move I made, he observed like someone examining an actor auditioning for a play. I said that I needed to make sure it was a good match. "Tell me what you are doing," I said, "so I can determine if I am the right man for the job."

"Sure. That makes sense. Let me tell you what it will be like." Erling paused to make sure I was listening. "We are going into the heart of Appalachia, the Cumberland Mountains in Tennessee to start a folk school. It's Danish in origin. It builds on folk traditions that are being lost in the rapid-paced urban and industrial society. The founder, Frederik Severin Grundtig, believed that the best way to spread democracy was to have all the people involved, to have all voices heard. He set up regional folk schools. People learned about the right of each citizen to have a voice. People also explored the rich folk traditions in each region. People were empowered to speak up. People learned of their rightful place in larger democracy.

"The same usurpation of local ways and the undermining of their way of life that was happening in Denmark is happening right now in Appalachia," he explained. "Coal companies have bamboozled local people, taken their land, strip-mined their mountains, polluted their streams, sapped their lives, and left them in poverty. Many go to the cities for work. I want to help them stay and preserve their folk traditions: their stories, their art, their crafts, their way of life. That's what we'll be doing."

He sat back and stoked his pipe, puffing on it, and continued, "It will not be easy. Some people will think we're communists. They may try to drive us out. It's not luxurious. We'll sleep in sleeping bags and wash in wash basins. Not for the faint-hearted. Could you handle it?"

"I think I could," I said.

His arms moved as if he were sweeping something out of the air between us. His eyes combed over me carefully—my Oxford buttoned down shirt, my Dockers slacks, and penny loafers with pennies in them.

"You sure?"

"Yes."

"It's not suburbia."

"I know."

He bowed his head and then lifted it quickly. His voice filled with intensity.

"Before you commit—I must tell you this—a lot of people's lives will depend on you. I have talked with a few families in Cross Creek." he explained. "Some are interested in the school. They're poor. They've seen strangers come and go. They've been let down. You need to be able commit fully, not half commit, to being there."

I asked him to give me more history of Cross Creek.

"There are three ex-nuns from the Glenmary Home Mission Sisters of America who have bought a place in Cross Creek Hollow and are working to start alternative businesses—ladies making quilts, folk carvings. It hasn't been easy for them. Ninety percent of the locals have migrated north to Chicago to find other jobs. Only ten percent have stayed. They're trying to get them work so that they can buy back their land. It's largely owned by a British coal company that defrauded local people and bought up all rights to their land, and, now have strip-mined it. Local people are skeptical.

"But, to their credit, the nuns stayed. Some accuse them of being communists. Some shot at their house at night. It was—and still is—dangerous. That's it," he leaned back in his chair and peered at me over his glasses.

I put my hands between my legs and mulled over my options for the summer—golf, a delivery center, or this folk school. The one option, the one I had done for years and required no thought, the other required some risk. I looked up. "I'm your man. I'll do it."

He smiled, stood up and shook my hand. "You sure?"

"I'm sure!"

"Then we have a deal," he said, smiling and turning to Jack, "Thanks for bringing him by."

Jack stood up, took Erling by the arm, and spoke in a hushed tone, one he intended I should hear, "I told you that I have some misgivings. I think you should reconsider and let me..."

Erling shook Jack's arm off and turned toward me. "Care to come to my room, Jason? Let me show you some books I'd like you to read."

Jack's lips tightened. "Erling, I need to talk with you privately, *now*," he said firmly.

"No, not now, Jack. Later some time."

"I just have—."

"Save it".

Erling motioned for me to follow him to his room. "We need to start making plans. I want to go over when it will start," he said, tapping my chest. "When would you be available?"

"When do we start?"

Erling laughed. "Start?! Right now, my friend."

Jack hadn't given up. He stuck out his hand like a patrol guard, waving it. "We need to talk first. Come on, over here. Would you excuse us, Jason?"

Erling glared at Jack's hand. "No, Jack, we don't. Jason is a good match. He was in my New Testament Theology class. I was impressed with his sensitivity and insight. He's a guy who hears something and embraces it. I like that."

That's where I'd seen him, but he was dressed up: a jacket and a scarf flung over his shoulder. He loved to question the professor. His range of knowledge initially intimidated me, but he enjoyed the exchange of ideas and was as good a listener as a talker.

"Do you think you could raise some money from your church up in Illinois?" he asked. He slung his arm around my shoulder.

"Sure," I said, "how much?"

"A thousand."

"Probably," I said. My church wanted to do more service work. "Anything you want. Just ask."

"It must be nice," Jack muttered.

Erling looked at him. "Jack, I thought you said you could pull in a bundle when we last talked."

"Hey, Jason," Jack said, stepping in front of me. "Don't you think you're being hasty. You just met the guy." He nodded his head toward Erling. "Let's get back to school. We can make it there for supper. And talk. Give you a chance..."

"No, but thanks," I said. "Catch you later."

His boots drummed across the floor. The screen door opened and slammed shut.

Erling told me about Whitman's and his own vision of America, how it included everyone, particularly those excluded from the American dream. He lent me several books. He spoke with a passion and intensity of someone who knew much and knew it well.

Jack usually met me for breakfast at the Divinity School's cafeteria before our Systematic Theology class. But the next day he didn't show. I saw him later in the hall. He paused long enough to ask, "What do you think of our idea?"

"What idea?"

"The folk school," he shot back.

"That's not your idea. It's Erling's. He told me about..."

I didn't get to finish.

He pushed me against the wall, "*I'm* the one who encouraged him when no one would listen. *I'm* the one who recruited you to attend. *I'm* the one who brought you over to see him. Don't forget that! Don't think you can barge in because you have Daddy Warbucks. I warned him about you. Don't think you can get what you want because you—"

I shoved him away, "Get out of my way! We'll talk later."

But we didn't. Erling and I did. He was full of plans for both of us. We put together a budget, staff, and housing for the folk school.

Jack kept visiting Erling. I'd seen him come and go. He volunteered to help with fundraising—or so he said. Erling never mentioned their conversations. Whatever Jack had against me, I had to prove him wrong. And planned to do just that.

The Test

Early in March, Erling showed me a map of the Cumberland Mountain region—the town of Clearfork, and Cross Creek Hollow where he planned to have the folk school. "I'd like you to see it," he said.

"Anytime," I said.

He said, "Let's go!"

He threw together some food, a cooking stove, and a sack with odds and ends; I gathered some notebooks and several textbooks, some clothing, and a towel, and we headed off. He drove five hours from Nashville clear across the state to the Smokey Mountains. He wanted to visit a waterfall that he loved. He described it: nestled in a hollow, a ribbon of water that fell first down one ledge, then another until it sprayed out and cascaded into a pool where we could swim. Locals mostly skinny dipped. They waited for those who were in it to clothe themselves and leave before they stripped and slipped into the water. It sounded enchanting.

Late in the afternoon, exasperated with his aborted efforts to find a back road to the falls, he pulled off by a TVA reservoir.

"We're lost," he said. "We'll camp here."

He heated beans in a can on a burner and said we would sleep in the car, with a frayed quilt to cover us.

Over beans, he bragged that he was a great boxer. He challenged me to a match. The last time I fought I had lost terribly. My father bought my brother and me gloves because we fought so much. He laced on the gloves and told us to fight. We could barely lift the gloves. We flailed, swatted overhanded at one another like pillow fighting. A straight-out punch, because of the gloves' weight, caused us to topple forward, missing the other entirely. Bigger than I was, my brother swung a round-house and his glove whapped my head. I was out.

I wasn't so sure I wanted to box. But Erling pulled out his gloves and handed me a pair. He took off his shirt and tightened up the belt on his trousers above his belly-button. I took off my shirt and let my jeans ride where they were. I was thirty pounds heavier than he was.

"You sure you want to do this?" I asked. "I'm much bigger than you are."

"Don't worry," he smiled, flinging a fake punch at me. "I can take care of myself. You're the one who needs to worry."

Once we laced on the gloves, he circled around me, peppered jabs at my stomach and face. I cautiously backed up, kept my gloves in front of my face as I'd seen Muhammad Ali do in his heavyweight fights against Liston. I figured that if I could keep moving, since I had a longer stride, I could make our encounter more a dance than a real fight.

I soon learned otherwise.

As I was bobbing to the left, Erling's glove smacked my temple. It staggered me. He laughed and gestured with his fist, "Come on, try and hit me."

I backpedaled. He came at me, hit me on the side of my head again and then slugged me with an uppercut that practically knocked me out. I staggered backward and ended up on one knee. I stared in disbelief at him. He bounced around me to the right and left. "Come on. Come on!" My head ringing, the bruise on my face stinging, I stood up but was still woozy. He laced me in the belly with four quick punches. He knocked the wind out of me. I toppled back, nearly fell over but caught myself with my glove on the ground. I propped myself up and darted away to get some distance from him.

"Come on. Fight. What's wrong with you? Don't be a sissy."

I wasn't a sissy. I was afraid of my rage.

In seventh grade, when I was shooting baskets in the gym to perfect a left-handed layup, a younger boy flung basketballs at me, taunting me. I told him to stop. He pelted me again.

"Leave me alone, okay?" I said.

He nailed me in the back as I shot a layup.

The next thing I remember was seeing his body recoil, his hands pressed against his face, blood oozing though his fingers, lying on the floor beneath me. The coach raced into the gym and glanced at my clenched fists. He called my name, "Jason. Jason. Stop it! Stop it!" He pushed me aside. "What the *hell* have you done?"

I couldn't remember what happened. A button was pushed, rage erupted, my body took over.

The coach told me that I better watch myself. I'd been watching myself ever since. I'd nearly lost it several times, but always kept my rage at bay. I took walks to cool off.

If I could keep the fight just a playful dodge, if I kept breathing, I could keep the rage at arm's length. I paid more attention to it than Erling, the quick moves he made, his punches at my face.

"Come on!"

He came at me, moving in, his hands up and his fists, one after another, jabbing me.

The blows hurt. The bones in my cheeks smarted. My jaw was sore. The thick gloves pummeled my scalp, numbing it. If I pulled my head back to protect it, he'd land a flurry of hits to my stomach. I was in a fight for my life. "The son of a bitch," I thought, "wants to knock me out."

"Hey, I've had enough," I yelled and put my arms up in surrender.

He slugged me right in the face. I fell back, stumbled for several yards, my eyes blurry. All I could see was his eyes and his gloves in front of him. I straightened up and jabbed at him. He ducked down, bobbed to the left and slammed me in the stomach.

He laughed and circled to my left. I saw an opening and hit him in the jaw. It sent him back about four feet. He smiled.

"Good. Good," he said, encouraged. He was pleased; we were a match, each given over to the fight.

I dodged to the right and left, avoided his best punches. When I could see an opening in his gloves, I thrust a jab at him. My gloves felt as if someone had poured cement in them. It took more and more effort to hold them up.

I had to act fast or he'd knock me out. He was crouched down, bobbing to the right and left. For an academic—someone I thought to be totally non-athletic—he was tough. He skipped to the right, ducked, and then to the left. I realized that he had a set routine. Move one way, then the other, jab with one fist and then the other. I waited until I was sure. We had been boxing for fifteen minutes before I saw him move where I knew one glove would be down. I threw a hard punch at his head. He toppled backward, only the whites of his eyes showing. I quickly lunged forward and grabbed him before he slammed into a tree. I held him against me, both of us drenched with sweat. As he came to, he looked me in the eye, "Good punch."

I asked, "Can we call it quits? I'm exhausted. Come on, the game's over."

"No," he said firmly. "It's *not* over yet."

He jabbed me in the stomach and leapt back three feet. He maneuvered more consciously, his feet not as quick as they had been, but his arms just as powerful. He tossed jabs at me. He wove and bobbed and ducked lower, forcing me to throw my punches downward. It put more stress on my upper arms. My hands dropped. He hit me four times in the jaw, twice in the head. It sent me back-pedaling, reeling. I stumbled to one knee.

But he came at me like a bulldog, growling. I stood up and back-pedaled.

His eyes bulged. He was looking for a knockout punch.

I dropped both my arms, shaking them to loosen them up, relieving the pressure on my neck. I danced to the right and left, nearly bumping into the car. I was running out of time. He wanted to knock me out. My body moved as if I were dancing with fire. He pursued me, a few jabs landed on my belly. I let my arms dangle. My legs were giving my arms a reprieve. He surged at me; I fluttered to the right and left. He didn't let up. He had me on the run.

He walloped me with an uppercut to my jaw. I shook my head: he was trying to kill me. He wanted a knockdown. This was no game; it was for real.

Somewhere in my head something snapped.

I felt a surge of energy. My left arm landed on his upper chest. He tilted slightly to the right. My right hook landed on his jaw. The impact knocked me off balance. I swirled back to my right and turned around. As my upward gaze caught the scarlet tint of last light in a maple, I failed to see what happened to Erling. By the time I turned back, I saw him topple as if he were going downhill, his head gazing upward. His legs wobbly, with the suddenness of a puppet whose strings are snipped, he slumped forward, shoulder first, then his whole body, crumbled in a heap. He hit the ground with a thud, then sprawled out. His head thumped on the pavement and his body bounced a few feet and then settled, motionless. His head was turned sideways, his arms at his sides, his legs grotesquely spread out like a frog about to leap.

"Damn." I muttered and ran over to him, knelt, picked up his head which had lolled to the side, a large black and blue bruise visible on his cheek, and held his head in my hands, gently lifting him up, cradling him in my arms. His eyes were open but unresponsive, his expression vacant. I called his name, "Erling, Erling." I continued to cradle him for several minutes, then let him down, careful to put his head down gently. Quickly shucking off my gloves, I went to get the canteen. When I lifted him up again, his body was surprisingly heavy. I pulled him into my lap and splattered water on his face. He looked awful, his skin pasty white. He wasn't moving. I put him down again, gently, and grabbed the comforter from the back seat and covered him, rocking him back and forth, looking at the car. I had no idea where we were, where the nearest hospital was. Whatever rage snapped in me—and this time, I was conscious of it, using it---was dissipated. It was replaced with dread. I may have killed him, or if not him, since he was breathing erratically, may have damaged his brain. It took about ten minutes for him to come to. First, he twitched, his muscles reflexively tightened, then his eyes focused on me. He lifted his left arm to wipe his face and realized that he still had his gloves on. He smiled weakly and shook his head, "Not a good idea: might knock myself out."

He lay back more comfortably, stretching out, relaxed in my arms. He breathed more intently, taking longer breaths, moving his jaw around, sorting out the effects of the blow and his tumble to the pavement.

"I didn't see it coming, but it was a good one," he said. "Can you get these gloves off me?"

"I thought I'd killed you," I whispered as I unlaced his gloves, not looking him in the face.

"Yeah, I thought you did too!"

"I'm sorry. I really am."

"No, no, don't be. It was a good punch, solid," he shook his head. "Face it, if you had missed me with that one, I would have clobbered you and been damned delighted to have done it."

I laughed, "So we're done?"

"Yep. Done. Good fight. For a country club kid, you're better than I thought you'd be."

We sat down on an embankment and analyzed the fight. He thought that he had me when I shuffled back on my heels and tried to avoid him. He was sure he had me when I angrily charged at him. My guard was down. He had a perfect opening but miscalculated. He sawed his jaw back and forth. He'd been taken down.

One good punch was all it took to win Erling's confidence. I felt proud.

The sun had settled in the trees. We drank water from a canteen. Our breathing returned to normal. Torrents of sweat still poured over our bodies. He motioned to the water. We walked down to the reservoir, stripped, and swam into the sunset sprawling across the water.

"Where do we sleep?" I asked after we had toweled off.

He patted his car. "In Mabel."

"Mabel?"

"That's her," he said, rubbing the faded blue finish of his Rambler. She was called Mabel because the 'r's had fallen off the front of the hood. He transposed the 'm' and 'a' leaving her name: *Mabel*. A fold-back seat came in handy. He reclined it. We pulled out the quilt and two pillows and had a comfortable bed.

The next morning, we sat over a kerosene stove. The water boiled. Two cups of coffee warmed us. We drove to Cross Creek Hollow to meet the people who lived there.

Cross Creek Hollow

After getting off I-75 north from Knoxville, he exited at Jellico, the last town in Tennessee before the Kentucky state line. We took Route 9, which joined up with 25W as it rose into the mountains and skirted along the Kentucky border on the Cumberland River. The road wrapped around the mountains, carved snugly against its slopes. It unwound in a valley and meandered along the river. We came to Route 90 which took a serpentine path deeper into the mountains.

At the town of Clearfork, Erling turned left on a dirt road. It was filled with ruts. Dust billowed up. Some homes were set a few feet from the road. Some were set back, up on knolls or down by creek beds. The undersides of the ones on risers were exposed. Some were painted, many were not. On a particularly steep incline, he pulled up into a yard. The house was set on posts. It had an unscreened front porch.

"This is it," he said. "The future home of the folk school."

"But, look"—I pointed at a boy on the porch— "somebody lives here."

"Right."

"Who lives here?" I asked.

"Peggy Lester and her family," Erling said. "They have another house up the hollow and want to move back to it. They've agreed to sell us the house and the land."

A teenager with a mop of blond hair waved at him.

"That's Bobby." Erling waved back and called out, "How are you?"

"Fine," he said and stepped down the front steps to greet us.

Erling introduced us. I shook Bobby's hand, which was soft yet strong. He smiled at me and told me Erling said that I played football.

"Is it true?" he asked.

"Yes," I said.

He raced off and grabbed a football. He tossed it to me. I flung it back at him. He grabbed it. "Go out for a long one," I told him. He sprinted off and I launched a long one right into his hands.

"Well, you've made a friend," I heard someone say. Standing on the porch was a large woman, her hair pulled back. She had a beautiful face. Not the beauty of a fashion model, more the beauty of someone who'd lived a hard life. She had deep-rutted crow's feet at her eyes, a sturdy jaw and a bold square face. Her smile radiated a warmth and humor that made me feel at ease.

Bobby trotted back and said, "Nice pass." We walked up the yard, his body inches from mine, his arm brushing against mine.

Erling introduced me to Peggy who said, "Pleased to meet you," shook my hand, and gestured for us to come in. The front door swung open to a hallway between two front rooms, a bedroom to the right and left. We walked down the hall past two smaller rooms to a kitchen.

Peggy said, "Erling told us a lot about you."

Not sure what to say, I leaned back against the door frame and joked, "I'm not sure what he told you, but none of it is true."

She laughed and pointed to a chair at a kitchen table, "Set yourself there. Get a load off your feet. Hey Bobby, get him a chair. Bobby's been anxious to meet you. He loves football. You played it?"

"Yes, I did."

Bobby placed three chairs at a long wooden table. I sat down next to him. He looked at me. A wide grin lit up his face, his cheek lined with wrinkles, his eyes full of delight.

Peggy asked, "You hungry?"

"No, that's fine."

"I'll not hear it. You've driven a long way. A feller your age, he needs his food. I'll fix you some vittles. You eat if I fix some?" Her tone led me to believe there was only one right answer.

"Yes, ma'am."

"That's better. Nothing better than a feller with a good appetite."

She carried herself with graceful dignity. Her dress, clinging loosely to her, denoted the plainness of her nature. She pulled out an iron skillet and shoved wood in the stove. I liked her manner: She said what she thought and expected the same from me. Later, Erling told me that she had twelve children and raised them all even when her husband, George, had black lung disease. His lungs had become coated with the fine coal dust that, over the years, clogged the lungs just as smoke did, but worse, so that he was out of breath and tired most of the time.

She plopped a dollop of lard in a skillet and threw in large thick slabs of some bacon. After cooking it until it browned, she set it aside and cracked several eggs in the pan. They sizzled in the grease. She flipped one after another on a plate, set several slices of bread on the stove top to toast them, slapped butter over them, poured some applesauce from a canning jar in a bowl, and set plates in front of Erling, Bobby, and me. She filled a cup with black coffee and leaned back to admire her handiwork.

We gobbled her food. I said, "Best eggs ever."

"I know," she said. "Used to be a short order cook. I served thirty at a time."

Bobby scooted his chair by the window and tossed crumbs out the window. He'd stuck tobacco in his cheek and spat tobacco juice at the chickens. They 'baaaked' and skittered away. He laughed and spat some more.

"Lord sakes leave them alone, Bobby," Peggy scolded him. "You torment them so."

Bobby's dark eyes were sunk deep in his face. With dusty brown hair sticking out at odd angles, he looked as if he'd just woken up. He had the same problem with his hair as I did. He'd comb it, pat it down with water, but it never cooperated. He walked across the room with an easy lope, his hips naturally swaying like a dancer's, carrying his weight lightly on the balls of his feet. He rarely stood still. He always wanted to be doing something to show me something he'd found, and ask me questions what it was like in the city. He chewed tobacco, as did his younger sisters.

Peggy introduced me to the girls, who'd been playing in the creek. She stood by each, patting them on their shoulders as she told me their names.

"Come on, don't be shy. This is Donna, and that's Katie, and the two young ones, they're twins, Janet and Joanie," she said.

I came up to each and shook their hand (they giggled) and told them what a delight it was to meet them. They were skinny with long angular faces. Their hair was cut short. They scampered off to the backyard and chased the chickens.

Bobby stood by the door tossing a football up and down. He eyed me so that the minute I'd scooped up the last egg yolk with some toast and cleaned my plate, he could toss me the ball.

We went into the dirt yard with a chicken coop at one end and a large fenced garden at the other. Quick on his feet, he darted up and down the yard, snatching my throws. He had good hands and could snare them high or low.

He treated me like an older brother and Peggy fed me like her kin.

I felt at home. It wasn't a society circumscribed by social events—parties, golf tournaments, bridge games, cocktail parties—where everyone was obsessed with keeping up appearances. No one had to wear the latest style clothes. It wasn't a place where I needed to pay attention to how I looked and what impression I was making. I could be who I was without putting on airs. I tossed one pass after another. The ball sailed over the parched red earth to Bobby who could have played all afternoon if my arm hadn't given out.

Bobby wanted to show me the swimming hole. Erling drove up the road where it narrowed to one lane. There was no guard rail. The side of the road fell off hundreds of feet into a ravine. The tops of scrub pines poked up from a creek bed.

Bobby yelled, "Pull in there." He hopped out of the car and raced down a rocky path. "Come on!"

In a clearing, a creek flowed off a jut of rocks and pooled in a basin. Dammed up with rocks, it looked to be fifteen feet deep. Tall poplar and ash surrounded the pool.

We sat by it and threw rocks into it. Bobby asked if we wanted to go for a swim. Erling begged off. I stripped off my clothes and stepped into the ice-cold water. I pulled out my foot.

"No time for wimps!" Erling cried.

Bobby had already jumped off a rock. He was paddling around. I dove in. My skin felt shrink wrapped. Every muscle contracted. I took several strokes and Bobby splashed me. I splashed him back. He leaped at me, trying to dunk me, and I dodged him and pulled him under. Wiry, he squirmed away. We played in the pool for fifteen minutes. When we hopped out, Bobby sat on a rock in the sun and I joined him. Bobby was self-possessed, comfortable in his skin. It felt natural to be in my body, too. Once dried and dressed, we headed back to Peggy's house. Peggy gave me a big hug and told me how glad she was I was working with Erling. She invited me to come up anytime. Her home was my home.

We waved goodbye and drove off. I asked Erling if she was sincere, if she meant what she said.

He said, "Yes," he said, "that's how she is."

Before we'd gone too far, he stopped the car. He turned off the engine. The evening light clung to the high ridges in the distance.

"Hey, I've been thinking," he said, "I need an Assistant Director, you know, someone to help organize the day programs, to fund raise, and to work closely with me in selecting students."

"That's what I thought Jack was supposed to be."

Erling laughed. "No, no, never. That was *his* idea, never mine."

"Really?"

"Yep," he said. "Even before he got the job at the church that pays him so well, I never wanted him as an assistant."

"That's not what he said."

"Jack has a unique way of seeing the world," he said, slung his arm on the back of the seat, and turn to me. "You want to do it?"

The dust behind us had roiled up and swept over the windshield. It settled and the view was clear again.

"All right," I said.

"Good, then I want you to meet several others. They're important. We need their cooperation," he said. He started the engine and drove down the hollow.

Erling introduced me to Marie Cirillo, the nun whose work developing jobs and programs for local people he'd told me about. Longtime residents like Peggy found that they could sometimes keep their homes, but the land around them, land that had game and fresh running brooks with fish and crawdads, became wastelands, contaminated with sludge from strip mines. Marie wanted to rebuild the communities and preserve the land.

Erling supported her efforts and wanted to work with her. He asked her to be on the board of the folk school. She agreed. With that last commitment made and with Marie on board, we headed back to Nashville. On the long drive back, he told me what he needed from me in terms of money. Erling had lined up three students to attend the folk school, two college girls and one local girl. He had also purchased a cabin for us to stay in. The other students would stay in a Methodist lodge near the Kentucky border. Folk school classes would meet there in the mornings and evenings. We'd have our summer arts and activities up in Cross Creek during the day on Peggy's land.

Money Matters

In late March, I drove back to Glen Brook to raise money. A church trustee, Mr. James Hook, agreed to talk with me about the project.

His house sat in an old residential community across from the Glen Brook football field. I wandered to the field I used to play on, walked by the bleachers, and stood on the grass, the white 10-yard-lines ribbed in the grass. I remembered how when the band played we burst through a large hoop with Glen Toppers painted on a large screen. Just on the other side of the hoop, cheerleaders with pompoms screamed at the top of their lungs. Spectators stood and clapped. For an hour or two, we'd give up our bodies for the team. We'd slam into the ground, only to get up and go at it again and again. It seemed so long ago. Yet my right knee remembered it every time it rained.

Mr. Hook, a bespectacled man, greeted me and told me to have a seat in his living room. His wife, a white-haired lady with a matronly build, yet the graceful movement of a former dancer, offered me a Sprite. We talked for an hour about the town, the church, and my project. Mr. Hook seemed interested, but wanted to know what my career interests were— "The ministry, perhaps?"

"Not sure," I said.

"What do you mean?" he asked.

I was at a loss as to what to say.

His wife had brought out chocolate chip cookies and more Sprite. She interrupted her husband's line of inquiry.

She said, "I think, whatever your career interest, what you are doing is noble. In my mind, it's very Christian. Serving the poor—isn't that what Christ asked us to do?" She directed her question not at me but at Mr. Hook. It took a moment for it to register with him. She continued, "Then it only makes perfect sense that the church supports him in his endeavors."

Mr. Hook nodded his head and winked at me. "She has a way of making her point, don't you think?"

She admonished him, "Now, dear, you know I always allow for differences in opinion."

He put his hand to the side of his mouth and whispered, "'Allow' is the key word. 'Permit' is quite another thing."

"Did you say something, dear?" she inquired.

"Nothing, my dear, just confirming our support for his work."

He agreed to do the fundraising. By the end of the holiday, he had a fifteen-hundred-dollar check cut for the folk school. I drove over to his house, rang the doorbell, and practically hugged him. Nonplussed, he invited me in and offered me a Sprite. We talked about the civil rights movement and the antiwar fervor on colleges. I was struck by his open-mindedness. His one requirement of me was that I keep a journal of my "mission" to Appalachia and that I come by again before I left.

Several days before I left, my parents took me to dinner at the club.

I put on my usual uniform for the occasion: blue blazer, tie, and slacks.

When I came downstairs, my father was at the back-porch door. He was still wearing his black pinstriped suit. He leaned over the porch, tapping his cigar on the railing and letting the ashes fall to the patio below. His dark hair had streaks of grey at his temples. He patted the railing next to me, noting where he wanted me to stand. He asked me to step out and offered me a cigar.

"No, thanks."

He pressed on with his concerns. "Your mother tells me that you're planning on working in Tennessee, some sort of school, is that right?"

"Yes," I said. I hadn't informed him for fear he might object.

"Well, we're worried about your decision," he said. "Does it pay well?"

"No, not at all. But room and board are free."

He plodded by me and faced the backyard garden, and, beyond it, to the bank of trees, and, further, to the faint headlights of cars on Butterfield Road. He paused there and puffed on his cigar.

"Sure you don't want one?" He held one out to me.

"No."

"Is this part of your program at the seminary?"

"No. But it's something I want to do, Dad. We're working with the people in Appalachia. They have it pretty hard"—

"I know all too well," he said and tapped his cigar on the railing, knocking off its ash, taking a long puff on his cigar. I'd forgotten that his father had worked in southern Ohio during the Depression. My dad had hated it. His mother had committed suicide there.

His face looked drawn, his lips tight. He shook his head.

"I think it would be better—your mom worries you know—for you to work here. Mr. Selman has a good job with benefits at his warehouse. I told you earlier it could be arranged. It pays quite well. It's time you start earning a living. And you'd be out by three and could play—"

"I don't want to do that."

"Money, son, is what makes this world go around," he said. "You'll come to—"

"Dad, this is part of *my ministry*," I said.

"Ministry?"

"Yes."

He cocked his head sideways and held his cigar at a distance and looked at it.

"Ministry?" he said more to himself than to me. He was trying to find his way around the word.

"Ministry," I said.

"I see," he said and took a long puff on his cigar. "This is a very good brand. Cuban. Sure you don't want one?"

"I'll take one for the road."

"Here," he said, passing me one. I put it in my jacket pocket. "You sure, son, you know what you're getting into?"

"I've been there. The people are great..."

"I've lived there. And, believe me, they're not as great as you think."

"Dad, I really want to give this a shot. I'll earn money at school. I have a job as a dorm advisor during the year."

He furrowed his brow. "Well—"

"Dad, it's what I *want* to do."

"All right. But keep us informed. Your mom's worried."

"I will."

"Here take another one of these," he said. He held out a cigar. "They're from Havana. Don't ask how I got them!"

"You're trying to get me addicted," I said.

He laughed. "How did I raise such a puritan!"

"Thanks, Dad."

"Any time," he said. "Look, your mom is waiting for us. Doesn't she look stunning!"

He pushed back my unruly hair which had begun grown over my ears and down my neck.

"You should get a haircut before you leave," he said.

Mother reached out to take his arm. "Everything all right?"

"Fine," he said.

—

I sat in the back seat as my parents sipped their martinis in the front of the car.

At the club, my father drove under a vaulted canopy. A valet opened the doors of the car. "Good evening, Mrs. Follett." "Good evening, Mr. Follett." And my door opened, too. "Good evening, Mr. Follett."

A red carpet led to the main entrance. The door was opened for us.

Cocktails were served in the Green Room. Dinner would be served in the formal dining area. The Green Room overlooked the 18th green. I had several beers. The conversation—how the course was opened, who shot the best round of golf, who was winning the latest PGA tournament, what the weather was like, or was forecast to be like, what the dog had done—bounced from topic to topic.

Our dinner guests, the Johnsons, joined us. Mrs. Johnson wore thick make-up. Her face looked like a mask. In the caddy shack, she was known as a "ballbuster." If she didn't like where a caddie stood, if his shadow transgressed her line, if he moved an inch while she prepared a shot, she'd shriek, "Young man!"

We were paired off at dinner so that each woman had a man by her side. Mrs. Johnson sat beside me and asked what I was doing for the summer. I told her about the folk school.

She smiled and said, "Why, yes. I remember when I was your age. I worked with the poor in Cleveland. For a summer, I took a bus to a shelter, served meals, and provided day care for some women. Very pathetic. Ignorant people, really. It was such sad work. Those people, I learned, will never amount to much. Born poor, they'll die poor...."

I interrupted. "I'm sorry but I *totally* disagree. From what I've seen—and I have only been there once—people want to regain control over their lives. Their homes and land were bought out from under them..."

"Such idealism," she spoke over me, her voice pitched higher. "Yes, it *is* commendable for a person your age, and natural, I suppose."

"I don't consider myself an idealist." I responded. "I see myself more as a person who wants to learn and who..."

She smacked her hand on the table and glared at me. Her mouth tightened so the muscles in her cheeks bulged. "Jason, listen, I don't want to discuss this matter. But let me say that—and mark my words..." She pointed at me, one long pink-tipped index finger at me. "in a year you'll tire of them and their sad lives and move on, as I did, as we all do." She pursed her lips together and glanced around the table for approval. "You must eventually find work with

80

more reputable people." She smirked. She was pleased with herself, and, surely, delighted that others felt the same way she did. She made one last declaration. "Those sorts of people wouldn't get a lick of my money, or anyone else's if I had my way." She nodded her head, smiled, and asked my father about his plans for the summer.

The waitress brought our salads. My mother shuffled her cucumbers onto my salad plate—she never ate them— and patted my hand. She whispered, "That's just Hilda." She raised her eyebrows and sighed. She added, "Your dad and I are proud of you."

I finished the meal hurriedly and excused myself, careful to thank the Johnsons for the meal and tell them how *nice* it was to see them. I would just as soon have told Hilda to stuff her damn money up her ample ass, but put on a polite face instead.

I walked down the fairway. When I thought about golf, I could block out anything and just think of each shot, how it would fly, land, spin back, and settle on the green.

My parents had finished their coffee and were saying goodbye to the Johnsons when I came back in the club. Hilda sashayed by in her purple dress (she loved purple, "doesn't everyone love purple?" she was fond of saying.)

I snuck in behind my parents. My father was talking to my mother. She saw me coming before he did. "That's the last time I'll have dinner with that pompous ass!" I didn't let on that I heard him. It would have upset my mother. But I smiled all the way home.

Before I headed back, Mr. Hook invited me to come for a chat. Since his wife was out of town, he asked if I'd like a Bud. I did. We sat in his living room and talked about the present antiwar demonstrations and his youth. Before Pearl Harbor, his friends were protesting our entrance into the war. The one beer led to two and two to three. He talked about himself and his life, his work as an accountant and his wanting, most of his life, to paint. He showed me his landscapes; they were good: the lake, near his house, misted with fog, in different seasons.

He was a thoughtful man who was honest about his own struggle with finding the truth about his own faith, or lack of it. He lived what he called two lives: his work life, the one he had to do to raise his three children— all grown—and the artistic life, the one he kept to himself.

He said, "I learned some things over the years."

He took off his glasses and wiped them with a napkin. "It seems that each generation believes that it has staked claim on The Truth. Some of my business friends say that the world comes down to money. Money makes the world go round."

"My dad tells me that!"

"He's right in many ways. There's some truth to that. But as a painter, I work alone. Oh, I have a few artist friends and mentors. We agree it's not about money. It's beauty that's most satisfying. I could be happy with just my paints and a landscape."

"That's how I feel when I write a good poem," I said, although I realized that I barely had written anything in the last year.

"Bet you would."

"Being an artist is never easy."

"You don't make a living out of it."

"No. I've wrestled with it my whole life. Sometimes I think I have myself figured out. But it's not so. The older I get, Jason, the more I come to see that I may come across some wonderful revelation that makes me more aware of something in myself—how I always strive to be the best and, say, as a result, overreach and do poorly—and discover that, much as I think that I will not make the same mistake again, I do. Have you noticed that?"

I laughed. "Every time I think I have myself figured out, I discover I'm just beginning to understand how I'm not what I expected. Who I am seems like a vanishing trick, one day this; another day, that."

"Exactly," he said, tapping his bottle against mine. "It seems that as I come to see something is true, I think, 'Yes, this is so,' only to get busy with my life and then forget what it is I saw. Years later, in a different time and a different place, I discover the same truth again. But it means as much to me the second time as it did the first time I discovered it, because the second time around I know better how to use it." He took another drink from his beer.

"Do you want something to eat?" he asked.

I did. He put a frozen pizza in the oven, and we sat in the kitchen. As we ate the pizza, he went back to our conversation.

"The truth, it seems to me," he said, "is more an accumulation of insights, each coming in different ways. The more I can expose myself to different situations, ones that push me out of my convenient ways, that shake up the same routines, the better I will be at coming to see what my truth is. The real truth comes to me when I'm vulnerable and filled with doubt. At those moments, whatever I have forgotten in my past, the little truths will come together in my heart..." He tapped his chest. "right here, and I'll know what I only guessed at was there all along, waiting like a stranger, to greet me and say, 'Here, this is your Truth,' and, finally, I will know it too and am able to accept it."

Not sure I entirely understood him, since what he was saying seemed very personal. I simply nodded my head. He thanked me for the talk and admitted, "People of my generation generally never talk much about themselves. They're doers. But me, I'm different."

I thanked him. Hilda's words had left a bitter taste in my mouth. His words felt sweet. Instead of shaking hands, he gave me a hug. He said that he'd share my reports with the church.

I felt lucky to know him, lucky to be on my way to some truth that I hoped to find in the mountains.

Goodbyes

Once back at Vanderbilt, I checked in with Michael and Sam. I'd miss Michael and Sam hanging out in my room. But I felt good that Michael had endured his trauma and found a friend. Odd how some guys had violated him, and another boy saved him, how men could be so cruel to one another, yet also be so kind.

Bob's efforts to get a conscientious objector status had failed. He'd go into the service. Because of his facility with language, he'd been assigned to a special unit for decoding enemy messages. He had to report for boot camp, but he didn't have to be in combat.

He threw a goodbye party. Eight professors and their wives came, along with several students. By the end of the party, his apartment looked like an air raid shelter after a bomb exploded. People were strewn on the floor and couches, everyone drunk and maudlin. One couple after another hugged him and slipped into the night. Ann and I stayed overnight. We sat up until one or two talking with Bob and his latest girlfriend.

Next day, after breakfast, I drove him to the airport. He was my one consistent college friend. I felt as if he were a brother. But I didn't want to let on that I had a knot in my stomach. I bantered with him about how hung over we were and how Ann and I wouldn't have a place to crash on the weekend.

When he stepped to the curb to wish me goodbye, he was looking at the cement, not at me.

"Something wrong?" I asked.

He lifted his head to me. His eyes were filled with tears, his face contorted with pain. Without thinking, I opened my arms. We hugged. I sobbed helplessly.

He whispered in a raspy voice, "I need to go."

I held him tight. "I know. I know."

"I do need to go; but, Goddamn, this is hard." He rubbed his hand across his face.

"I don't want to lose you," I said and pushed him back slightly, staring at his face—angular with high cheekbones, blue eyes, and a mop of curly brown hair. I brushed his hair back like he usually did.

He blinked and grabbed a hold of me. "Damn. Damn. I maybe should have just kept my 4-D. I never thought it would come to this."

"We're looking pretty pathetic," I said, trying to joke. I noticed that several men hopping out of cars were glaring at us, just as they had when Paul and I embraced at the airport months ago.

"Yes, we are." He laughed and looked at the other men. "They must think we're a couple of queers!" He waved at them, kissed me quickly on the lips, and gave them the finger.

"Figure we should give them something to talk about," he said. "They don't know what love is."

He held my hand and said softly, "I do love you. You know that?"

I bit at my lower lip. "Yes, yes, I do."

He said he'd write; I must write too. The mindless regimentation of boot camp was going to be hard.

"I'll miss our conversations," he said, "and the—" His voice trailed off.

"Being together."

"Yeah."

"Me too."

"No more times like we had," he said.

He stepped back and picked up his bag. I wiped my tears away, my chest torn open. I watched him go through the turnstile. Once inside, he waved once. He entered a line and turned away. I got in the car, touched my lips with my hand, looked at him once more, and drove away.

I saw Ann the next day. She asked how it had been and I cried again. I told her that he said that he loved me and no guy had ever told me that before. I couldn't get over it. He said it as if it were the most natural thing in the world. Yet, for me, to say it—or even to think it—brought up fears and doubts about my own sexual feelings. No matter how deeply I had buried them they broke through the crust of my denial. I said nothing of what I felt to her. But she knew Bob had cracked my shell. Grief worked its way out. We went back to my dorm room. She held me most of the night while I cried. She understood that I'd lost a part of me that I could not name.

Her fingers traced lines down my chest and belly. My fingers glided over her nipples and her soft round belly and legs. We stopped to kiss and then, almost without thinking, made love. Never had I felt as comfortable as I did with her.

She left the next day for a summer job in Seattle. I felt as I had with Bob, choked up. I drove her to the airport. She took her two suitcases to the ticket desk and waved. I watched several planes take off, clear the hills, and head into the clouds. Life was a long goodbye.

I drove home and worked at the country club pro shop. The pro taught me most of what I knew about golf, about how to swing and make trick shots. He liked me and put me in charge of starting times. I also worked around the yard at home and weeded my Mom's garden. I went out with my friend Jerry, who liked to try to pick up girls. He mostly just drank too much and we drove home at an ungodly hour with a sizable bar bill for all our efforts.

In June, I packed my bags, including my journal and writing paper. I looked at a map of eastern Tennessee for Clearfork to make sure exactly where to meet Erling.

Too Old

A few days before I left for the folk school, my mother said, "Before you go, dear, your father and I want to take you to the club for dinner."

I was standing at the kitchen window, looking out at the daisies alongside the driveway, and replied absently, "Thanks. That would be nice."

The tone of her voice changed, "Good, then you need to get a haircut."

I ran my fingers through my scruffy, dense hair. It now covered my ears.

"No. I don't want one."

She pressed her hands on the counter, turned away, and began to weep, her hand over her eyes.

"What is the problem, Mom?" I asked. I stayed halfway across the room.

"You can't go looking like that. It's embarrassing. You know what that does to us. People..."

"Talk," I completed her sentence.

"Yes."

"Let them."

"I can't. It's much more difficult than you know," she explained. "Not only do they talk, they gossip, they say things, and it hurts your father and his relationships with important people..."

"Is that all you care about?"

"Yes, dear, it is. Friends *are* very important. We cannot change that."

I stared at her. "Why?"

She looked directly at me—but, as I later realized, not at me but at who she wanted me to be—and said, "We're too old to change."

"Too old?" I scoffed.

"Well, will you?" she asked.

Pain was in her eyes.

Not knowing what else to do, I said, "I'll think about it."

I didn't get my hair cut. I put my bags in my car. I called my friend Rick who had offered to let me crash at his apartment, and said I was coming early. I left a note on the kitchen table. "Needed to leave early."

Confession

I pulled up a narrow driveway pinched between two apartment complexes. Scorching heat hit me when I opened the car door. My shirt was drenched with sweat before I entered the apartment. Linda welcomed me with a hug and said, "Just in time." She waved her hand toward the kitchen table which was filled with food—a big pot roast, a bowl of mashed potatoes, and a mixed fruit salad. I put my suitcase on the floor, gave Rick a hug, and sat down.

We talked about the Apollo 10 flight around the moon and John Lennon and Yoko Ono doing a 'bed-in' in protest of the war. Rick mentioned *Midnight Cowboy*, a movie I'd seen in Chicago. It scared me, especially the scene when Joe Buck couldn't make money hustling women, offers himself to men, and after sex, beats them up.

"What did you think of it?" Rick asked.

"It was okay," I said.

"Okay?"

"Well, I must admit that scene when Joe beat up that old man, and when he beat up that young kid and took his watch was disgusting," I said.

"The homosexual scenes bothered you?"

"Not that. It was just that I felt sorry for those guys, you know," I said. Trying to change the subject, I asked if they'd watched the Apollo 10 launch. Rick didn't take the bait and pursued his questions about *Midnight Cowboy*.

"You felt sorry?"

"Yes, I—"

Linda, sensing I was uncomfortable, intervened. "How were your parents, Jason?"

I was about to reply when Rick said. "Linda, you changed the subject?"

She shot back, her tone decisive, "Rick, can't you see he's bothered by it?"

"Sorry, honey. I just—"

"Just nothing," she said emphatically. "Now, Jason, do you like chocolate or vanilla ice cream?"

"Both," I said.

"Oh, a gourmand," she said, "I suspected it," and winked at me.

After dinner, we lounged in the living room. After an aperitif, Linda excused herself. She kissed Rick and me goodnight.

Rick talked about the course he was taking in liturgy.

"You wouldn't believe how sophisticated they are. The whole Eucharist, for example, must be staged carefully, the bread held up, the wine poured. Each is sequenced. I've seen it done a thousand times, it seems, but I always bungle it. I have to look at my crib notes. I feel like an idiot," he said. "You're lucky. Many Protestants don't even use wine."

"You forget I'm not going be a minister."

"Right," he said and lowered his voice. "Sorry I pressed you about Joe Buck."

"It's okay."

"It's just—I don't why I'm telling you this—but back in college I had a crush on another guy. Very intense. I couldn't get him out of my mind. I wanted to be with him all the time. It disturbed me. I saw a counselor. I didn't want to be...you know, a—"

I added the word, "homosexual."

He wanted me to say more, to tell him that I, too, had the same feelings, and, in fact, found him attractive. I wondered if he knew about me? It would have been easy for me to say something. He was married. I didn't have to worry. But I stood up, shoved my hands in my pockets, and told him, "That must be rough." I felt like a Judas, turning my back on him.

"It was," he said. "You want another drink?"

"No thanks."

"That's just between you and me, right?" he said.

"Sure."

"It gets better," he said. "Linda is great."

He sat on the couch, his head down. "Thanks for listening," he said in a small voice. He wiped something off his shoe. I got up, sat next to him, and put my arm over his shoulder.

"Hey, it's all right. No big deal. I..."

He tilted his head toward me. The sadness in his eyes seemed immeasurable. The left side of his mouth lifted in a half-smile. He waited for me to go on.

"I...I understand."

He nodded his head.

In the morning, Rick seemed distant and Linda took me aside and asked if something was wrong. I told her, "No, everything's fine."

Rick walked me to the car and said, "Sorry about last night."

"Hey, as I said, *no* big deal."

He shook his head. "Still friends?"

"You bet."

I reached over to hug him. He grabbed hold of me and held me tight.

"Have a good summer, and write, will ya?"

"You bet."

PART III

What might have been and what has been

Point to one end, which is always present.

"The Four Quartets," T.S. Eliot

Road to Clearfork

Driving was torturous from Nashville to the Cumberland Mountains. Rain ricocheted off the windshield and flooded the highway. In the mountains, the pelting rain made it impossible to know how sharp the turns were. In Jellico—the foothills of the Cumberland Mountains—the rain slackened. Driving was slow on mountain roads. Road signs jumped out at sharp curves. One pointed in one direction; another in the opposite direction. My foot rarely left the brake pedal. A large boulder appeared with yellow lettering and a jagged cross painted beneath the words, "Jesus Saves."

Erling had told me to turn at "Jesus Saves." By then, the road was clear. No rain. I stayed on that road for twenty miles. I downshifted up the steep rises and braked on the way down. Some curves were so severe I wondered if I'd meet myself coming from the other side.

I was to meet Erling at one o'clock. The last twenty miles put me behind time. I gunned it down a straightaway. At the small pitted sign "Clearfork," I knew that I had to take the first right before another hill. The side road was ribbed like corduroy.

I pulled up to the Clearfork Post Office five minutes early. I stood on the front porch. Yellowish-white dust rose from the road. It caked the trees, shrubs, plants, and stairs. Just off the porch, under a large maple, its leaves whitened with dust, a man in bib-overalls stood beside a green rocking chair with his rifle, staring at me.

"What you doing?" he asked.

He had several badges on his overalls. His black hair, unkempt, shoved under his blue cap.

"I asked you, mister—what's your business..."

The front door squeaked; I turned around to see who was there. A husky lady with gray hair stood behind the screen door. She peered at me.

"Can I help?"

"Yes ma'am, you can," I said, "but, first—" I nodded toward the sheriff.

She stepped out the door, noticed him, and gave a big guffaw.

"Oh, Brady, put that away. This man means no harm. Get off now," she scolded him. He bowed his head and sat down under the maple, the gun in his lap.

"It's not loaded," she said, smiling. "Now what's it you need?"

"I need to meet Erling Duus," I said.

"Why didn't you say so? He's expecting you. You're at the right place. I'm Ida Handford, Postmistress," she said, extending her hand. "Y'all come on in. I'll get you something to drink. You thirsty?"

"Sure am."

She looked at me closely, "You look it. Lemonade—will it do?"

"Yes. Thank you, ma'am."

"Land's sake, call me Ida."

"Okay, Miss Ida."

"It's so damn hot likely to kill a man. Fan keeps me going these days." The post office was more like a home than an office of the United States government. There was a small booth with a counter just like other post offices. To its right was another screen door. It opened into a living room with a couch, chair, desk, and huge fan.

"Make yourself at home." She aimed the fan at me.

"Mr. Duus is hunting for you, too. Been here twice. He's at the Community Center just up the road apiece. He's got the girls with him." She handed me the lemonade—cool in my hand, dripping with condensation. "Should be back soon."

I wondered, What should I say? Tell her about myself? Where I came from, how I knew Erling?

I didn't have to worry. Words poured from her. She told me about the community, the excitement about the folk school, and how folks liked Mr. Duus.

"He's just regular folks," Ida said.

There was a knock at the door. Erling came in, put his hands on his hips, "Well, well, here's my golf buddy!"

My outfit: golf shorts, golf shirt, and golf hat.

I replied, "You wanna play nine or eighteen?"

"I wanna just shake your hand," he said. "You made it."

"Yes."

"You met Mrs. Handford?"

"Ida, please," she chastised Erling.

"Of course."

"She's been gracious," I acknowledged, "and she's told me a lot about the community too."

"As Postmistress, she knows pretty much everything about everyone in Clearfork. And she has the biggest, kindest heart of anyone I know."

Ida smiled. "You're too kind."

"It's true."

"Darn right," she grinned. "I make it my business."

Erling chatted with her and thanked her for taking care of me.

"Drop by any time," she said. "Gets pretty lonesome here."

We squatted on the porch steps and surveyed the road. He wore a white shirt, rolled up at the sleeves, and beige slacks, which made him seem too well dressed for the setting. The thick cloud from his car had not settled. He pointed to a parking spot in front of the post office.

He said, "That's the center of town."

Dust swept over my car. I coughed.

"You get used to it," he said.

I leaned close to him and pointed at the sheriff in the chair with a gun. "What's with him?"

Erling signaled me to follow him.

"Brady," he said five feet from the man, "this is my friend Jason. Listen up: you need to take care of him. He's a good man. You understand?"

Brady nodded.

I stepped forward to put my hand out. Erling blocked it. "Not a good idea," he said. We walked a few yards away.

"Brady is—well—limited," Erling explained. "The local sheriff deputized him years ago. He gave him that rifle. It can't shoot. Brady watches out for Ida. He lives in back in a little two-room cabin. He wouldn't do any harm. At least not yet. He can fly off the handle. Especially if he doesn't know you, if you get too close. He's a little edgy. He's at all the big town events. He stands guard. He delivers papers too, to those who live nearby."

He pointed to his car. "Mabel's doing fine." It looked the same, a faded powdery blue shaped like a shoebox.

"Would you like to see our accommodations?" he asked. "They're five-star. A golf course right down the road. But I'll tell you right off I'm not caddying for you!"

At the head of the road, a tall, rusted metal structure on iron stilts loomed. It looked like an enormous canister with its bottom gouged open. Erling noticed my quizzical look and explained.

"It was used to load coal into train cars. They'd pull under it, fill it, and it would go west." He pointed past the tracks, to a road that swung up a hillside. "That's where they mined and stripped off the whole top of it ."

Three mountains triangulated around us, each sloped upward like a green pyramid. Beneath our feet, the dust puffed like gunsmoke with each step.

"What do you think?" he asked.

"Don't know. Not like the plains of Illinois. Never been in any place like it."

"I'll show you the digs. And then we'll meet the girls. They'd like to swim."

"I could use one," I tugged the shirt off my chest, damp from perspiration.

He moved gracefully around his car, stopped at the front grill, brushed off some dust, and dipped his head down from under the rims of his glasses. He sucked his lower lip in and pointed at my outfit, said, "Well, you *do* look comfortable...But," he inhaled sharply through his teeth, "there aren't too many golf clubs in these parts."

He drove up to the main road to a narrow road that dipped down and twisted around several hills and curves carved precariously from the shale hillsides. He parked along a wire fence. Our cars teetered on an embankment that sloped off at a thirty-degree angle down to a log cabin. Gravity flung my door open. It nearly slammed against a fence.

"Watch your step there, bub," Erling said. "Can't afford to lose you this early."

He opened a gate and escorted me to a two-room cabin. It rested on the slope of the steep pasture and overlooked a farm and a white house. Farther on, Route 90 snaked along the valley. Honeysuckle vines climbed on one side of it. Knee-deep grass grew around the cabin.

"That's the golf course," Erling joked. "Deep rough. Nothing you can't handle."

He stood in front of the cabin. It was a pale brown, aged. It had a green front door. To the left, an old tool shed sat under the shade of two sycamore trees. On the right, a gnarled apple tree sagged slightly to one side as if it were drunk.

The front room was ten by twelve with windows on each side. It had two chairs in it—wooden chairs with frayed wicker seats. Erling's sleeping bag was rumpled in one corner and his brown suitcase lay open next to it. A side door opened onto a stoop.

The next room—behind the first—was down three steps. It was small. It had one window that faced the pasture and a back door to the right. Peeling wallpaper had come loose and hung in long strips the color of rust. A musty smell pervaded the interior. Out back, down a grassy path, was the outhouse with a quarter moon window on the door which sagged on its hinges.

"The lady who owns it—hers is the white house down the hill—says there's a well in the back by the creek. But I can't find it. We'll need to locate it. It's our water source," he said.

"How do we wash up?" I asked.

"Oh, here's the bathroom," he said. He stepped out the side door on the first floor.

"I have a washbasin on the side stoop. I do my daily ablutions here," he chuckled. "Not exactly Triple-A-approved!"

I unloaded my sleeping bag and suitcase from the car and set it on the other side of the room.

Another car pulled up. Erling took me lightly by the arm.

"Come meet the girls," he said.

Girls? I thought. *He called them girls.*

He swung open the gate, tapped on the roof of a yellow Mustang. A woman let down the window. He leaned in the window and pointed to a young woman with straight black hair and a dark complexion in the front seat. "That's Lois—you may remember Peggy mentioned her."

I peeked through the window and said, "Hi." I wasn't sure I remembered her, but she looked familiar.

Before I could ask her a question, he pointed to another woman sitting in the back.

"That's Lorraine."

She waved at me. Finally, he tapped a woman in the driver's seat, "This is Emily." A petite woman with a ponytail, she reached out to shake my hand. She had a strong grip. "My pleasure," she said, her mouth in a tentative smile. Her eyes had the steely acuity of a police inspector.

I pulled my hand back, "Nice to meet you." I'd lost some circulation in my hand.

Erling declared, "Hey, girls, let's take him for the scenic view."

Lorraine chimed in, "Good, we love it there." Emily winced but she pasted on a smile.

The Dead

As Erling backed up Mabel, dust billowed into a white cloud. He waited for it to settle, drove down the road for a mile, and turned onto a road with even more ruts and washouts. It looked more like a creek bed than a road. His car hiccupped down the road.

He pulled up the embankment and parked. From the surroundings, much the same as it had been for the last ten miles, I was baffled as to why he stopped. Nothing but a few trees and shrubs canopied the roadside. But I hadn't paid too much attention to the road because I was busily trying to remember the names of the new folk school students.

He hopped out of the car, the three women behind him.

He called back to me, "Come along. Be careful. There's lots of poison ivy."

I stopped in my tracks and looked for the plant. What did that jingle say? "Leaves of three, let it be" That didn't help. What did the leaves look like? Bending over, shielding my eyes from the sun, I couldn't find a three-leaved one, but, nonetheless, was careful to stay on a worn path. I was highly allergic to it. And I had shorts on.

I hurried after them. We trekked a quarter of a mile up a steep embankment. At its steepest point, it became a stone stairway. Stepping stones were lodged in the hillside, each one a different size. I watched each one to make sure I didn't trip.

"Where're we going?" I called out, out of breath.

"To a cemetery," Lois replied, turning her head slightly to answer.

"A cemetery?"

No sooner do I get here, I thought, *then he takes me to a cemetery.* I'd never been in one. I'd seen them from the road—particularly that huge one by the East-West Tollway in Illinois. As a kid, I'd avert my eyes when I passed it. If I looked too long, I'd be the next headstone on the lot.

The cemetery was enclosed by a raised picket fence at the far end. It took up about half a football field, small by Chicago standards, with forty or so graves with granite and sandstone headstones. It was nestled under gnarly pin oaks whose wide branches overshadowed the cemetery.

The headstones were cracked. Weeds had overgrown them. Vines fingered up and obscured the inscriptions. Blanched plastic flowers drooped by them. "Gone but Not Forgotten," were etched on two stones.

I laughed out loud and said, "These graves are *long* forgotten!"

Erling glared at me. Lois looked away.

"This is a place," Erling hesitated to gauge his words, "where your bourgeois cynicism needs to take a break."

He motioned to me to button my lip. "Why don't you quietly look around." He pointed to the mountains in the distance. "Give some thought to Lois. She happens to live here. Her relatives are buried here."

Lois had bent over a grave and parted some weeds. She was trying to make out the names on it.

The sunlight stippled the ground by the gravestones. Off in the distance, dark splotches lay on mountainsides where clouds hid the sunlight. Gray-blue mountain ranges were visible through openings in the trees. Below, a truck wound along a road. Dust rolled up behind it, lifted skyward, then dispersed in a brownish smoke.

I felt embarrassed that I'd made a fool of myself.

Erling placed his hand on my shoulder. "It'll take a while. It's not suburbia."

He went over to Lois and discussed the lettering on the gravestone. I looked at the dates on tombstones. Many had died in their teens, most in their thirties and forties.

On the way back to the cars, Lois asked me questions, one right after another. Do you believe in God? Why did you come here? Why is your hair so long? Do you always wear shorts? Is blue your favorite color?

I held up my hand and told her to slow down. We had plenty of time to get acquainted. I wondered why she wanted to know so much about me. She acted as if she had the *right* to find out.

Erling called out, "Let's head to the lake."

I trotted to the car. Lois tried to keep up with me. I sprinted to get away from her and everyone else.

Erling drove directly to the lodge fifteen miles away, nearly to the Kentucky border. It was nestled in tall pines on a ridge overlooking a lake. The lodge was where we'd meet in the mornings to discuss "The American Experience."

The lodge's cook, an attractive guy with a winsome smile, introduced himself. "I'm Will. I'll make your breakfast, lunch, and dinner," he said and extended his hand.

"You any good?" I asked.

"The best!" he said. "I aim to please."

His hand, soft, lingered in my hand.

Erling went into the bathroom to change into his swimsuit. Will asked if he could join us.

"Hurry up," Erling said. "I want to beat the girls to the beach." Will and I went into the bathroom.

It was the size of a broom closet. Will shed his clothes quickly. He leaned against the door, his trunks in one hand. He had a wiry, athletic frame with a dark, furry chest. I almost said—"beautiful"—out loud. I hadn't yet undressed.

"Something wrong?" he asked.

"Not really," I lied. I was unnerved being only a few feet away from him. I was aroused. I tugged on my shirt which had stuck to my back.

"Here, let me help you," he said. He grabbed the shirt and pulled it off.

A narrow fringe of pubic hair formed a line to his belly button. His penis had stiffened slightly. He was chewing gum. Spearmint. "Hurry," he said. "Erling doesn't wait." He pulled on his trunks.

Off came my shorts and underwear; I hopped into my suit.

Erling rapped at the door. "What's keeping you?" he asked.

Will pushed the door open. "Ta-da, we're ready!"

The road to the lake was fringed by pines and hickory. A sandy beach was packed with families, some in the water, others stretched out on towels. Will flung out his towel to join them.

Lorraine called out, "Over here!"

Erling slapped his thigh and muttered, "Figures."

The three women and I waded into the water and swam out toward an island in the middle of the lake. We treaded water and chatted. Loraine attended Wheaton College in Maryland. She wanted to be a doctor. Lois, the elder daughter of Peggy Lester (that's why she looked so familiar!), had graduated from high school. She planned to go to Bethel College. She wanted to teach. Emily majored in philosophy and wanted to teach it. Her father, an English professor at Indiana University, had taught with Erling for a semester at a small college in the Midwest.

Lois, short with piercing eyes, still peppered me with questions.

"Do you believe in God?"

"No."

"No?" She was startled.

"No, I don't"

"But you're in a seminary, aren't you?"

"Yes."

"What *do* you believe in?"

"Not much. I suppose I believe there's good and evil. We must try our best to do good although, even with that, it's likely we'll fail at that."

"I don't get how you don't believe in God."

"It's easy. Who needs Him?"

"God?"

"Yeah."

"You some sort of nut?"

We waded to shore as we talked. I asked her about Peggy and Bobby. It turned out Bobby had cut his foot badly playing chicken with a knife; Tommy, his older brother, had tossed the blade a little too close. It went right into his foot.

"Were they barefoot?"

"Of course," she giggled. "Silly boys!"

She joined Lorraine on a blanket. I spread a towel by Emily. Lois muttered to herself, but loud enough for me to hear, "I can't believe he doesn't believe in God."

Emily overheard our conversation. A lanky woman nearly as tall as I was, she spoke quietly. She asked how I had met Erling. She wondered why he hadn't recruited more women from Vanderbilt.

"There were only two women in my class," I told her.

"Figures," she said.

"What do you mean?"

"Sexist," she explained.

"Why do you say that?"

She furrowed her brow and said, "Can you count?

"Yes."

"How many students are in your class?"

"Thirty or so," I said.

"And only two women." She shrugged her shoulders. "I rest my case."

She had a good case. Only one woman, Evie, had been in my New Testament class and she was bright and asked more questions than any other student.

Emily leaned close to me. "Do me a favor," she whispered. "Call us women, not girls."

Will beckoned for me to move my towel by him. "Catch some rays," he said. His body needed some sun. Milky white except for brown rings around his neck and on his lower arms, he looked like a monk. He offered to rub some suntan lotion on my back. He massaged my back and legs.

"You're tense," he said.

"I've driven hundreds of miles," I said.

"Time to let go," he said and patted me on the back. I crawled onto the towel, careful to keep my feet from soiling it, and, closed my eyes.

Water splashed my face.

I shot up. "What the—"

Lois stood over me with a sand bucket in her hand. "Hey, sleepyhead, wake up!"

Will offered his towel so I could dry off. "It wasn't my idea," he said on the way to the car.

"Whose was it?"

He whispered, "The dark haired one."

"Lois?"

"That's it. Think she has a crush on you," he said. "You should see the way she looks at you."

"Not sure it's a crush," I said, "or a curse."

After dinner, Erling read Walt Whitman's "A Cradle Endlessly Rocking." There were yawns and a desultory discussion. A fan whirred in a corner. The kitchen lights went off. As did others. Will said, "Good night." A door closed. Night fell.

The women went to their rooms. Erling and I drove to the cabin.

The Ropes

The next morning, we looked for the well so we could shave and wash. With a plastic bucket in hand, we walked to the bottom of a path.

There was a wetland with tall grass and several dung heaps. There was also a metal pipe about four inches in diameter sticking up out of the ground. But no well.

Erling decided to ask Peggy where to find the well. Bobby took me to the side yard, a bucket in hand. He walked over to a cylindrical pipe like the one we saw protruding from the ground at our place and said, "This is it."

"But how do you get water out of it?" I inquired. The pipe had a lid, but, unless it worked on suction, it didn't seem possible to get water from a pipe.

He showed how another cylindrical contraption about three feet long that was inserted in the pipe, dropped down by rope into it until it plunged into the water reservoir. He pulled a string and a lever closed, trapping the water inside the cylinder. He hauled up, dumped it into a bucket, and lugged it inside.

Erling and I went to the Tibbitt's General Store and purchased a cylinder, some rope, and some string. We filled several buckets at our cabin, washed, brushed our teeth, and left the rest for drinking water.

The first week, Erling and I spent mornings and evenings at the lodge. With a kitchen, meeting rooms, and dorm rooms, it was the safest place for the women. The cook, Will, told us that he'd fix anything we liked. I asked if he knew how to make waffles.

"For you, mon cher, they'll the best you have ever tasted," he said. "Come let me show you the kitchen."

I followed him to the kitchen. A small room lined with cupboards, it had a huge black iron stove with burners on top. He pulled an old cast iron waffle iron from a cupboard. "This will do," he said.

He had long, feminine fingers with the nails perfectly trimmed. Aqua blue, his eyes were mesmerizing. His hair fell across his forehead. His lips, moist and full, seemed to invite a kiss.

"Something wrong?" he asked.

"No, no, sorry," I said. "Just got lost for a second."

He pushed out his lips. "Anywhere I've been?" he asked.

I blushed.

Every morning he prepared a cup of tea for me. Once a week, he'd fix different types of waffles—Belgian, Liege, rolled—telling me how the Dutch made the first waffles back in the 16th century. During breaks after lunch, we went for swims with the women—or, as Erling said, "the girls." Will joined us. His compact body moved through the water with effortless grace. He'd lounge on his blanket, me beside him.

Our daily routines were jam-packed. In the morning, Erling led us in Danish folk songs and then he would do a reading from Whitman, Wolfe, or McLeish. We'd discuss the readings. After breakfast, we drove to Cross Creek Hollow. The women set up tables to do arts and crafts. Children arrived by foot and car. I'd play touch football with the older boys. Most days, Erling and I explored the hollow. Roads wove like arteries into the mountains. We'd drive up a side road, mostly one lane, and discover narrower roads like capillaries going up a creek bed.

The deeper we drove into the hollow the more the roads were scarcely stitched to the sides of mountains. We abandoned Mabel and climbed up the slopes to talk with residents. Erling explained what he was doing: the history of the folk school, who was involved in it, and how he valued the history of the area. He told them about the kids' program, the bonfire on Fridays, and the upcoming potluck cookout.

The conversations often had long periods of silence. People weren't afraid of silence. On one ridge, an elderly man in bib overalls and a white shirt rocked in his rocking chair. He said, "Let me give you some history." He told us about a family feud. His brother had been shot while working just down the road. The next week, his folks shot the culprit who did it. There had been bad blood ever since.

He spoke with such ire I worried we were in the middle of a feud.

Erling asked, "When did it happen?"

The old man rocked for three minutes, not uttering a word, and then said, "Well, I'm supposing it was '38 or '39."

By Friday, we had met most of the families in the hollow and planned for the Saturday cookout to be at the old one-room schoolhouse. The food would arrive about noon. Everyone would gather and celebrate the start of the folk school.

Jack called to announce that he planned to come up for the big event. Erling drove to Jellico to have dinner with him and told me to relax and enjoy myself.

Come On

After he left, a blue pickup pulled up. Bobby hopped out of it with his brother Tommy. They sat on our cabin porch. Tommy, taller and stockier than Bobby, worked as a mechanic in a nearby town. He told me that Bobby said I was a good man.

He asked, "So what's up?"

"Not much doing here," I replied. "Erling's off to Jellico."

"You like to drink?" Tommy asked.

"That would be an affirmative," I replied.

"What's that mean?" he asked.

"Yes." I laughed at my pretentiousness. "I like a drink."

"Ever had moonshine?" he inquired, raising one of his eyebrows and giving me an impish smile.

"Nope."

"Well, then it's time for you to give it a try. Let's get drunk and be somebody!"

I had misgivings, but I liked his enthusiasm. "Come on," he said. He brushed his dark brown hair back but it didn't stay. It fell over his forehead. He tapped his knuckles at my shin. "Come on. No harm in it."

Bobby gazed up at me.

"You coming, too?" I asked him.

Tommy interjected, "He comes with me all the time."

"Really?"

Bobby said, "Yeah," and shrugged his shoulders.

"I'll drive," Tommy said. "Come on."

We drove to Cross Creek. Across a plank bridge was a rundown house in an unmowed yard.

Tommy said he'd do the talking. I gave him twenty dollars.

A man with a grey shirt peered out the front door. He asked Tommy several questions. He looked at Bobby and me. He said, "No." As he started to close the door, Tommy flashed him the money. He looked at them and closed the door. Tommy gave us a thumbs-up.

A mason jar with moonshine, the best you could buy according to Tommy, sat in Bobby's lap. We drove to the strip mine pit. A small pond with surprisingly clear water was at the end of a red scarred lane. We sat beside it and passed the jar back and forth.

The moon hung in the sky. Its milky face illuminated the pond. Dark shadows fell across the few remaining trees.

Bobby had been drunk once before. By his third swig, he yelped and staggered to his feet. He fell over, got up, and fell again like a doll whose battery had run out.

Tommy told him to stay by us. By our fourth swig, we were no better than he was. We stripped off our clothes—it was warm—and plunged into the water. We howled at the moon. We leapt on all fours. We chased each other from the shallow to the deep end. Midway into a chase, Bobby crumbled to his knees.

"I feel sick," he said.

I took him in my arms and carried him to the shore. He vomited in waves until his body became slack. We dressed him and carried him to the truck. Tommy and I found our clothes and dressed. He wanted to drink some more. "Come on." But I could barely stand upright. He drove me back to the cabin.

I aimed myself at the front door and missed it by four feet to the right. With my hands on the wall, I edged my way into the cabin and down to my sleeping bag on the lower level. I left Jack the upper room.

Hangover

In the morning, I heard voices speaking in the upper room. I squinted out of one eye. Jack, perched on a chair, was talking with Erling who was pacing back and forth.

"I told you that he was not reliable." Jack warned. "He's a relativist. He doesn't have a moral center. He'll do what he wants when he wants to do it. He's like a fraternity brat. Get rid of him."

"Why do you say he's a relativist?" Erling asked.

"It's easy. When he and I were discussing what someone would do if he were faced with the decision of supporting a friend who violated the law or obeying the law and reporting him, he said that 'it all depends.' He said that, in some cases, he might support the friend and in others he might back law enforcement," Jack explained. "He has no firm moral compass."

"But he's right. In many cases, it *is* relative," Erling countered.

"You're not getting the point," Jack insisted. "He thinks that he's the one who decides what is wrong or right based on what pleases *him*. I don't trust him. He'll bring down the folk school. What fool would get an underage boy drunk? Tell me that. How do you think he can explain himself?"

"I get it. He messed up, that's for sure. He has some serious explaining to do," Erling admitted. He stood by the window and looked out into the field. "Our program may be in jeopardy."

I must have moaned because Jack startled and jerked his head toward me. Erling walked over to Jack and whispered something. Jack, not happy with what Erling requested, left by the front door. He stood on the front porch, his eyes on me like a judge at an inquisition.

Erling sat on one of the steps, expressionless. "Not feeling too well?" he asked.

"No, bad hangover," I said, propping myself on my elbow.

"The word got around the hollow quickly about your escapade last night. I guess everyone could hear the three of you for miles," he said.

"Shit."

"Yep, that sums it up."

"I'm sorry. That was really dumb of me. I just didn't...." I didn't know what to say. I sat up.

"Not sure what to do about it. You may have cooked your goose and ours," Erling said. He went to the back door and gazed at the ash tree by the side of the house. "Some tell me that I should dump you. Not trustworthy. Too self-centered. Even immoral. What you did is too egregious. You're a liability."

I stood up and tucked in my shirt and brushed back my hair. "I wouldn't blame you. I fucked up." I walked over to the doorway and stood beside him.

"This is not easily resolved," he said, glancing sideways.

"It's not on you. It's on me."

Erling's voice became strident. "You don't get it. It's *all* on me. This is *my* idea, *my* dream."

"Fuck," I said.

"Exactly. What do you have to say?"

There were two clouds in the sky and then blue going on forever.

I took a deep breath. "I know it seems I'm untrustworthy. But I don't think I am. I learn from my mistakes. I swear this is the last one I'll make, if you'll give me a second chance," I offered.

My words, however, carried as little weight as the clouds.

Erling stared off for quite a while. The wind tickled the leaves. The two clouds moved on.

He turned to face me. He put his hand under his chin and, squinted his eyes. He asked several questions about the night before. I answered them. He nodded and turned away from me to look out the window. "Some say you are out for yourself—no moral center," he said. He took out his pipe and, knocked the old tobacco out of the bowl, and then took out a pouch, unlaced it, and poured fresh tobacco in the pipe bowl. His words sank in.

"I know. Jack accused me of that," I responded.

He lit a match and put it to the bowl, sucking in the first smoke.

"Is it true?"

"What?"

"No moral center."

I stepped back. "It may seem that way, especially now. But, Erling, I gave up a job I could have done at my country club. I raised the money you needed to fund the school. I've never asked for a salary. My parents were supportive but not entirely happy with my decision. I came up here because I believe in what you are doing and want to help. If that means I have no moral center, well, so be it." I turned away from him and slammed my fist into the cabinet.

"Hey, calm down," he said, turning me around to face him. "Listen, I get it. You made sacrifices. But we're in a quandary now. We're just getting started. This will cause problems."

"I know."

"Well, if you were me, what would you do?" he asked.

"Me?"

"Yes, you."

"Well, I guess I'd apologize to Peggy and admit I made a mistake."

"Okay, fine. But what would you do if you were *me*?"

"I'd tell me that I needed to step up and take leadership and see the implications of what I did and not act like I was some stupid fraternity bozo."

Erling was amused by my last statement. He put his hand to his chin again and paced back and forth. As he paced, he noticed Jack standing in the front doorway shaking his head, staring at us. Completing his ruminations, he pivoted and looked me directly in the eye.

"Well," he began, "I guess you better shave and put on clean clothes and get yourself up to the picnic, because you have apologies to make and fences to mend."

I rushed over to him and shook his hand, "You will not regret this!" Changing quickly into a fresh shirt and pair of jeans, I took out our wash basin, filled it with water and shaved. I refilled the basin, splashed my face, and combed my hair. Finally, I checked with Erling to make sure I looked okay. He gave me the thumbs-up.

I headed to my car. Erling was sitting on the front porch and Jack was speaking to him. Jack pointed at me and then sat down next to him, pulling his chair close. He looked like he was about to make a long speech. I knew who his subject was.

On the way to the picnic, I parked by a stream and hopped out. I made notes in a journal and worked out what I should say. I shouldn't blame anyone. I had to admit the wrong. I had to convince them that I would do better. I also needed to figure out why I didn't see how my actions could ruin our program.

Jack was right in a way. For me, getting smashed was perfectly okay. It was something I did to connect with other guys. That had to change.

Jack always knew what was right and did it. He would have said, "No," and have Tommy stay and drink a soda. He would never have touched the moonshine.

Jack might have my number. Maybe I wasn't worthy of Erling's trust.

—

At noon, I drove to the picnic and arrived well ahead of Erling and Jack. Twenty people were clustered around picnic tables nestled under the trees. Near the back of the tables under a large maple, Peggy was mixing something in a bowl with a wooden spoon, clad in a bright red and yellow dress. She focused intently on the bowl as she poured something from a jar into it.

My stomach growled. My head throbbed. My scalp sweated.

She seemed surprised to see me and raised an eyebrow. "Morning, Jason."

"Morning, Peggy."

"Just added the final touch. You want some potato salad?" she said. She spooned a large portion on a paper plate.

"That'd be fine."

"Get yourself more grub. There're some mighty fine hotdogs and sausages there on the grill." She pointed to Shady John, a thin, tall man.

"Peggy," I whispered, not looking at her but gazing down at my potato salad, "I need to say I'm sorry. I made a mistake. I should have known..."

"You need to speak up," she said. "I'm deaf in the right ear."

I repeated myself.

She leaned over, picked up my chin with her hand, motioned for me to look her in the eye. "I always tell my boys to look me in the eye when they talk to me. I know what they say by their eyes."

I looked at her. I couldn't tell from her expression what she might be thinking. She flipped the potatoes up with a spoon and folded them back in the bowl. She licked a finger to make sure it tasted right.

I repeated what I said with my eyes on her. As I told her this time, my eyes welled up. I had brushed the tears away.

She shook her head. "You like it?" she asked, pointing at my plate.

"Yes."

"Worried it had too much mustard."

"It's fine. It's really good."

She didn't seem to have heard me. Her hands on her hips, she nodded, "Good."

"I'm sorry," I repeated. "I feel really bad."

"You should," she said.

"Well, I *really* messed up..."

She nodded her head and looked over at the man at the grill. "Them dogs done? I got a hungry man here."

I started to repeat myself. She shushed me. "Now, my dear, it's not that bad. Hell, I'd be damn proud if I was you," she said. "It takes a lot for a man to admit he done wrong. And, hey, my boys, they know they done wrong too. I think all of you paid mightily for your shenanigans. I can see you don't look so hot. My Bobby, oh my, he's got a head full of thorns. If your stomach is up to it, get yourself something to eat." She pointed the spoon at me. "And, Jason, hold your head up. You have a nice-looking face. You should let others see it."

She was smiling. Pointing at the plate, she said, "Tell me what you think of my potato salad. Some claim it's the best in the county."

I took another bite. The potatoes had a sweet-sour tang to them. The sauce was creamy. "No, I think you're wrong," I said. "It's the best in the world!"

I ate several hotdogs, a second helping of potato salad, and baked beans. I chatted with fifteen or twenty people. Bobby was leaning against a tree trunk. He was shading his eyes with his hand. I squatted next to him.

"Not doing so hot?"

"Nope."

"How's Tommy?"

"He's at work," he said. "I'm sorry. We shouldn't—"

"Don't be," I said. "I'm the one who should apologize."

"Mom's okay, you know," he said. "She's mostly mad at us."

"I know. You should get some of her potato salad. It's good."

"I know."

Jack and Erling were enjoying the food, too. They made the rounds of all the tables. At first, Jack wouldn't look at me. I greeted him, however, with a handshake. He offered a weak, "Hello." Then, abruptly, he turned, his face inches from Erling, and whispered something to him. Erling nodded several times.

I felt lightheaded and sat on a picnic table, my head in my hand.

I heard a booming voice. Jack announced that he was headed back to Nashville. He must prepare for Sunday services. He had enjoyed meeting everyone. He shook hands with Emily, Lorraine, Lois and numerous others. He scowled at me and shook his head. He trudged down the hill to his blue Oldsmobile. He left behind a trail of unsettled dust.

Erling took me aside and asked, "How did it go?"

I told him that it was fine. She wanted to get a good meal in my stomach.

"We dodged a bullet," he said. "They like you and seem to have grown to trust you. Remember," he tapped my chest, "you're no longer a student out for a grade and a good time. You stand for more than that. You have to be a bigger person. Trust is a perishable commodity."

I shook his hand, "Thanks." Tears welled up in my eyes again.

"Hey, no tears," he said. "They'll think you have a screw loose!"

"Heaven forbid."

"You have a sense of humor, I like that," he said. "That's why I chose you." He hugged me around the neck, slapped me on the back and said, "Now, why don't you go back to the cabin. You don't look so hot."

I started to walk away but caught myself, intent on leaving yet drawn back to have him answer one question.

"Erling, I need to know something."

"Okay."

"You *did* choose me. But I don't get it. I really messed up. Lord knows Jack opposed me from the start. Jack told me that he wanted to be assistant-director. He always seems to know what to do and would be a far more experienced and better choice than me. I don't get it. He's managed a big company, is ordained, and runs a big church. Why didn't you choose him as assistant director? Why did you not take his advice?" I asked.

"Oh, you overheard us talking this morning."

"I did. I thought my goose was cooked."

"I thought you heard," Erling mused, then asked me pointedly, "So are you a 'relativist'?"

His question stunned me. I bowed my head, not knowing what to say. But I admitted, "To be honest, I don't know what that is. It sounds bad."

"I don't have the faintest idea either," he said, laughing. "I was hoping you did."

He put his hands on his hips and shrugged, "Suppose it's relative!"

We laughed together. I put my hand on his arm and pulled him close to me. I wanted one other question answered.

"I still can't figure out why, with all Jack said, you stood by me. Why?"

He slapped his hand on the side of his head. "Oh, Jason, that's a no-brainer. Jack is a bright guy; an earnest guy; a guy who has offered support with tons of experience; but, to tell the truth, he's also a pompous ass, full of himself. He promised to get money for the school, to come help us get it started, yet all he does is give me advice and tell me that he knows Dean so and so of some big university, and some president of a bank—but it comes to nothing. He has an opinion about everyone and a doctorate degree in self-righteousness. But his word is no good. You, my friend, have kept your word every time I've asked you."

Startled, I winced and felt dizzy, losing my balance.

Erling grabbed me by the sleeve.

"You all right?"

"Dizzy."

"Sit over here." He sat by me at a picnic table. "Listen," he said, "you have your flaws. But you don't need, as Jack does, someone listening to your grand ideas and someone patting you on the back saying how wonderful and bright you are. You listen to others. You care about them. I'm much more interested in having someone who can learn than having someone who already knows it all. Now, sit tight, let me get you something to drink." He went over to a cooler and pulled out a Coke.

"Drink this," he said. "And go back to the cabin. Your breath stinks. I mean outhouse bad. If you stay here much longer, you'll kill someone. Besides, you look like hell and need some rest. I need to check in with the girls."

He went over to them. They were sitting under a beech tree, plates in their laps, and five teenage boys with plates in their hands stood over them.

I said goodbye to Peggy, Bobby and the girls and drove back to the cabin. I stripped to my underwear and slipped into my sleeping bag. The cool skin of it was like a soothing bandage.

I made notes in my journal. I remembered the words of the theologian Dietrich Bonhoeffer. In times of great upheaval and even greater evil, a man must 'come of age' (that was his term). A man cannot rely on old palliatives to resolve his moral questions. Rather, he must determine what was right for him. He had to act and trust in what he thought was in the best interest for everyone. As an assistant director, I had to put aside my own needs for the larger good of the folk school.

I thought of Mr. Hook's words, how he had to learn time and again the same lesson.

The apple tree leaves whispered outside. I fell asleep.

The Classes

Monday morning, I shaved on the porch, my razor in the cool water. We had no mirror. I rubbed my cheek and neck to discern where the whiskers stuck out. I dressed and waited for Erling to perform his morning ablutions.

He usually drove toward the Methodist Lodge, but on an unfamiliar road, he took a side trip. He drove a mile or so and pulled over, parked, hopped out, and said, "Follow me."

"Where are we going?" I asked.

He motioned for me to keep up with him. We trekked up a narrow path between a dense grove of hemlocks that nearly blocked out the light. He climbed a cliff that had good footholds and, on the top, followed another path around the side of a mountain. On the far side, east where the sun had nestled in the sky, there was a deep ravine cut through two cliffs. Only forty feet wide, it dropped straight down. At the bottom was a stream. He picked up a rock and told me to count when he dropped it. It was ten seconds, hundreds of feet.

"I think about the animals—I've often seen tracks here—that frequent this trail in the dark," he said, "and they never fall in. They have a sense of the danger. We are not as adept." He peered over the rim of his glasses at me.

I looked down.

He added, "One false step and it'd swallow you up. No one would be the wiser."

"What's it called?" I asked.

"The Grand Abyss," he said, a smile in the corner of his mouth.

A chill went through my body. I shuffled closer to the edge, cast my eyes down to the dark ledges along the effacement.

"Is there any way down there?" I asked.

"I'm sure there is. I've never seen it. That stream starts at that large mountain and dips down and, over the years, has cut this cavern. Something, isn't it?"

"Hmm," I responded, woozier than I liked to feel.

"We'll head back," he said.

At the Methodist Center, several missionaries had gathered in prayer at the end of the room. They took our space.

Erling waited for them to finish. He went over to the lead minister to chat with him. A plain-looking woman in her forties introduced herself to me. "Now who are you?" she asked in singsong voice.

"Why, I'm Jason, and who are you?"

She pasted a huge smile on her face. "I'm Joan. I'm a missionary. I leave for Africa in several days. I've never been to Africa. Have *you* been to Africa?"

"Not recently," I said.

"You have been there. That's nice. Did you like it there?"

Holy shit, I thought, *this lady speaks a Dick and Jane primer.*

I told her I was a revolutionary.

"Oh, isn't *that* nice," she said.

"Yes, it is. We plan to overthrow the government."

"That must be a lot of work.""

I asked, "May I ask what you used to do?"

"You certainly can," she said. "I was a first-grade teacher for twenty-eight years."

"Twenty-eight years," I said. "Amazing."

"I loved every minute of it."

"I'm sure you did."

Will had overheard her as he picked up dishes. His eyebrows raised, he shook his head back and forth and out stuck his tongue. I laughed.

"Are you all right?" she asked.

"Yes, yes,"—I frowned at Will—"I just remembered a funny joke that someone told me."

"Really, do tell."

"It's a little off color."

"Well, then you should keep *that* to yourself."

She invited me to tell her more about the revolution; I told her that I had to "take a pee-pee really bad" and excused myself.

"By all means," she said. I half expected her to take me by the hand and escort me there.

Erling had started the class. He read a poem by Philip Larkin called "Church Going." It was about someone in an abandoned church. It ended:

A serious house on serious earth it is,
In whose blent air all our compulsions meet,

Are recognized, and robed as destinies.
And that much never can be obsolete,
Since someone will forever be surprising
A hunger in himself to be more serious,
And gravitating with it to this ground,
Which, he once heard, was proper to grow wise in,
If only that so many dead lie round.

We discussed the usefulness of religion and of a church. As a Jew, Lorraine thought that religion was central to her sense of self. Not just the rituals and the Old Testament history, but also being part of a larger community, were vital. Emily didn't have much use for religion. She agreed with the poet. Maybe it once served a purpose, but for her, she preferred philosophy—Bertrand Russell and Ludwig Wittgenstein who argued that the world had an underlying structure that mathematically could be discerned.

Erling puffed intently on his pipe.

"Well, young lady," Erling interrupted her. "If your Mr. Russell is so right about his arguments, then, I suppose you'd agree about his being a profligate. He had affairs while married and flaunted it."

Emily's cheeks flushed. "I don't know about his personal life," she countered. "But I have great respect for his ideas."

"A person's personal life doesn't matter?"

"I didn't say that. I said I didn't know about it."

Erling had her on the defensive. He had to prove her wrong, as he had once tried to outmatch me in our boxing match.

"Well, once you find out, will *that* change your opinion?" he inquired.

I jumped into the conversation.

"Erling, I for one wouldn't change my opinion. I know Paul Tillich, whose theology I admire, was a really dirty old man, too. He grabbed any graduate student he could get his hands on. But his writing is beautiful and his ideas make sense to me," I said.

Erling laughed. He had heard the story about one of Tillich's female students. She said that Tillich might have a big mind but wasn't well-endowed in other parts. Everyone laughed.

Lois had been quiet. Erling asked her what she thought about the poem. She gripped the seat of her chair tightly. "I don't understand it," she said.

"What part?" Erling asked

"What does 'blent' mean?"

Her honesty allowed us to have a more casual discussion of religion, its good and bad sides.

Will called, "Lunch time." We hustled into the dining room.

For the remainder of the week, we followed the same routine: breakfast, class, lunch at the lodge, and, in the afternoon, arts and crafts at the hollow. On Friday night, we had a campfire with food, football games, story-telling, banjo, and dancing.

On very hot days, we broke up the morning with a swim. I enjoyed undressing with Will. He'd sit naked on the edge of the bathroom sink. His penis had a hood like a sweatshirt. He noticed me inspecting it. "Never seen one?"

"Couple of times. What's it like?"

"Works the same as yours," he said. "Want to see?"

"No, no, that's okay," I said.

But I did wonder what happened to the hood when it was erect.

"If you ever do," Will said. "I'll show you."

"Thanks," I said. He knew something about me, something that I tried to hide from him, from everyone, including myself.

Snipers

By the second week, we were in the public eye. The afternoon folk arts and crafts activities had attracted children up and down Cross Creek, and beyond. Mothers joined in. They wove lanyards, made baskets, and painted watercolors. The boys played football, or softball.

On the periphery of the property, sitting in cars with the windows down, men would stop to check out what we were doing. Erling engaged them in conversation and invited them to play baseball. Some joined us, but mostly they watched from a distance.

Erling felt sure we'd made it over the hump. We'd been seen around town. Parents gave us positive reports. We'd gone to Tibbets' Store to buy snacks and soda for the day program. The Tibbets owned the only grocery and gas station. Anyone who needed something had to go there.

A young man at the counter, who was in his twenties, waited on us. He was a wisp of a fellow. A mop of muddy brown hair fell across his face. Whenever he spoke to us, he'd shake it back. He took a great interest in us the minute we came in the store.

An off-kilter screen door banged shut. A few flies rose from the window sills to herald our entrance. He'd straightened up like a watch dog.

"What you want today?" he asked.

"The usual," we said. We picked up a case of soda, chips, pretzels, and assorted candy bars. He sized us up, craning his neck over the counter to see what we were doing down the two aisles of the store. The black and white-keyed cash register tallied our items. One day, he leaned over as if he wanted to make sure no one noticed him and whispered, "Where you boys from?"

Erling told him that we came from the Cross Creek Folk School. "Come up sometime," he said. "It's lots of fun."

The clerk said, "Yeah, sure it is, but, honest now, where you from?"

When I told him Illinois, Erling shot me an angry look.

Erling asked him, not unkindly but with an edge, "What's it to you?"

"We don't take too kindly to outsiders," he said. "You with the feds?"

"Not on your life."

"Well, that's good," the clerk said and went back to ringing up our total. I sensed that the "good" he said was more a mockery than a sincere reply. I was about to say something when Erling squeezed my arm hard. I turned to see what was the matter. He shook his head. I picked up the cartons of soda and headed to the car.

Later that night, after coming back to the cabin from the lodge, I got into a t-shirt and gym shorts, prepared for bed, and asked Erling, "Why shouldn't I tell people where I'm from?"

"We're outsiders and we're dangerous. Some outsiders like Drug Enforcement Agency try to catch moonshiners. Years ago, union operatives tried to unionize mines. They ended up getting men fired and families kicked off their land. Your telling him that you came from Illinois is asking for trouble," he said. "Keep the focus on what we're doing here."

A moonless night was upon us. I slept soundly because, when I woke up and gazed around the room in the morning light, I noticed that Erling wasn't there. His sleeping bag was gone. One of his sneakers was by my sleeping bag. Why would he go out without one shoe?

I pulled on my pants, one leg at a time, tossed off my t-shirt, pulled on a shirt, grabbed my socks and, skipping to the front door, slipped on my socks and shoes. Mabel was parked by the gate. I called his name. I circled the cabin. I walked to the outhouse. I looked at the well. I called his name again, louder. I trotted to the road to look for foot prints. A cluster of prints was by our gate.

He might have gone to a ridge to watch the sun rise. I sprinted to the hill. He wasn't there. This was not like him. He kept to a schedule. Up by six; out on the porch for his morning ablutions; over to nudge me awake; then to the chair on the front porch to read. All was done in sequence. He never varied no matter how late we were up the night before.

There were different tire tracks on the road, larger than ours, on either side. It might be from the family living down the hollow. I stood on the road, stuffed my hands in my pockets. What could have happened to him? At the gate, on a whim, I glanced into his car.

There he was, snuggled in his sleeping bag.

I tapped on the window. He stirred, stretched, his arms emerging from the bag. His head lifted. He pulled on the door handle, unlocking it.

"What's going on?" I asked in a tone that, once I spoke, I realized was severe.

"Hey, calm down," he said. He scrunched up and sat upright, rubbing his eyes. "Where are my glasses?"

I picked them off the front console. "Here."

He put them on and looked at me. "Didn't you hear them?" he asked.

"Hear what?"

"The gunshots," he said.

"Holy shit!"

"Two or three blasts."

"When?" I asked.

He tugged on the steering wheel and scooted his legs down so he could pull on his trousers. He patted the seat next to him. "Sit."

I did.

"Last night," he said, "midnight, maybe later, I heard noises. There were voices. I got up and looked out the window." He shook his head. "There were four or five guys. And shotguns. I couldn't make out how many."

"No."

"Yes. And I tried, I honestly did, to wake you up. I mean I even threw my shoe at you. You didn't stir." He sat upright and turned to look up the road, his neck craned.

"What'd they do?"

"You didn't hear?"

"No."

"They shot at us. Two or three times. It splattered against the outside wall. I called your name. Told you to keep down. I thought we were done for. I saw other guns, too. Shots hit the door hard. It cracked open. Some shots hit the window. Glass shattered. I slammed the door shut. I yelled, 'I know who you are.' There was a scuffle. Car doors slammed. They were gone."

"You knew who they were?"

"Have no idea. It scared them."

"Holy shit!"

"Yeah," he said and shook his head. "You slept right through it. Never flinched. For a while, after the shots, I thought you were dead. I crawled across the floor and poked you. You muttered something. I told you we had to get out. But you never woke, even when I called your name."

"Really?"

"Slept like a baby."

"Why'd you go to the car?"

"Figured it was safer. If they came back, you know, they wouldn't think to look in the car."

"And left me here."

"Well, you were like a corpse," he laughed. "I thought they'd never notice you there in the corner."

"You left me?"

"I gave it my best. I pushed you. Called your name. You didn't budge. If they shot you, you'd die in peace." He shrugged. "And, well, if you must know, I was scared to death!"

We told Peggy about the encounter. She said there were rumors we were communists, outside agitators. There was talk about trying to scare us off. They were not in Cross Creek folks, but from another hollow up the road. She knew who they were and planned to give them a piece of her mind. She would tell them to let us be.

For the next few days I barely slept. Erling said we should have a sentry. I stayed up well into the night, posted by the door, listening for any car sounds, the grinding of gravel, the hum of a motor. I heard every groan of the wood in the cabin. Every susurration of a branch startled me. After a few nights, we gave up sitting sentry at night. If they were going to get us at least we'd die with a good night's sleep. But sleep was hard to come by.

However often Peggy told us, "There's nothing more to worry about," the cabin door and walls had peppered indentations as a reminder. Buckshot would fall out and tink on the floor as a grim reminder that we weren't welcome. Dreams of falling off a ledge came at night. No one reached out to save me when I called out. Erling heard me several times and nudged me awake. I looked at the cracked window panes. I tried to convince myself everything was fine. But once back to sleep, I fell off the ledge again.

When I asked Erling about it, he said, "It's the abyss. You've come to face it. We all have to."

The dream came less often, but it never left. Some mornings I woke in a sweat, hands aching from grasping at something that wasn't there.

Grace

One afternoon, I was lounged on the front porch in a chair when I spied two children, a mop-haired boy and a younger girl with pigtails, at the slats in our fence. I waved at them. The boy perched on his tiptoes and waved. "Come in," I called. But they stood by the fence, either frightened by the sight of me, or hampered by something. I put down my journal and walked toward them.

They scurried off down the hill, their feet kicking up puffs of dust. I went back to the porch to write a long letter to Mr. Hook as I had promised, and a shorter one to my parents to let them know our progress. I didn't mention the shotgun blasts

Every evening about six, the boy and girl would creep up to the fence. If I got up to greet them, they'd run off. At sunset, I'd hear a woman singing "Amazing Grace." Her voice would well up from down below. The air filled with the tranquility of her voice. I'd never heard a hymn sung so passionately.

"Amazing Grace, how sweet the sound

That saved a wretch like me

I once was lost but now I'm found..."

I'd sing along with the mysterious voice. I wondered who she was.

One evening, after the serenade, Erling and I walked down the hill to introduce ourselves and tell her how wonderful she was. The house, a gray shingled structure, had cardboard in some windows. It had a wire fence around it and a front porch with three chairs on it. An older man, perhaps in his seventies, sat in the larger chair next to him, an older woman, and, right next to the smoldering rag, a younger woman with a gaunt face and shoulder-length dark hair. She had several front teeth missing. And her right cheek was swollen. We asked if we could join them. They invited us up.

"Hi, I'm Erling."

"Pleased to meet ya," the man replied.

"Your names?"

"This here's the Missus. I'm Jack. That there is Melinda. She's the mother of them two rapscallions."

Erling stepped forward to shake his hand and introduce himself. I shook each of their hands too. They seemed bothered by the formality.

"Sit a spell," Jack said.

"That'll be fine," Erling said. He motioned for me to sit on the stoop, while he stood, looking very much like a politician on a campaign. He talked about how dusty the road was. The smoking rag caused me to cough and squint my eyes. They laughed at me.

"That keeps the mosquitoes away," Jack said. "Smoke does the trick."

We talked about how little rain we had. We talked about their garden, its two rows of corn barely waist high.

The boy and girl came out of the cabin and sat on their haunches in the yard. Melinda called them over. With one on either side of her, she introduced them: Travis and Alice. Clearly proud of them, she brushed back the boy's hair from his forehead and tugged on his shirt to straighten it out. Jack was taciturn, but Melinda loved to talk. She told how she became pregnant with Travis. His father had gone north to Chicago, and she had not heard from him since. She had Alice by another man. He got sick—black lung—and died. She worked as a clerk at the Tibbets' Store.

By and by, the boy edged his way over to me and sat in my lap. The girl scrunched up to me too. I reached over and held her under my arm. Melinda seemed pleased. To hear her tell, not many men were in their lives except Pa but "He weren't much for little ones."

I asked who sang. Jack spoke up and told us Melinda had a mighty fine voice and sang in a choir. He never had much luck keeping her quiet. She agreed, but stated proudly that was the way she was.

As we were leaving, Melinda rose to walk us to the gate. Her left leg, atrophied and stunted, dragged as she leaned sideways to compensate for the shorter leg. Polio, we learned later, was the cause.

Travis and Alice raced ahead of us like two pups as we walked up the road. They opened our gate and followed us to the front door. Inside, we sat with them for several minutes and asked them about school—what grade they were in. (Second grade for Travis. Head Start for Alice.) We asked what they liked to do. (Read for Travis. Play dolls for Alice.) Then we heard a voice calling them—their mother—and they fled.

One afternoon when I was writing in my journal, the two of them came to the fence. I waved them in. They sat on the stoop while I continued to write. Alice held a little doll with a white frilly dress and blonde hair with a red bow in it. She was telling it a story. Travis sat beside me.

125

"What you writin'?" he asked.

I told him that I was writing about the last week: what I did, how I felt. He studied the page.

"You don't have very good writin," he noted. "Them looks like chicken scratches."

I laughed. He was right.

He leaned over my shoulder, ran his fingers in my hair, and put his arm around my back and mused, "What if everything cost only a penny?"

What a wonderful question, I thought. "That would be something. What if everything cost a penny?"

His face brightened. He came around in front of me and sat, cross-legged at my feet, and put a finger to his lips.

"Let me see," he pondered, frowning, "everyone'd be happy since everyone would have what they want."

"That's true."

Excited now, he stood up and squirmed between my legs. He sat on my lap, face to face with me.

"You could have a boat and sail to Paris, France. You could own a plane and fly to Florida. See them alligators. I've seen 'em in books. And you'd never have to worry or work," he said, and tapping on my chest, asked, "What you think?"

"If everything costs a penny, the poor would be rich and the rich wouldn't know what to do because money wouldn't matter," I said.

Travis added, "If you had a lot of money, you wouldn't know what to do with it, so you'd give it away."

I was impressed with how imaginative he was and how he loved to toss out ideas. I folded my hands around his waist. We thought of all the things that cost a lot of money—mansions, boats, fancy cars, exotic food, and even wild animals like a giraffe—and considered how anyone might have them for practically nothing.

I had a strange feeling with him there in my lap. The father, the feeling of having a son, had its first spark in me. I couldn't name it entirely, but it was a kind of love for a child that felt true to me and was entirely different from anything I'd felt before. It overwhelmed me. Eventually his mom called him. He hugged me; I hugged him back. He ran off, pulling open the gate, and let it slam shut, his sister trailing behind him.

I checked my watch. I was late for dinner.

The Abyss

After breakfast, Erling began each session with a Danish song. His favorite was Jakob Knudsen's psalm "Behold the Sun is Rising."

> "See the golden sun from the ocean rise,
> Glitter on the waves and the flaming skies!
> Silent happy moment when night is o'er
> And the dawn is landing upon our shore."

Once we had sung and chattered about the previous day's events—what some kids had done, how'd we thought the day camp was working—Erling introduced us to different writers in the American tradition. He loved to read Walt Whitman's "Passage to India." The poem poured over us. Its repetitive lines and shifts in tone and mood were spellbinding to us.

> Passage, O soul, to India!
> Eclaircise the myths Asiatic, the primitive fables...
> The far-darting beams of the spirit, the unloos'd dreams,
> The deep-diving bibles and legends
> The daring plots of the poets, the elder religions;
> O you temples fairer than lilies pour'd over by the rising sun!
> O you fables, spurning the known, eluding the hold of the
> known, mounting to heaven!
> You lofty and dazzling towers, pinnacled, red as rose,
> burnished with gold!
> Towers of fables immortal fashion'd from mortal dreams!
> You too I welcome and fully the same as the rest!
> You too with joy I sing!

He asked what life passages we were making. How had we tried to break with our family's expectations?

"Look at your own soul and find what it's calling you to be," he said. "Find

127

ones closest to your heart. Don't just look through the eyes of materialism and of social expectations."

Following the class, we'd have to be by ourselves, to write, and take walks.

The most memorable and baffling presentation Erling gave was one on "The Abyss." To him, "The Abyss" was real. But it wasn't just a geographic aberration. It was something deep inside each of us. To make his point, he read a number of poems, Dylan Thomas's "Do Not Go Gentle into That Goodnight" and William Stafford's "Traveling Through the Dark." In Thomas's poem, he pointed out how a son pleaded with the father not to go into the dark. In Stafford's, a man must decide whether to dispose of a dead doe with a fawn in her womb or to let the fawn live.

None of us had much to say. Maybe it was the heat. Maybe we didn't want to look at the darkness. Maybe it was Will's pancakes that lay in our stomachs like cement. Our silence riled him. He took off his glasses, held them by the bridge and launched into a sermon. He spoke about how each of us had to face The Abyss. We couldn't avoid it. Someday we'd have to decide whether metaphorically to push doe and fawn off the cliff or let it suffer. We'd have to face the good night of death.

"What is it? What will *you* do?" he asked. He pointed his finger at Lois. She said she wouldn't want to kill the fawn.

"That's *not* the point," he said. "Those are only metaphors, analogies for a deeper, more personal abyss you live with every day."

She dropped her eyes. "I don't know what you're talking about."

"You don't?"

He sat back down, pressing his arms between his legs, rocked back and forth.

I looked at my shoes. They were dusty. I had no idea what to say. Maybe it was my attraction to Will. Perhaps that's what he meant.

Erling dismissed the class and told us to write in our journals. Maybe we'd come to see that the abyss did exist. Maybe it had to do with the emptiness in our lives. He said, "Find a place where life and death *truly* mattered. A place where a need or a want that couldn't be fulfilled by a pretty dress or—" He glared at me. "A new set of golf sticks." He picked up his books and stomped off.

I was irritated that he picked on me. But I was amused that he didn't even know what to call golf clubs. I wrote extensively about the abyss I'd experienced just a few weeks before when my happy-go-lucky party self clashed with my obligations as a leader of the folk school. But I couldn't, or didn't want to find anything more than that.

It wasn't that summer, but the one after the next, that another abyss shook my life to the core. I'd stand on one side of a chasm and find I couldn't, like Tarzan, grab a vine and swing across to the other side. I'd have to go into the dark unknown. At the bottom, I'd have to claw my way up the other side. I'd have to find the strength to get back to the light.

In early July, Erling suggested that I read James Agee's *Let Us Now Praise Famous Men*. Not familiar with Agee or Walker Evans, the photographer, I became entranced with the tenant farmers portrayed in the book. Agee and Evans' mission was to expose how landowners exploited tenant farmers. Agee wrote with compassion about a woman's daily work.

...how is it possible to be made clear enough...the many processes of wearying effort which make the shape of each one of her living days...the accumulated weight of these actions upon her; and what this cumulation has made of her body; and what it has made of her mind and of her heart and of her being.

I felt a new appreciation for what Peggy did raising her children. I discovered someone who saw the world in an entirely different way: not just seeing the appearances but inside their souls. I fell in love with him and his sensibilities.

When I was reading Agee one afternoon on the porch, Erling pulled up and parked by the gate. He practically leapt over the fence, bubbling with excitement.

"We're going to get national news coverage!" he exclaimed.

"From who?"

"From none other than Walter Cronkite, CBS News," he shouted. CBS wanted to do a series of stories about Appalachia. They wanted to meet with Marie and talk about her efforts to promote economic development. They had also heard about the folk school. A woman correspondent would fly to Knoxville with a crew. Erling agreed to meet them in Jellico and drive them to Cross Creek.

We discussed what he could say, who they should interview—certainly Peggy, her neighbor Bonnie, and some of the kids, maybe Lorraine since she would be enthusiastic.

The day of the meeting, Erling made sure his clothes were washed and pressed. He even polished his shoes. With a national news story, he could promote the folk school not only in Appalachia but across the country—in the Dakotas, in his home state, Nebraska, and even in North Carolina. We washed Mabel.

At midday, he headed off. I played hide and seek with Travis. Alice sang "Amazing Grace" to the hills. Her voice closed the day into night.

Erling was as enthused as I had ever seen him after he had met the correspondent. Words poured from him: the CBS correspondent was gorgeous, just plain gorgeous—tall, with brown hair, and sexy in a reserved way—and they had hit it off, gone out for drinks, several of them. She liked him. She listened to him and flirted with him—yes, he was sure of it—flirted with him and, yes, he would gladly have gone back to her room. It might be love. He was not sure. But, no, he needed to be professional. She was doing a story. That would not be right. But, oh God, she was something, never met a woman like her, powerful, bright. She was a confident, beautiful woman. He could fall for her, no doubt. They had so much in common. Her father had been a minister and she was quite well versed in the latest theological thinkers—Bultmann and Tillich—and loved Whitman. His face glowed. Unable to sit down, he paced back and forth and talked for an hour or more, basking in the pleasure of knowing her. After he settled down, he said that he was to meet her the next day at Marie Cirillo's house. They would give her and her film crew of four a tour of the area. He rubbed his hands together and kept saying, "This is it. This is the break I've been waiting for. Man, I could fall for her." He looked over at me. "You like Agee?"

"What?"

"Agee."

"I love him."

"You'll love her, too. I'll bring her by. Let me know what you think," he said. "What a classy girl. Never met one like her."

"Can't wait."

Neither of us slept. Erling said I should be interviewed. I wanted to call my parents and tell them— impress them—that I'd be on the nightly news.

In the morning, I pulled out my best shirt, rubbed the wrinkles out of it, made sure my jeans were clean. I shaved twice, pressed down my cowlick, and dabbed on some Old Spice.

I set up the afternoon program with Emily, Lois and Loraine. They had planned to make leather purses. I brought the wiffle ball and football. When the kids arrived, we told them that CBS News would be coming. Bobby agreed to be

130

interviewed; Tommy drove him home to put on his Sunday clothes.

The afternoon dragged because we kept anticipating the crew driving up in their big white van. But they didn't come. We sent the kids home. I drove back to the cabin. Erling was reading on the porch.

"What happened?" I asked. "Where were you? We waited *all* afternoon."

"Hold your horses," he said.

"But—"

"Calm down," he said. He set Whitman's *Leaves of Grass* down and told how, once the crew arrived, the bubble burst. The whole plan fizzled.

He smirked. "Oh, you know, what you would expect from New York."

I sat on the edge of the porch. "Tell me."

The crew with cameras and lights had arrived at Marie's house. The lead correspondent, the dazzling woman, wanted to go over the story that she wanted to do.

Marie interceded, "What do you mean by 'story?'"

The correspondent proceeded to tell her that Mr. Cronkite wanted to do a story about poverty, how the people struggled against poverty, their desperate situation.

Marie explained that she wouldn't do a story about poverty. She would tell how the people, against all odds, lived in a land that they loved. She would tell how they were rich in many ways.

The correspondent told her that may be the case, but what was their annual income? Wasn't it below the poverty line? Marie said yes, but she wouldn't allow these people to be stereotyped. The mining companies had taken their land and abused it. The residents were fighting back. They were very touchy about the use of the term "poor."

The correspondent told her that she had a storyline approved and that was what she was going to do. She'd gone over it with the front office; they agreed to run it. Wouldn't they cooperate? It would be great coverage. It could benefit their programs.

Erling said that he hadn't come to Appalachia to work with "the poor." He'd come to promote their folk traditions.

The correspondent tried to change the topic. She didn't want to do a story on his program or on mining companies—it wouldn't sell.

Erling jumped on the word "sell" and asked her what she meant. She told him that he knew damn well what it meant: certain stories weren't appropriate. Mining companies were too controversial.

"Walter Cronkite would give them five minutes," she said. "He wants to do it. I'll make it a good story."

Marie told her that she wasn't interested. Erling, despite his attraction to her, concurred with Marie. No poverty stories. The broadcaster said she didn't have all day to haggle. She had other stories to do. Marie offered a compromise. They could talk with some of the people in Cross Creek. But the story couldn't be just about poverty. The correspondent shook her head.

"Look around," she said, "just look at the rundown shacks, the pathetic state of the roads. Clearly, poverty is everywhere. Don't you see what is in front of you?"

Marie and Erling refused. She needed to change the storyline. The correspondent made several calls to New York. It was a "no-go." She had other leads and took her leave.

"My moment of fame," he concluded, "up in smoke. Lost in the abyss. Too bad. Had she not been a robot, it'd been nice to know her." He sighed. "Love lost." He laughed.

At home, when I watched CBS News, I had thought that news emerged from the daily events. But it wasn't as Cronkite said, "That's the way it was." It was more, "That's the way we'll sell it." Anyone, it seemed, who dared to tell a story different from what everyone wanted to hear was ignored, silenced, or shot.

Erling and I went, one after the other, to brush our teeth, to take a leak off the back stoop, and to read until the dark fell and crickets offered the final news of the day.

Night Dip

One evening, after discussing Thomas Wolfe's vision of America, Erling suggested we go for a drive. Lois had gone back up the hollow. The twins were sick. Will, Lorraine, Emily and I crammed into his Rambler. We drove by the Clearfork Post Office, and from there, across the tracks to the western side of the mountains, a region I'd never seen.

A narrow mining road climbed up a ridge. At the top, in the twilight, far in the distance lay another deep blue mountain range far as the eye could see. To our right, a quarry with steep rock effacements dropped into a pool of water. Darkness swept quickly over the hillside as the last light slipped away.

Erling suggested that we all go skinny dipping. Will stripped off his shirt. "Hey, I'm game."

Erling chided the girls, "Come on. No one can see you. Get a little daring!"

The girls refused and perched on a set of rocks over the quarry. They called back, "You can if you want. We wouldn't look."

We stripped off our clothes and piled them on a rock. Erling went down a pathway toward the quarry. Will followed him. At one point, Will stopped and looked back at me. "Cool, huh?"

"Sure."

We crept forward. Erling muttered, "Those girls will end up just like every other bourgeois girl. They'll marry a rich guy, move to the suburbs, and watch the nightly news, their brains turned off, their souls dried up."

Will whispered to me, "I kinda like them as they are."

"What'd you say?" Erling called back.

Will responded, "How far are we?"

"Not far."

But it was a far way to the water. Diving into jet black water from twenty feet worried me. What about rocks?

Erling assured us, "It's safe."

Along a slate path, two feet wide, he walked. He tapped where we should put our feet. He stopped on a ledge that jutted out from the cliff. A thin reflection of the moon spread on the water below. The night air caused me to shiver.

Will put his arm around me. "Hey, it's okay. Trust him." I felt his thigh against mine. My hands over my groin, I said to myself. "Down, down."

He looked over at me. "You all right?"

"Sure."

He was aroused too. But he didn't seem to mind.

Erling stepped out on a rock, smooth and rounded like a tooth.

"You scared?" Erling asked.

"Some," I admitted.

"Not me." Will flapped his arms as if he were about to fly.

"Follow me," Erling called.

Erling went to the edge of the rock. "Ready?" he asked. "No worries."

"Uh-huh," Will said.

Erling leaned out and disappeared into the darkness. A sploosh. Seconds later, "It's great!"

I rested my hand on the rock outcropping behind me. I couldn't do it.

Will put his hand on my shoulder, squeezed it. "Come on, hold my hand," he said. He extended his hand to mine. Although I felt as foolish as a child, I took Will's hand. We walked side by side to the edge of the rock. Ripples moved in the water below, ridges of white on ink.

"Count to three with me," Will said.

"One. Two. Three." We were off. At the last moment, I let go of Will and raised my arms. Just as I wondered where I was, since I could see nothing in the dark, I felt the water smack my feet. My legs submerged, my shoulders hit the surface. My legs, stretched out as I entered the water, knifed downward. I twisted upward quickly to avoid hitting bottom. My eyes were open, but at first I could see nothing. I kicked my legs like a frog. I reached up and pulled my arms back like a blind man with only instinct to guide him. I felt a blissful serenity in the black void and stopped. I treaded water beneath the surface. I blew out bubbles that caught the moonlight and pushed upward to the surface. I followed them. Except for little glints of light in the bubbles, I could see nothing. Yet I felt the water around me and felt my naked body inside it. I ducked underwater again, diving down, blowing out more bubbles. No sound. Only my arms straining to keep me underwater. I swam on. Then, when my breath gave out, I surfaced and heard Will call out in a soft voice, "Jason, Jason. You there? You there?"

"Yes," I whispered back.

"Thank God," he whispered back. "You all right?"

"Yeah."

"You let go."

"I did!"

He swam over to me and dunked me. I pushed away from him, but he grabbed on and his body clung to me, his genitals pressed to mine. We were both aroused, but no one could see us, no one knew what we were doing. I let him hold me like that. I pressed my lips to his neck.

From the shore, Erling called out, "Where are you guys?"

"Over here," Will called out.

"Come on, let's do it again." We swam to him. Once we got to shore, we whispered. We didn't want to disturb the quiet.

We pulled ourselves onto a rock ledge and followed it to the top. We sat down and called to the girls. We told them that no one could see anything and urged them to try it. "Besides, we'll get out and let you do it by yourselves."

They giggled and called back, "No, thank you. We're fine."

We jumped and dove several more times. Landing feet first proved to be more exciting since the water, once it smacked against your feet, caused a momentary resistance and then, as if someone pulled a plug, sucked us into a tube, and our bodies would dart down into the void. I learned to leap with my arms up on either side of my head like I was diving so that I shot like an arrow to the bottom where I would resist coming up for a few seconds. Deep as it was, there was nothing but blackness, like swimming in ink. After each jump, Will swam over and splashed me. I'd swim away. He'd grab my foot, pull me toward him. We laughed. We embraced. Our secret was hid in the night.

Finally, we dried off, pulled on our clothes, and told them we were decent. Erling drove them back to the lodge. He lectured them: someday, they needed to loosen up, let go of the bourgeois mentality and just be. They would never experience freedom unless they dared to be free.

We dropped Will off by the road to his cabin.

"Great night," Will said to Erling. As he scooted out of the back seat next to me, he slid his hand down my arm to my leg and squeezed it. "See," he said. "Listen to Erling. You can do it. You just need to let go."

"That's what I keep telling him," Erling said.

I said, "Let go. Let go. Where's caution in this world?"

"Hey, get in the front seat," Erling said. "It's late."

Erling lamented how the girls were uptight rich girls who basked in the complacency of wealth, not ever considering what life was like for the largely invisible poor. By the way he spoke about them, I knew he was also talking to me. I knew, by inference, what might lie ahead for me if he dared to be honest with me.

I had other thoughts about Will. It felt wonderful to leap with him off the cliff and to have him hold me. I was afraid, however, of what it might lead to, what might happen if I wasn't more cautious. I didn't want to step into another Abyss. I opened the car window and took in the night air. I remembered how it was under the water, the way it embraced me and carried me into the dark. It was an underworld I craved but only faintly understood, and I feared it would swallow me whole.

Fairy Tales

By the fifth week, our weekly routine drew even more people to us. On Friday evenings, as an alternative to Friday night at a bar, we had campfires. In late afternoon, the whole community gathered on the ridge by Peggy's house. The men made a large circle with boulders. In the middle, they built a bonfire. Before sundown, the boys would play intense, but fun tackle football. When they tackled someone, they dragged him down gently. I'd often play quarterback. My favorite target was Bobby, who could leap four feet into the air and snatch the ball.

One team would start down a slope, from a hickory tree at the end of the field. Boys eleven to sixteen, and men twenty-one to forty wrestled each other for the ball. They high-stepped in foot-long grass to the end zone.

When the sunset—yellow, purple and faded pink—blinked out, we ignited the bonfire. Usually Cecil, a tall man with a lucrative moonshine business, doused it in gasoline. He'd light a newspaper and toss it on the pile and, whoosh!

Bud Terry, who sang despite his asthma, played the fiddle. A few would dance on an old tabletop set in the dusty perimeter of the fire. They'd clog on the wood, while everyone else would clap, whoop, and tap their toes. To add to the festivities, I told stories. I had memorized several Appalachian folk tales. The kids loved for me to tell "The Twins and the Dark Evil Witch."

The twins were poor children whose family was starving. The children heard about a mysterious land with fabulous riches. They told their mother that they wanted to go there to bring back money for food.

They set out on their journey, traveling to the strange, enchanted land. On their travels, they encounter a fox caught in a trap and they release him. He gave them several of his teeth to use if they ever are in trouble. They came across a pine tree that has fallen. The tree asked them to straighten it up. The tree gave them one of its cones. As they crossed a mountain pass, they found a stream that, because of landsides, was stopped up. They rolled rocks away until it flowed freely. It gave them a cup of its water.

Finally, they came to a magic land where gold and silver glistened on the hillsides. They stuffed their pockets and satchels, enough to be rich forever.

But an evil witch caught them in their thievery. She cast a spell over them. She locked them in a room in her castle where they had to await their fate.

They could smell the fire burning in a stove. They heard the cries of other victims. From time to time, the witch would poke them to see how plump they were getting and how soon they'd be a fine morsel for her dinner.

One night, the twins heard a tiny voice. It was a tiny mouse that showed them a trap door in the cell. The twins escaped, running as fast as they could.

But that wasn't the end of the story. (This was the part where I'd have the children pretend they were the twins.) The evil witch heard their footfalls on the road and took off on her broom to capture them.

The children cheered the twins. "Hurry, hurry!" The last part of the story was filled with "Oohs" and "Ahhhs." I'd give some children pine cones, buckets of water, and chalk (as teeth). As the witch cackled, "I'm going to get you, little ones, hee, hee, hee," and flew after the boy and girl on her broom, they'd toss the teeth. They sprouted into an enormous teethed fence to block her way. But she'd smashed through the fence. They'd toss the pine cone which sprouted a gigantic forest to block her way. But she would swerve around the trees. She'd nip at the children's feet. Finally, they'd throw a bucket of water at her (and on me). An ocean would rise with waves that swallowed the witch. The boy and girl arrived safely home. Their mother welcomed them with open arms, and, as in all good fairy tales, good won out over evil.

The story concluded the evening. People dispersed. Several men lingered and helped extinguish the fire. Then the girls, Erling and I would get in Mabel and drive back to our sleeping quarters.

Bad News

The program became all consuming. Rarely did we read the newspaper and know what was happening in the world. The girls told us that Nixon had pledged to withdraw 25,000 troops from Vietnam and had also appointed Warren Burger to the Supreme Count.

Will and I had several conversations about the war (he opposed it, too) and civil rights (he'd been in several marches). One night, he wanted to tell me something important and asked if we could take a walk.

"There's been a riot," he said on path toward the lake below the lodge.

"Where?"

"Right down the street from where I live," he said. "You might be interested in it."

"How so?"

He spoke in a hushed tone. "The gays in Greenwich Village rebelled. The police harass them all the time. Arrests. Beatings. Finally, some drag queens at a bar called Stonewall had enough and fought back. It's big. It made national news."

I pulled back from him. For weeks, I'd seen him hiking the roads. Rain, sun, day, night, he walked ten miles home and back. His endurance amazed me. He was always upbeat. He made me smile. We'd gone swimming every week, changing in the same room. He was easy to look at. And I did look. He told me his family, strict Catholics, wanted nothing to do with him—too radical. But he never said what "radical" meant. I hoped he wasn't gay. Maybe he was just lonely or was starved for affection. And horny, like I was. That's how I rationalized my relationship with him, how I kept him at bay. But he was telling me about some gays in New York.

"Why tell me?" I blurted out.

"Just thought—"

"Thought what?"

"Thought you'd like to know," he said. "That's all." He shrugged.

"Thanks," I said and excused myself.

He knew something about me from our first encounter. That's what scared me. What was it that tipped him off? I didn't flirt with him. Or at least not consciously. I was curious about his being uncircumcised, but that was only natural. I never said a word about being attracted to him. True, I found him attractive. He wore a Speedo. His body was like marble, with a hairy chest and chiseled muscles, probably from his long hikes. Somehow he did know. The night in the quarry, I gave in. I tested the limits. But I wasn't going to just give into those feelings again now.

I kept distant after that. I didn't want Erling to suspect my interest in Will. That would be a big problem for the folk school. And me.

A week or so later, the girls, particularly Lorraine, were in tears one morning because Ted Kennedy had nearly drowned. But worse, one of his aides had drowned. His car toppled off a bridge at Chappaquiddick. Lorraine's family was close to the Kennedys. She had gone to school with one of them. She asked if she could spend the day at the lodge listening to reports on the radio and making telephone calls. Erling let her and told me, "Those Kennedys are always out to get laid. Looks like he got screwed this time instead."

By late July, the lodge was abuzz about the moon landing. There was one TV in the lodge. Many people who frequented the lodge, including several ministers and their wives, and some of the kids from the folk school, Bobby and Tommy, pulled up chairs and watched the lunar capsule. Once it landed and the dust swirled out across the rock-strewn landscape, Bobby, who was sitting next to me, said, "Looks like the road from our place."

Tommy asked, "You think it's real?"

"I'm sure it is," I said. "I've seen the rockets take off from the Cape."

"Looks like some movie to me," he said.

Two astronauts climbed down the ladder and pranced on the surface in their inflated spacesuits. President Nixon got into the act.

"I just can't tell you how..." he said, "proud we all are of what you have done. For every American this has to be the proudest day of our lives, and for people all over the world I am sure that they, too, join with Americans in recognizing what an immense feat this is. Because of what you have done the heavens have become a part of man's world, and as you talk to us from the Sea of Tranquility, it inspires us to redouble our efforts to bring peace and tranquility to earth. For one priceless moment in the whole history of man all the people on this earth are truly one..."

One of the ministers chimed in, "I think the president forgot another priceless moment in history."

"What's that?" I asked. "It's pretty darn big if you asked me."

He tilted his head to one side and said, "How about Christ?"

"Oh, yeah," I said. "Can't forget him."

The minister shot a glance at me and muttered something to his wife.

Will had walked out of the room and was looking up at the moon. With the atmosphere in the room more heated than I liked, I joined him.

"Pretty amazing, isn't it?" he said.

"Right out there," I pointed at the moon. "They are on it, hundreds of thousands of miles from here."

Will came over to me and put his hand on my shoulder. "Hey," he said. "I didn't mean to scare you."

"It's fine," I said and stepped away.

"I just thought..."

"You thought wrong," I said.

He was silent. I kept looking at the moon. When I turned to say something else to him, he was gone. I went back into the room and watched Walter Cronkite interview a scientist. I drove Tommy and Bobby back home. On the way back to the cabin, I stopped by the road and walked by the creek. A sadness had come over me. The water cascaded over the rocks. I didn't mean to hurt Will. I wanted to hug him. Maybe I would have, if he had stayed. *I could be such a creep,* I thought. *I'd tell him the next time I see him.*

When we had our next class, I learned that Will had gone back to Greenwich Village. His friend had been beaten and arrested. He told Erling he'd write, but he never did. I never heard from him again.

After the morning meeting, Erling pulled me aside to talk in private. He was puzzled by the abruptness of Will's departure.

"Did something happen between you two?" he asked.

"No, *why* do you ask?" I shot back.

"Hey, calm down. I just thought you were close, that's all," he said.

"We were," I said. By the look in Erling's eyes, I could tell that he knew more than he was saying. He chewed on his cheek, waiting.

I broke the silence. "It might have been something I said. I don't know."

"I'm sorry," Erling offered.

I tried to be casual. "It's fine."

"Well, they have another cook," Erling said, trying to be light. "It doesn't matter, as long as he knows how to cook!"

But it did matter. I missed Will terribly. He was as far away as those men on the moon, orbiting two hundred and thirty thousand miles from the earth.

Here I was on earth watching them in their spacesuits that looked impossible to move in. They seemed just like me with the full weight and gravity of my own fears dragging me down. There was nothing I could do to change it, go back in time and make it different. The abyss I'd feared was not only of my own making but based on my own mixed-up feelings.

Erling looked at me and asked, "Is there anything I can do?"

"Fuck, I don't know. I guess it's just..." My voice trailed off. I was crying.

"Hey," he said. "Take the rest of the day off. You need it."

I did. I drove back to the cabin, pulled out my journal and wrote about what happened. I reconstructed what he said, what I'd said. I tried to make sense of it. But no matter how many words scattered across the page nothing changed. They couldn't assuage the fears that stood in my way. No way around it, I'd made an irreconcilable mistake.

Ending

Two days before the folk school closed for the summer, Erling and I drove through the Smoky Mountains. He wanted me to see Thomas Wolfe's boarding house, the site of his famous novels *Look Homeward, Angel* and *You Can't Go Home Again*. The boarding house was in an old residential area. The looming three-story house had a wide porch and expansive façade.

I understood why Erling made such pilgrimages to his literary heroes. I saw how Wolfe shaped his stories from what he'd experienced and seen. Words became rooms we walked through. We walked up the stairs where his dad, Gant, had raged, staggered drunk and hemorrhaged; we sat in rooms his mother Eliza had cleaned for her guests; we looked at the bed where Ben lay with his failing lungs and died. His descriptions of the rooms—the dining room where guests ate, the porch where he gazed to the hills—had, by the magic of his pen, stopped time. I could imagine him coming out of the kitchen. His enormous hand around a sandwich, he'd tell us to sit down. He'd tell of his life, of what he dreamed.

Erling read passages from the book and told me that, if I read well and if I trusted in the voice of those I read, that soon—maybe not in a year or even in a decade—I would find their voice would meld with mine. He said too, that if I followed my heart, I could make a break, as Eugene did in the novels, and discover I couldn't go home again. Eugene realized: "You can't go back home to your family, back home to your childhood ... back home to a young man's dreams of glory and of fame ... back home to places in the country, back home to the old forms and systems of things which once seemed everlasting but which are changing all the time – back home to the escapes of Time and Memory."

I wondered if that was to be my fate too. Each time I went home, I felt more like a stranger. Yet I felt that, to leave my home, I had to have someplace and some people I could claim as my new home. Until I had such a place, I was a wanderer on a voyage to a new continent of my heart without any clear destination or final place to settle. It was as if, deep inside, I knew that I had to have a place to say hello to before I could say goodbye. I yearned to open a door and look out and see the face of someone who loved me as dearly as

I loved them. Right now, when I opened doors, there were people who cared deeply for me, as deeply as I cared for them. But they weren't my lovers and they didn't really know me any more than I knew myself. I knew I was still a long way from finding home and how to be true to myself. I thought, too, of Will and how in an instant he had left my life because I'd denied his love for me. I wasn't ready for his love and he knew it.

Erling and I drove back through the Smokey Mountains and slept in Mabel under the dog-eared comforter. We hiked deep into the forest to stunning waterfalls. We perched at the headland of a waterfall and sat quietly, each of us taking in the view down the valley where the stream dove and darted through pines, its spine visible for miles as it bent along the forest floor.

Suddenly, a mother, father, and their young son charged up the path to us. The mother had a camera around her neck; the father, a trail map in his hand; the boy, a miserable look on his face.

The father stepped in front of us and shouted orders to his son, "Stand here, Jerry," and to his wife, "Alice, get his picture."

The heavy-set wife stood in front of us, straddled our legs, and took several photographs. Once she did, the father brought the boy to the precipice and said, "Take a good look."

"Got the pictures?" he asked his wife.

She nodded. He said, "Let's go." They hurried down the trail. The whole encounter took three minutes.

"What is it about the American need to capture everything on camera?" Erling asked. "Nothing seems real to them unless they have it in a snapshot. Trouble is they never stay long enough to experience what they see."

We waited until the family had gone far down the trail. Once they were out of sight, we followed them back to the parking lot. We drove toward Clearfork where, the next day, we'd meet the girls to say goodbye.

The Dare

On our trip east, I'd bought several newspapers and a *Time* magazine. I wanted to find out what had happened while I was isolated. The news was bizarre: Muhammad Ali was convicted of evading the draft and stripped of his boxing title. Nixon was getting tough on antiwar activists. Charles Manson and his "family" in California had brutally killed an actress, Sharon Tate and others. In upstate New York, 400,000 people gathered for a music festival. Naked people splashed in the rain. It was gratifying to see how uninhibited they were.

We parked and ran under the covered front porch of the Clearfork Post Office. Torrential rain battered the roof. The road was a giant mud puddle, tire tracks filled with a milky coffee-colored pudding. Silver curtains of rain whipped by. The sound was deafening. We arranged a rendezvous there to say goodbye to the girls.

"This is no place to say goodbye!" I shouted.

"No, it isn't. Horrible weather," Erling agreed.

Loraine's yellow Mustang drove up to the post office. Lorraine and Emily bolted out of the car to join us on the porch. They looked as if they had been dressed by Christian Dior himself. With a white blouse, tight blue and green pants, and pink sneakers, Lorraine looked regal. Emily had on a red blouse with a matching skirt and white loafers. They had abandoned the jeans and workshirts Erling insisted they wear.

They shook hands with Erling and told him that it meant a lot to them to be in the folk school. Not wanting to miss this last opportunity to warn them of the societal trap that they would fall into, he hoped someday they'd break out of their bourgeois shells and experience true freedom.

"I wish you girls well," he said.

"Erling," Loraine said in a calm yet stern voice, "I used to be a girl; since you have known me, I have always been a woman. So *please* call me a woman."

Nonplussed, Erling said, "Well, of course."

"Good."

Erling took a deep breath. "Glad you came here. I hope it was a good experience."

"It was."

"I wish we could have done more, and I do hope that someday you can find the gumption to be fully yourselves."

Lorraine asked, "What do you mean by that?" She seemed intolerant of his patronizing manner.

He explained that they were still uptight, not willing to let go, but that was expected given their background.

"Let go, be less uptight?" she asked.

"Yes," Erling said, "and, well, stop worrying about appearances. How you look." He motioned at their outfits and turned down his mouth. "You always look as if you were about to go to a swank Boston cocktail party."

Loraine blushed and started to thank him, to concede his point, and then caught herself and repeated Erling's phrase, "Let go, huh? Is *that* what I need to do?"

"Yes," he affirmed. "I hope you can do that someday."

She mimicked him, "Someday."

Grabbing Emily by the hand, Lorraine shouted to Emily, "Someday *is today*," and sprinted off the porch, right into the rain and into the quagmire that once had been a road. The two girls stomped and leapt, the rain lashing at them, the mud splattered on their outfits. They yelped and splashed back and forth. Their hair splattered across their faces. Lorraine's blouse was soaked. We could see the clear curve of her breasts and her nipples. She was, indeed, a woman. We stood in awe of them.

They raised their arms and whooped and hollered so much that the postmistress, Ida, came out to see what the commotion was about. She stood, her hands on her hips, and said, "Well, I'll be."

It reminded me of the photographs from Woodstock, naked hippies flopping in the mud, free of all restraints.

Erling seemed genuinely befuddled. Yet he couldn't help but smile and looked at them in admiration. They were like wild beasts.

"What the hell?" he gasped, not comprehending what precipitated the girls' romp in the road.

I laughed, took off my shirt, and joined them. The girls screeched and grabbed my hands and we swung around in circles. We didn't expect it, but Erling came out too. He took off his shoes, socks and shirt, piling everything neatly on a chair. We raced back and forth. We threw mud at one another. The

146

postmistress laughed and called out, "It's better than 'Hee-Haw'!"

When we finished, we stood once again on the porch. The girls asked Erling, "Like that?" He smiled, "Yes, like that." We hugged one another and they drove off. Erling and I stood and watched them go.

PART IV

"Neither flesh nor fleshless;

Neither from nor towards; at the still point, the dance is."

"Four Quartets," T.S. Eliot

Alone

Erling drove back to Nashville to complete paperwork for his degree. I drove northwest out of the mountains across Ohio and Indiana back to Illinois. The patchwork cornfields broken by railroad tracks, and the vast expanse of sky from horizon to horizon made me feel at home.

My parents had gone to bed, although my dad, a light sleeper, heard me come in and came out and said groggily, "Good to have you home, son." With less than two weeks before the new semester began, I typed up my letters to Mr. Hook. We met with some parishioners to talk about my experience. They committed to support me for another summer.

I went back to familiar routines: playing golf, going to the club, going out with Jerry to find girls, and contacting Bob, Ann, and Paul to catch up with their lives.

Bob was excited about decoding enemy messages. He couldn't tell me much for security reasons. However, he stayed on the east coast and played golf with a number of senior officers. I imagined that they came to his pad on weekends for parties like the professors had at Vanderbilt.

After the presidential campaign, Paul moved out west, joined a commune, and met a woman. Nixon, he believed, would tear the country apart even more than it already was. His interest in politics ended with the election. He advised me to drop out too.

Ann wrote a lovely letter. She looked forward to seeing me. She planned to move out of the dorm and wondered if I wanted to get an apartment with her. I told her no because I was still a residential advisor; but I did look forward to seeing her. Several nights I went to Old Town, the upscale neighborhood near Chicago's Lincoln Park, to drink and, later, to haunt The Hidden Treasure, an adult bookstore. Wandering down the magazine rack with photographs of men, randy and beautiful, my old urges came back to me. I bought several magazines and hid them in my room. I fantasized about being with one of the men. He'd take me back to his place. We'd slowly undress. I'd fall into his arms as if they were Will's arms.

In the morning, I'd hear my mom call me from downstairs. "Time to get up. You have a tee-off time with your dad." I'd splash water on my face, slip on my golf shirt, shorts, and shoes, and head off to play. Pars. Bogeys. Birdies. Numbers. Missed putts. The Oak Room. Drinks. Shower. Change. Dinner. Coat and tie. Stand when others came to the table. Seat mother. Smile. Make small talk. And thus, August ended.

In September, I left home on the day the *Chicago Tribune* condemned the "Chicago 8." They were indicted based on charges against them at the Democratic Convention. My father made a point to tell me that they were unpatriotic. I was happy to get away from him.

A long day's drive. New dorm room. New students to take care of. Books. Schedule. Classes. A call from Ann. Her new apartment with another girl, Jenny. A long overnight. "I love you." One of us said it. Every weekend I went over. We wanted the old magic back. But it wasn't the same without Bob. We knew it. No one said anything. Parties with mostly students lasted late into the night. We slept together. Something was missing. I couldn't say. Perhaps, I didn't want to know. Her roommate told Ann I wasn't good for her. Maybe they were right. I went back to my room to study. Deep into the night I read Kierkegaard, a man as troubled as I was about a relationship.

Innocence

In October, Tom Winters, a fellow second-year divinity student and dorm advisor who was also in several of my classes, came to my room to study some terms in the Phenomenology of Religion class. Skinny and awkward, not an athlete, he carried himself like an adolescent, flinging his apish arms around as if they were in free flight from his body.

We discussed how to distinguish "world-view" from "lived-world," two concepts that the professor had introduced. In college, Tom majored in English with a minor in philosophy. He was familiar with recent trends in literary criticism that had its roots in phenomenology.

One evening, he brought a bottle of Jack Daniels. He poured shots of it, one for every question we answered from the last class. We kept our focus for an hour. We went over the textbook, read and re-read pages, and deciphered what they meant. Bracketing. Lifeworld. Intentionality. Noesis.

Our scholarly conversation waned, and we reverted to storytelling. I sat on my bunk against the wall by the one window. Tom pulled his chair up next to me and continued to pour Jack.

I said, "You're a good bartender."

"I'm tending you."

"You've fucked up."

He pulled back, offended. "How so?"

"You're getting me very drunk!"

"Oh, no," he said. "You don't get it. That's my intentionality, to use a phenomenological term."

"Aren't you the brilliant one!"

Tom told about a girl he dated in high school. His hand was on my thigh. It was a casual gesture. I hardly noticed it since it was holding out a full glass of whiskey. He asked if he could sit on the bunk. We could drink from the bottle. I motioned to a spot. He sat down. He leaned back and looked into my eyes.

"I like to look at someone when I talk to them," he said.

"That's fine."

We talked about dating, how frustrating it was. He put his hand on my

155

stomach. I let it be. It sat there. It wasn't doing anything. It felt comfortable, a good place for a hand. But I soon felt an increase in pressure as if it were trying to get me to sit up. I scooched up more. He looked at me. He wasn't talking any more.

My penis bulged in my pants. I twisted my hips to the side to cover it up. He could see what I saw. There was no use hiding.

"That excites me," I said. I pointed to his hand and noted that I had an erection.

"Oh, I'm sorry!" Tom apologized, lifting his hand high in the air.

"Oh, it's okay. Feels good." I half realized what I said and wanted to disown it. I leaned back and closed my eyes. I let myself go. *To hell with it; I'm drunk, very drunk. This is bad, I know, this is bad. But I don't care.* He caressed my stomach. It felt good. *If it feels good, do it.* His fingers were on my cock.

"I'll just lie here," I said to myself, "and pretend it's Ann. I don't know what he's going to do next. If I'm still, he can do what he wants. He likes it, fine, but I'll have no part of it."

Tom asked, "Are you awake?"

I opened my eyes. "Somewhat."

He unzipped my pants. As he unbuttoned my shirt, I leaned up, his hand around my neck, supporting me. I unbuttoned his shirt. In one quick moment, we were undressed. I lay on Tom and kissed him. I felt the bristle of his beard and thought how different it was from Ann. Tom was larger than me. I wondered why he was queer because, in my mind, men were gay because they didn't measure up to other guys. But clearly, he did. I rubbed Tom's dick. How odd another man's penis felt—like rubber, no life in it. I wondered what I was doing; it seemed so perfunctory

This is sick, I thought. But I couldn't figure out how to get away since I was plastered. I laid back and hoped the dizziness would end. I looked up at the ceiling.

Tom took the initiative and took me in his mouth. I closed my eyes and soon it was over.

After wiping me off with a towel, he sat up and said, "Nice."

I reached for my underpants in a vain attempt to cover up. I felt embarrassed. Too little, too late. I knew Tom was probably expecting me to do the same favor for him. But I didn't want to. I felt disgusted. Tom had a mouth like a giant fish that craved to suck in something. His face was narrow. It looked to be starving. Gaunt. That was the word: gaunt. How was it that I just noticed that? He put his hand on my cheek and said, "Lovely."

What was I doing here with him in my bed? It wasn't right. I lay back and awoke with Tom by my side, caressing me. He began again, and I let myself go. It was over soon. He kissed me, dressed and left quickly, leaving the bottle. "Good night." The door closed behind him.

After that encounter, I couldn't face him. I kept on the opposite side of the seminar table from him. I'd been in the hands of the devil. I had given into temptation. It was the whiskey. I let down my guard. I wrote in my journal: "I WAS IN THE HANDS AND MOUTH OF THE DEVIL!!" I was ashamed and angry at myself. I'd stepped over the line. I avoided him, claimed I was too busy.

Late one evening, when I was standing in jockey shorts in my bedroom preparing for bed, Tom knocked. Before I could refuse him, he entered. He was drunk and held a bottle in his hand and cradled two glasses in the crook of his arm. He staggered toward the chair and said, "Oh, I'm sorry."

"Can't you..."

I pulled on my pants, looked at him, and said flatly, "Don't think you're..."

"No, no."

"Look, sorry, man." I said. "I have to study."

Tom sat down in the one chair in the room. "You hate me," he said. He set the glasses on the floor and poured the liquor in the glasses. He picked one up, kneeling, pleading, "Come on, have a drink. Come on. It'll do ya' good—Here. Here."

I looked out the window. I turned back to see how pathetic he looked, penitent, trying to make up for a mistake. He mixed the drinks, poured in soda, and didn't look up. He talked as he poured, "Come on, let's drink, just one for old time's sake."

He offered a drink to me. As he held the glass up to me, it slipped from his grasp and shattered on the tile floor.

"Oh god. Oh god, I'm so sorry. I'm sorry. I'm such a fool."

Tom bent over and muttered to himself, "Asshole. Asshole." He scraped the glass together with his hand. The liquor ran in all directions in quick rivulets. The side of his hand was bleeding.

"Listen," I burst out, "Forget it. I'll clean it up. Just get out! I'm *not* innocent any more. Just get outta here. I don't want to. I made a mistake. Do you understand? No more. I'm not like *that*. So don't try it again. Just, go."

He didn't seem to hear me but continued to pick up glass shards. Both hands were bleeding.

"Do me a favor. Get the hell outta here, now!"

He kept picking up the shards, muttering to himself.

I leaned over, grabbed him under his arms, picked him up, and shoved him against the wall. He gasped and cowered, looking as if he were going to faint. The glass shards fell from his hand.

"Forget it," I said, softening my tone. I grabbed a T-shirt on my dresser, wrapped it around the bottle, placed the bottle in Tom's hand, and put the remaining glass in the crook of his arm.

Tom repeated, "Let me clean it up. I'm so sorry. I'm such an asshole. I'll get a towel. I'm sorry. Let me..."

I opened the door. "Forget it. It's okay. Just get out of here."

Gently, I pushed him out the door. The puddle of Jack Daniels covered the floor in a huge arc. It seeped under the bed, the desk.

Once he was outside, I took a deep breath. How could I have been involved with him? He was disgusting. I could hear Tom stumbling down the hall, bumping into the wall, muttering to himself. I thought he'd probably go out and pick up some other guy tonight. He was so drunk he may have succeeded.

I mopped up the booze with paper towels from the john and, wide-awake, went back to my studies. I could hardly focus. I had a strange urge to kill him, I hated him so. I hated what he made me feel. I felt embarrassed just as I had with Stephen in college, that time in the adult bookstore with the guy (what was his name?) in Chicago, and Will just months ago. I was shocked that I should be as aroused as I was with Tom. He did it twice. More than I'd ever done it with Ann. When Tom came in the room, it was as if the devil had barged in and unmasked my disguise. I didn't like it. I had to see Ann. I had to make it right.

The next day I asked Ann over to my room. We studied together. After a few hours, we lay down together. With music on my stereo playing, we made unhurried love. I felt as if I were whole again. I liked her perfume, her breasts that were firm and sweet and, how, as we made love, she moaned and kept pace with me, holding onto my back, whispering, "Yes, yes, yes." We settled, kissed, and fell asleep.

She came over regularly. She lounged on the bed, read her books, and made notes in a journal. We listened to the radio. One night, President Nixon had a special broadcast. We opened a bottle of Merlot that she liked, curled up in bed, my arms around her and listened. We hoped he might be withdrawing more troops. But that's not what happened. In his faux sincere voice, he called on "his fellow citizens" to hear his plan for peace. He noted that some might disagree with him.

"Honest and patriotic Americans," he said, "have reached different conclusions as to how peace should be achieved. In San Francisco a few weeks ago, I saw demonstrators carrying signs reading, 'Lose the war in Vietnam. Bring the boys home...'"

He made it seem that any of us who disagreed with him were not only letting him down but were also letting the nation and the peace process down.

"And I want to end the war for another reason," he continued, "I want to end it so that the energy and dedication of you, our young people, now too often directed into bitter hatred against those responsible for the war, can be turned to the great challenges of peace, a better life for all Americans, a better life for all people on this earth...

"So tonight, to you, the great silent majority of my fellow Americans, I ask for your support. I pledged in my campaign for the Presidency to end the war in a way that we could win the peace. I have initiated a plan of action which will enable me to keep that pledge. The more support I can have from the American people, the sooner that pledge can be redeemed. For the more divided we are at home, the less likely the enemy is to negotiate in Paris."

Ann jumped out of bed. She pointed at the TV as if I hadn't noticed it.

"He's threatening us."

"I know," I said, motioning to her. "Sit down. Let's see what he says next."

He concluded, "Let us be united for peace. Let us also be united against defeat. Because let us understand: North Vietnam cannot defeat or humiliate the United States. Only Americans can do that..."

Ann bolted upright. "He's not ending the war! He's going to expand it," she exclaimed. She was right. The president started "Vietnamization" that expanded the war. His "Silent Majority" raved about his speech. Yet protests to end the war increased to a fever pitch. Ann and I didn't make love that night. We just held onto one another. Something awful was about to happen and we couldn't make it right.

Several days later, Tom came back, sober this time, to apologize. He sat in the same chair he had the other nights. With his arms and hands caught between his legs, he asked what I meant about having "a loss of innocence." I told him that I learned that sex had to be more than just getting someone off. It had to include commitment. And I couldn't see commitment between two guys. It just wouldn't work. It wasn't right.

Tom explained how the same thing once happened to him. An English professor had been attracted to him in college. One afternoon the professor asked Tom to his apartment. They talked and drank. Before he knew it, the professor had him undressed. They had sex.

Before that, Tom had been "innocent" too. He never had had sex with anyone. A few days passed. He was enraged at what the professor had done to him. He confronted him. The professor invited him over to his house to straighten it out. They had a long talk. The professor said he knew Tom was queer. He could see it in his eyes. Tom denied it. That couldn't be. How can you see it in someone's eyes? He couldn't believe it. But a few weeks later, as if drawn by a magnet, he came back to the professor's house.

"I tried to deny it," Tom said, "but I found myself attracted to him. I ended up there one night, then a week, a month. I couldn't help it although I tried. I even dated a girl after that with some success."

He went on to explain. "One night at a party where I was supposed to meet my girlfriend—we had a lot of friends in common—I met a lawyer who told me my girlfriend was real hot. And she was. We'd been getting it on for months. He pointed to a young girl who looked like Twiggy, and told me that they'd hooked up. We drank together as a foursome. After the party, he invited me to go to his apartment. The girls had left early (they were both in college and had to study for an exam). When we got there, one thing led to another and you can imagine what happened. I stopped dating the girl. That's the way it has been for me. I tried to deny him, but I couldn't. He went after every young guy he met, but I didn't care. For a while, it was me. That's all that mattered." He shrugged his shoulders and offered a sour smile. "I've never found someone, as you say, someone to be with who feels the same as I do. It's just sex, and goodbye." He glanced around the room and fidgeted with his hands.

I didn't say anything. I wanted to know one thing. "When you came over here that first night," I asked. "Did you see something in *my* eyes?"

He blinked several times. "I don't know. Maybe I did. Maybe I just had the hots for you. Not sure."

"It's different for each of us, the knowing," I said, gazing at him.

"Well, at least you see how it's been for me," he said. He straightened up and was ready to leave. *He was right,* I thought. *There are some things that are in you. But I wasn't sure that was the case with me.* I said, "I'm sorry."

"Oh, don't be. I've accepted it; and, if the gay revolution actually gets some steam behind it, I'll be okay."

"What do you mean 'revolution?'" I asked.

He laughed and said, surprised, "You don't know, do you?" He started to tell me about the riots in New York, the ones Will mentioned.

160

"Wasn't it near Christopher Street in Greenwich Village?" I asked.

"You know about it?"

"A friend told me," I said. "I want to go to Greenwich Village, 19 Perry Street, to visit Father Flye who I was corresponding with—"

"Is he gay?"

"No."

"He may be: That's right in the middle of the gay district."

"No, I don't think he's gay. He's a priest and a friend of a writer I like, James Agee. But go on. Tell me what happened."

"Well, it was pretty common for the New York cops to raid any gay bar to beat, harass, and arrest people. But Saturday, June 22nd was different. Judy Garland had died. Her funeral was held on June 27th in Manhattan. It brought out all the 'friends of Judy,' you know, guys in tight trousers, like me." He pointed to his revealing pants. "20,000 came out to mourn her death. The next night, when the police raided a bar—I went there several times—no one was in the mood to put up with the bullshit. It was like Judy's rainbow died. The drag queens and patrons revolted and threw lighters, beer cans, pennies, and even parking meters at the pigs. The cops retreated into the bar until reinforcements came. But tourists and gays, hundreds of them, joined in and crowded the street. They blocked traffic They called for "Gay Power." It was amazing. I wish I'd been there. Cops tried to take one boy, cute too, and beat him. That's when the 'queens' attacked, calling out "Save our Sister" and reclaimed him. Eventually the crowd dispersed. But the word got around. Now, at least for some of us, it's a new reality." He smiled. "That's your history lesson."

I wondered if that boy who'd been beaten up was Will's friend. No wonder Will left. He'd left to take care of him in ways I never could have taken care of Will.

I thanked Tom. He reached out for me to give him a hug. I did, but I angled my body sideways to his. I felt his lips kiss my neck. He stepped back, smiling weakly. His right cheek quivered slightly. I opened the door for him. Once he was in the hall, I closed and locked it.

I did have coffee with him several times. We went over our notes from class. He spoke about his battles with depression and how he wanted to find someone. I couldn't make it right for him any more than I could make it right for me. But we did have a similar need. I had no idea how it would turn out for either of us.

Internship

For my internship, I decided to work at the Edgeville Methodist Church. The minister, Jim Warren, was a leader in the civil rights movement. In Nashville, Edgeville, once a thriving black community, had been cut in two, severing the heart of the community. When the city commissioners determined the best location for new Interstate 24, they routed it through the middle of the black community. They bulldozed stores and restaurants and, divided the southern side near the river from the northern side near Vanderbilt.

Reverend Warren was a short stocky man with the build of a middle linebacker. He explained that, for years, the only place blacks were permitted to move to was property by the river, susceptible to spring floods.

"That's how it works for blacks. They get together and the white establishment divides them, strips them of their homes and community."

He showed me around the church. Compared to other Methodist churches I'd seen, it was small. It had three tiny classrooms, a large kitchen and a meeting room in the basement, and a small sanctuary with a simple wooden cross at the front. There were no fancy windows. Only pennants that children had made of cloth, with Love, Justice, and Forgiveness written in bold colors on them, decorated the walls.

He told me that I would drive their bus, taking kids to parks and on hikes out of the city. Since he needed someone to supervise a group, he asked me to be the youth group's advisor.

I hated to go to Sunday services, but Jim insisted that I come every Sunday to meet the parishioners. In my blue double-breasted jacket and red tie, I sat in the front row at the first service. An attractive woman sat next to me. She introduced herself as Julie and pointed to the pulpit. "I'm his wife."

I shook her hand. Their two children, a boy with an impish smile and a girl with pigtails, giggled as I shook their hands. During the service, which ran rather efficiently, Julie occasionally let out long sighs when her husband explained about the next march in Memphis, one in solidarity with Reverend James Lawson. After the service, I asked her what bothered her. She confided that Jim spent more time out on the streets than in the house. His kids barely knew him. She asked about me. I told her I was a poet. Her ears perked up.

"That's nice. I'd love to see your work," she said.

"What do you do?" I asked.

"I'm an artist too," she smiled. "Mostly pen and pencil drawings."

I told her that I'd love to see her work as well.

We agreed to meet during the next week.

She came over to my dorm room. She wanted to get out of the house. Her children were at school or day care in the mornings.

About ten in the morning, I heard a tentative knock on my dorm room door. I had been at work on a long exegetical paper on the Sermon on the Mount so I was distracted. I opened the door and her radiant greeted me.

She carried a bag of goodies. Once inside, she surveyed the space. She asked if she could set out some food. Before I could say yes or no, she cleared part of my desk and put down a loaf of French bread, a chunk of cheese, and a bottle of wine with two wine glasses, each wrapped in a napkin. She sliced the bread and put it on a plate. She used a short knife to cut the cheese, which smelled like Boursin.

"Here," she said and held a piece of bread with cheese.

Its flavor spread throughout my mouth.

"Good, isn't it?" she said, smiling. She poured the wine.

"I don't normally do this," she explained. "Most days I'm busy with the kids, getting everyone off to work, doing laundry and, you know, groceries, cleaning up. It never seems I have any time to draw, to do things I want to do. I hope you don't mind, but, when I met you, I felt an immediate connection like a kindred spirit, another artist."

I put my hand on her knee, "Hey, this is great. I'm glad you feel so comfortable."

She leaned over and kissed me on the cheek.

"You're sweet, really. Quite sweet."

We talked about her life, how she met Jim. She was involved in the Nashville sit-in movement. She went to downtown stores and sat with blacks at lunch counters with other Nashville seminarians. Jim was one. They both spent a night in jail, and then started to date. They married. Before long, she had her son and daughter. He had the movement, day and night, meeting with local officials, coordinating with the Southern Christian Leadership Conference, Dr. King's organization, planning rallies. Wonderful work. Important work. She knew it and she believed in it.

She was proud of him. But they'd drifted apart. She asked to read my poems. I gave her several. She read them, looking up at me as she did. After several glasses of wine, she asked if I ever thought of modeling.

"What do you mean?" I asked.

"Well, you have amazing shoulders—I can see their definition though your shirt—and I would love to draw you, if you're willing to sit," she said.

"I'm not sure if I can sit still that long," I said.

"I can draw very quickly. Here, take off your shirt and let me have a sheet of paper and pencil. There. Now time me," she said, sitting back on the bed as I stripped off my shirt.

I was embarrassed. I'd never had anyone look so intensely at me. Her eyes took in every muscle in my body. Her gaze seemed to slide up my chest, over my neck, back and forth, following the contours of my body. Not a word was spoken. I let myself look back at her.

With soft, light brown hair and a wide peaceful countenance, she radiated warmth. Her voice, mellifluous and deep for a woman, conveyed a quiet confidence. She finished and handed me the gift: my head, partial and in profile, my neck and then the shoulders, each striation of muscle and curve of flesh on bone. As she left, she thanked me and asked if she could kiss me. I put my hands on her hips. We kissed for several minutes.

We met often, some mornings, some afternoons, all dependent on her schedule. Several times we came close to making love, but were restrained— or I was—because I was working with her husband. One afternoon, when we'd drunk half a bottle of Merlot, as my hips pressed against hers, I pulled back slightly, and she grimaced. She knew I was aroused, but I'd withdrawn from her advances.

I held onto her. We kissed until our tongues grew tired. She leaned back, put her arms around my neck, and asked, "Are you gay?"

I paused. "Why do you ask?"

"I've been coming here for months and, today, as several other days, I knew you were aroused and yet you did nothing."

My face flushed. I looked at her and said, "It's just awkward, you know. Awkward being with you and working with Jim." She looked at me and held my hands, rubbing them to ease my distress.

"It's okay. I didn't mean anything by it," she said. "Relax." She kissed me gently. "I'll be going," she said and picked up her purse and left.

Julie became fascinated with the long-haired students who hung around my room. She asked me if I smoked pot.

"Of course," I said.

"What's it like?" she asked.

I told her time seemed to slow down and had a heightened sensuality. She wanted to try it. She arranged for me to come over to her house when Jim was off to Memphis with Reverend Lawson. She put her children to bed and called to let me know it was safe.

She welcomed me with a gentle hug, but one less uninhibited than the ones in my room. She scooted me in the door and glanced out to make sure that no one saw me. I offered her a bottle of wine, which she promptly returned to me with a corkscrew. I nestled the screw in the cork and twisted it until the cork popped out.

"Voila!" I said and poured her a glass.

Although neither of us admitted it, we were colluding to commit a serious transgression. I'd played the part of the young Casanova. She'd let herself be seduced.

I'd had misgivings, particularly about Ann. But she was involved in her final year and graduation preparations. She wanted more time to be with her classmates. Julie was a safe bet. No real commitment. Just an interlude. Something wild. Unconventional.

The tension in the room mounted with every gesture. We sensed that every touch, every word spoken, was an enticement. We hoped the sweet-sour taste of the wine and the perfume of the marijuana would help us shed any inhibitions. We said nothing of our mutual fantasy. I'd wanted to prove I was definitely not gay. She wanted to discover that she was still alluring to another man.

Dressed in a loose blouse with no bra (I could see her nipples as we passed under the overhead light) she meant business. I pulled out two joints and put them on the coffee table. The room had a large photograph of Dr. King—it must have been at the March on Washington—and several others of what appeared to be African paintings with vivid reds, oranges, and blues. They portrayed women dressed in long one-piece dresses carrying large water jugs on their heads. Julie told me that they were her work. We sipped wine and chatted. She ran her hand down my thigh. I caressed the back of her neck. We did our best to play our parts in the affair.

"Shall we?" she asked, glancing at the joints. She got up and opened a window, turned on the fan.

"Just in case," she said.

I lit the joint. I showed her how to hold it pinched between her fingers, and to inhale it, and to keep the smoke in her lungs as long as she could. The effect was instantaneous. She asked me to take off my shirt. Her hand traced an S pattern on my chest and stomach.

"You're quite beautiful," she said. Her fingers were cool from the glass of wine. The chest muscles twitched with her feathery touch.

"It tickles," I said.

She pinched my nipples and traced around each of them. Her fingers tiptoed down my abdomen and tugged on my belt. She knew what she was doing. She unhooked my belt buckle. My cock strained against the fabric of my shorts.

"My, my," she said, smiling. "You're a normal boy after all."

I groaned, pleased with myself. "Here," I said, "Take another hit," and passed her the joint. Smoke swirled around her head. Thin strands of it wove through her hair.

"What do you think?" I asked.

"Nice." She kept her one hand on me, gently stroking me. I scooted down on the couch. She loosened her blouse. My hand traced across her breasts mimicking what she'd done to me. She took a deep breath and shook her head.

"You all right?" I asked.

Her mouth open, her eyes glazed, she appeared terrified. Both her hands flung to her mouth. She raced from the room.

I quickly pulled on my shirt. Had she seen the children? I hurried after her.

A bathroom door was ajar. She was on her knees vomiting. Her whole body shook violently.

I asked, "Can I help?"

She shook her head. The sight of her heaving, her shoulders jerking, her belly torqued, frightened me.

"Should I call a doctor?" I asked.

She waved a hand at me as if brushing away a fly.

"Should I go?" I asked.

She paused for a moment and turned, her face wan, angry.

"Yeah. Go. Go now!"

I didn't stop to pick up the last joint or the bottle. I don't know why. I felt sick, too. I left her one of my poems, one I'd written for her, a short one about the eyes of a painter being her fingers, and placed it on the coffee table.

The next day she didn't call or come by my room. I went to classes and then drove over to Edgeville Methodist to meet with the teen meeting. Three girls and two boys came to plan a spring break picnic for the younger kids. Jim saw me when I came out of the group. He asked how it went. We talked about the park with the lake and how I'd need to drive the old school bus—mostly practical things.

"You're doing good work," he said. He patted me on the shoulder. I was about to thank him when his face hardened, his jaw tensed. "Julie's okay. She had a bad time of it."

My mouth must have dropped open because he grinned at the sight of me. "Hey, kid, no blame here. She gave me the scoop."

"I'm—"

"I know. I know."

I had shoved my hands in my pockets. My face felt as if it were roasting.

"Relax." He took me by the arm and walked outside to the side yard. "Someday you'll have a marriage, kids and all. Believe me, it's not *Father Knows Best*. There are rough spots. But you get through them."

All I could focus on was her blouse, unbuttoned. I bleated out several times, "I'm sorry."

"No need for sorry. Just know she's okay. She wanted you to know that," he said. "And, kid, I'm okay too. Some things can't be helped."

When I got back to the dorm, I pulled out the drawing she'd done of me. For her, drawing was a kind of lovemaking: how the hands that penciled the line across the page had also caressed my chest and belly and cock. Careful attention to the other is, for an artist, lovemaking. She took what she saw and gave herself over to it. I pinned the drawing to my bookshelf.

More than any woman I'd known, I loved her way of seeing me, of not just seeing the surface, but my inner self. If I went back, I feared I would destroy her, and her marriage. I kept the drawing because I saw in the face and eyes a young man who didn't believe in himself, but who someone had seen as real. It was through her eyes I had come to see myself that way too.

For weeks, she didn't call. One afternoon, she did. She'd gone away, the whole family had—Jim and the kids. They'd spent time at the ocean. They walked the New Jersey beaches and built sand castles. She drew. She read. For that week, she saw Jim as the man he once was, vital and passionate. She realized how I was like him in so many ways and how she missed him. But now he had returned. They were both happy. It was a lovely reincarnation of what had drawn them to one another when they were younger. She said that she couldn't see me again. She knew that now. Whatever she was attracted to in me, she couldn't resist. She hoped I'd understand. I told her I did. I was sorry.

"You'll find another woman," she said.

"Not like you," I said.

"I thank you for that," she said.

Divided

With Julie gone and Ann busy with school, I met another woman, Cheryl, who advertised on the Divinity School bulletin board as a typist. A receptionist for the Upper Room, a religious group that offered training and workshops, she typed my papers for the Kierkegaard and the Sociology of Change seminars. She was fascinated by my thinking. I told her that I wanted, more than anything, to be a poet. I'd written a poem about Dietrich Bonhoeffer as he waited in his cell to be hanged. She liked it.

We exchanged books of poems. I gave her Eliot's *Collected Poems* and she gave me D.H. Lawrence's *Selected Poems*. She invited me to her apartment for dinner. She cooked braised chicken with mustard and wine sauce, beans with buttered almonds, twice-baked potatoes with cheddar cheese. She had lovely wines, merlots and pinot grigios.

We'd read from T.S. Eliot's "Four Quartets":

> "In that open field
> If you do not come too close, if you do not come too close
> On the Summer midnight, you can hear the music"

It spoke to me about the need to keep my distance, to be an observer, to be free from obligations. To her it meant letting what you loved be as it is.

We argued what Eliot's "still point of the turning world" meant. Why did he say "neither flesh nor fleshless, neither from nor towards"? I felt it meant that we could separate ourselves from our experience and merely observe it. She believed that it had to do with the dance, how two bodies could become one. She pulled me up and we danced across the room. She pressed her body into mine. At that moment, I could have made love with her. But I was afraid. There was Ann, and, weeks ago, Julie. I couldn't take another affair. I stopped the dance. But we talked well into the night

One night Cheryl and I tore open several pomegranates. We peeled off their skins and picked out the dark purple fruit. Our hands were stained with sweetness. She sucked the juice off my hand, and I off hers. My fingers in her mouth aroused me. She could tell. She leaned in to kiss me. I pushed her away. I had no idea how to balance all my relationships and all my feelings for each lover. I wanted to be close yet was dreadfully afraid of being too close and being taken over by her needs.

As we parted, she asked for a kiss. I complied. But she stuck her tongue in my mouth. I pulled away. "Please, give me some time," I said.

She bowed her head. "So sorry. I'll be good."

A short time later, she outdid herself. She prepared salmon with some vinaigrette, tomatoes with pesto and a fruit salad, followed by a pecan pie. I loved it. She plied me with wine. I became blissfully intoxicated. She listened to me talk about my love for James Agee. We talked late into the night. She snuggled next to me. We had another glass of wine. She asked if I wanted to stay the night.

"Friends, that's all I want," I said.

She pouted, "Why must it stop at that?"

"Look, I love our talks. But I need distance. I need independence, space to write and think," I told her. I'd told Ann the same thing. I poured more wine for myself.

She clinked the glass, "Hey, I love that you're an intellect, that you love to read. But what does that have to do with us?

"It's simple. If I'm involved with someone, I give myself as much to them as I do my own work. I invest all the emotional energy that I have. If we get involved, I'm going to give myself to you entirely, and I don't want to do that."

"I would," she said.

I pinched her cheek. "I know you would."

"Well?"

"I'm serious. I don't want to be dependent on you or have to worry about you. I want to be my own self. That's not an easy thing to be. I put up fences. But they have gates. As long as you and I know where they are, we can be as close as we choose to be," I said.

She pulled her knees up under her and straightened up on the couch. She took a folder from the coffee table. and pulled out a sheet of paper. "Let me read this to you. It's from Rilke's *Letters to a Young Poet*. You recommended it.

"And if we only arrange our life according to that principle which counsels us that we must always hold to the difficult...then that which now seems to us most alien will become what we most trust and find most faithful..."

She finished reading, sipped her wine, and asked, "Maybe it's possible that we might find that we trust each other: you trust me, I trust you?"

"Yes, but what he's talking about is those aspects of ourselves, our inner voices, that we must trust. He wasn't talking about relationships."

"But what if he was? What if you're wrong?"

I picked up the wine bottle. She had a point. He might have been talking about both.

"You may be right. But for me, at least now, the freedom not to worry about others and to explore what is in me is the ultimate freedom. I need boundaries. Can't I have them?"

She flung her arm around my neck and kissed me on the cheek. "I've never met a man so certain about relationships."

"I have to be."

"How so?"

She was making me think about myself. I liked that. But I was intimidated, too. I wasn't sure if I could explain what I only partially understood. "If I don't, I'll get lost and, if I get lost in what I want to do as a writer, given the demands of time on me already—working on a degree, getting the folk school started up for another year, doing my internship—I'll forsake my writing."

"Your major concern is your writing."

"Yeah. Why shouldn't it be?"

She poured herself another glass of wine and stood up. She wandered around the room, her hair draping over her face, only one eye peeking out. She stopped across from me, swaying slightly, her face squinted in pain.

"What the hell can you give *me*?"

I set my wine glass down. I stared at her for a moment. She continued to sway, slightly out of focus. An inexplicable rage burned in my chest. I said, "When you stop asking *that* question, then you'll have something," and walked to the door. She flung herself on me, turned me around, and kissed me hard on the mouth. I recoiled, pressed my hands on her arms, and pushed her away. "Let's call it an evening," I whispered and left.

As I walked back to the dorm, I noticed that bell tower said 2 o'clock. A few cars drove down the street. The street lamps looked like stage lights, one after another.

If I had wanted to make love with her, I could have. It would have been nice as it was with Ann and Julie, to have a woman who wanted to give herself to me. But I couldn't shake what I was feeling. Mostly I felt alone, afraid, and misunderstood. In some ways, I wanted as much intimacy from them as I could get, their adulation of me made me feel more like a man, surer of my masculinity than I had ever felt before. I liked how they touched me, how their hands lingered on my shoulder or face or waist. I felt reassured. This is what it was to be a man: to have women want you and need you. Or at least that's how I'd come to see it. But maybe it was like that saying of Jesus about the city on the hill. Maybe I was only seeing part of the city of love, the part I'd been raised in, the part others, especially my father, had told me I needed to live in. And yet there were other parts of the city, hidden ones that Will and Tom told me about, parts that I was afraid to enter, parts like those sections of Nashville that I was warned not to go, parts I might someday need to enter.

Yet there was something holding me back, something pulling me away from them. Cheryl told me that when she first met me she sensed a mystery and danger; that I was like a wild animal, untamed and beautiful, free and powerful. I wasn't sure I was all that dangerous. Something in me wanted to be close. But I feared that she'd possess me, and I would lose the freedom to live alone, to be as solitary as I wanted to be.

Relief

As an escape from women, on weekends, I drove to Cross Creek and stayed with Peggy and her kids. The mountains roads wound back against themselves and reflected how I felt inside.

I lost myself as Peggy told a story of how she nearly drowned—her lungs full of fluids— from pneumonia. Tommy drove her forty miles to the emergency room. Bobby told a story of how he cracked his skull diving into the creek and his ma had to sew him up with her own needle and thread.

The bedtime routine was the same every night. If someone started to undress, others averted their eyes until they were in a nightgown or pajamas. In Bobby's room, two beds accommodated anyone who slept there: Tommy in the one on the left, Bobby and I in the one on the right. It seemed strange to sleep with Bobby. But he loved it. He tickled me once I got in bed. Once he quieted down, he snuggled next to me and fell asleep, his arm across my chest.

The moonlight cast a milky glow on Bobby. With his hair over his forehead and his eyelids closed, he never budged. It felt nice to be where affection between men came as natural as love between a man and a woman.

In the morning, we'd work in the garden, nudge the potatoes from the ground, pull up six-inch carrots, and tote pumpkins to the back porch. We'd feed the chickens and toss leftovers to the pig. The labor dictated the pace. If I wanted to sit on the porch and write, fine. No one bothered me. If Bobby wanted to toss the football, I'd jump off the porch and we'd throw it back and forth. By the time I got back to Nashville, I felt as though Peggy and her kids had stitched me back together.

Baxter

When I returned to Nashville, the university students were outraged that the Pancake House refused to serve "long-haired, hippie-type" students. The restaurant was across the street from the campus. Many students went there for meals. A long-haired law student tried to reason with the owner, but he became enraged, called the student "un-American," and threatened to call the police.

Reverend Baxter Bryant, the longtime leader of the civil rights protests in Nashville, called a meeting at a small coffee house. My hair was long, so I went.

Dressed in bib overalls, Baxter strutted back and forth, anxious to see if enough people would show up for a protest. Fifty students packed the house.

He had an infectious laugh that made anyone near him break into a smile. He called for a peaceful demonstration. If it was done well, and lasted long enough, he argued, it would dissuade the regular customers from going to the restaurant.

The next day, a Sunday, we picketed, carrying signs that said, "End Discrimination Now," "Jesus Had Long Hair," and "Pancakes for Everyone." For a week, we demonstrated in shifts. Pickets marched in a circle around the front of the restaurant. Instead of this discouraging business, customers lined up and waited for a seat. The customers were well-dressed and apparently enjoyed the spectacle of slovenly dressed long-hairs.

One day after church, I carried a sign with the other long-hairs. I had finally worked up the nerve to protest, even though I worried that my father, if I were arrested, would be outraged and cut off my tuition payments.

Baxter chided the customers who waited in line. He read selections from the Bible that addressed civil rights.

He was well-dressed for this protest. He had a long white beard that framed his wrinkled, ruddy face. He had large shoulders and an enormous chest. With his black jacket, heavy leather boots, and holiday red scarf, he was a spectacle.

Baxter was no fool. He knew how to chafe and irritate the clientele. He would crane his head back and blare questions at them as they tried to avert his eyes and scurry into the restaurant. He preached without hesitation, engaged people, smiled at them, and greeted them as if he worked for the restaurant. He was on stage, doing what he did best, standing like God's advocate, castigating the smug and affluent.

It was early December. In the holiday spirit, children were dressed in red and green. Baxter happened to catch the attention of a young couple with a cute young boy. They sat at the table at the front window. The little boy waved at the bearded man. Baxter waved back. Since the boy and Baxter were center stage—one on each side of the window—all the protesters outside and the clientele inside watched them. The procession of marchers halted.

The mother and father refused to look at Baxter. They had a brief conversation. The father pointed his fork at the mother and then at the boy. The mother cut off a tiny piece of her omelet and ate it. The father tapped the boy's plate and told him to eat his pancakes.

The father parted his hair in a perfectly straight line. He wore black framed glasses and a gray, three-piece suit with a red tie. He shooed Baxter off with his hand. Baxter wouldn't leave. He offered a peace sign to the boy who imitated him, putting up two fingers in a V. The protesters cheered. The boy smiled back, enamored by the attention. The boy's father eyed Baxter and pointed his finger at him with his lips set in a straight line.

Baxter smiled at the dad. The dad gave Baxter the finger. The protesters booed. All this time, the boy focused on the man with a white beard who kept smiling at him. His mother cupped her hand around his back and pointed at his plate. The father stabbed one of the pancakes and shoved it at the boy. The mother reached over to pat the boy's hand.

Baxter stepped back and put his hands on his hips and gave a hearty laugh. The boy smiled. Baxter tapped the window, saying as loudly as he could, as he gave the boy a peace sign, "Let's exchange signs. You do this. Yes. There you have it. And I'll do this. Good." The boy made a V again with his fingers.

All the customers in the restaurant as well as all the protesters watched as Baxter gave the whole restaurant the peace sign.

The father glowered at Baxter and gobbled two quick bites of his pancakes. The tiny boy, not much older than four, looked once more at Baxter. His expression brightened. His father turned from watching the boy to chat with his wife. The boy looked directly at Baxter and spoke directly to him. Everyone could hear him. "*You're* Santa Claus!"

Baxter cocked his head back and laughed. He put his hands on his belly and cried, "Ho. Ho. Ho, I sure am!"

His father had turned as red as his tie and the scarf around Baxter's neck. He shook his fist at Baxter and cursed him. He grabbed his son's head and forced him to focus on his pancakes. The boy broke into tears. The mother wrapped her arms around the boy. Baxter crouched by the window and looked sad to show the boy that he sympathized with him. The father called the waitress over to the table and asked to be moved. The mother took her son in her arms. He waved at Baxter as the family repaired to the back. The protesters cheered and waved.

After the protest, Baxter asked several of us to go for coffee. He'd lived a remarkable life. When John Kennedy flew into Dallas, Baxter had greeted him. Kennedy asked him if he should ride in a covered or an open vehicle. Baxter told him that the people of Dallas loved him. "Ride in the open vehicle."

"There is not a day I do not regret my advice," he said. "Think of what would be different now. No Nixon. Bobby would be alive." He brushed something off his jacket. "There's no way you can get out of this life without getting dirt on you."

Someone asked him about his work with Dr. King.

"I'll tell you something you've never heard before," Baxter said. "You remember the sanitation strike in Memphis?"

Some of us had, some hadn't. He gave us some background. The FBI set up disturbances to create public outrage against the protest. It was unsettling for King. He was supposed to speak to rally the workers. He'd been ill, so he sent Ralph Abernathy instead. The crowd clamored for Dr. King. Abernathy called to tell King he had to come. The crowd roared their approval when King arrived. But he hadn't prepared remarks. He rambled about Abernathy, about history, about Egypt and the Promised Land. He struggled to find his way, leaping from topic to topic. He talked about Aristotle, Martin Luther, Abe Lincoln, and even Franklin Delano Roosevelt.

That's when his tone changed. It became darker. He spoke of Jerusalem and of the road Jesus walked. But he paused and changed topic again. He spoke about being stabbed in New York, the tip of the blade near his heart. If he had sneezed, he would have died. He spoke about all the major civil rights events he'd have missed. Someone whispered that King was being rather morbid. Baxter agreed. It wasn't like him. He didn't talk in public about threats to his life.

King paused again. His voice became more impassioned. Something had struck him, and his voice rose as he spoke about the threats to his life:

"And then I got to Memphis. And some began to say the threats, or talk about the threats that were out there. What would happen to me at the hands of our sick white brothers?"

King shook his head as if trying to shake something out of it. He spoke of mortality. He wanted to live a long life. He abruptly ended with those famous lines:

"I just want to do God's will. And He's allowed me to go up to the mountain...I've looked over. And I've seen the Promised Land. I may not get there with you...I'm not fearing any man. Mine eyes have seen the glory of the coming of the Lord."

"What happened next," Baxter said, "was eerie. When he spoke the last words, he turned abruptly. At first, we didn't rise to greet him. We thought he was at a fever pitch and was going to go on and speak more of the strike. He lunged at us, not waiting for applause. We knew something must be seriously wrong for him to cut off a speech. His eyes looked strange. They were filled with fear. He headed to his seat.

"Abernathy hugged him. We took his arms and led him to his chair. He confided that he had seen his death. He looked ashen. We tried to lift his spirits and say, 'It's all right. We'd heard that before.' But he said, no this was for real.

"Later, he asked to be left alone. He needed time. By the next day, he had recovered from the shock. He was lively and engaged. A burden seemed lifted from him. He was shot that day."

Baxter sighed and said, "I often wonder if I...if we'd been more vigilant, if we'd kept him off that balcony, whether he might be with us today." I listened intently. I remember that Lincoln also had had a premonition of his death and I wondered whether Bobby Kennedy had. The hatred in the eyes of the father at the Pancake House came to mind. Such hatred fueled violence. But I also remember the boy waving to us, as if he knew something was wrong and he wanted to make it right.

Cut Short

"I'm late," Ann said. "Two weeks."

She sat on my dorm room bed, her legs folded beneath her. I sat in the desk chair across from her holding her hands. Early that day she'd called and told me we needed to talk. With all the weeks we'd been apart except for several nights after Tom in my room, and with her upcoming graduation, I thought she'd wanted to break off our relationship. But not this.

"Have you seen a doctor?" I asked.

"No. I was hoping—"

"Sure."

"What'll we do?" she asked. She looked at me intently.

"Punt," I said.

"What?"

"It's a joke. You know in football if you don't know what play to call, you punt," I said.

"This is *not* funny. This is serious, Jason." She jerked her hands back. "We need to decide what to do."

"Sure."

"Well?"

"I don't know. I mean, can't we wait a little longer?" I said.

When the door slammed, I wanted to get up, go out, grab her, and tell her that I would stand by her no matter what. But my feet stuck to the floor. I sat in my chair and gazed out the windows at the yellowish green leaves. It was spring already. Months had passed.

I called her later, but she didn't answer. I went over to her apartment; her roommate told me she wasn't in. I remembered Travis who sat in my lap and talked about everything costing a penny. Having a kid in my arms didn't seem too bad. I'd have to find a job, risk getting drafted, and settle down. I hated the idea. But it couldn't be helped. I wanted to tell her I had changed my mind. She didn't call. One week, two. No word from her. Maybe she was going it alone. It was most likely my child. As far as I knew, she'd been exclusively mine. I had to start acting and looking like an adult.

One Monday afternoon I went to a local barbershop and told him to give me a haircut. "Long or short," he asked.

"Short," I told him.

He cut it short. My ears stood out and I looked like a new army recruit. When I got back to the dorm, kids asked, "What happened to you?" I wondered the same. Ann would be surprised. But she wasn't at her apartment. I went to a party that a mutual friend had invited us to weeks before.

When I arrived, I saw Ann with another student, a young man I'd seen at antiwar protests. With long wavy hair, he was strikingly handsome. I walked over to her. She glanced at me, "Oh, hi," she said and continued to talk with the man.

I grabbed her arm. "Can we talk?"

She pulled my hand off her. "Later," she said. "Can't you see we're involved here?"

After three bottles of beer and a shot of whiskey, I was more drunk than I'd been in months. I bumped into the table with the refreshments, lost my balance, and put my hand in a bowl of onion dip. I licked it off my fingers.

Ann avoided me most of the night. She must have seen me staggering around. I was singing to myself, "We shall overcome..." and dancing in a circle, holding onto a bottle of beer as if it could keep me upright.

Someone stuck an arm under my arm and pulled me to the side of the room.

"You're making an ass of yourself," Ann said.

"You bet I am."

"And the haircut, it looks awful. You look like a frat boy."

"You don't like it?"

"Are you kidding?" she said. "Lower your voice, please."

"It's my responsible father look," I said.

"I said, lower your voice!" She jerked me toward the front door. We went out and stood on the stoop. A cool breeze wafted across my face.

"Listen," she said. "You don't have to do the dutiful father routine with me."

"But—"

"You already made it clear where you stand."

"Sorry, I—"

She smiled. "Besides, I'm back on my cycle."

"You're what?"

"Not pregnant," she said. "Now, go back to your room and sober up." She kissed me on the cheek. I leaned over to give her a hug. She stuck her arm out. "Whoa, horsey," she said. "Not so fast."

I lost my balance and fell into a hedge. She laughed so hard she bent over and held her stomach.

"Perfect," she said. "That's perfect." I struggled out of it, straightened up, and walked away. The traffic on the streets had quieted, only a few cars passed by. I felt a strange exhilaration. I also felt like a fool. She had made me see how petty, and insensitive, I could be. Why she had not called me earlier, or when she had known, seemed immaterial. I was free. I could do what I wanted when I wanted. No kid. No marriage. I rubbed the stubble on my head. In a few weeks, I'd be myself again. Maybe we could even date again.

Nixon

Rick and Jane asked me over to their house to watch the Kentucky Derby later that spring. Rick made a mean mint julep. The night before the race, he got out three chilled silver cups and placed them on the counter.

"We must make them the night before so the ingredients make love with each other in the cool quiet of the night," he said. Then he added two cups of sugar to a pitcher and stirred in two cups of water and crushed ice.

"Now the important ingredient," he said, pouring what seemed to be an entire bottle of bourbon into the mix. He stirred it with a spoon. "Can't forget this," he said, adding sprigs of fresh mint. He put crushed ice in a glass and poured the mixture over it. The rest of the mix he set in the refrigerator.

"This is to die for," he said. He passed the glass to Jane who sipped it.

"Wonderful, honey," she said. "Decadent southerners. That's why I married him." We passed it around, each letting the sweet-bitter taste wash over our tongue. We had dinner, chicken with Dijon mustard sauce, and some carrots with honey ginger sauce. With these two, I saw how a marriage could work, how he, even with his misgivings about his sexuality, seemed quite happy.

Even though he was against the war, Rick was excited because Richard Nixon was to be the first president to attend the Derby.

"It's nice that he's coming. Our Derby is really a national institution. But I'm afraid if he thinks we southerners are going to welcome him with open arms, he's in for a surprise," Rick said. "Protesters will greet him. He'll not have an easy time of it." The next day Rick's predictions proved right. Nixon had to be escorted in a decoy car into and out of the race. Once he had gotten onto the track grounds, some patrons cheered him. He waved and made the best of their support. But the antiwar movement had reached a fever pitch. He couldn't go anywhere without someone shouting at him to end the war.

After the scare with Ann, I worked on an exegesis of the saying from Christ's Sermon on the Mount in Matthew:

You are the light of the world. A city set on a mountain cannot be hidden. Nor do they light a lamp and then put it under a bushel basket; it is set on a lampstand, where it gives light to all in the house. Just so, your light must shine before others, that they may see your good deeds and glorify your heavenly Father.

I'd been thinking about it since that last night with Cheryl. But I had come to see it in a different light. I realized that the saying seemed ironic, almost a play on words. Of course, a city cannot be hidden on the hill. Why would that be important to Him? What could it possibly mean to his followers?

I came to see that if someone didn't want to hear what He had to say because it disturbed his world-view, he could deny it and hide it from himself. He could go on believing what he'd always been told. He could go on acting as if the penthouse he lived it, the swank restaurants he frequented, and the wealthy friends he hobnobbed with were all there was of the city. If he wanted to see what was *really* happening around him, he had to let the lamp shine on the *whole* city, places he may not even want to look, places on the southside living in poverty.

My ruminations jived with what was happening on campuses. Ever since Nixon ramped up the war, campuses had rebelled. But the rebellion was soon to reach a higher pitch.

President Nixon appeared on all three U.S. television networks to announce that, "It is not our power but our will and character that is being tested tonight," and, "the time has come for action." He launched American forces into Cambodia. Their objective was to capture "the headquarters of the entire communist military operation in South Vietnam." Nixon hid behind high-minded rhetoric as a ruse to escalate the war. But students saw it for what it was: an escalation of the war. Protests broke out. Kent State students ignored Ohio Governor Rhodes' threats to bring in the National Guard. His statements only incited them. Pounding on a desk, he sounded like a petty tyrant. He called protesters un-American. He said they were revolutionaries set on destroying higher education in Ohio. He said,

We've seen here at the city of Kent especially, probably the most vicious form of campus-oriented violence yet perpetrated by dissident groups...who were worse than the brown shirts and the communist element and also the night riders and the vigilantes...the worst type of people that we harbor in America...They are not going to take over the campus. I think that we're up against the strongest, well-trained, militant, revolutionary group that has ever assembled in America.

To him, the students were worse than Nazis or revolutionaries. He didn't hear what students were saying. He missed the point: it was the United States that was acting as Nazi Germany did in Poland with our incursion in a sovereign nation that was, according to international law, illegal.

Rhodes and Nixon wanted students to be as silent as the silent majority. Nixon didn't want his foreign policy shaped by protesters on the streets of Washington or on the campuses. He wanted us to unite behind him "for peace," while he waged war. It enraged me. When he called activist students, "Bums...blowing up our campuses," many of us felt insulted.

At Vanderbilt I'd heard students threaten, as they had at Kent State, to burn down the ROTC building. Not a bad idea, I thought, although the building was adjacent to the Divinity School and right across from the Law School.

I blocked out the hubbub and attended my English class on Milton.

In my English class, I sat next to Jackson, an undergraduate with whom I'd had several conversations after class. A poet and and antiwar activist, he asked me about the Divinity School—what I studied, who I knew, if I'd met James Lawson. He was thinking of going into the ministry. He sat next to me during the seminar. We'd become friendly. His rusty brown hair fell over his shoulders. He wore Army fatigues and a bandana across his forehead. During class, he scooted his chair next to mine and whispered commentary about the poet we were studying. We'd read Yeats's "Leda and the Swan." He nudged me. "You ever had sex with a swan? It's great." He rubbed his fingertips like a feather across my thigh

I chuckled and whispered back, "Not yet."

"It's fun!"

I remembered how Tom had lured me into having sex with him. But I felt relaxed with Jackson. His touch was playful.

After class, he asked me to go have coffee so he could fill me in on the protests that day. He was worried about the students in Ohio. The governor had declared martial law and brought out the National Guard. "He's a major nut case," Jackson said. "Not to worry. It's all talk and no action. We have big plans for today. You should come."

Allen Ginsberg was to speak at an antiwar rally. Jackson suggested that we go together.

A phalanx of students surrounded Ginsberg as he walked across campus. He was arm in arm with his lover Peter Orlovsky. He wore loose multi-colored pants, sandals, and a white shirt. Once on the stage, Ginsberg chanted a long antiwar poem. He played his sitar and danced, his arms waving back and forth over his head.

The crowd made a loud "OM" sound. Jackson slung his arm over my shoulder, put his cheek next to mine. We strutted and pranced to the sound. We grabbed a Peace sign and pumped it up and down.

After the protest, Jackson told me to come over to his dorm room. He had a new poem that he wanted me to read. On the eighth floor of the new high-rise dorm, he asked me to sit on his bed while he rummaged through his papers. His room looked as if someone had detonated a bomb in it: papers, magazines, books, clothes on the chair, bed, and his desk. When he found the poem, he told me to lie down. He jumped on the bed beside me, lifted my legs and scooted under them, and then let them down over his legs. He leaned over to read his poem. He had lovely hazel eyes.

His poem was about a man lost in a dark wood. I listened intently as he rubbed his hand on my chest to keep rhythm to the poem's oracular beat.

"What do you think?" he asked

"I like it. Love the image of the creek. 'It shimmers under the dark ash.' Perfect image," I said.

"You have a nice body." He rubbed my belly.

I put my hand on top of his. I'd become aroused and didn't want to let on. "You do too." I rubbed his fingers.

He scooted close and ran his fingers through my hair. He placed one finger on my lips. "I've wanted to do this since you first came in the class. Did you know that?" he asked.

"No," I said. He reached behind my head and pulled me upright. His head was now resting on my crotch.

"You feel good." He rubbed his cheek on my erection.

"I don't think I should go there," I said.

He pressed himself up, his chest against mine, and put his lips on mine and kissed me. He swung his legs around, so he was sitting next to me and said, "I get it. It's all right. Let's just cuddle, you know, hold onto each other, man to man."

He lit a joint and offered me a toke. I took it. He stretched out, his body against mine. We finished it. He pulled me close to him, his chest against mine, his leg nestled between mine. He brushed back my hair and kissed me lightly on the cheek. He put his head next to mine and looked into my eyes.

"We could be good friends, you know," he said.

"I think we already are," I said.

He leaned over and kissed me. "You may be right. You know if other men felt as we do about each other, there wouldn't be any wars. We'd be seeking how to connect and make love. And the only thing we'd worry about would be if the other guy was as attracted to us as we were to him." He pressed his body against mine.

I could feel that he too was aroused. He took my hand and let me rub his chest, face and legs. He did the same to me. Eventually, he leaned up on an elbow, asked if he could kiss me harder and I told him yes. He pressed his lips against mine, his teeth hard against mine, and slipped his tongue inside my mouth. I moaned. Then he stopped. It was over. We sat up.

"Need to check on the protest for this afternoon," he said.

"We'll meet again?" I asked.

"Any time," he said.

I told him I had to get to my Synoptic Gospel class. But I wanted to continue being with him and his tutoring me in how a male could make love with another male.

At two o'clock, after I left my second class, I heard shouting. A large group of students carrying North Vietnamese flags marched toward the ROTC building. Outside the ROTC building, an officer and twenty cadets stood in front of the entrance. They had set up a barrier. Arms crossed and legs spread wide, they looked imposing. I asked one of the marchers what was going on. Word had spread about Kent State. Students had marched toward the National Guard; shots were fired. All hell broke loose.

Dean Harrelson rushed down the hill from the Divinity School with James Lawson and several other students, including Evie, the student I'd met at orientation. He motioned me to join them.

"Come on, Jason. There's going to be trouble," the dean cried.

As we raced down the hill, he explained that the Ohio National Guard had fired at antiwar protesters. From news reports, several students were killed.

The dean and Reverend Lawson arrived at the ROTC building before the protesters. They spoke to the officer in charge. He'd called Nashville and campus police. Sirens screamed, and four cruisers charged up the drive of the ROTC building—a one-story building with windows on each side. It looked more like a maintenance building than one used for military training. The police officers kept their sirens on. Eight of them strode up to the front entrance, armed with rifles. They spoke with the dean and the ROTC officer.

The protesters shouted, "Burn it down! Burn it down!"

I noticed Jackson standing in front of a group of protesters, a *Peace Now* sign in his hand. He led the chant to burn it down. He noticed me standing with the dean and police and narrowed his eyes.

The dean turned to us. "Do you know any of the activists?" he asked.

"Yes, one of them," I said.

He turned back to the officer and pointed toward the Divinity School. Sweat poured off his forehead. He took out a handkerchief and wiped his brow. The police officer came over to me. "Do you know one of these...thugs?" he asked.

My fist clenched. The dean interrupted, "Officer I told you he did."

"Okay. Here's the deal," the officer said. "We don't want trouble. Your dean here, he says he'll give up his office, if you and some of the other ministers can calm this down. Think you can do it?"

Reverend Lawson put his arm on my shoulder, "Yes, officer, we'll do it. We have some other students who are on their way to help."

The officer stepped back. He conferred with the ROTC officer and then signaled the dean with a simple nod. The dean and Reverend Lawson asked me to introduce them to the protester. We walked up the embankment. The crowd had expanded to several hundred students. I called out to Jackson and motioned him to come to one side by a large magnolia tree. I introduced the dean and Reverend Lawson.

"*THE* Reverend Lawson?" he asked as he shook his hand.

"The same," said the reverend.

Jackson looked at me. "You know him?"

"Yes."

The dean and Reverend Lawson explained to him that they'd like to see whether he and some of the organizers would be willing to meet with other students who are also against the war. The dean wanted to see if they could stem the violence and not escalate the encounter.

Jackson looked at me. "Will you be there?"

"Yes."

He asked if other authorities on campus, including the chancellor, could be involved.

"Yes," said the dean. "We can arrange for it. You will have my office, night or day. I assure you that you'll have access to the people you need."

"I'm not sure I can stop this," Jackson shouted. The chanting had increased as had the number of protesters.

The police force had expanded to eight cars. Eighteen armed police officers stood in a line in front of the protesters.

"Look," Lawson said. "I've seen worse. Would you let me talk to them?"

Jackson nodded. Pressing my hand on his shoulder, I thanked him. He pulled back.

Reverend Lawson was perfectly composed. His whitened afro showed his age. He went over to a police car and asked for a bullhorn. The lead officer went to his car and pulled one out. Lawson strode up to the protesters with Jackson beside him. He draped his arm over Jackson's shoulder. Jackson gazed up at him, clearly stunned by the strange turn of events. Lawson told the crowd who he was and how he had stood with Dr. King against the war. He believed it was an unjust war. He despised the recent incursion into Cambodia. But he also believed in nonviolence. He told them that they should be mad. Students were shot, killed for doing what every American had a right to do: protest against a war that they believed was immoral. The students listened intently. He told that the dean (who he introduced again) had graciously given up his office so that those who were leaders in the antiwar efforts could meet and find a non-violent way to resolve the issue. He encouraged them to protest in a peaceful manner.

He offered Jackson the bullhorn. Jackson put it to his mouth, but no sound came out. The officer showed him the switch to press. Jackson laughed and then told the crowd how angry he was, how other students, innocent students, had been shot down. He said that he wouldn't back down. There were cheers. "Burn it down!" started again.

"No, no," he said. "I'm a longtime admirer of Reverend Lawson. I'm also grateful the dean has offered us his office. I, for one, would be willing to give it a try." He held up his sign, *Peace Now*. "Will any of you join me?"

Several others raised their hands. With support for the negotiations, Lawson asked that the protest move away from the ROTC building—there was to be no vandalism—and he would gladly lead them to the Student Union building where he'd let them speak.

Three students joined Jackson. The dean motioned for me to join them. He also asked three ROTC students to join us. Jackson glared at them. Ten of us headed to the Divinity School. The protest headed to the center of the campus. The officers stood their ground.

The four protesters, three ROTC students, and three divinity students headed to Dean Harrelson's office. He asked his secretary to have the cafeteria set out coffee and snacks. He pointed to a long boardroom table and suggested that we sit down. But Jackson interrupted him. "Mind if we sit in these chairs?" He eyed the leather chairs surrounding his desk.

The dean chuckled. "You don't mind luxury, do you?"

"We have a heap of work to do. We might as well be comfortable," Jackson said.

"Go to it," the dean said.

A girl who wore a red bandana who had been leading the march took one of the chairs. Jackson sat in another. Other students sprawled on the rug; some sat in the large chairs around the table. Evie sat by me and winked.

Once we'd all settled, the dean spoke to us.

"It seems to me," he said, "that you need to have a plan. The others, both those who value their ROTC experience and those who oppose the war, need to feel you have a better alternative to burning down the building. I suggest you appoint some members to be facilitators to make sure everyone's heard, some to keep track of your proposal (you can use the whiteboard over there), and some to speak to the crowd once you're in agreement. You don't have much time since that crowd isn't going to be put off for long."

We introduced ourselves and let the others know where we stood on the war. One of the ROTC students, a freshman, opposed the war. The other two believed that the president should never be questioned.

We decided that Evie should be the facilitator. Jackson became the scribe, writing down our proposals on a white board. Coffee and doughnuts arrived. The dean excused himself to keep the chancellor and police briefed about our proceedings.

Nothing came easy. Inflammatory accusations flew around the room. A ROTC student with a crewcut refused to listen to the protesters. "You're anti-American," he blurted out.

"Cut the crap," Evie said. "You're no better than the president. And look at what he said got him!"

"But we have an oath," the crewcut said.

"Listen, if I remember right, you took an oath to defend the country, not the president, right?"

"Yeah."

"Well, can you set aside your loyalty to him and focus on what might be right for your country?"

The crewcut nodded his head in agreement.

Evie said, "One of the rules: no name-calling. Let's cut the bullshit and work together."

Jackson proved to be a major problem. He demanded that the university make a statement against the incursion into Cambodia. "That's why we're here," he insisted.

"Not me," the crewcut said.

"Well, you're a—"

Evie jumped in. "Jackson, not another word!"

The freshman ROTC member offered a compromise. He suggested that the university sponsor a forum and let students hear different points of view.

"You miss the point," Jackson said. "You're acting as if Nixon's view is legitimate. It's not. You know it. For Christ's sake, how can you offer such a proposal?"

"We need to compromise here," I said. "There are others who don't share your point—"

"Share?" he burst out and stood up. "Share?! My God, he's invaded another country without the consent of Congress. Fuck compromise. Fuck this whole process. We need to make a stand."

Evie stood up. "Let's have a break, shall we?" She asked Jackson if she could talk with him. He grabbed a coffee and they walked into the hallway.

After meeting with Jackson, she asked the dean to get us some soda. He also had pizza, chips, and coleslaw delivered. But he said, "Not a word about this."

As we helped ourselves, Jackson sat next to me and whispered, "Sorry."

"Hey, this is intense," I said. "Hold your ground. But let others hold theirs too."

At the Dean's suggestion, we broke into subgroups with members from each faction. Evie divided the groups with mixed members from each faction. She put Jackson in my group. We met in different parts of the room.

Evie told me, "Work with him. I think he has the hots for you."

"No!" I was startled that she'd seen something going on between us.

"Oh, yes," she said. "And I believe you are quite aware of it." She smiled. "He's cute. I don't blame you."

I headed to a corner with large windows facing the central campus. Jackson, another protester, the crewcut and I sat in a circle on the carpet. Graduate students were the group's facilitators.

Before the subgroups met, the dean asked us to have a moment of silence. Before that, he said he wanted each of us to dwell for a moment on what brought us to this room. What was of most importance to us? What could we do to bridge the divide?

"When you came in here, you came as part of a group." He glanced around the room. "When you entered this office, you were just twelve 'I's,' separate persons with your own loyalties and faiths. Now it's time for you as an individual 'I' to find something in common, a 'we' that respects each of the 'I's,' including yourself."

There were several groans. We sat quietly. I thought of Jackson who sat beside me, and Will, and of my torment about being attracted to them. I thought about the war, how my dread of serving in it had brought me here. I knew that some, like my high school friend Duffner, who wanted to serve his country had died. I needed to respect that call to serve.

The consensus of the groups was that students wanted the university to make a statement denouncing what happened at Kent State.

The dean told us that a statement by the university would require a meeting of the board. It was unreasonable to think that it could be done quickly. Jackson offered an idea that the university sponsor a forum in which both the pros and cons could be heard. He also advocated for the university to allow protesters to present their concerns about the war to the board at their next meeting. I was surprised how he'd taken on the role of conciliator.

The dean got the chancellor to hold a special board meeting where the protesters could be heard. The university would sponsor a forum that the dean agreed to spearhead. The Dean congratulated us. We left to inform the protesters about what we'd done. There were cheers and celebration. Reverend Lawson who had been with the group told us the gruesome details of the Kent State shootings and the chaos on campuses across the nation.

After the crowd dispersed, Jackson took me by the hand. "You want to go back to my room?" he asked. When I hesitated and said, "I need—" he added, "We could always compromise and go to yours." I laughed. He could be so charming. We went to his. I spent the night in his arms.

Start Up

The semester wound down as my work with the folk school increased. My big worry was my relationship with Jackson. As much as I was attracted to him, he would soon go home to upstate New York. He took his exams and left early. He said goodbye and promised to write. Eventually, he wrote short letters about his hometown, the grocery where he worked, the local fair, and his boyfriend. They'd been together for years. I let him go.

Ann was still in my life. I hung onto her because she made me feel like I was all right. A man. A lover of women. We studied together. She told me about her job applications and an interview she had with a company in Connecticut.

Erling and I made plans for the summer. We brought boxes of books to our newly owned folk school. He purchased Peggy's land and home. He had four new students and more faculty.

Earlier in May, Dr. Compton, my former philosophy professor, invited me back to Ashbury College to read my poems at his house and recruit students for the folk school. He posted a notice in the Philosophy Department about the reading and the folk school. Thirty students came to the reading and talked about the folk school. Stephen, Adam, and Alicia volunteered to come to the folk school.

Attractive and petite, Alicia asked me to meet with her at the Double Decker café after the reading. She was taking a course in modern poetry and wanted me to explain "Sunday Morning" by Wallace Stevens to her. She read it aloud, her soft, sensual voice enunciating every word. I wanted to tell her, "Listen to yourself; you *are* the poem." We then went over it line by line and, as we talked about the lines, she asked what he meant by,

> She dreams a little, and she feels the dark
> Encroachment of that old catastrophe,
> As a calm darkens among water-lights.
> The pungent oranges and bright, green wings
> Seem things in some procession of the dead,
> Winding across wide water, without sound.

I didn't give her answers. I asked her what the "old catastrophe" could mean. She figured out what the poem meant to her, how she'd often felt constrained as a sorority girl. She lived as if she were just some pretty object when inside she felt full of loss. Despite the bright colors and elegance of her sorority house—one of the most beautiful on campus—it seemed meaningless to her. She became excited about how the poem spoke to her. She called her parents to convince them to let her go to the folk school. They did.

After a brief visit home to drop off my books and records and to see my parents, I headed back to Nashville in my air-conditioned car. I pulled into the driveway of Rick's house and walked to the door. In seconds, my shirt was drenched with sweat. Rick and Jane had gone to Louisville. The key was under a ceramic frog.

I planned to spend that night resting before heading to Cross Creek where I would meet Erling who had already arrived. The students would arrive Friday.

We had seven students. Two young women, Grace and Betty, came from Maryland. Stephen, a member of my old fraternity; Adam, a cross-country runner; and Alicia, the sorority girl, came from Ashbury College. A foreign exchange student from Sweden, Ingrid, came from a small college in Appalachia where Erling taught American Literature. Maddy, a local girl, who played the guitar, went to Bethel College and would head the music program. Erling enticed a divinity student, Dylan, to come. A first-year student, he wanted, in his words, "to explore the primitive heritage of the mountain people." I thought he was odd. But Erling liked him.

We also had one faculty member, Erik Cline, a professor of history from Vanderbilt University with a specialty in American Studies. He used a lot of three syllable words. But he had a genuine interest in history as lived experience. His wife, Ellen a tall, thin woman who looked like Audrey Hepburn —she exuded sensuality—was the activities director. She was a painter and would coordinate craft programs.

Everyone would stay at the new folk school. Erling had purchased bunkbeds for co-ed dorms. A library was in one room that also served as a bedroom for Erling, a meeting room, and living room.

Since the house sat on the crest of a steep hill with a great view, some of our group sessions were held on the front porch. Despite the desolate quality of the immediate terrain—no pines, no grass, nothing—there in the moonlight, you could see far beyond the soft slopes of the mountains to the grayish blue light on the horizon. I liked to think about cool evenings on the porch with Erling discussing how we would arrange the daily schedule.

I opened the door to the narrow flight of stairs to Rick's apartment. Stale, dank air slammed into me. Once inside, I went to the window with the air-conditioner. I turned the knob on high and stood in front of it. It would be the last time for months that I'd have the luxury of cool air on my command. I lifted my shirt to let the cool blow over me.

Over the last months, I'd been busy trying to sort out who I was and who I wanted to be with. I'd finished my second year at graduate school. But what had it gotten me? I felt stalled. I'd gotten out of the suburbs. Yet I was mired in uncertainty. Will. Tom. Jackson. Ann. Julie. Cheryl. I was experimenting with life. I dabbled. I never committed. I hoped to land one true passion.

It would be good to get back to the mountains. At least I was comfortable there.

Erling called me at Rick's to make final arrangements. His voice seemed distant, almost as if we had a bad connection.

I told him I'd gotten more money from the church. "Another grand. Can you believe it? They really like what we are doing. Mr. Hook may come to visit us!"

"Hold your horses," Erling said.

"What is it?"

"Bad news," he informed me.

"What?"

"The folk school burned down last night."

The air conditioner droned on. I stared at it.

"Arson," he said. "By the time the fire department came—and they didn't rush—it was engulfed in flames. I couldn't get in. Old as it was, it went up like tinder. Nothing left. Nothing."

"Shit," I said. I crumpled on a kitchen chair.

"You got it," he said. "Shit is the right word. 'Damn' would work too, and 'fuck'."

"What will we do?" I asked.

"Already on it. Peggy told me about a house not far from the folk school that's empty. We may be able to rent it. It's furnished. Beds, furniture, kitchen, the whole works. I looked in the window. It would hold most of us, not all. Some would have to sleep up in the log cabin, which is nearly done," he explained. "The grand may make the difference."

"Do I need to get anything?"

"No. Drive up as fast as you can. We can outfit the house if I can rent it."

After the call, I drank some cold water and sat in the lounge chair. Who burned the school?

Grief settled over me. I had to get some rest. There would be much to do.

Rick and Jane would be back late. "Don't wait up," they said. But I did.

When I heard the door open downstairs, I helped them carry in their luggage.

Jane seemed tired and excused herself—the long drive. When she closed the door to the bedroom, Rick said that she hadn't been well.

"There a problem?" I asked.

"Not exactly," he said.

I waited for him to continue. He was restless. He picked up something on one counter and set it on another and then moved it back again as he unpacked.

"I might as well tell you," he said. "You're the first. She's pregnant!"

"Really?"

"Early on. But it's real."

Since he stared at me without expression, I didn't know how to read him.

"And..."

'She's due next fall."

"Rick, how are *you* feeling?"

"Oh, that," he said, wincing. "That's more complicated. Still have school to complete. A parish to find. Being a dad, you know, that's hard for me to get my head around."

"Mixed reviews," I said.

"Very."

"Let's have a drink," I said. "You can unpack later." We spoke for several hours. His father had been absent, caught up in his job. Rick didn't want to be like that. But he was starting a new career. It would take him time to learn the ropes. He hoped that he'd be a good dad.

By the time Jane came back into the room looking surprisingly refreshed, he seemed more relaxed. He fixed us cheese dip and corn chips.

I told them the bad news. They were shocked and listened to my concerns.

Rick excused himself to unpack his bags.

"He's a bit nonplussed," Jane whispered. "Men don't get pregnant the way we do. I mean for us, it's there. What can we do? For them, it's like inviting a stranger into the house. He'll get used to it."

She had such a unique way of putting things. I suspected that she wasn't really tired at all but just knew that Rick needed to talk. She was right about our bodies. I was reminded of a woman I'd met in Chicago.

Last January, we went on a double date with my friend, a medical student, to a drive-in. Before the previews, she had her hand in my pants. Her name was Darla but she preferred to be called "Pussy." She slipped off her panties. If I hadn't been inhibited by my friend and his girl in the front seat, I would have had sex right there. Later she invited me to a party at her house. Before the guests left we'd hopped into bed. I was amazed how willing she was, how much she enjoyed having me enter her body, how comfortable she was making love. I began to feel that maybe my confusion about sex grew from my inexperience or not finding the right woman. Rick had found Jane. He seemed happy. Maybe that could happen to me.

The next morning, after Jane fixed a big breakfast of hash browns, eggs, sausage, and toast, I wished them well. I gave Rick the address at Clearfork Post Office. He hugged me, whispered, "Thanks." Jane gave me a hug too. She escorted me to the car, "You worked your magic. He's fine now. He'll be a great dad."

PART V

Footfall each in the memory

Down the passage which I did not take

Toward the door we never opened

"Four Quartets," T.S. Eliot

Ashes

When I arrived where the folk school was to be located, the plot was blanketed with white ash. Whoever torched it had done a good job. A chimney rose from the middle of a slab on one side of the house.

A year after the first visit to Peggy's house, I sat in the same place, my books burned and ash all around me. The surrounding trees were scorched and dead, the stove pipes twisted like melted plastic tubing. The hillside was denuded—red clay wounded and bled.

I picked at chunks of ash and realized that they were burnt books, each page like flakes of French pastry dough. One book was intact. Chardin's *The Divine Milieu*. As I broke the pages they blew away like white wings of a moth.

I remembered bringing boxes of books to the house, setting up a bookcase and alphabetizing them: James Agee, Teihard de Chardin, and Thomas Wolfe. I opened my journal to make notes about how beautiful the book ashes were, how fragile they were. If I hadn't loved the books, I'd have found the ashes more stunning in appearance than the books themselves.

I wiped the perspiration from my forehead. The afternoon sun had lodged at its apogee in the sky. I had to find Erling and find out what he wanted me to do for orientation.

A car came up the hollow. It turned in the driveway next to mine. Out popped Bobby and his sisters, Janet and Katie. They scampered up the driveway. They called out, "Jason! Jason!" I almost burst into tears. My joy at the sound of their voices, and their pleas with me to go swimming in the strip-mine pool, dashed my sadness.

I raced down the hill to greet them. Bobby had gotten his driver's permit. He pointed at the keys in his hand; I patted him on the back. The girls tugged me, "Come on, come on," and told me to hurry. I got my suit. Bobby and I chased after them. Bobby and I scooted behind a crop of saplings, stripped, and put on our suits. We jumped into the cool water. Their indomitable spirit and capacity for joy astounded me.

Bobby hopped on my shoulders and Janet hopped onto Katie's shoulders. We tried to topple each other. We were taller by a foot than the girls. The girls giggled and shouted, "No fair!" I fell so the girls would win. Bobby glared at me, I winked, and he smiled. We played for an hour. Then they took me to the new house that would be the home of the folk school.

Erling greeted me at the front porch, which was less than five feet from the road. It hung over a gentle ravine with its back set on four posts. A set of stairs out the back door led to a backyard and a meandering brook. Erling hugged me, and pointing up the road, said, "Sad sight." While the kids roamed around the new location, he told me what he thought we should do to organize the house. Bobby, the girls, and I helped Erling move some bunk beds into different rooms. He'd bought some more cooking sets—pots, pans, fry pans and kettles—along with dishes, glasses, and silverware for fourteen. We dusted and washed the cupboards, putting down yellowed shelf liner. We set the plates, bowls, and pots on the shelves.

Toward evening, Erling met with Marie Cirillo. He told me that I could do what I wanted. The Lester family had moved to their other home deep in the hollow. Bobby heard that I had a night off. He invited me to come visit. I drove up the road that, in some stretches, was hundreds of feet above the creek bed. The farther I drove into the hollow, the steeper the drop-off became. We took the right branch of a fork to their house. Constructed much like their other home, it had a front porch that led into Peggy's and the girls' bedrooms. Across from it was another room with a bunk bed where Bobby and Tommy slept. Just beyond Peggy's room was the kitchen with a wood-fired cookstove and a kitchen table.

There were no toilets of gleaming white porcelain. I couldn't just push the handle and flush. I couldn't step to a mirror, smile my face shining in light, and wash and dry my hands. I couldn't ignore my body in an antiseptic world. I couldn't open the door, step into a hallway, and go back to where everyone pretended nothing had happened.

In the outhouse, the olfactory senses told a different story. That sense of bodily reality was reassuring. It wasn't based on social status, political affiliation, the clothes I wore, the car I drove, the money I had in the bank, or the name I had. It was based on my being with other bodies like my own. Martin Luther wrote about this communion with others. He spoke graphically about the body. He believed it was a great equalizer. On winter nights, as I scampered to the outhouse, I believed him. On hot summer afternoons, even more. Being in one's body was the primal connection that brought us together. Individually, we had immense differences but they did not divide us as much as they made us unique in our camaraderie. Being with Peggy and her family brought me back to that awareness.

Shady John

We oriented the new students and set up the house, then determined that Stephen and I would sleep in the new cabin that had been constructed on folk school property. The program started: Classes in the morning. Lunch. Outdoor activities in the afternoon by the burned-down school or in the new cabin. On Friday evening, a campfire. For the first two hot and humid weeks, we spent many afternoons in the pond.

The new students organized the arts and crafts program under the guidance of Ellen. The two Maryland students, Grace and Betty, both athletic, joined the boys in football games. Dylan liked to play checkers and chess under the shade of a maple.

In the morning group discussions, Dylan liked to be right. Short, with the remnants of acne splattered across his face, he impressed Erling with his familiarity with the day's reading. He liked to impress others with his intellect.

If I made a statement about Thomas Wolfe, he interrupted me. "No, that's not what he said. Haven't you read him? In the chapter you're referring to, he actually said..." I had an urge to punch him in the face, but decided, instead, to ignore him, a decision I'd come to regret.

The Swedish student, Ingrid, involved students in writing workshops and painting watercolors. Along with Ellen, she showed local kids how to weave baskets from sapling bark. Everyone, including Erling, joined in. He said that he had an interest in short story writing. That Ingrid was stunningly beautiful may also have attracted him. I was certain that the three younger and two teenage boys who joined the group never complained when she leaned her shoulder into theirs to see what they'd written in their journal.

With a larger crew of five men, four women attending the folk school, we had managed in three short weeks to create even stronger allegiance in the community than we had the year before. The core of our community events was the Friday bonfire. People brought potato chips, potato salad, chicken, fresh-made loaves of bread, and cookies. There was plenty to eat.

Erik, the history professor, and Mandy, the musical wizard, played the guitar. Bud Terry and Otrel, two local musicians, played the fiddle and guitar.

We'd sing folk tunes and danced around the fire. I told folk stories. Robbie Metzler, a teenager who became a regular in the day program brought his banjo and soon enough we had a jamboree.

Before the bonfire, we had baseball and horseshoe games, horseshoe and shooting contests. We played wiffle ball with the kids. Erling played with a vengeance. He'd pick the teams and pitch for his team. If his team was down, he'd slap their backs and embolden them to play harder, run faster, score more often. He'd stand at the pitcher's mound, slap his fist in his mitt, lean, eye the batter, and whip the ball to home plate. His motto, "No one on, no one scores." When he batted, he crouched so low it was hard to get a strike across the plate. On offense, he batted balls over everyone's head and charged around the bases with his arms up, chiding the runners on base to hurry up so he could plant his own foot on home plate.

Horseshoes brought serious betting for some adults. The locals would challenge members of the folk school, betting five or ten dollars. The horseshoe pit would be lined with kids watching the horseshoe fly end over end toward the stake.

We wanted to draw more local men. If the word got to others, we'd be safer. We added a turkey shoot contest to draw them in. We'd put bull's eye targets on a maple tree. Everyone chipped in a buck. We drew up a lineup. Three shots, two rounds. The one with the highest points won.

The first round went to the younger set. Tommy and Bobby had two bull's-eyes. "You young Turks are whipping these old guys," I said.

Tommy shook his head, put his hand over his mouth and whispered, "Don't be fooled. Shady John will clean house. He's the best shot in the country, probably the state."

Squatting on his heels beside his red Ford pickup, Shady John worked his plug tobacco and spit on the ground. He wore a baseball cap low on his forehead. He owned a piece of land down the hill from the folk school; he had a small pond next to his driveway and, beyond it, an extensive garden with a sizable corn crop, squash that twined among the corn, beans, carrots, chard, lettuce—you name it. Most of the day, he posted himself under a pin oak that loomed beside his house. He held a rifle in his arm. He'd pick off any varmint that snooped around. He could have been any age, forty to seventy. His face was like the land he labored on, worn like clay, streaked with crevasses that ran along his eyes down to his massive jaw.

Rarely one to smile or even speak, he came to church every Sunday and sat in his front pew, dressed as he did most days in bib overalls and a white work shirt. It was rumored that in his youth he'd shot and killed a man. He'd been rowdy and mean-spirited. But he met his wife, had a son who was his pride and joy, and settled down. He'd developed a case of palsy and his hands had a slight tremor. He kept his hands in his lap, or, as he did that night, on the butt of his rifle.

I laughed out loud when Tommy told me that Shady John would clean house. "Christ," I whispered, "He can't keep from shaking. How's he going to sight a gun?"

"Watch him."

I called Shady John up to shoot. Most everyone stopped to watch him. He was a legend. He set his legs wide and lifted the rifle to his shoulder. The tip of it jittered up and down. He put his eye over the barrel and sighted on the target. He must have stood in that posture for several minutes. He squeezed the trigger and everyone looked at the target. Bull's eye. Dead center. He rested his gun. There was applause. A smile creased one corner of his mouth. He proceeded to squeeze off two more shots, bull's eye each time. "Much appreciate the turkey," he said. "and what you are doing with my boy." He came back every week.

Squeaky

Rumors spread the third week of the folk school: Squeaky wanted to kill me. Squeaky, a young man newly released from prison, didn't like our being in the hollow. He thought we were communists. He threatened to take a knife to me. He didn't like my looks. He resented that I took the boys skinny dipping in the creek. He called me a "faggot."

Erling told me to be careful. "Don't go off by yourself. Keep someone else around," he said. "Let's just check it out and play it safe until we identify if he actually made the threats."

With Shady John on our side, and more people coming each Friday, Erling and I were surprised to hear that Squeaky was making threats. He carried a switchblade and bragged how he'd gut me with it. He had a proven record: He'd gone to prison for knifing someone: manslaughter.

Erling made plans to protect me. Stephen, Erik and, Adam were to keep an eye on me. One was in front of me, one to the side, one in back. Wherever I went, they followed me. They kept their distance, so they didn't look conspicuous. I was aware of them as I passed the football, when I got up to tell a folk-tale, or during the folk dance. They were there, joining in but also looking for Squeaky.

The trouble with the plan is that none of us had ever met Squeaky. We knew that he had been released from prison, that he was a cousin of J.B. Terry, and that he was only twenty-one. But no one from the folk school had seen him. For all we knew he could have been any of the younger men at the bonfire.

One evening, Grace told me that Squeaky had arrived. As we were doing a circle dance, she kept hold of my arm when I was supposed to swing her to her next partner and, instead, pulled me aside.

"That's him," she pointed to a young man standing at the outskirts of the campfire.

He was short, and his head darted back and forth and up and down like a startled turtle peeking out of his shell. He had long black hair and a plain, almost childlike face. His outfit was nondescript: a plaid shirt opened in the front, jeans and cowboy boots. He chatted with several guys his age. They all laughed. An unfamiliar girl hung on his arm. He was self-assured, even cocky with his hands shoved in the front of his jeans.

Grace signaled my bodyguards. They moved closer. Stu came over to me and put his hand on my shoulder.

"Erling suggests," he said, "that I take you back to the cabin, just to avoid trouble. Okay?"

I told him to wait. "He's not making trouble, let's see what he does." I spoke with the fiddlers, then squatted on a log and fed the fire. The Lester kids—Bobby, Tommy, Donna, Katie and Janet, gathered around me. They took turns tossing sticks into the bonfire. I knew they were protecting me.

Squeaky and his friends came over to the campfire and stood on the opposite side. They were laughing, tossing sticks in the fire, stomping their feet to the music. Squeaky eyed me with quick furtive glances. He talked with his friends who clustered around him. I crouched and gazed into the embers; an orange light welled up from the gray ash. As the timbers and logs burned down, the fire hushed as if sleepy, no longer snarling and snapping as it had at the start.

Stephen came over again. He knelt beside me, "You sure you don't want to go?"

I could feel the tension in my neck. For a week, I had kept my guard up. I was careful not to go anywhere alone. I was easy prey sleeping outside the cabin on the hillside on hot nights without someone with me. I lay out my sleeping bag and worried that he might sneak up and stab me while I was lost in a dream. I could not imagine how it must be to be the president, knowing at any moment that someone could take a shot at you. I remember how both Dr. King and President Kennedy had joked about someone taking a shot at them. It made no sense to me. Why would anyone want to kill me?

I picked up a stick, broke it on the ground with my foot, and aimed it at the fire.

"What is it?" Stephen asked.

"Wait here," I said.

I stood up and walked to Squeaky's group gathered by the maple. I'd decided that if Squeaky was going to knife me, he'd have to do it in public. He saw me coming and gave one of his buddies a nudge. Katie was at my right shoulder, Tommy at my left, Bobby next to him. Stephen, Erik and Adam watched from twenty feet away.

I came up to him, extended my hand, and said as calmly as I could, "Hi, I don't think I know you. What's your name?"

He had a soft cautious grip. "Squeaky."

"Mine's Jason. Nice to meet you," I said. I wasn't sure what to say next, but I followed the script that I had used at parties that my mother held for my dad's corporate friends: ask something personal about them.

I asked him where he lived. He told me that he was staying with his uncle for the time being. I thanked him for coming.

"We do this every week," I said. "We need help in getting the bonfire going. You good with an ax?"

"Yeah. Pretty good, I'd say, but even better with a chainsaw." He smiled at his friend. He stared at me, his face fixed. I felt an odd affection for him, for his boyishness, his round soft features and long curly hair, sticking out in several directions. He seemed vulnerable, as if he had been picked on and had a chip in his shoulder. He was no more than five-two, nearly half a head shorter than I was. He had a frail build—slight shoulders and skinny legs. I could have picked him up with one hand. He must have been easy prey in the prison system. I took a risk and touched him gently on the shoulder.

"It would be great to have your help—and your friends too!"

I introduced myself to his friends, Taylor, Billy, Joe, and Squeaky's girlfriend, Jean-May. I invited them to help.

"Hey, we are going to roast some marshmallows. You want to get some sticks for the kids? We need a lot of them. You can join in!"

He frowned at first and shoved his hands in his pockets. His girlfriend nudged him. He agreed, "Sure, anything for the kids."

Becky went up to him and started to chat. She asked him if he played guitar. He did. She invited him to come to the cabin some time to play. Tommy, Bobby, Squeaky, Taylor, Billy, Joe, and Jean-May joined her; they all headed to the saplings on the edge of the strip mine, pocket knives in hand.

Squeaky had a theory about not getting marshmallows too dark. Squeaky, Taylor, and Jean-May toasted two bags of marshmallows and passed them out to the kids.

They didn't come back the next week, but Squeaky came to the folk school to play his guitar with Becky. He became a regular. He became a good friend and confided in me that he wanted to get his GED. He asked me to help him learn some grammar and I agreed.

Fires of Hell

From the folk school porch on Sundays faint fragments of hymns carried down the valley. The tiny Pentecostal Church had a service each Sunday. Because it was such a small congregation, they imported different preachers each week. Many were lay preachers wanting to get a shot at the pulpit. Peggy knew I was a divinity student and urged me to come. She couldn't understand how a man of God wouldn't come to church. I didn't have the heart to tell her that at best I was a man in search of God.

After weeks of pestering, I finally relented in July. I donned my best slacks and white dress shirt, and walked up the crooked road to the church.

Peggy greeted me at the door. The church consisted of one large room twenty feet long and fifteen feet wide with a platform in front. A makeshift pulpit, painted white, sat on a platform in front. A vase of Queen Ann's lace and wild daisies was placed on a little table by the pulpit. Nine people filled in the first row of folding chairs. Shady John leaned against the back wall. Peggy ushered me to the front. A local boy who worked in a collision shop in Jellico was preaching for the first time.

"You'll enjoy him," she said. "I've heard he's a lively preacher."

When he arrived she introduced me. She told him I was at Vanderbilt Divinity School. Short, in a gray suit much too large for him, he offered his hand to me. The sleeves of his jacket were so long that I could not see his hand at first. He had a rotund face. A slab of hair that looked glued in place was pasted across his forehead. He bounced from one foot to the other as we talked. His eyes focused more on my Adam's apple than my face.

Peggy sang the first line of each hymn. Everyone followed, repeating the line. She sang, "He has the whole world in his hands." She had a strong deep voice that reminded me of Mahalia Jackson's. Even children joined in. Peggy's twins loved to sing. As the service continued, three toddlers wandered in and out of the building. They'd scamper in, perch next to their mothers for a while, and, when they tired of the service, toddle out. Their playful screams outside could be heard through the open windows.

The boy preacher read some New Testament verses from a worn, leather-bound Bible. He thanked the congregation for the chance to preach "The Word." He emphasized those two words, his voice pitched high in a falsetto. Living in the hollow, he had fond memories of the church, although, he admitted that he was a wayward boy.

Peggy called out, "You certainly was," and several women echoed her sentiment, saying, "Uh-huh."

With the Bible held high, he slapped it with his hand. "I've come to Jesus," he said. His voice grew stronger. He crouched down, knees bent, and leaped up high in the air, still saying, "I've come to Jesus." He'd been saved by Jesus. His face flushed, the slab of hair on his head broke loose and flapped up and down as he jumped up and down. He managed to break the phrases. "I've come" would be called out as he rose up and "to Jesus" as he landed. Peggy and the other women shouted, "Praise the Lord!"

He stared at me and asked, "You ever seen an acetylene torch?"

I shook my head. "No."

"Well, I'll tell, you I work with one every day. I put a match to the flame and it's mighty hot, so hot it melts iron into liquid, a flame as hot as the flames of hell. Yes, it is! Hot as the devil's temptation, a flame that'll burn the flesh. I see it burn it black as tar, black as the soul without salvation. I know you're tempted—" He was still staring at me. Besides Shady John, I was the only male, the only one who might have been tempted as he had been tempted. But I wondered if he suspected something else about me. He kept on, "Yes, charred souls. The skin peeling off black as the sinners go against the word of God," and, each time, he said "sinners" he jumped straight up so the floor boards shook. When his shoes slammed down, he kept his legs wide open and popped right up again, up and down, calling out, "Yes! Yes, 'Ah, yes! 'Ah!" as if he was out of breath. But he wasn't because he kept right on preaching. "Hot as an acetylene torch. God roasts sinners! Burns them black as coal! Sinners! Mark my word. Yes, ah he will, ah, yes," another jump, "sinners, yes he will." My head bobbed up and down. Sweat poured from his forehead. He stared at me. I was sure he knew I was one of those sinners. As he continued leaping, I was impressed with his stamina. He looked like a man whose feet were being scorched on a skillet who had to leap to prevent from getting fried as black as his shoes. I kept nodding my head. He must have thought I was agreeing with him. He described the torch, its blue flame, and how he could intensify the flame. He held the Bible out in front of him as if it were a torch. He aimed it right at me. Then he scanned the congregation. Heads turned away, afraid to be scorched.

He sweated so much that he had to loosen his tie and shed his jacket. Peggy seemed to enjoy the performance. The children had gathered beside me. They seemed to want to see more of his calisthenics. His last pronouncements were about the wages of sin. He went back to the pulpit, put his hands on it, stared up at the ceiling, and offered a prayer. He asked us to accept the love of Jesus. I was surprised. Up to that point I was convinced that all our doomed fates were sealed. We'd burn in an acetylene hell. I even wondered when he was leaping up and down what Jesus would have done with an acetylene torch. He might have burned the temple down.

But the boy preacher erased those thoughts. He came back to love. He said Jesus's love washes away sin and quenches fire. He smiled and thanked us again for the chance to preach The Word.

Peggy called another hymn. The boy preacher fled to the entrance in the back. A basket was passed around. I put in ten dollars. I felt some obligation because it was the best entertainment I'd had in months. The preacher shook my hand. I told him that it was an inspiring sermon. He seemed pleased.

"I've been changed by the Lord," he said.

I'm sure he had. From what, I couldn't tell. But I suspected that it was rough for him. With him being as short as he was, it was likely bigger boys picked on him. But now he had his torch, a decent job, a new jacket, and Jesus, too. How it was someone "found Jesus," as if Jesus had been lost, never made sense to me. For me, Jesus was a historical figure with a distinct message: to heal the poor, to see the kingdom of God in the world before one's eyes, and to see that everyone knows they are a child of God. Jesus was never an intimate friend or a personal savior for me. I had several people who saved my life. Two were professors at Ashbury. They were living. They hadn't been dead for over a thousand years. I realized that it was mysterious how Jesus as a real-life personage became vital in some people's lives. I didn't think I'd ever understand how that happened for people like the preacher.

Peggy asked if I'd come again, and I did. She introduced me to several other regulars. Bonnie Hatfield lived a half-mile from the folk school. Her boys, Jay, Tyler, and Jesse, were regulars. Over the next few weeks, I visited her house several times, picking up and dropping off her boys. She ran a household of six. Her daughters worked. The boys were all in school, from elementary to middle school. She liked the church, too. "Gives me some peace and quiet."

Peace and quiet was never what I experienced at the church. The other itinerant preachers may have not been as entertaining as the one with the torch, but they spoke of sin and damnation and called for us to repent. No one came forward to repent while I attended the services. But the congregation enjoyed themselves; we sang gospel tunes that always lifted our spirits.

My being there gave me more credibility with the community. It only lasted an hour or so, depending on how revved up the preacher was. I came to find it refreshing. Sometimes I picked up Bonnie and her kids.

I skipped a few services as the summer days shortened. I'd been cashing in my wages of sin at a rate that frightened me. Much as I tried to deny it, my attraction to Stephen who slept at the log cabin with me became an obsession. I'd been attracted to him in college when he was my pledge son. I loved watching him undress before we crawled into our sleeping bags. I often drank too much in the evenings. I felt unhinged and overworked. I made daily excursions to the stores, helped set up the meeting room, ran laundry to the laundromat, and played with the kids all afternoon. The church became a refuge for me, as it was for Bonnie and Peggy.

They knew I didn't much care for the message most of the time and neither did they. They had an enormous faith in the goodness of people and they liked getting out of the house and seeing neighbors. That's what you did on Sunday mornings. It was probably the only time Peggy and Bonnie got away from chores, taking care of her six children. Sunday was a day of rest for women. There was something blessed about being free from the household, just as it was good for me to be away from the folk school

One evening, I went off by myself. I followed the stream up the ravine, so I could see the water at its source drop down into the valley. I was haunted by something that happened the night before. I studied what I had done like a riddle from different angles. But the more I thought about the incident, the more befuddled I became.

Late at night, I'd slipped my hand into Stephen's sleeping bag. If I half believed the preachers, it was the wages of sin. But it was not sin. It was me out of sync.

I climbed farther up the mountain to a graveyard and looked at the gravestones, dating back to 1840. The sun hung in the sky. The heat of the sun on my body was like the lust I had felt last night. Why was it that I felt a compulsion to be naked, to strip off my clothes, and to sit naked, free of all veneer? I unbuttoned my shirt, doffed my sandals, and slipped my jeans off. I kept low to the ground in case anyone might see me. I lay on the ground letting the sun bake me. I caught myself being shy and realized that my shyness was almost instinctive. When I finally started to get dressed, the wind felt good as it fingered across my legs and my jockey shorts.

When I was with other guys who enjoyed being naked, I felt no shame. I lay back now, and let my mind wander to the previous night when I snuggled next to Stephen and placed my hand lightly on the cotton of his underwear. I waited. Stephen was quite still. The moon showed in cracks in the logs. A milky yellow light spread over our sleeping bags.

There was a stirring. My hand snapped back. Stephen rolled over to face me. "What are you doing?" he asked.

I pretended to be asleep.

"You awake?" Stephen said, nudging me. He leaned over me, propped on his elbow. Getting no response to his question, he turned over and slept.

The wind stirred. I put my hand back on his sleeping bag, feeling the rise and fall of his breathing. I was aroused and groped for the warmth of his body under the palm of my hand.

He sat up, turning to me, "What *are* you doing?'

"Nothing," I stammered.

"How long have you been awake?"

"Awake?" I looked at my hand as if it were a foreign object. I cringed. "My hand must'a fallen on your sleeping bag."

"I don't think so."

"Sorry."

"What *is* going on?"

"Must'a reached out in my sleep."

"But you were awake. Weren't you?"

"Yes." There was no avoiding it, I had to admit it. "I was. I'm sorry."

Stephen looked at me and shook his head back and forth. "Keep them to yourself, okay?"

"Okay."

I rolled over into a ball, closed my eyes, and wondered what Stephen would say the next day. I wanted to creep off into the night and disappear.

In the morning, Stephen's sleeping bag was empty. Just the corner of it was folded back. I sat on my elbows. He was sitting on the front stoop, looking at the sunrise. When I unzipped my sleeping bag, he turned around. With a beautiful smile, he said, "Good morning." I wished him the same.

The Runner

Adam and I were out on a run one afternoon. Although I could not keep up with him if he kept a regular pace—as a cross country athlete he could run for hours—he slowed down so I could point out where different people lived. When we crested the hill, I could hear Bud Terry's guitar playing and we slowed down to listen to it. He waved for us to come in. We pushed open the gate and went to the front porch. We chatted about the heat. He showed us a pistol that he had on a table by his chair.

"Feel it. There that best gun in the hollow. It rests in your hand like a glove," he boasted. He picked it up and asked Adam to put several bottles on the fence. Once they were perched there, he took aim and hit one, missed another. His hand was shaking. He shattered one more and missed yet again.

"Twern't the gun," he said, apologetically. "My hands ain't no good. My breathing's so bad I wonder if I'll ever catch another breath."

When he started to complain about his health, Adam turned away and walked to the other end of the porch. Bud handed me the gun. "You much of a shot?" he asked.

"Don't know," I confessed. "Never shot one, except toy pistols when I was a kid."

He told Adam to line up a set of bottles, six of them in a row. "Let's see what you can do."

I asked him how to site the gun. He told me to use my strong eye to pinpoint the target and to squeeze the trigger gently. I held it out in front of me, closed one eye, and aimed. I'd learned from Shady John at our shooting contests that a lighter finger lets the gun work as it was intended and doesn't jerk it off the target. The gun fired and the bottle shattered. Pleased with myself, I blasted one after another: six bottles, six shots.

Bud laughed, "Well, I'll be. For a city slicker, you've got a steady hand."

He coughed several times and complained again about his lungs. Adam moved off the porch and was pacing back and forth. I apologized for Adam. Bud said, "Oh, I remember that age when it was hard to sit still. Be off with you."

I handed him the gun and Adam and I returned to the run. After two hundred yards, I told Adam that it was rude of him to ignore Bud when he was complaining about his illness. Adam said, "He's not ill."

"Yes, he is. He's got emphysema, compounded with black lung," I told him.

"He's fine. He's just fine." He picked up his pace, jogging yards ahead of me. I looked at him, his lean body and the scars on his legs like marbled rock.

When he was twelve, a chemistry experiment at his house exploded. It covered his legs with a flammable liquid. He ran down the street and collapsed in a neighbor's front yard. The neighbor covered him with a blanket to extinguish the fire. He suffered third-degree burns. The doctors said he'd never walk again. But he walked and ran and won the state cross country meet. He also converted to being a Christian Scientist. He claimed that the religion saved his life.

Earlier in the spring, when he came for a weekend visit to Nashville, he stayed in my dorm several nights. One night, we got into a heated argument about how many decisions were neither good nor bad. He stood up—his arms folded across his chest, his face flushed—and started to leave the room. I asked him not to walk out in the middle of a discussion. He changed direction and leaned against the window, his feet tapping the floor. I told him that sometimes to produce more energy to help the economy grow, we damage the environment. That's how a good thing can also be a bad thing. He shook his head. He claimed that there was only good: a right way which meant there was a wrong way and he wanted nothing to do with it.

He was standing by my window. I noticed a large magnolia with a shadow under it. I pointed to it and said, "Look at that tree. See the shadow under it? Notice how the dappled light mixes with the dark? That's how it is for most things: it's not dark and light, good and bad. There is always a gray area where most decisions are made."

He looked at the tree and shook his head, "All I see is shadow and light." I put my hand on his shoulder and pointed at the light changing under the tree from the branches blowing and shifting the light. He refused to see it. That's where we left it.

As I followed him up the road, his legs pumped in long strides, I knew that his running gave him a way to block out anything that interfered with his reality. I also knew he'd keep running for miles and miles. He'd keep going higher up the hollow, onto steeper, more rutted sections.

I called out to him to let him know I was turning around. Sweat poured off my back. My shirt was drenched. I thought how hard it must be to keep the world in a black/white, right/wrong dichotomy, but how convenient it was too.

As long as you were on the right side, there was only shadow and light. The dappled subtleties of life couldn't exist; they were conveniently ignored. Up in the hills with little access to the news, it was easy to lapse into complacency about the outside world and to imagine that everything could be reduced to black and white.

At night, I'd often go off and read. Sometimes I spent time with Alicia. We'd walk off by a creek that ran behind the folk school, stick our feet in it, and talk about the other members: how Ed, the history professor, made up terms to sound more impressive like the "thwartedness of the American Dream." We wished he'd speak more from his heart than his head. We also talked about what we would do after graduation. She had one more year at college. I had one year at the Divinity School. For us, the future looked bleak. I'd probably be eligible for the draft. She majored in history and had no idea what she would do for a career. She'd slip her hand into mine. She remained the one person I felt I could genuinely talk to. Vibrant, with long brown hair and an impish expression on her face, she wanted more of life than what she'd been told was her fate: marriage, housekeeping, and children. She wasn't about to let that happen. At times, I felt I could fall in love with her. But I knew that couldn't happen—at least while we were at the folk school.

Security

Midway through the summer, we heard that a local group claimed that a bunch of "communists" and "outsiders" had come to Cross Creek and were introducing "socialist" programs. They threatened to root us out and planned to crash our Friday night bonfire. They had guns and meant business. Erling talked with several members of the board of the folk school about it. We had not encountered such threats since the first weeks of the program the year before.

But this new threat came from a gang that had guns and clubs and committed serious assaults up and down the valley with anyone who crossed them. They'd even assaulted members of another baseball team that had beaten their team. (They were usually undefeated for good reason.)

Erling and I discussed calling the police, but Peggy and Bonnie, along with other board members, told us that the local police often covertly worked with the feds. No one wanted feds up in the hollow with so many families relying on moonshine to supplement their incomes. Peggy downplayed our fears and said that it would be all right. "We'll provide security," she said.

Friday night, as I was walking up the hill to set up the bonfire, I noticed Cecil Marlow, the biggest and most successful moonshiner in the hollow, on the side of the road.

I was indebted to him. The previous summer, he'd sold me a quart of moonshine. I brought it back to my father, who told me he loved the taste of it. It seemed so out of character for a businessman to like rotgut moonshine. He'd poured it into a shot glass and took a swig. He claimed it was the best shine he'd ever had. After we shared a couple of shots apiece, I discovered some interesting family lore. During Prohibition, my dad had drunk a lot of moonshine in Ohio and set up a small still himself. It gave me a slightly different picture of him from his role as a prominent businessman.

Cecil's black 1967 Lincoln Continental was parked at the base of the hill. I stopped to chat with him. He was an enormous man, broad shouldered and well over six feet tall, with white hair that was in stark contrast to his young, sturdy face. He wasn't someone you'd fool with. I asked why he had parked his car on the side of the road. I'd never seen it there before.

He smiled at me and said, "Don't worry about tonight. Everything is going to be fine."

"What do you mean?" I asked.

He motioned for me to look in the back seat. A long baseball bat leaned against the seat.

"That should take care of them," he explained.

"I heard they have weapons," I interjected.

"Well, I wouldn't worry about that," he said, lifting his shirt, revealing a revolver. He took me by the arm to the back of his car and flipped open the trunk. He had a range of rifles, some with clips attached to them. He told me that if our country was invaded, I should come right up here to Cross Creek. There were more arms per capita than any other place in the United States.

"We could hold an army off for months," he claimed.

I didn't doubt it since, on most weekends, when they had dances at local bars, inevitably someone was wounded. Cecil was never involved in those altercations. He was well-respected and well-armed. Everyone knew it.

When I got to the top, Stephen, Adam, and Alicia, along with Jay, Bobby, and several other boys, had piled up wood in tepee-like fashion. Erling was pacing back and forth.

"Worried about tonight?" I asked.

"Yes, who wouldn't be. It's one thing if they take a potshot at you like they did last year. But there'll be thirty or more of us tonight. Cars drive by all the—"

"Don't worry, we'll be—"

"Hey, don't tell *me* not to worry, I'm—"

I put my hand on his shoulder. "Let me finish, Erling." I told him about Cecil parked down the road, the only entry into the hollow.

Erling laughed. "Best moonshine in the hollow, they say."

"Best armory, too!"

Erling drove down the hill to thank Cecil. They swigged moonshine while they stopped each car to check the occupants. Erling was gone for nearly an hour and by the time he came back he was in a good mood.

If anyone came into the hollow to threaten us that night, I never heard about it. The campfire went off without a hitch.

The next week, Erling and I found out the names of the boys who had made the threats. We checked with the postmistress and found out where they lived, and drove fifteen miles to meet with them.

Erling acted like a career diplomat. He "calmed their fears" and, to my surprise, challenged them to play a softball game the next weekend.

I told him that they didn't take too kindly to losing. Erling brushed me off. "It will be just a friendly game." He winked at me.

The wink bothered me. When it came to baseball, Erling was relentless. He'd do anything to win. And, if we won, I suspected that we'd have a real gun fight.

Several young men from the hollow— Tommy, Bobby and a few of their friends along with some of our staff—eight guys and four women fielded our team. I wasn't worried about the women. Betty and Grace had played softball in college. Mandy could wallop the ball. The professor was nimble but uncoordinated. Dylan hated team sports. Adam could run, but that was about it.

Our opponents were all strapping young men, eighteen to twenty-six years old. Their size made us look like pygmies. When I shook hands with several players, I nearly had my hand crushed.

Erling stationed us deep in left and right field since he expected our opponents to slug the ball a long way. And they did. He had a relay team to bring the long balls back to the infield. If we failed to catch the bombs, he had players stationed every twenty feet to relay the ball and prevent them from getting to third base. Erling pitched and knew how to spin and jig the ball so the big brutes couldn't get a smooth swing at the ball.

They hit enough home runs to keep them comfortably in the lead most of the game. I was relieved. By the seventh inning, I suggested that we concede the game. Erling wasn't willing to give up. He'd wagered a keg of beer on the game. By the eighth inning, we were only down three runs—13 to 10. Betty, Adam, and Grace were quick and stole bases any time they got a hit. Erling had the shorter girl, Betty, come to bat. Their pitcher walked her. He was used to pitching to taller players. He told her, "Don't go for a home run. Get on base."

When I came up to bat, the other team had their players deep in the outfield. I had hit a home run in the third inning. My line drive got me on base now. Stephen followed me. He did the same, and we lobbed one single after another, scoring three runs, putting us in the lead 14 to 13. The next inning, their big hitters knocked balls over the tracks, putting them up by two.

Erling was unfazed. In the bottom of the ninth, he had another plan. He wanted us to load the bases, leaving him the fourth batter up. A good hitter,

Erling had swung from his heels and gotten a home run, a double and a triple on his previous three at bats. Their pitcher, a tall, lanky kid with a powerful arm and graceful athleticism, liked winning as much as Erling. He planned to make short order of our lineup. Manny, another short player, came up to to the plate. Erling instructed her to crouch down as low as she could and get a walk. But Manny, not one to lay off a good pitch, knocked it over the fence. Adam struck out. I hit a line drive for a single. We had a long pop fly which allowed me to get to second base. Stephen singled.

Always one with a flair for the dramatic, Erling took ferocious practice swings like Babe Ruth. The outfielders backed up. On the first pitch, Erling made a mighty swing, catching himself with his hand before he toppled over. On the second pitch, he made another grand swing and came up with air. The infield moved back slightly in case he caught hold of a line drive. On the third swing, just as planned, I took off as soon as the pitcher threw his pitch. Erling bunted the ball, dribbling down the first base line. The pitcher sprinted after the ball, hoping to make a quick flick for the final out. Erling ran right by the ball. The pitcher had to slow down to avoid him. When the pitcher reached to snatch the ball, Erling screamed "Ahhhhhhh." It startled the pitcher who looked up to see what was the matter. He missed the ball. Erling darted toward first base, his arms out at his sides. The pitcher threw by Erling's outstretched arms and over the head of the first baseman. Meanwhile, Stephen and I crossed the plate with my hands over my head in a victory salute.

The pitcher slammed his mitt on the ground and charged at Erling, shouting "You fuckin' asshole, you can't—"

Erling held up his hands and said, "The victors *must* buy the keg."

What might have been a disaster became a celebration. He had already bought a keg and, once we opened it, Erling offered it to the other team. They became our drinking buddies. We played baseball with them at Clearfork Park. Despite Erling's conniving, we never won again. We lost the next game 28 to 10. But the other team bought the keg, so winning didn't matter. By the end of the summer, we drank before, during, and after the games. Teams were mixed and everyone got to play.

The Invitation

On hot afternoons, the boys skinny dipped in the basin below the falls. Local men often joined us to sit, watch, and chat. They joked about the nudity: how we looked like we'd been chased out of a whorehouse. Sometimes they joined us. They'd strip off their shirts but keep their pants on. When they climbed out and sunned on the hillside, their wet pants clung to them like a snake's skin.

Jonathan, Bonnie's oldest son, took a liking to me. He'd met me several times at Bonnie's house on nights I stayed for dinner or slept over. Bonnie worried about him. "He takes too kindly to the drink," she said. "And not enough to work. His wife's the one who makes things work. Afraid he takes after his dad." Bonnie warned me not to get involved with him. "Most the time, he's up to no good."

One afternoon at the stream, he invited me to come with him to a really good whorehouse. "They have real pretty girls there," he said. "None of your old biddies."

"Nope. Although I appreciate the offer," I replied. I learned that anything you did in these parts became common knowledge.

"Hell, I wouldn't say a word. My wife, she don't even know. It'd be between you and me. I promise," he whispered.

His secrets were known to pretty much everyone. Bonnie complained about it to me. His wife, from what I heard, didn't care about his trysts. She hadn't much use for him.

I told him that I would love to do it and let off a little steam but not tonight. I'd made a promise not to jeopardize the folk school. The younger boys went off with Erik—he offered to drive them home. Jonathan told me, "Just you wait here. I'll be back in a spell."

"I need to head—"

"Just a spell, you hear?"

"All right."

I pulled on my jeans and sat by the stream, listening to it lapping over the rocks. The afternoon light glinted off the water. Adam paddled around in the water. He was off in his own world, probably imagining the positive ions radiating into his body.

Jonathan came back with a brown paper bag, a bottle—no doubt moonshine—and his cousin, Barry, who introduced himself. I'd seen Barry before at the bonfires. He was a slim fellow with soft brown hair parted down the middle. He had been married to Jonathan's wife. It didn't last long. There weren't hard feelings; it just didn't work out. Rumors were that he couldn't consummate the marriage.

"Since you don't want to take me up on the chance to meet some real sweet girls, at least join me for home brew," he rejoined. "I'll show you the best way to drink it."

He took a big tomato out of the paper bag, sliced it in half with his pocket knife, and salted it---held it up to me like an offering. With his other hand, he put the bottle to his mouth and swigged it. Immediately afterwards, he chomped into the tomato—in one seamless swift action.

"That's the way to do it," he gasped, twitching his head back and forth.

Barry followed suit. He passed me the sliced tomato and the moonshine, clear as the stream.

At first, I begged off, since I was that apprehensive about making a fool of myself again. Yet Erling had told me to take the night off and do what I wanted to do. He had nothing planned. Most of the other folk school members were hanging around the house playing guitars. He told me to have a good time: I decided that a little drink wouldn't hurt.

I took the sliced tomato, shook salt on it and, as deftly as possible, gobbled the tomato and took a swig from the bottle. It felt my ears pop. My eyes watered. I gasped and coughed.

Jonathan and Barry laughed.

"We make it strong," Jonathan said.

Barry patted me on the back. "There you go," he said. "You got it." I had to admit that the acid of the tomato took the sting from the alcohol. I had several more tomatoes and slugged down several more swigs. Night was teetering on the edge of the mountain. An hour, maybe more, passed.

We decided to go back to the cabin and see if anyone wanted to drive to the top of the mountain where you could see the faint lights of Kentucky. At the cabin, three girls—Maddy, Ingrid, and Alicia—joined us. Adam came along, too. They packed up some hot dogs, potato chips, and soda.

Jonathan took me aside. "Sure you're not interested?"

"I'm sure."

"Well, much as I like picnics, I need to take care of business, if you know what I mean." He grabbed his crotch. He stepped into his truck, hit the accelerator. A cloud of dust roiled across the porch.

Adam, Alicia, and I jumped into Barry's jeep. The others followed us in Maddy's chevy, an old, dented 1965 Impala. At the top, we piled out. I got the Coleman stove lit and put on a pan to fry the hot dogs. Maddy pulled out her guitar. We sat around the stove singing Bob Dylan songs, "Blowing in the Wind," "Mr. Tambourine Man," "Like a Rolling Stone," and "It Ain't Me, Babe." Our off-key voices occasionally blended in harmony. Barry, Adam, the girls, and I foraged some sticks and a dry-up log to start a campfire. Its embers emitted a gentle light: Maddy's large sweet face shone. She went about her business—helping in the kitchen, sitting with the youngest of the children, teaching them crafts—without calling attention to herself. By the fire, she stirred the coals and gazed up at the stars, content with being in the moment. I wished I knew her better.

Alicia, bending over the fire, stuffing in little sticks, had a glow on her face. She asked if I wanted to talk. We strolled to a rock overlooking the ravine that ran along the road.

"What brought you up here?" she asked.

I was frank. "I hated my life: playing golf, going out to get drunk—"

"Like you are now," she jested, sliding her arm inside mine and pulling me close.

"Yeah, like now."

"Sorry, I couldn't resist," she said, leaning over on my shoulder.

I put my hand on her shoulder and pulled her close.

I asked her, "What brought you here?"

"When you explained what we would be doing—working with mountain people, learning about folk traditions, and studying about the American tradition—it seemed like an adventure, something I'd never have a chance to do again. I jumped at it."

"I'm glad you came. You're the one girl I can talk to," I told her.

"Why is that?"

"Oh, I don't know. I just feel awkward with girls," I admitted.

"I thought you did. You spend most of your time with the boys and Stephen, and, when you're all business, Erling."

"Is that weird?"

"No, most guys aren't real comfortable with girls." She looked up at my face and brushed back my hair.

221

I leaned over and kissed her lightly.

"Hey, what are you two lovebirds doing over there?" Barry called out. "You having an affair?"

He came over with a bag of potato chips. "Here, have some before Maddy and Adam eat them all." He dropped the bag in my lap.

I looked over at the campfire where Maddy and Adam were poking at it. Little sparks rose up, wavered in the air, swirled around like fireflies, and went out. Ingrid was standing, her arms folded across her chest, gazing at the fire. With her blond hair flowing over her shoulders and down her back, she seemed to be made of moonglow.

"Beautiful, isn't she?" Alicia said.

"Amazing," I said. "Yet she wears it so naturally. It almost comes as much from inside as outside."

"When you get to know her, and I have these past weeks, you appreciate how unpretentious Swedes are, not caught up in appearances. Or so it seems from being with her. She's quite thoughtful."

"I wish I had more time to get to know her. By the time dinner is over and everyone has settled down, I'm heading up the hill to sleep. I don't get as much time as others to be with you at night in the house," I said.

"Why not make more time?"

"I may."

"Always on guard, huh?"

"You got it."

"A loner, right?"

"Something like that."

"We should be getting back to the fire," Alicia said. Holding hands, we returned.

For the first time that summer, I felt close to a girl in the folk school. She was right that I should spend more time at the cabin, just hanging around. I spent much of my time working: doing errands, going to the store, preparing for classes. I hardly knew Erik, Ellen or Grace at all. I felt like an outsider whenever I arrived. It was as if I'd walked into the middle of a conversation and didn't know what to say. Of course, I had volunteered to sleep in the cabin. Stephen agreed to join me in case someone threatened me again and because he was an introvert and liked being off by himself. I missed the late-night socializing, the sitting on the porch when locals came down, parked their cars, and strummed their guitars.

Taking her advice, after that night on the mountain, for the next week,

I did spend time on the porch, singing along with everyone else. I'd grown fond of one of the regulars at the cabin. He was a local guitarist named Otrel who lived several miles away in another hollow. He loved country music and played a mean guitar. He'd arrive before we ate supper and stay most of the evening. He'd tell stories about bears and raccoons, about the feds chasing moonshiners, and about endless feuds.

A gaunt man with a light spring in his step, he rarely sat still. He invited me to dinner several times. He had five kids—four of them living at home, one off in Vietnam. We'd pick buckets of blackberries on the hill behind his house. His wife made a thick preserve that we put on ice cream. We sat on his porch talking about how he wanted to start up a band and how he would help me with the folk school the next year. He also told me to watch out for J.B. Terry, Squeaky's uncle. J.B. often came to the folk school jam sessions but never said much. He chewed on a toothpick and spit on the ground. He was trouble.

I wasn't thinking about J.B. or anyone else when I was drunk and sitting on a log by the fireside that night. Everyone—Adam, Peggy, Ingrid, and Alicia—seemed mystified by the way the sky, drawn nearer to us on the mountaintop, pressed down on them. Peggy, Ingrid, and Alicia wanted to head back to the folk school. It was nearly ten. But they made no attempt to get up. It was too beautiful. The moon had risen over the mountain and the stars seemed close enough to touch. Maddy, tired of strumming, poked at the fire. Silence settled over us. We sat around the fire watching it crackle and spit up sparks.

Barry turned on a radio. From the mountain top, we could hear Chicago radio stations broadcast a Cubs game: from Lake Michigan, far northwest of us, across Indiana and Kentucky.

Far off, the blackened outlines of mountain ranges extended endlessly across the orange-tinted sky. Barry offered me another drink. I took a sip. Although I hadn't drunk for an hour, the amount I'd drunk before had begun to hit me. It made me feel woozy. I stood up to pee but lost my balance and stumbled against the front hood of the Jeep. Alicia hurried to me.

"You all right?"

"Perhaps too much so," I said.

I held onto the jeep as if it was a tilting ship. She took me by the arm and steered me toward the woods.

Barry called out, "Might be better for me to do that. Let me help you." He swung quickly around the Jeep to where I was standing. He put his arm around me. I slung my arm around his shoulder. We walked to a ledge. I tried to unzip my fly but couldn't find the zipper. I hopped around.

He said, "Mind if I help?"

"No, go right ahead," I replied.

He unhitched the tab and pulled the zipper down.

I fumbled, trying to find my penis.

He asked again, "Need more help?"

"Help yourself," was as much as I could say.

He deftly opened the slit in my jockeys and fished out my penis.

"Steady as you go," he said as I leaned back and let out a long stream, the arch of it disappearing in the dark.

After I finished, he joined me. He found his zipper like a pro, even while holding me up. He peed like a racehorse.

At the campfire, Alicia put her arm around me and kissed me. I hugged her. She hopped in the backseat of Maddy's car. Ingrid slid into the front. The red rear lights of the car snaked down the mountain, dimmer and dimmer, and vanished around a curve.

Barry plied me with several more sips as we listened to the ball game. The Cubs were losing 6-5 in the ninth inning, a long game. I pressed my head into my knees. My head felt as if someone had yanked part of it off. I must have passed out because I awoke to find myself in the jeep.

Adam had wandered off. He was perched on a rock up the side of an incline. I could see his silhouette; he looked like a scarecrow. Adam called out, "Hey, it's time to get back."

Barry called back, "Hold your horses. We've got some serious drinking to do. Moonshine always tastes better when the moon shines overhead. I bet you can touch it."

I must have passed out again because I woke up with Barry slapping me gently on the face. "Come on, don't be a spoilsport," he said. He offered me a tomato. I chomped into it. The juice dribbled down my chin. Barry and I sat in the jeep. We shared a tomato and a swig.

The stars pressed down from the sky closely. I started counting the stars in one corner of the sky and got to 358 when Adam interrupted me.

"Jason, you're drunk and need to get off this mountain now." He used the same condescending tone of voice as my father.

"Why don't you loosen up, Adam? Cool your heels. We've got some serious..." I raised the bottle in the air. "Have a drink."

"I don't drink." he glowered at me.

I took another swig and offered the bottle to him again.

"I said I don't drink."

"Oh, I forgot."

Adam whipped around and grabbed Barry by his shirt, "Listen to me. You got the assistant director drunk. You better get him back to the school. I don't want to hear any excuses. We need to get off this mountain *now*."

"Yes, sir. We're getting ready to go," Barry said, saluting Adam. "Just get your big mouth in the Jeep, sir, and we'll do as you command."

Adam guided me to the front seat. He got into the back and said, "We better hurry. It's late."

The road, mostly one lane, gripped the side of the mountain like a rope stitched around a tree trunk. On one side, rock wall rose straight up and seemed to stick clear into the clouds; on the other, a ravine, hundreds of feet down, pines and saplings clinging on to it. Barry knew the road well. The cool night air caressed my face.

Barry's jeep was humming along when it jagged, jerked, made a wheezing sound, coughed several more times, and sputtered to a stop. Barry pressed on the accelerator. Nothing.

"What the hell is going on?" Adam called out.

Barry tapped the gas gauge and raised his shoulders. "Plumb out of gas."

"Well, coast down," Adam implored.

"Not a good idea. No lights either."

Adam jumped out of the jeep. "I'll get some help. We can't stay here; some logging truck might hit us."

"Do many come this hour of the night?" I asked.

"Not likely. Some do, ones that want to get ahead of traffic," Barry said. "Don't worry. We'll see 'em coming. Might as well enjoy the pretty night. We can camp out here and get some help at sunrise."

"Are you nuts? I'm not risking my life," Adam said.

With that said, Adam charged down the road, his head bobbing as he jogged. I had little doubt he could negotiate the six or seven miles down the mountain. But it would take some time. Who knows who he could scrape up at this hour of the night.

Barry brought out his bottle and toasted to Adam. "Here's to Mr. Do-No-Wrong!"

An hour passed. Rescuers never showed. We drank the last of the moonshine.

Barry asked, "Mind if I lie down?"

"By no means," I said. "Go ahead."

A long angular man with no fat on his body, he leaned over. He snuggled on the seat, near my thigh, his hands under his head. I patted him on the back and let my hand rest on his hip.

"Make yourself comfortable," I told him. "We are going to be here for a while, I suspect."

I stretched back in the seat and extended my legs. I lifted his head onto my lap and he fell asleep. I stared up at the roof punctured with lighted holes.

He shifted several times. He turned on one side, then another, trying to get comfortable. He finally nestled into a somewhat comfortable position. But it didn't last long. He rubbed his head one way and another.

I felt aroused. I shifted my hips to the side. He tilted his head. His cheek was against my erection. It felt good—his face against my crotch. Here I was with another guy, feeling aroused when hours before I had felt close to Alicia and was behaving like a guy should.

If I had not been so drunk, I would have gotten up and strode down the mountain. I must have passed out again. When I awoke, I felt Barry's head on my lap. He was asleep. But he tilted his head up and then put his mouth right where my erection was sticking up. Ever so slightly he moved his head back and forth. I put my hand on his head. His hand loosened my belt and unzipped my pants. He managed to get my pants partially down. He hooked his lips on my erection. I let myself go and enjoyed his ministrations. He wasted no time and got right into it.

I remembered that Larry, the man who married Barry's wife, said how Barry never consummated his marriage. The suspicion was that Barry was inclined the other way. Barry looked like a normal guy. But then so did I.

"You okay?" he asked after stopping to get air.

I noticed a thin flicker of light darting back and forth in the trees. It was a large vehicle coming toward us.

"Shit. Lights!" I pushed him off me, pulled up my pants and buckled. I shifted upright in my seat to try to see what was coming. It was a logging truck. It was moving fast. The headlights bobbed up and down.

Barry moaned, "Shucks, just when it gets interesting."

I shouted, "Let's get out of here!"

I hopped out of the jeep, stumbled, and fell to my knees. Although dizzy, I managed to stagger up the road. I had to get clear of the jeep. I found a turnout and pressed against the side walls.

A logging truck would obliterate the jeep. I didn't want to be anywhere nearby. I waited for the collision.

Barry was scampering behind me on his hands and feet like a dog.

"Hurry up, it's coming fast!"

Lights barreled toward our jeep. Lights swung around the bend. I put my hands over my ears.

Nothing happened.

A large Ford truck with someone standing on the sideboard came around the curve and stopped. It was Adam. He leapt out and two figures followed him—Bobby and Tommy Lester. Tommy had a gas can in his hand.

"Mission impossible!" Tommy yelled at us. He poured gas into the jeep's tank. Bobby told Barry to get in the back of the Jeep. He hopped in the driver's seat. I sat in the front. He glanced at me.

"You alright?" he asked.

"Fine."

"You don't look fine."

I admitted, "You're right. I'm out of it."

He said, "I can see that."

Bobby drove down the road. Tommy backed the truck up. He came to a turnout that allowed us to pass by the truck. Tommy angled the truck back and forth, turned it to follow us. The four lights crisscrossed the trees. It made me cross-eyed. I closed my eyes. The jeep swayed back and forth and its engine moaned as we came to the bridge over the creek and up the hill to the school.

Bobby held me up, brought me to the cabin, and stretched me out next to Stephen who had opened my sleeping bag. Stephen took off my shoes and pants and stuffed me into the bag. He patted me on the head and said, "Go to sleep." He told Bobby, kneeling beside me to hold up my head while he put the pillow under it, "Careful, put his head down real easy."

Bobby asked, "Is he going to be all right?"

Stephen whispered, "He's not going to feel so good tomorrow. But he'll be fine. Thanks for taking care of him."

I could hear Bobby walk away. Barry asked where I was. He wanted to say goodnight. Tommy told him to get back in the jeep. Arguing occurred. A raised voice. A smack. Then gears grinding. An engine loud, then fading and soon as the sound slipped over the hillside, silence. I stuffed my hands between my legs where Barry had been. I turned on my back, I felt my cheek where Alicia had kissed me. I smiled. She loves me, I thought, and fell asleep.

The Conversation

At times, Erling would join Stephen and me to sleep in the log cabin or out on the ledge. With mostly women in the house and guitar music until eleven at night, he needed quiet time. We read by a kerosene lamp in the log cabin until the mosquitoes, beetles, and moths became so thick in the air that it was impossible to read.

When the morning sun crested the hill, its rays were muted by the firs. Stephen was asleep in a corner, his pillow pulled over his head.

Erling sat up on his elbow, "It's like old times."

I mused, "Yes. This is how it was every morning."

"That was a great year, not as crowded as this year. It had a more leisurely pace. I miss that."

I remembered how, after sunrise, we took turns washing, shaving and brushing our teeth on the side stoop, the pasture down to the road and the lull of the cars, each with its distinct sound along the road. We'd take several hours to wake, write in journals, and drink coffee brewed on our kerosene burner. Not like this year with an infant mewling, guitars playing and people chattering dusk to dawn. Erling and I barely had time to talk with one another.

After Erling and I folded up the sleeping bags, we sat on the porch of the log cabin and looked at the scraggly trees and vines that wove through the hillside. I asked where he was going at the end of the summer. As far as I knew, he had no place to call his home.

He said, "Oh, I'll do a pilgrimage to Sandburg's house in Flat Rock, North Carolina. I'll go to his birthplace too in Galesburg, Illinois. I can visit you if you'd like."

"That would be fabulous," I said.

"That'll work out. From there, I suppose, I'll go back to Iowa and visit my mother. Nothing fixed. Just traveling." He asked what I was going to do when I got back. I told him that I would play some golf and visit with college friends.

A scowl creased his face.

"What?" I asked.

He stood, shifted his weight on the porch, and bit lightly on his cheek.

"I don't see how you can keep on going back there and calling it 'home.' Down here, do you hear them?" Erling said. "The people tell you to come back, to stay here with them because this *is* your home."

"It's lovely that they feel that way about me," I said. "But I've no job. No place to live."

"Bonnie or Peggy would put you up if you stayed. You know that."

"I suppose I do."

"So?" Erling asked.

"Not ready for that. Not yet."

Erling tapped me in his chest. "Not ready, huh? There's something I should like you to explain to me: How can a fellow produced by upper-middle-class America, the capitalist economy, keep going home to a place corrupted by all its false values? I ask you, how are you going to live in that society and still be able to separate from its claims on you?"

"I don't know," I said.

"I can tell you how: You've never actually confronted their false ideals and tastes, and by not doing so you avoid having to deny that world. I should think the very idea of playing golf would be abhorrent to you now. It's a game for the moneyed elite, a fat cat's game. They play it on the backs of the poor."

I knew that he didn't understand how complex golf was, because he'd never played it.

"I don't have to explain why I like golf. It's simple: I'm good at it. I enjoy the challenge. It's a demanding game. I work hard to play it well."

"If you were good at killing people at war, does that mean you should keep killing them when you leave the Army?"

I stood up. "That's *not* fair. We're not talking about murder here. You don't get it. When I play golf, I can do this solitary thing—hitting shots, seeing how many balls I can land close to the pin. For a while, I am in a world of my own. I can leave behind expectations of me—acting nice and looking nice. I'm just a kid with a club perfecting a move."

He laughed. "The quest for perfection is one of the last vestiges of religion. Since we've given up the idea that we are flawed sinners and replaced it with some mawkish idea that all we need to do to be saved is strive for perfection, we can pretend religion doesn't matter. Look at yourself. Look how you dress. Look at the high-end car you drive, a Volvo no less. You emulated your elders, falling lock-step into line, conforming to some belief that doing something well absolves you of responsibility to those who suffer while you play," he told me. He tipped his head, peered over the edge of his glasses, and raised his eyebrows. "Right?"

What was I supposed to say? He had a point. I'd seen how the ground crew at the club lived in near poverty. Many of them were alcoholics, perhaps their only consolation.

"I'm not giving up a game I love. Not now. Playing it doesn't make me into some monster. I'm getting pleasure, just as you do going on your pilgrimages. And, besides, when you play baseball, you love it. Admit it. And you're good at it. What's the difference?" He tried to interrupt me, but I went on. "For me, golf has kept me sane. I go into an altered state, a place of my own, where I can put aside the world. And that is not a bad thing," I said.

He stood up, shook his head, picked up a stick, and broke it, tossing half of it to the side. "To my ears it sounds as if you use this private spot for yourself removed from family, occupation, and friends as a form of escape," he said. "We all need that, I agree. That's why I come up here some nights. And, you're right, baseball does that for me. It's fine to indulge in occasional self-aggrandizing activities in the search for perfection. But where does it lead you?"

He turned back to me and drew a circle in the clay and tapped it.

"Here's Jason Follett, the lawyer, member of Glen Brook Country Club, a member of the establishment with a charming wife and obedient children. His son is a star halfback on this fall's Oak Lawn High School eleven. Oh, he'll have a life apart where he writes poetry. He prides himself in a game he plays well. While he hits shots, he removes himself from the world. That'll work if you just want to be an aesthetic writer, making pretty verses, but not if you want to write about larger moral issues."

He walked back to his sleeping bag, picked it up, and shrugged his shoulders. "We need to get back to the school. I need to prepare for our discussion of Eugene Debs. You might find it interesting," he said.

I put my sleeping bag back in the log cabin. "I'll be there," I said, and added, "And I hear you. It's just that you're asking me to change some things that are dear to me."

He turned and nodded. "I know. That's my job," he offered, smiling out of one side of his mouth. "I'm a gadfly in the ointment of complacency."

He strode off and I woke Stephen who was still sleeping, his hair tousled in knots from tossing and turning.

Materialist

During the discussion on Debs and the labor movement, Dylan sat next to me. It was unusual. He often parked himself across the room. He asked how I'd been sleeping up on the hill. I told him that it was fine unless it rained. When we had a break for coffee, he asked if he could borrow my car; Erling wanted him to run into Jellico to pick up some supplies.

"I do that," I said. "That's my job."

"Well, I also need to meet a friend who's coming into town," Dylan said.

"Sorry, it's not a rent-a-car."

"So the rich boy won't let anyone play with his toys," Dylan snarled.

"Right," I said. "You got it."

"Listen, I'm sorry. I didn't mean that. I just would really like to see her. We're close, if you know what I mean, and she—"

"I'll think about it," I said.

Later, Erling asked if he could talk with me. We went out on the porch.

"I heard you're not letting Dylan use your car," he said.

"Not really. I just have to think. It's new. I don't know what kind of driver he is. And—"

Erling took hold of my arm forcefully. "Look," he said. "Remember what we were talking about this morning? It's time you let go. He needs your car. It's no big deal. Besides, all you've done this summer is ignore him. Why don't you give him a break?"

I pried his fingers off my arm. "I'll think about it."

At lunch, I asked Dylan if he'd ever driven a stick shift. He said, "No problem."

"That's not what I asked," I said, staring at him.

His eyes shifted to the right. "Yeah, a number of times."

When he came back later that day, he parked the car and tossed me the keys.

"Thanks," he said and strutted into the front door.

From the porch, I noted a mark on the back panel of the car. I inspected it. Dylan—or someone—had dented the car. A foot-long crease ran along the panel an inch deep. I flew across the yard and into the house.

"What the hell did *you* do to my car!" I yelled at Dylan. He was helping himself to a cup of coffee.

He laughed. "Took a curve a little too fast. That car has a lot of pep."

"Is that all you have to say?"

"Yeah, what's the big deal? It's only a scrape. I didn't wreck the car."

Before I knew it, I had him by the collar. "You little bastard," I shouted. "You will pay for it. Every cent."

He shoved my hand away from him. "Hey, cool it, man. I'm not paying a dime. You let me use it. I did—"

I pointed my finger at him. "You think you don't have any obligation to pay?"

He laughed again. "I'm a fuckin' student, man. I can barely afford to pay for my tuition. I'm not some rich dude like you—"

"Rich dude?"

"Right, Erling says you come from money."

"He does?" I said. "That's interesting."

Erling heard the fracas and came into the room. "What's going on?"

Dylan stepped by Erling and said, "He's all fuckin' uptight because his pretty car has a dent."

"A dent you caused," I said.

Erling looked at me and then at Dylan. "So what's the problem?"

In a whiny voice, Dylan said, "He wants me to pay for it!"

"You're damn right," I said.

Erling put his hands on his hips. "Let me see it."

We walked outside and I pointed to the dent. Erling groaned. "Jason, that's nothing. Hey, look at Mabel! She's got so many dents and bruises she looks as if she'd been in a roller derby."

"What are you saying?" I asked.

"I'm saying you need to let go of your materialism. It's no big deal."

"It's not a big deal that he—" I pointed to Dylan who stood on the porch smirking. "That he isn't responsible?"

"He doesn't have the money—"

"Money, is it?" I said, barely able to control my temper. "It's okay to damage someone's car if he has the money. Isn't that, Erling, a bit of a contradiction? What if *I* didn't have the money and *he* did? Would he have to pay?"

Erling winced and said in a low voice, "But you do. And probably insurance, too."

"You're right, I do and it's okay for you use me to raise money for the program. Is that right?" My fists were clenched.

"Yes. But that's—"

"Yeah. That's the point, when it's convenient to you and Dylan. You..." I started to say something else but stopped. I opened the car door and hopped in. There were two cigarette butts in the ashtray. Dylan didn't even ask if he could smoke. He knew I didn't smoke.

I headed out of Cross Creek on the main road, going no place in particular. The word "materialism" throbbed in my head. Was I materialistic? I was. But what was so bad about that? I respected people's property. It seemed to me that Dylan was no better than a coal company: he took my property, damaged it, and blamed me for being upset.

When I got to Jellico, I pulled into a motel, paid for one night, and pulled out my journal. I wrote for hours. Inside me was a sea of doubts. I wanted badly to break with my family, to be someone different. But I had no idea who that was. Perhaps I was too materialistic. I valued the things I owned—the car, the record player, my books, golf clubs, clothes, and shoes. Maybe I was too caught up in my appearance, how I presented myself. But I did care about others and respected what they had, even if it wasn't the same quality as what I had.

I knew I had to go back to the folk school. I had to let go of my rage. I wanted to punch that snotty, smug face of Dylan's. I wanted to tell Erling off. Let him know that he was dead wrong. But I wasn't so sure he wasn't right. I walked to a local diner. A stocky waitress with a large round face and a soft Southern drawl asked me, "What'll it be, hon?"

"Not sure," I said.

"You look like you need some good loving," she said.

"You're right about that," I said.

"Well, I can't offer you that. But I can get you some good food."

"That'll have to do," I said.

"We have a great burger here with everything on it—tomatoes, onion, cheese. And our fries—I swear they are the best in the state," she said. "How about it, hon?"

"You're persuasive," I said.

"What's that?"

"The burger it is, and fries, and whatever's on tap."

In the cool yellow light of the diner, I listened to customers chatting and watched the cook work behind a window, sweating and flipping burgers. My rage was doing nobody any good. I sipped the beer, and another, put my fingers around the giant burger and lolled away an hour. The waitress kept coming back. "How's it, hon?"

I told her "Great," and it was.

"You look a mite better," she said. "That's what our burgers and fries do to ya!"

By the time I got back to the motel, my rage had cooled to a simmering exasperation. I turned on the TV. All the excitement was about astronauts walking on the moon. No one mentioned Kent State. I'd even forgotten about it. I changed the channel. It was a Cary Grant movie. He dodged an airplane. In most of the movie he seemed to be on the run, fleeing from some guys trying to kill him, much like I was fleeing from mixed feelings that were tearing me apart.

The next day I drove back to Cross Creek to participate in the day programs. Kids ran up to me, crying out, "Where were you?"

I said, "I don't know."

I didn't want to tell them it was a strange place called rage. I joined them and passed the football, and got involved in what really mattered to me.

Midweek, after dinner, when we all sat on the folk school porch to play folk songs, Erling sat by me.

He said, "Glad you're back."

I nodded.

"I talked to several other people. They told me what Dylan said. I spoke to Dylan, too. He owes you something, and not just an apology," he said.

"We'll see," I said.

"I need you here. I count on you more than I can say," he said.

"Even though I'm a materialist?"

"Get over it. You got me. I overstated my case," he said, pressing his lips together.

"I suppose," I said. I didn't look at him. Several people had pulled up outside the house. They hopped out of their trucks, guitar and banjo in hand. It was going to be quite a night of music.

Dylan spoke with me at the bonfire. He talked to his parents. They might be able to pay for some of the repairs. "They don't have much money," he said.

I kept my mouth shut.

"So you expect me to pay?" he said. He kicked something on the ground.

I didn't say a word.

"Fuck it," he said. "Just tell me what it is."

"Give me your phone and address," I said. "I'll let you know."

We shook hands, but I had no use for him. I'd become bitter and didn't know how to get beyond my resentment.

More Bad News

At our campfires, Otrel and his band member, Bud Terry called the folk dances. Bud would stand on a log and call the steps; his deep, gravelly voice carried well into the mountains around us. Then he'd join Otrel, and they'd do a medley. Not much of a looker, Otrel was unshaven and swarthy, but had uncommon charisma. People whooped and joined in whatever he played. I admired him. He managed to keep his house on the mountain top together by doing odd jobs, by driving trucks across the cross-country and back, and by performing whenever he could. Give him his banjo or guitar and he was a happy man. His thumbs, callused and dry, were split from fingering and strumming the strings.

Every evening, Otrel joined Maddy's songfest on the porch of the folk school. With new cowboy boots and a western shirt with gold buttons, he was pleased with himself. His band had done five shows and brought in some good money. He spoke to me about coming to Nashville and getting a record deal. He was talented and able to pick, strum, and play practically any song. His high pitched nasal voice made every song a lament.

After Dylan dented my car, Otrel sensed something was up with me. He joked with me. "Come on, sourpuss," he'd say. "Sing a few bars."

He asked me to come over to his house. He had something he needed to discuss. His house was on a ridge with a huge field in back that rose up the mountain. Betsy, his wife, poured her blackberry preserves over bowls of ice cream. Otrel and I stood in the middle of the front room with the TV in the corner. A heavy rain trampled the roof. The alabaster sky melded with the dusty earth. The grass was stiff and desiccated. We needed rain. When the rain stopped, his boys scrambled up an apple tree and picked ripe apples.

Otrel said, "Erling is worried about you."

"I imagine he is," I said, not letting on about my resentments.

"He needs you. We need you. You're too important to drop out now," he said.

"Oh, Otrel, it's no big deal. Doesn't someone have a right to be upset?"

"About your car?"

"How'd you know?"

"Everybody's talking."

"I just—"

Otrel interrupted me. "You know what I'd have done, had it been me? I'd have punched the squirt in the nose."

I laughed. "I thought about it."

"You're too nice, that's your problem. You take things to heart."

"I suppose I do."

"Well, piss on 'em."

We sat on the front steps. The rain had let up. He mentioned Bud Terry, the fiddler who always play at the campfires, and reminisced about the fun times they'd had playing at the Friday night bonfires and at gigs around the state.

"You talk about him as if he were dead," I said.

"He is."

"What?"

"He died Wednesday," Otrel said.

"But he just played last Friday!" I said.

"You know he was pretty sick," Otrel said.

"I knew he had the shakes."

"I told Betsy he'd not make it this time. His eyes, they were set back in their sockets. You notice?" Otrel asked.

"Can't say I did."

"They were, believe me. He shook sometimes like a headless chicken," Otrel continued. "He lost weight. Couldn't eat. He went to the hospital Monday. What killed him was his stomach. It burst, folks say, from moonshine. Drank pretty near two quarts a day."

"I liked him. He let me shoot his pistol once. He made our bonfires something special." I tossed a pebble into a puddle. "Shit."

"He liked doing it. But folks called him a drunk. No one paid him much mind. He never hurt no one. He wasn't like his relations. That J.B. Terry is always out to get something. Yet Bud never hurt no one. An alcoholic, I suppose. But he was a good man too. Never an angry word from him. And he played a mean fiddle. I'll miss him. Won't you?"

I nodded. "Yes." I'd never seen him obviously drunk. But I'd probably never seen him sober. He could talk, look you in the eye, and walk as steadily as a marine. His death wasn't unusual. Many men had lost their jobs, had little to do but make moonshine, and had filled their lives with drink. They died quietly and young.

Before I left, Otrel shook my hand and said, "Now you and Erling need to mend your fences, hear me?"

I tried to pull my hand away. He held on. "Hear me?"

I smiled. "Okay. Okay."

"I weren't supposed to tell you," he said and pursed out his lips.

"Tell me what?"

"Erling wants to move on."

"What!?"

"That's what he told me," he said. "So now you know why it's important that—"

"Christ! Why didn't he tell *me*?"

"You haven't been yourself lately, now have you?"

"Not exactly."

He smiled at me. I smiled back.

"There, my job's done." He patted me on the back and handed me the quart of blackberry preserves. "Get back there. See that you talk with Mr. Duus!"

I intended to do just that. I was irate. How come he didn't tell me about his plan? Had he decided to have some else run the school? It better not be Dylan. Why was he quitting? We'd just gotten started.

I drove off the mountain, the preserves on my car seat. I knew that I had to get over my anger and wondered what I'd do if Erling left. It would be a big change. If he wanted me to take over, I'd have to do all the recruiting. By next summer, I'd be done with Divinity School. I'd need a salary. The slow back and forth—taking a curve to the right, then to the left—made me pay attention to each turn. In a way, it released tension in me. I knew that nothing is as straightforward as it seems. I had to take the bad with the good and move on.

Erling and I took the next day off and drove up to Cumberland Falls State Park. We watched the water cascade over the rock ledge and fall to the pool below. I told him what Otrel had told me.

"Sorry you got it indirectly," he said. "But let me say that if the folk school is to continue, you're the man to keep it going."

"You want out?"

"I need to move on. Don't get me wrong. I think we've had a great two years. But I need to see if I can make it work somewhere else. I believe you'd be better off going it alone," he said.

"I don't think I'm ready."

"Don't underestimate yourself. You've got what it takes. You've learned a lot in the last two years. Besides, I think you can find the funds better than I can."

"Materialistic, huh?"

"It has its merits."

I told him I would do my best.

He said, "We need to make some tough decisions about this year's program. We're nearly out of cash." With a shortage of funds due to the fire and the cost of renting the house, we needed to close the folk school in mid-August. I wanted to stay longer, as did others, but we couldn't afford to feed everyone. We decided to end it with a big campfire and cookout the next Friday. The day after the cookout the students and staff would pack up and head home. Erling and I would stay to plan for the following year.

The folk school staff cooked all day: pies, macaroni, beans, corn from our garden, hamburgers and hotdogs. As carloads of kids and their parents arrived, we had a wonderful spread for them. Erling rounded us up for a last softball game. The kids, as usual, helped us start the fire under Squeaky's supervision: pour on gasoline and let it explode. After dark, the bonfire blazed in the sky. Otrel played his guitar. We sang, danced, and roasted marshmallows. But a sadness hung over us because we knew that, come morning, we'd all pack up and go our separate ways.

Erling was right. People liked me, and I had a home in the mountains. I knew that I had to work with the folk school board. Marie Cirillo gave me an idea for funding. The folk school board could apply to the feds for a daycare grant. It would provide childcare year-round and fund a position for me. I could direct the Cross Creek Daycare Program and also, in the summer, lead my own folk school.

On the last day, I drove around the hollow to say goodbye to everyone. I also helped clean up the house for the new tenants who would arrive a week after we left. We stored supplies in a shed at Peggy's house, including the kitchen supplies.

The Visitor

I spent the remainder of the summer at my parents' house. I worked in the yard, dividing my mom's iris beds, and played golf. Erling promised to come by and spend a few days before I went back to Vanderbilt.

Returning home was a welcome relief. I could shower every day, go to the pool to swim, play golf, and read. My dad worked most days. My mother was busy with projects or her bridge club. I often had the house to myself. I got an estimate to repair the car and sent a bill to Dylan. A check arrived a week later. I'd nearly forgotten that Erling planned to visit until I came home one day and Mabel was parked beside the garage. Erling was stretched out under a maple, reading. My mother and I were just getting back from the grocery store.

"Who's that?" my mother asked.

"That's my friend Erling," I told her. "The one who started the folk school." He was wearing an old, wrinkled white shirt, open at the neck, rolled up at the sleeves and old wrinkled white slacks. She was not impressed.

After I pulled into our garage, I raced over to him. He roused himself from his spot under the tree, closed his book, and greeted me with an extended hand.

"Good to see you," he said and added, motioning to the yard with the long blacktop driveway. "It's what I expected."

"What do you mean?" I asked.

"Bourgeoisie," he said dryly. He curled up his mouth in a grimace.

I ignored him and took him by the arm. "Let me introduce you to Mom."

My mother, ever gracious, asked him to come in. She hoped he could stay for dinner. We were going to the club. She was sure that I would like to show it to him. I helped mom put away the groceries. She told us to get a drink and go downstairs to relax. I took Erling to the game room where we had a billiard table. Erling loved to play pool. We played several games, fiercely fought. When my father came home, dressed in his blue suit, he came down to meet Erling. They eyed each other like gladiators standing side by side in a coliseum. Each noted the relative size and strength of his opponent. They chatted for a few minutes. My father peered at Erling's attire and said, "We're going to the club, Mr. Duus, and, well, we need to dress up. I would hope...."

I interrupted him, "I know, Dad, we need to dress up."

"Good. Coat and tie."

"Right," I said.

My dad went upstairs to have a martini. When he was a young executive and went to the Mayo Clinic for a check-up, he was told by the doctors to have a martini every day when he came home from work.

I explained how it worked to Erling, who smiled. We played another game of pool. Much to his pleasure, he won. Before we went to the club, I had Erling bring his suitcase, a wicker contraption tied together with rope, to my room. I told him that we really *had* to wear a coat and tie. Dumbfounded, he looked at me.

"Coat and tie?"

"Yes."

"What is this club?"

I explained that it was the Glen Brook Country Club. It had a full dining room, swimming pool, tennis courts, and eighteen-hole golf course.

"Oh," he said. "'How the other half lives.'"

Erling pulled out a wrinkled white jacket, one like Bogart wore in "Casablanca" except that it was yellowed and frayed. I asked if he had better pants and he did, wrinkled but cleaner. He wore tennis shoes and no socks. I gave him a tie but he said that he never wore them. They caused him to choke.

We came downstairs to greet my parents who had finished two martinis, already. I wore a blue blazer, red tie, brown slacks, and dress shoes. They stared aghast at Erling as if contemplating where to leave him off on the side of the road.

When we pulled up to the front entrance of the club, before my dad hopped out of the car, a senior valet opened my dad's door and two valets my age opened the doors for my mother and for us. My dad left the keys in the car and we headed inside. Erling whispered to me, "Aren't you allowed to open your own doors?"

I explained, "It's a service."

In the clubhouse, my parents passed right by the Green Room and made a beeline for the dining room. My father approached the maître d' who smiled and greeted us, "Good evening, Mr. Follett. May I help you?" My father, pulled him closer and whispered, pointing to a corner table. The maître d' said, "Certainly, Mr. Follett. Come this way." We headed to the far corner where we'd never eaten before; my father generally enjoyed eating by the bay windows where he could watch any late golfers coming up to the eighteen hole.

Over dinner, we attempted polite conversation, talking about golf, how I'd finished second in the club championship; how lovely the summer had been; and how happy they were that I'd done some good work with the people in

Appalachia. To engage Erling, my parents asked him what his plans were for the rest of the summer. It was a mistake. He explained how he'd wander. He planned to see Eugene Debs' home. He asked if they knew who he was. My father said that he'd certainly heard of him. Over salad and drinks, Erling explained how he was a labor organizer and socialist.

My father said, "Mr. Duus, if I recollect, I voted in those elections when he was a candidate. I can't say I thought much of his views."

"You didn't? May I ask—"

My dad shot me a dagger-like glance that I knew meant "change the topic." I did. We discussed the folk school, how well it had gone, how we had made do despite the fire. By the end of supper, I could tell that my parents had had enough of Erling. He seemed quite oblivious that the poor, social class, and the inequities in society were not my parents' favorite topics.

After dessert, my parents suggested that I show Erling the clubhouse and golf course. They excused themselves to talk with some friends. I showed Erling the Oak Room, the exclusive room for men, with its wood paneled walls, ceiling-high mirrors, and wall-length mahogany bar. It had every liquor imaginable on glass shelves. There was a painting of the eighteenth green over the bar. We ordered two more beers and Erling surveyed the scene, the men at the tables drinking and playing cards, the large bay windows with the putting green and practice range beyond it. I took him into the men's locker room through two swinging doors. For half a block, on either side of the room, there were lockers, many with polished golf shoes in front of them.

Samuel, one of the attendants, greeted me. "Good evening, Mr. Follett, how are you?"

I greeted him and turned to Erling, "Sam, this is my friend Erling" and they shook hands.

"Can I do anything for you, sir?" he asked.

"No, I'm fine, just showing my friend around," I reassured him.

Erling sipped his beer and gestured to the long row of lockers and the white-tiled bathroom, "So this is where Mr. Follett calls home."

"Well, yes, you're right. I do feel at home here. I've spent more time here than at home," I admitted.

"I suspect you would. Why, people treat you as if you were important. That must be gratifying," he said, giving a sideward glance at me.

"Never thought much about it."

"No, I suspect you wouldn't," he said. He noted the wood paneling; the gold-plated faucets in the bathroom, cloth hand towels, hand lotion, a glass jar with combs in it, and a bottle of aftershave. Every need was anticipated, every amenity there for the asking. He looked at a pair of shoes in front of the lockers.

"Do these attendants shine your shoes?" he asked.

"Of course. Why do you ask?"

He stared at me. "Why don't you ask?"

"I don't get what you mean," I admitted. I looked around the room I'd been in hundreds of times since I was a little boy. My father would bring me in to go to the bathroom countless times. I changed clothes here, took a shower after playing a round, and got dressed up to eat in the dining room. Sure, I knew that it was a privilege, but I also had long-standing attachments here.

"This whole place stinks of money, of privilege and of pampering," he said. "It's the conspicuous consumption, the inflated materialism, that leaves people who you and I know, those people in Cross Creek, with nothing and people like your father and like you with everything you want just for the asking."

"That's not fair," I retorted. "My father didn't cause their poverty. You know as well as I do it was those mining companies, some of them British firms."

"But he's a part of the system, the larger system of greed that makes it possible for those companies, and ones like the one your father works for, to use the workers, to wring sweat and blood from them at the lowest wage. Then they reap the profits and build these palaces to their enormous egos," he said, swirling around, looking at the stained-glass windows, filtering in red and blue light. I didn't know what to say. I knew that on one level I agreed with him and resented how many members of the club acted as if they were better than everyone else. But that wasn't how my family behaved.

He spoke in a hushed tone. "Oh, I'm not blaming you, Jason. Not for this. This *is* amazing. I've never been in a place like this before. Yes, it would be nice to come in here and have an attendant say, 'Is there anything I could do for you, Mr. Duus?' calling me by my last name, while I call him, a man older than I am, by his first. But if I did accept it, and didn't question it, and went on living in this illusory world, I'd be fooling myself and betraying my own beliefs."

"Well, you don't have to because you're not a member here," I said. "We need to go." I felt disappointed that he didn't like the club. I didn't want to feel defensive about the club. Despite my own misgivings about my background, I felt proud that I belonged, that people, yes, even attendants, recognized me, knew I was a good golfer, and that I was my father's son.

We walked out of the locker room and the bartender called out to me. "Oh, Mr. Follett. Your father was looking for you. He wants to go."

I hurried into the lobby where my parents were chatting with the Johnsons, who eyed Erling and me, then turned back to finish their conversation with my parents.

Without bothering to acknowledge Erling, Mrs. Johnson said, "Nice to see you Jason." She smiled weakly, took her husband's arm, and walked out to their car.

My dad went out to hand his ticket to the valet who ran off and retrieved the car. My father had a martini glass in his hand. He obviously had added another drink to an evening that, I suspected, he wanted to forget ever happened.

On the ride home, my father asked whether Erling enjoyed the meal and what he thought of the club. Erling said that the meal was fine and the club was quite impressive. My dad nodded his head, pleased. Although I did not like to admit it, I felt as if I'd brought a rube to my high school prom and felt embarrassed.

I left Erling in the basement to play billiards with my father while I changed. As I walked down the stairs from my room, I could hear Erling berating the business mentality, how corporations cared little for individuals, and how they were solely driven by the quest for profit. By the time I arrived in the basement, my father was hunched over the table, cued up behind the white ball. He hadn't responded to Erling's diatribe. Erling leaned against the paneled wall, his arms folded and his face screwed up, looking intensely at my father, waiting for a reply. My father hit one of his classic spin shots that sent two balls in the pocket, leaving him only one more to close the game. He stood and studied the table and spoke to Erling without looking at him.

"You know, Erling," he said. "Who was it you called a capitalist? Did you say, 'the privileged class?' Let me say that I had to come up like anyone else. I worked as a clerk. Oh, I had my fun. I spent more hours than I care to admit in a pool hall and while away my time. But I worked for next to nothing for years. Twenty dollars a week. Couldn't even afford a car."

Erling said, "I'm sure you did, Howard. That wasn't my point. What I was saying is that the economic system, as it is set up, creates a sub-class who do all the heavy lifting so that an elite class can enjoy it."

"Elite class, you say," my father said, mulling over the term.

I knew that my father didn't like anyone calling him "Howard" if they were younger. Earlier this summer, another friend of mine, a junior member, had played golf with my dad and me, and called out, "Hey, Howard, nice shot."

My father glared at him and said, "My name is 'Mr. Follett' to you."

My friend, startled by his steely tone, said, "Yes, sir," and never called him Howard again.

My father glanced at me. He settled into his next shot and smacked it into the pocket. He took his stick and handed it to me, "Your turn."

Without looking back at Erling, he said, "Nice to have met you, Mr. Duus." He headed up the stairs.

Erling had a puzzled smile on his face. "Well, your father plays a tough game of pool," he said.

"Did you win any?" I asked.

"I skunked him the first game," he said, pleased with himself. "But then he got down to business. Based on our conversation, I think he'd just as soon cut my throat. I must hand it to him, he showed me a thing or two."

I wanted to find out what Erling had said because I knew my father would certainly tell me his side of the story.

Erling said, "We discussed inequities of the economic system. He made some points, good ones, but ones that confirmed his own views and also the narrow-mindedness of corporate leaders who only see the bottom line—profit." He shook his head and hung his pool stick on a hook on the wall.

"What's wrong?" I asked.

"To be frank," he said, "I'm shocked to see how much you feel at home here. I don't think that you are being altogether honest with yourself. The question isn't whether or not you'll love and seek to understand your parents, but whether or not you will declare your independence."

"I have," I protested. "I have made a commitment to work in Cross Creek. I haven't taken a job here, as I could, in the business world like my brother."

I was agitated and didn't want to have my parents hear me argue with Erling. "Let's go out for a beer," I said.

We climbed the steps, said goodbye to my parents who were sitting and talking intently, and drove to a local bar. It was a quiet spot with booths and with few people in it. We sat down and continued our conversation. I told him that I had broken with my parents, not having my hair as short as they wanted, not dressing exactly as they wanted, and not doing as they wanted by being for two summers at the folk school.

"Yes, yes, you have taken some measured steps; but they are half measures. What shocked me was how easy it is for you to blend into their world, how thoughtlessly you expect others to wait on you, to call you by your last name. In my mind, you haven't even come close to doing any real separation. You would rather go through hell than deny them. Yet is it not clear, that you like all men, must do so—must separate. With each year that passes, you are rapidly coming to an age beyond which it cannot be done."

"What do you want me to do, tell them off?" I shot back. I looked at my clenched fist. It surprised me. He glanced at it, too.

"Have another beer. Calm down. Let me explain. Just hear me out, okay? What I experienced in you is a near paralysis of will around your parents, and you might see that as just being an obedient and respectful son. But it seems much more than that. Of course, I know that you maintain an important measure of individualism." He took a sip of his beer. "Do you want to order some potato skins? Do they serve them here?"

"Sure."

He called the waitress over and asked for one order.

"I dip them in ketchup. Left over from my childhood. Now where was I?"

"Individualism."

"Right. I think that's good: you're your own individual. I can see that, especially compared to your older brother, who has resigned himself altogether to the expectations and values of your parents. But here is the thing: I found in things your parents said to me a singular lack of respect for you. I could see little resemblance between the Jason I know and their own view of Jason. It's not only that they don't understand you, but that they are unable or unwilling—I am not sure which—to grant you a world apart from theirs. Do you hear what I'm saying?"

"Yes," I said. "Sort of."

"Here's how I see it: they judge you by your ability or inability to accept and to be at ease with their world. And thus—this is hard to say—your mother sighs tolerantly, and says, "Oh, Jason has so many things to learn," and your father self-righteously upbraids you for language you use at the dinner table. That they can do this so confidently indicates that you have not made a break with them. They are unaware of any rebellion"

"What am I supposed to do? Tell them to get fucked? I'm not going to do that."

I glanced over at the counter behind the bar. Our potato skins were sitting there. I tried to catch the waitress's eye. My fist clenched again. "They've paid for my schooling," I said. "I *do* have some obligations to them. And that they don't understand who I am, yes, it frustrates me. But I don't know that there is anything I can do about it. They see the world through their lenses and only their lenses. I do too. So, quite frankly, I don't know what more I need to do to break with them."

The waitress brought the potato skins with dipping sauce, but Erling asked for ketchup.

Erling followed up my question, "I broke from my father, and, yes it was difficult and painful on both our sides, as I imagine yours will be, but now I'm treated with respect, and instead of his world imposing on my world, my world imposes itself on my father. He has come to know who I am. I was about your age when this finally happened."

I drank some beer, cooling my mouth after eating several more potato skins.

"I don't know how I would start. I just don't...."

He interrupted me. "Jason, it's not just what you say. It's about what you want them to say about you. You do know, don't you, what you want? Tell them."

"I'm not sure I know."

"That's important to know, because the character of this independence is that it can't take place simply inwardly. It demands outward manifestations. The power of the father over his son, particularly a father like yours who is so successful and aware of his success, must be outwardly and openly challenged or it remains intact. There's no way that you can spare him or yourself. "

I leaned on the table and looked at him. "You make it sound inevitable. I'm not sure it is. At least not for me. My parents have their reality. I have mine. How is it that I'm going to change their life? It's so all encompassing. You don't know. They are literally possessed by its demands: going to this party, that party, this meeting, that meeting, traveling to Portugal and Hong Kong, caught up with all the demands of their lives. Even if I tried to make an outward break, they probably wouldn't notice. And, well, I'm still beholden to them. I won't have a real job until we get that grant for the daycare."

Erling dipped a potato skin in the ketchup. "You should try this," he said. "Nothing better."

I poured ketchup on my plate and tried one. I preferred mayonnaise and went back to dipping them in it.

"If that's how you see it, you seem to be resigned to living as you do. But know that it is a choice whether you have a job or not. Not making the outward break, of course, you are forced inward to a psychological thing and an inner rebellion that plays itself out in your soul. Then it's you who suffers and everyone else only sees the public mask you offer and assumes you are fine, which is what you are doing now. You can maintain an inner life that is your own. But there is also an outer life, and it has a way of getting after the inner life. Sure, you can be like the poet Wallace Stevens, whom you admire, and busy yourself, as he did with the outward guise of success, being a well-paid corporate lawyer for an insurance company. To most of his peers he was unknown as a poet. This was no oddity because they couldn't care less about art. He lived a compartmentalized life. While being a poet living the aesthetic life, he lived in another reality, which was unrelated and meaningless to his artistic life. He gave over his outer life

246

to a worthless preoccupation. He dabbled in poetry on the way to work, and at home. Because of his enormous genius as a poet, he managed that split life rather well, and successfully. You could follow his example, but I'm not sure you have his genius. Or you can move toward a compelling view of reality that calls forth your whole life and effort."

"I like his work," I said. "It's amazing that he could live in those two worlds. But I agree. I'm not sure I could do it." I thought about my dual sexual life, feeling one way at one moment and entirely different at another moment. I added, "It's nice to know that it's possible to be possessed by one reality and still live in another."

Erling held up a potato skin and pointed it at me.

"I cannot believe that you really mean it when you speak of reality as something to possess. When you speak of it in terms of this man's reality and that man's reality that would, of course, be convenient; but is it truly what's going on?"

"For me it is," I said, thinking about how I felt about Alicia and how I responded to Barry. His voice rose and tugged me back from my reverie.

"I don't buy your premise about reality. For me reality possesses us to the extent that we live close to it, and that must be the case for you, me, Mr. Stevens, or an Alabama sharecropper, or Mr. Howard Follett, Vice President of some corporation."

I drank my beer, not looking at him. My brain was stuffed with too many thoughts. We ordered another beer and finished the potato skins. He noticed my silence. I felt torn apart. On the one hand, I felt loyalty to my parents. But, on the other hand, I wanted to be free and seen as my own person.

"Listen, Jason." He reached across the table and tapped my hand. "The problem is a serious and demanding one. Very demanding. It's maybe your misfortune that your parents have been so loving and lovable and that your dad is so secure with his authority and his right to determine what's best for you. They've given you enough freedom to grow intellectually, but you have to do the hard part: rebel. Your existential freedom appears to me to be seriously curtailed."

He shrugged his shoulders. I must have looked distressed because he then said, "It's not the end of the world. You don't *have* to do anything. There are plenty of people who would give their eyeteeth to have what you have."

I agreed with him. I told him I wanted to change, but now wasn't the right time. He acknowledged that it would take some courage, especially with such a formidable man as my father.

"And one other thing," he said. "It's not good news."

"What?"

"It's never the right time."

We paid for the food and he asked me where the nearest river was. I directed him to where I used to go ice skating and where, when I was in middle school, a friend and I used to take his boat to an island on the river and pretend we were Native Americans. That ended when I was told to start caddying to earn money. We drove to the park, walked down to the river, and sat on a wooden bench by a bend in the river.

"When I'm not sure what to do with my life," he said, "I go to a river and watch it. Look at it. It moves gently through these trees, finding its way. Oh, the Army Corps of Engineers may try to force some rivers to bend to their will, but, in the end, rivers make their own way. They don't take any prescribed path. They meander. My life is like that. I go where I can find my way. You don't have to live as your parents think you should live."

I looked at the water's surface shimmering with flecks of light. The current eddied along some rocks. The moon skated over the water mid-stream. What Erling had said about my parents was true. Their love had certain demands built into it. I knew I wasn't ready yet, to do as he had done. Maybe his bringing me here was his way of saying that I would, as he had, find my way to the river. We sat quietly for an hour, then walked upstream where I pointed out several islands where I had spent one summer. I showed him the inlets where two kids had fallen through the ice and drowned.

When we got back to the car, I said, "Thanks."

He looked at me and winked. We drove back to my house, where he stayed the night. He left early the next morning, well before my parents awoke. He wanted to go to Terre Haute, Indiana to visit the grave of Eugene Debs.

Before he left, Erling shook my hand. "Glad I had a chance to meet your parents. Let's stay in touch as you make plans for next year's folk school. I'll be in North Carolina at the Joseph Campbell folk school. You're invited to come any time. And if you ever want to go there," he said. "Debs is buried in the Highland Lawn Cemetery in Terre Haute."

"I may just do that," I said.

Mabel left the driveway, turned right, and disappeared. When my parents woke, they didn't mention him. They asked what I planned to do. I told them I was going to the club to hit some balls and maybe find a game. My dad, dressed in his suit, seemed remote. He ate his cereal quietly. He paged through the financial section of the *Chicago Tribune*. I could almost hear him thinking, "What in the world drew Jason to such a man?" I took the sports section and went out on the porch. As I read, and listened to what sounded like a cardinal in the oak tree, I noticed my old friend the squirrel, who was leaping from limb to limb. He stopped on one limb and peered down at me. "I know, I know," I said. "You want me to try it. Just be patient. I'm not ready yet."

The following evening, we talked about Erling. My dad was worried about me. He believed Erling was not a good influence.

"He's an angry man, not at all at home in this world," he said. "I don't understand, son, what you see in him."

I tried to explain, but ended up being tongue-tied, spouting platitudes that didn't reflect my indebtedness to Erling.

"I can tell you," my dad said. "I'm not willing to support your working with him for the summer. I don't think he's a stable person."

"I'm not," I told him. "I'm writing a grant and plan to start a daycare program."

"That's a relief," he said. "I found him..." he searched for the right words, "...very misguided." He paused again. "And a very arrogant young man."

I didn't reply. Later that night, I went to my room.

Dear Dad,

After talking with you tonight, I thought it was appropriate to lay down a credo, and theoretically, at least, to explain my relationship to Erling Duus, which for me is important. But I need to start by making it clear that I am by no means a 'disciple', as you called it, of his.

First, Erling is a wonderful teacher. Until I met him I was very unschooled in the American intellectual tradition especially Ralph Waldo Emerson, Thomas Wolfe, Carl Sandburg and Walt Whitman. Erling was the catalyst for me to read them. He has dedicated his life to the study of these men, particularly Whitman, whom he considers an American prophet.

Unfortunately, he cannot tolerate the economic and social discrepancies between the wealthy and the poorer classes. He distrusts people who have money because they represent the inequity of our society. For him, you, as an executive in the corporate world, are a threat to his ego. If he could argue with you and beat you with his arguments, he'd feel that he'd defeated at least one corporate power. I didn't foresee that he'd try to do that with you. So I was disappointed when I walked into the basement and found him wholly distorting some of his thoughts in order to rile you up. I later asked him why he did it.

He said that he had to express his disdain for our lives. It was a moral question. He said I shouldn't live the life I do, but should forsake it. I asked him what I should do and where I should go, if not here with you. He never could figure out where I should go or what I should be. I told him that his judgment was certainly correct—there are inequalities—but that I had to affirm, not deny my own life. If I was ever to address those wrongs and work to change some small portion of them, I'd have to decide to do that my own way. I have, since that conversation, split with Erling.

I wrote this to appease my dad. If I was done with Erling, it would make the rest of the summer better for both of us.

I learned from his knowledge about literature, but I have also learned that I have my own life. I learned that some wrongs are not just the fault of individual men, but are the failure of generations and the result of distorted values that have led to some injustices that no one intended. I know that you are a good, intelligent man and ...

I broke off writing the letter. It wasn't any use. My dad would grow more incensed that I had anything to do with someone who opposed capitalism. Even worse, he'd be enraged that someone was trying to pit son against father. I folded it up and stuck it in my journal. We never talked about Erling again. It was as if he had never visited our house. Our life went on as it should. I played golf with my dad in a father-and-son tournament. We came in second, the best finish since I was a teenager. I worked at the club and helped the pro with starting the players off the tee. We went to the club for dinner, sitting in our regular table by the window overlooking the eighteenth green.

But what Erling said bothered me like a dark splinter under my skin. He was right. I had no idea how to break away, to tell my parents that I didn't want or need them, that it was too much of a demand to expect me to continue as I had to live my life as if it were their life.

The summer wound down. I prepared to head back to school for my last year. I would figure out what to do once I was back at school. This was the year I hoped to set off on my own once I had my graduate degree.

PART VI

What might have been and what has been

Point to one end, which is always present.

"Four Quartets," T.S. Eliot

He understood that men were forever strangers to one another, that no one ever comes really to know anyone, that imprisoned in the dark womb of our mother, we come to life without having seen her face, that we are given to her arms a stranger, and that, caught in the insoluble prison of being, we escape never, no matter what arms may clasp us, what mouth may kiss us, what heart may warm us.

Thomas Wolfe, *Look Homeward Angel*

Big Plans

I returned to school and started classes. I saw Ann once, on her way to a lucrative advertising position with Gillette. She lived in New Haven. I promised to write and to visit. But when I kissed her at the airport, it was as if she'd already left.

On Marie's advice, I began to apply for a grant to set up a daycare program in Cross Creek. I needed to explain the purpose of the grant to the folk school board. They had to write letters of support.

My idea was that our Folk Center, the log cabin we had built the previous summer, would be renovated to meet state guidelines for a daycare center. Several men agreed to insulate the cabin and put in running water. We also razed the old Lester house that had level ground to make space for a fenced-in playground. With a daycare center, mothers could work and supplement their husbands' income. folk school students could supervise daycare in the summer, as we had in previous summers.

Helen Goya who worked for the Department of Human Services helped me put together a grant application. Meanwhile, we did fundraising in the hollow, with a Thanksgiving turkey shoot. Cecil Marlow ran the shoot.

I'd brought enough prizes to make it worthwhile. We advertised at the local stores. We had eleven turkeys, ten hams, and six chickens as prizes. Once again, Shady John won first. We raised $208.85. For the kids, we had a horseshoe contest.

The board—which consisted of Peggy, Bonnie, Cecil, Marie, Greta (a mother with five young children), James, J.B. Terry who had shown interest in the project, and Otrel—met to discuss next year's program. The grant could give us up to $60,000.00 to start the program, if we met federal guidelines. J.B. had questions about the board's obligations—did they have to do anything? I told him that the board merely had to approve what I'd written.

"That's all you need us to do?" he asked.

"Well, yes. You need to approve the grant application," I said.

J.B. nodded his head and smiled. I didn't like his smile. It looked like the smile someone made before they pulled a gun to rob a bank. But he didn't say a word. I figured Otrel would keep J.B. in check. He wouldn't let him get out of hand. He kept engaged as we discussed building a rifle shoot on the property and continuing the crafts programs and folk school in the summer. With everyone excited about the possibilities—and three staff members that we'd hired from Cross Creek—I headed back to Nashville to write.

Ninety-degree heat with eighty percent humidity had walloped Nashville. I called Linda Stone, a woman whom Helen suggested I meet. She had a degree in early childhood education. Might she want to work on the grant?

"Sure. Sounds interesting. Why don't you come over?" she said.

Her third-floor apartment was hot and perfumed with the sweet smell of marijuana. Three guys lounged on her sofa, stoned. Chicago's third album played over and over.

I want to be free
I want to be free
I want to be free of all hurt
Free of all pain

"Want a hit?" she asked and passed me a joint. I joined the other three on the couch. She squeezed in next to me. With her hair parted down the middle and tiny wire-rimmed glasses, she looked like a female John Lennon. She didn't introduce me to the others. I picked up their names on my own.

Heat permeated her apartment. If anyone moved, sweat poured off their body. Linda filled our glasses with cold lemonade. Bill, a philosophy major, suggested that we fill the bathtub with ice and take turns sitting in it.

I went to the grocery and bought eight bags of ice to fill the tub. Linda slipped off her clothes and hopped in the tub. Her eyes popped out as she sank in inch by inch. Bill pulled off his shorts and shirt. Once Linda emerged from the tub, Bill quickly followed her in. I followed Bill and Jack, a short stocky guy who played guitar, followed me.

For a few hours, we alternately cooled off and sat in the living room, smoking and listening to the traffic outside the window. We hoped for a breeze. It was no use. We got back in the tub.

Once the numbness from the cold water wore off, my skin tingled, as if someone tickled it. Too soon, the heat took over. I'd be perspiring. I spent several days in and out of the icy bathtub and lounging around. I'd go to class and come back.

We drafted the grant application. Linda used early childhood education language to write learning objectives. As she helped write the grant, I was having the time of my life.

Perhaps that was because I wasn't involved with another woman and wasn't worrying about which one would be the best for me. She had four of us as friends, and she seemed indifferent as to which one she claimed as her special friend. We enjoyed being together and never crossed the line into sex.

Moonlight

One long weekend later in the fall, I drove to Cross Creek to stay with Bonnie and her kids.

Her sons loved to play wiffle ball and football and swim in the creek with me. The youngest, Todd, nearly drowned one day. He was paddling from one side of the swimming hole to another when his head dropped like a stone. For several seconds, everyone waited for him to emerge.

"Where'd he go?" Bobby asked.

"Ah, he's playing around," Dylan said. "He'll come up."

I sensed something was wrong. He didn't dive under like someone who knew how to swim. He sank. I dived in, grabbed his limp body from the bottom, and pulled him to shore. I gave him mouth to mouth resuscitation. He coughed up water and revived quickly. Word got out and Bonnie felt indebted to me.

About a quarter of a mile into the hollow, a narrow lane followed a small creek to her house. I dimmed the lights and parked the car. Snow fell lightly. One lightbulb slung from a tree cast a damp reflection on their truck. I walked toward it. The stillness surprised me after leaving Nashville. The humming of tires over pavement still vibrated in my ears. A dog growled. The house was perched on a ledge, up a steep incline. A full moon had risen above the trees, casting a soft glow on the house.

I ascended the stairs, careful not to slip on the snow. The dog scampered off the porch into a stack of wood under the beech tree. Bonnie opened the door. She welcomed me, pointing to the couch. I put my bag in the bedroom in the back and returned to the main room. Once I took off my jacket, she offered me coffee. She had brewed a pot just in case. I went into the kitchen as she poured me a cup. She eased herself into a large chair. We sat before a black and white image of a television program, some sitcom, which we ignored.

On some nights, when I'd come to visit, her family sat around the woodstove. Her family—all boys, Howard, her youngest, Jay, a pre-teen, and Larry, her eldest—would sit around the stove, ignoring the TV. They told stories. Some about Shady John and his feuds with the Witcombs up the road. Some were about city boys at school who didn't know a thing about hunting and fishing. But this evening the boys were asleep.

Our conversation fluctuated between storytelling and concerns about the grant for the daycare program. I read her the preliminary applications. She liked what I'd written. She wasn't sure everyone would. I planned to meet with the board the next day to go over the application process.

She smoked four or five cigarettes while we talked, lighting each new one from the nub of the last one. She told about the time she had a rattlesnake in the kitchen. She was reaching into the cupboard and it bit her.

I asked her, "What did you do?"

She laughed and said, "Why I killed it, of course!" She wrung its neck. Instead of going to a doctor, she cut the bite, sucked it, and spit out the venom. For a few days, she didn't feel so good, a bit nauseated, but she'd been bitten before, so her body was used to it. She fried that snake up. It made a pretty good supper.

The hour was late. We'd grown tired. She told me to sleep in the bed on the left.

"That's where Howie sleeps. He sleeps so sound, nothing can wake him," she said. While she prepared something in the kitchen, I slipped off my pants and shirt and slipped into bed.

Bedtime always surprised me. Just as at Peggy's house, everyone respected the other person's privacy at her house. Earlier in the summer, she told me that I'd be sleeping with the boys. The three of them showed me the beds, two of them against the wall. I was unsure what to do. There were no other rooms to undress. I watched them. They slipped off their pants and shirt, folded them over a chair, and hurried under the covers, Jay and Larry to the bed on the right and Howard and I to the bed on the left. As the last one, I slipped off my pants and shirt. I kept on my t-shirt and jockey shorts and flopped in beside Howard. He rustled and settled down, his small pre-pubescent body with gangly arms and legs pulled in close to keep warm.

On this night, I whispered, "It's me, Howard. I'm staying over." He craned his head without moving his shoulders, offered a wan smile and snuggled, as he did with his brothers, near me. I smelled his tobacco breath, pungent and sweet. His hair had a musty odor, the smell of clay and bark. He'd probably been helping his brothers cut wood for winter. The charcoal smell of the potbellied stove wafted through the cool night air. I wished him goodnight. Jay and Larry groaned.

The cool lemon light from the kerosene lamp cast a faint glow from the other room where Bonnie changed into her nightgown, crawled into bed and put the lamp out. The soft breathing of the boys pervaded the room, a lazy rhythm that grew quieter as a deeper sleep overtook them. Before I could fall asleep, Howard shoved his hand into my face, his little fingers brushing against my cheek.

My brother and I used to squirm in bed, fighting for the spot in the middle. I chuckled to myself. It was as if Howard, used to staking claim on his nocturnal territory, unconsciously set his boundaries with a quick right to my head. Soon he had fallen back to sleep. I tossed and turned several times. My nose and toes were freezing. I pulled my head under the blanket. Howard scrunched next to me, spooning his body into mine to get warm.

I looked across to Jay and Larry. They too had crawled together, gathering heat from one another as the stove cooled. They made the best of this small home, the beds, the potbellied stove. Their futures would not come easy. They'd have to make their way in a school system that considered them hillbillies and prove themselves, excelling academically or athletically in order to find a niche outside the hollow.

I realized that Erling was right about me. I'd grown accustomed to living a life where I assumed that people would take care of me and treat me as if I was important. I never questioned it. When I wanted to play a round of golf, I picked up my shoes in the dressing room, retrieved my cleaned clubs from the pro shop, and walked to the tee. I expected the pro to make small talk with me and send me off playing as if I owned the course. I'd play as long as I wanted, hitting two and three shots a hole. I was a member, one of the elite.

But here in Bonnie's house I was also accepted as one of the family. I felt as comfortable here as in the Oak Room. They liked me, not because of whose son I was, but for who I was with them.

I lived in two worlds. At some point, I had to make a choice between them. I had to reconcile the privileged life with this new life. I was like a man holding onto a limb for fear of falling who didn't recognize that he was standing firmly on the ground. I couldn't let go. I enjoyed the free golf at the expense of my father as I set out to create a life apart from that with my work in Appalachia.

My mind crowded with the voices of Erling, Ann, my parents, and Will. I went over what I'd said to them. I wondered sometimes if I were play acting, never quite sure of who I really was.

I slipped out of bed, tiptoed quietly to the kitchen, sat at a table by the woodstove, and looked out the window at the night. I liked to stay up after everyone had gone to sleep to look out on the snow-covered ground. The shadows and stillness added up to a timelessness, a sense that, although I was there, as I looked onto the scene, that I was also not there. The night always enchanted me. As I gazed outward, it was as if I could also gaze inward. My thoughts quieted. The snow was letting up; it had come too early. Hours such as these were designed for introverts, the one time when the extroverts were asleep. Alone at the table, the moon illuminating my journal, I felt more myself than I did in the day, more present and complete.

For a moment, I was off the ambition train. I let my thoughts rest. But soon enough, I thought about what must be done in the days and weeks ahead.

If the daycare project didn't work out, if we didn't get the grant, I could move on and find another job. My dad was right about work. I needed to have a job. He wanted me to be successful so I could continue as I had as his son, living the good life. But these children sleeping beside me would struggle to find jobs that could keep them going. Their struggle was mitigated by their closeness, snuggled close on cold nights.

When I went back to bed, Howard held onto me. His embrace soothed me; sleep came easily.

The morning light splintered through the cracks in the walls. I heard the frying pan sizzle and smelled bacon. I lifted Howard's arm. He opened his eyes and smiled at me, then turned over, pulling the covers over his shoulder. I went to the kitchen and pulled a chair up to the stove. Larry and Jay sat by it. They watched their mom fix us breakfast. Most of the snow had already melted. They looked at me. "Welcome home," they said. I was like one of their kin. We sipped coffee and talked of school and the latest row at the dance. That's when I heard that Randy Hatfield—a blond boy who wanted to be the first in his family to go to college, whom I'd encouraged to keep his grades up—had been shot at the dance. It was bad. He lost his leg. But that wasn't all. When I saw him weeks later, he'd lost his ambition to go to college.

His story weighed on me as I met with the board. I told the board that I wanted a program that would give kids like Randy a better chance. They approved the preliminary application and agreed to meet again once I had completed it.

Mixed

With the end of the semester fast approaching, Ann called me to see if I would come visit her in Connecticut. I wrote her a letter and let her know my ambivalence about any long-term commitment. I still felt attached to her and, more than any other woman, felt safe with her sexually. I feared that, if I continued to see her, I'd fall so in love with her that I'd want to marry her. I wasn't ready for that, not yet.

I couldn't afford it. Not in the state I was in.

My parents, who had met her twice, liked her. Sweet and polite, she made it easy. She knew how to carry on a conversation, defer to elders, and smile when she needed to do so. I tried to spell out my mixed emotions.

> Dear Ann,
>
> I'm not sure I can tell this you face to face, so I'll tell you in writing.
>
> I have said before that I need freedom. I must be free in going where I need to and when I need to go there. I feel like a sailor who leaves the land he loves for the sea. But unlike that sailor, I have no distant port I'm heading for. I have only the promise of what may be.
>
> What does this all mean?
>
> I must be free of any long-term commitments.
>
> That is blunt. But it is true.
>
> I do want to see you. I'm still in love with you. It's just that I'm confused. I need to sort out who I am before I commit to you. I don't want to disappoint you.
>
> I'm planning to make a trip to Greenwich Village to see a priest, Father Flye. He's invited me to meet with him to discuss James Agee. My graduate thesis is on Agee's vision of tenant farmers as complex, authentic human beings. I'm excited to meet him. We've talked on the phone. After seeing him, I'll drive up to New Haven. I really look forward to being with you.
>
> I did and still do love you. I say this because, like it or not, I love you more than any woman I've known. But, because I cannot settle down, we can no longer go on as we did. We need to figure out, if you are willing, what our future will be.

It is much easier to say this to a page than to your lovely face. My ability to set limits comes in fits and starts. Much of me hates to break away. I can feel your skin on mine. It is as if we're one.

For now, I speak of our lasting relationship, not as it was before, but as what we make of it. I'm afraid the fault is in me. I just cannot commit. My heart is split. I must find the cause. I don't want to leave you with only half of my heart. I want you to have my whole heart.

Your friends Jay and Carol who had us over to their house several nights last year were right. You should have listened when they told you how I wasn't good for you.

Those who have never loved, who have loved but never broken apart, cannot know the agony I feel. There are no rings to return, no pins to unclip, just a word, "unsure." It's as if dark clouds settle.

You understood how I need freedom. Before I said, "I must be free in a certain way. But the present is good." Now I say, "I must be free. The present demands it. So, we must separate more than you would like." This is not "breaking up." I never liked that term. There is part of you that will never be separate from me. It will remain a part of me no matter where I go.

I'm afraid I've not been good to you. I have, however, been honest. You needn't read anything between my sighs. Let me know if I can visit. I say this with

Love,
Jason

I'd made plans to take a trip to meet Father Flye. His apartment was at 19 Perry Street in Greenwich Village. After my visit with him, I'd visit Ann. She agreed to meet with me. She wasn't happy with my letter and told me so. But she was willing to hear me out. She wanted to understand why I needed distance. She was far more understanding of me than I was of her.

I drove the same roads my mother drove every summer when I was a kid, heading to Long Island to visit her parents and her brother. I found the right tunnel, turned on the right street, and parked two streets from 19 Perry Street. Father Flye had corresponded with Agee throughout his life more than anyone and, including Agee's wives, knew him longest and best.

I was standing in the same Greenwich Village where the Stonewall riots took place. A tall man with long hair and the same stride as Will hustled across the street. If I ran into Will, what would he say? He'd probably keep on walking.

I wouldn't blame him.

19 Perry Street was a four-story brownstone with steps leading to a large black door. I pressed the apartment three button. Footsteps hurried down the stairs.

A little man greeted me. His white hair stuck out as if an electrical current had just surged through him. He made a quick gesture with his hand.

"Come in, come in," he said. He wasted no time with introductions, but took me by the arm. "You must be Jason. Yes? Good. Good. Now come on." He pointed up the stairs. "Two more flights. Be there in no time. I must tell you," he said, shaking his head, "I believe there are two types of people, don't you know. There are those who are concerned with material things." We had made it to the first-floor. The staircase, narrow and dark, had a single bulb hanging from the ceiling. "And there are those who are more concerned with spiritual things, the life of the mind," he said as we came to the second landing. "Now, I'm one of those who is more concerned with spiritual things," he said as he opened the door of his apartment.

Scattered on the chairs, on shelves, on the floor were piles of books and newspapers. Some piles looked as if they might topple over at any minute. "Come in, come in," he said. His words shot out in bursts as if, had he not said them, they would escape and flee from him on their own. He picked up a batch of newspapers from a large brown wingback chair. The kitchen, off to the right, had books piled in the sink, on top of the refrigerator, and on a small table. His reading tastes were eclectic: theology, literature, current events, poetry, and science.

"There you are." He motioned to the chair. "Sit down, my boy. It's so nice to meet you. I enjoyed your letter very much. Yes. Very much."

Being in his presence, knowing that he knew James Agee and after he had taught him in high school, how he followed Agee's career, overwhelmed me. I managed to say, "It's nice to be here. Thank you for taking the time."

"Oh, no. Thank you for coming all this way. Would you like some tea?"

"Sure."

He went into the kitchen, pushed the books aside, pulled out two cups, put a kettle on the stove and came back. "Now where were we?"

His hands clasped together in his lap, he leaned forward. Clad in his Episcopal priest's attire, with white collar, black jacket, and matching trousers that were too long, the cuffs covering his shoes, he was almost too much to absorb. His intense gaze made me flinch. I began to perspire and wiped the perspiration from my forehead.

"Are you all right, my boy?" he asked. The kettle screeched. He pattered to the kitchen, talking over his shoulder at me. "Don't mind me. I'm always in a rush it seems. Never enough time, you know."

Once he passed me the tea, he settled back on a couch. He piled newspapers in one corner so he could sit in the other side. "Now tell me what do you find most interesting about Jim?"

I was not sure how to reply. I offered him my ill-formed thoughts. I told him about my thesis on the imagination. As I started to speak, he held up his hand. "Now, would you mind if I recorded this?" he said.

He pulled out a reel-to-reel recorder, tested it, pressed the record button. The tape recorder made me even more self-conscious. I told him I thought Agee had seen more humanity in the tenant farmers than anyone else. He entered their lives and came to see in their daily tribulations how they were far grander than people who lived in mansions.

I asked him what he thought caused Agee's untimely death at forty-three. My question distressed him. He bent his head, rubbed his forehead, and repeated, "I don't know. I don't know." I changed the topic and asked if he had any recordings of Agee speaking.

"Why, yes, I do," he said. "He had a beautiful voice, rich and deep with a slight southern lilt. Here let me play you a recording I have. Jim was as fascinated with the tape recorder, new back then, as he was with film."

He played Agee reading the Lord's Prayer and several poems. His voice, calm and measured, brought Agee into the room. Father Flye's face changed as he listened. His eyes crinkled up, and his thin lips curved up in a wistful smile. "Lovely. Lovely. Isn't it? That was Jim. He made words come alive, almost sing. You know he played the piano. Had a wonderful singing voice. Much talent..." he sighed.

There was a knock on the door. A young Asian teenager came in. Father Flye stood up and motioned for him to come in. The boy carried several books under his arm. "This is Vinh. He's a student of mine. Wonderful writer," he said.

I stood and introduced myself. He bowed.

"Be right with you," Father Flye said to Vinh, then turned to me. "He comes every day. We read together. Then he writes. Quite extraordinary."

From his enthusiasm for Vinh, I saw what the shy, fatherless, teenaged Agee saw in him. Father Flye championed Agee, encouraged him, and, even when Agee's life went on the skids—failed marriages, dead-end movie projects, and heart attack— stood by him, believed he had a calling. After Agee's death, Flye was his tireless advocate, published a book of letters, and, as he told me, got his voice recordings made into a record album.

The student glanced our way, then perched on a chair, and opened his book. I was taking up his time.

Father Flye walked down the stairs with me. "Is there anything else you need?" he said as he opened the door. I thought how I'd love to sit for an afternoon with him to hear him recount more stories of Agee. But he'd given me enough.

"No, I'm fine. I really appreciate your taking the time," I said.

"Time is the one thing we're all given," he said. He patted me on the arm. "We just have to take care how we use it."

I stepped into the street and saw a sign for Christopher Street, the one Will mentioned. Traffic going up one street was heavy; horns blared. Pedestrians scurried across an intersection. Along the side streets, old stunted maples shaded the sidewalk. I could see why it was called a village. It was a mix of big city and small town. Men walked arm in arm down the street. I must have stared. A man, passing by me, asked, "You have a problem?"

I left. I wanted to see Ann. New Haven was a couple of hours away. I gazed at my map, noted the streets I should take, and headed north.

Ann's apartment complex, ensconced in a stand of majestic oaks on a ridge, was in a new development. New three-storied brick homes with long driveways lined the street up to her apartment. She roomed with another woman who had a man's name, Sam, and a masculine air about her. She scanned me from foot to head, and grunted, as if convinced that what she'd heard about me from Ann was confirmed by the impression I made standing in the doorway.

Ann, quick to break the tension, offered me coffee and suggested we sit down. Ann and I sat on the couch in the living room. Sam squirreled herself away in an armchair, her cup clasped between her hands.

"So what brings you east?" Sam asked.

"To see Ann," I responded.

"I thought that was secondary," Sam shot back.

I smirked at her. "I did visit a Father Flye, friend of a writer I know," I said.

"Why aren't you honest?" Sam snapped.

I sipped my coffee and turned to Ann. "What you say we go for a walk?" Sam caught Ann's attention, shaking her head. Ann hesitated.

Sam pursued her inquisition. "Why don't you answer my question?"

I blew the steam off the coffee and stood up. "It seems like there are lovely places up here. Can you show me around?"

Ann stirred. I reached out to take her hand. Her fingers touched mine, but didn't close.

Ann turned to Sam.

"Do you mind?"

Sam laughed. "Ann, you can do what you want."

"We'll be back in a bit."

"Yeah," Sam intoned, her thin lips turned down, scowling at me.

Once outside, Ann took me by the arm. "Let's go over there," she said, pointing to a pathway through the trees. The path went upward. In the distance, broken light from the sway of leaves danced on the ground.

"She read your letter," Ann said.

"What?"

"It was accidental. I left it on the kitchen table."

"That's great," I said, pulling away from her. "She had no—"

"She's a good friend."

"She's a creep."

Ann stopped. "You didn't have to come."

"I wanted to. I still love you."

"Really?"

"Really."

"You shouldn't send letters like that," she said and walked off, following the path to an open field atop a hill. I watched her go. Her body, strong yet soft, moved with the grace of a fine racehorse. Her brown hair, draped over her shoulder, caught the sun and glistened. She was quite beautiful. I hurried after her.

"Ann," I said as I caught up with her. "I've been the creep. I'm sorry. It's just—"

She put her finger to my mouth, tapping it. "Shush. Let's just walk. It's lovely up here. You'll like it."

After dinner at the Golden Wok and plenty of wine, the rapport that we'd had at Vanderbilt came back. She spoke about the challenge of promoting merchandise that seemed to demand that the consumer buy the latest improved razor when the previous razor was probably all they needed.

"We always have to find the right sales pitch," she said, "to convince them that what they're using is outdated. What's new is always better. What is infuriating is that they know that thirty-three percent of their products are no good mechanically, yet still, they sell them. It seems everything about the consumer and what they want is so meticulously researched it's nearly impossible for anyone to resist buying them. It makes me sick."

"That makes no sense," I said. "I use the same razor I've had for years."

"Profit," she said. "That's what drives it. New product, more sales. It's hard. The selling more, finding new markets is what we do. There's this hungry desire for consumption and figuring how to push the American people into wanting more of it. That's what's frustrating to me. But the work itself I kinda like. It's fast paced. The staff is smart. It pays very well. I'm going to buy a horse. Get back to riding."

"I'd love to see you ride!"

"I'm in another world. It's like profit and greed and 'hurry-up and do this and that' all recede. Would you like to go for a ride with me?"

"Wish I could. But I do need to get back to Nashville. Grants to write. Classes. Papers to do."

"I remember. I miss the academic life, the challenge to think deeply about ideas. People here don't seem to think. Yet they appear to be so happy and content. Sometimes I think that maybe ignorance is bliss and I'll try that for a while—of course, to no avail."

"Can you quit?"

"No, not now. I keep thinking that somewhere there will be a thread of honesty and beauty and I keep searching for that," she said, rubbing my hand between hers.

"Don't you feel as if you're compromising yourself?"

"I hope not. I must admit I'm still confused as to what I'm doing. A few weeks ago I thought I was having a mental breakdown because all I did was work late, come home, and read. To be honest, I still don't know whether I want to go to graduate school, keep this job, or what to do," she said. She let go of my hand and scooted back. "But one funny thing." She laughed, putting her hand to her lips. "I met a man from Survey and Research in our company who knew your dad."

"Really?!"

"Yeah, and listen to this. You wouldn't have believed it. He started talking about the war and came up with the brilliant comment that we shouldn't end it because all those boys would be brought home and there'd be a great rise in unemployment."

"Asshole."

"A big one. I told him I'd rather work to reorganize or redistribute the economy and industry than have friends and family killed," she said. "But not him. That's the type of people I have to work with."

"Why don't you come down this summer, if just for a week or so, and meet the people in Cross Creek. They're not like that. They're decent people," I said.

"I'd like to. But I'm still not sure what I'm looking for. It's like that quote you sent me about going nowhere rapidly, half-frightened that you'll reach some place and know it's wrong but not know enough to stop. Remember? Who said that?"

I puzzled for a moment. "It might have been Rilke. Or maybe Camus."

"Anyway, I thought a lot about it and think it calls us to seek that which has not yet become something for us but still challenges us. So for now, I want to cultivate the seeker, not the sought. I don't need another destination. I need to explore what I've got here and find out if it's something I can do well before leaping into something else. See what I mean?"

"Sure, I get it. I wish I had the same tenacity. But I don't."

"Jason, you'll figure it out. Be patient."

She curled up next to me, letting me hold her in my arms, her head pressed back against my neck. I admired how she allowed herself to live with the uncertainty while she kept focused on her work, remaining open to other options.

Sam came in later, paused briefly, and asked, "You're still here?"

"It's okay," Ann said. She kissed me on the cheek.

With a shrug of her shoulders, Sam said, "Catch you in the morning."

In the morning, after we made love, the light from the window by her bed inched up the bed until it covered us like a sheet. I felt complete. Her naked body coiled, leg over leg, around me. My cock nestled against her belly. She traced her fingers across my chest, circled around my nipples and down the narrow furry line to my belly. I cupped my hands on her breast, feeling its soft yet firm swelling. Her lips touched mine just barely. The thick smell of love emanated from our bodies. I wondered why I questioned my love for her. She caressed my chest and belly. I became aroused again. She slid back and I entered her again. It was slow and deliberate. The light embraced us.

We showered and dressed late that morning.

Sam sat at the kitchen table. "Well, here are the early birds," she said. "And he's still here!"

"Sam," Ann said. "It's *fine*, really."

"Well, lovebirds, I've fixed you French toast and bacon, just to show there are no hard feelings," she said.

Ann reached over and hugged her. "My special friend," she said.

I offered, "Thanks."

She smiled at me, the first time since I'd walked in the door. "Dig in," she said.

Warmed in a pan, the maple syrup perfumed the room. We ate at the table. Sam asked me what my plans were. I told her about the daycare application and the folk school. She wished me well and went off on an errand. Ann and I had the rest of the day together. I stayed one more night, making love again. As I packed to leave, Ann sat on the bed, her legs folded under her.

"I hate to ask," she said. "But where do we stand?"

"I love you," I said.

"I love you, too," she said, smiling softly. "But— "

"I know. You want me to say something and..." I couldn't bear to let her down.

She came across the bed, stared at me, took me in her arms, and kissed me.

"When you can," she said. "When you can."

I kissed her goodbye again and again and was in tears. She stood by the car and waved. I knew that what I felt for her was unlike anything I had ever felt for another woman. It was real. She was wise and compassionate and honest. Yet I was heading back to Nashville. I was leaving her and I wondered what, if anything, would bring me back to her. "When you can," she'd said. I turned onto Interstate 95 and headed southwest. Well into the night, I pulled up at Linda's apartment. She let me curl up on the couch to sleep the few hours before dawn.

Grants and Strings

Linda and I met with Helen, the regional director of the Department of Human Services who helped us write the proposal. She'd grown up in eastern Tennessee and wanted a good program up there. She offered suggestions that would give the grant a better chance of approval, including statistics and some narrative describing the poverty in the region. Linda and Helen collaborated on writing different sections of the grant. We found statistics on unemployment in the Clearfork area. I wrote some descriptions of the area and the people. Helen looked over the grant application. It had good statistics, clear goals and objectives, but was missing a better picture of the people and the community. Could we add some quotations? More graphic descriptions of the poverty? The neediness of people?

I added descriptions of Bonnie's house and included quotes from some people I'd heard during the summer. One man said, "Now don't just go off and forget about us." I described how Bobby, his shirt unbuttoned, greeted me with a handshake, and Peggy invited me in for breakfast. Linda found facts about the average annual incomes, the rate of unemployment, the lack of health care, the incidence of mental retardation—all elements of the general poverty in the region. We filled in multiple forms, including ones with questions about mental retardation and mental health. We called schools in the area to get the number of students who qualified for free lunch which would increase the grant's credibility. I made some notes and extrapolated, based on kids I knew who were having trouble in school, like Squeaky who'd gotten in trouble with the law, and kids who had been suspended for one thing or another. Helen had said, "Give me numbers." The picture I painted didn't look pretty. It was what the grant required. Upon looking at the second draft, Helen gave a thumbs-up. We submitted the grant application in May. Since I had had the board review the general concept of the daycare program, I figured more approval for the application was unnecessary.

I put my energy back into completing my Agee thesis and several other papers. I also contacted students at Ashbury and Vanderbilt who had shown interest in coming to the summer folk school. I spent my free time with

Linda. She had visited Cross Creek several times in the fall. We planned how to advertise and hire staff. She agreed to work with me as co-director of the program.

We invited a gospel choir to perform at the folk school in early May and raised $60.00, which was added to the two thousand I had been promised by Mr. Hook to pay my salary for the summer and which we could use as in kind monies for the grant. I showed the completed grant application to Bonnie, asking her to read it before I showed it to the whole board. I felt sure that we could add to what Marie Cirillo had begun to do years ago: provide hope for a community that had lost a sense of hope and give mothers an opportunity to work while we cared for their children. Bonnie looked at the grant and squinted, "Mighty big."

"Sorry. Federal applications require you to document everything."

"I'll give it a look."

A few weeks later, in the middle of final exams, Cecil Marlow, who had joined the board because he had several pre-school grandchildren and liked the idea of the grant, called me. There was trouble. He claimed that rumors were being spread. Several mothers—he would not name them—said they saw a list with names of those who were "mentally retarded." It frightened them. I told him that the application had no names attached to it. I'd included statistics and mentioned difficulties some students had in the regional schools. He said I had better get back to the hollow. They called a meeting of the board and elected J.B. Terry as chairman.

"J.B.?"

"How the hell did *he* get the grant application?" I asked.

"Bonnie gave it to him. Seems he heard she had it."

"Shit."

The previous summer, J.B. had been released from prison. He spent hours on the folk school's front porch listening to impromptu jam sessions. I had never spent time with him. In fact, I'd worried about him being more interested in Ingrid than in the program. Cecil told me that J.B. read them a page which talked about "mental health." He claimed that I was saying mountain people were "mentally retarded." I knew the exact page he was referring to, the one where Helen suggested that we include some numbers. The board voted to oppose any proposal with any mention of mental retardation in it. They also voted that any proposal had to be read by all the board members. In addition, they voted that Erling, not me, be asked to run the folk school.

272

"They're after your hide, Jason," Cecil said. "J.B. has them on the warpath."

That evening, I drove up to J.B.'s house. I wanted to go over his concerns, page by page, before the Board Meeting. I felt I could explain what the terms meant. Having driven from middle Tennessee clear across the state, I didn't arrive until 9:30, but decided to see if he was up.

The air was heavy. A thick fog ebbed up from the roadsides. When I pulled into his driveway, my headlights shone on the front porch. I turned them off so as not to disturb anyone. I walked up to the porch. Illuminated by the gray light of the TV, I could see Karen, J.B.'s teenage daughter, and Squeaky on the couch, embracing. His legs were splayed open. They were taken aback by the dark figure on the front porch. They jolted upright. Karen stood, pressed her skirt down, and came out of the front room, her arm leaning on the door jamb.

"What you want?" she asked in a petulant tone.

"Wondered if your dad is up," I said.

"Nope. Went to bed a long time ago."

"Shit," I muttered and added, "Sorry to bother you."

She leaned forward, straightening her blouse, softened her expression, and murmured quietly, "Come in."

In back of her, behind the couch, Squeaky was adjusting his pants, shoving his shirt in, and buckling his belt.

I said, "Hi, Squeaky." He nodded in my direction. When my back was to him, he sat in a chair, closer to the TV, slumping low and motionless.

I gave her a copy of the latest grant application, the one I revised. I'd clarified the meaning of the term "mental health" in it and cut any reference to people in the grant. I kept the narrative as it was. I knew that I needed it to convince the granting agency of the dire need of the mothers in the region.

"This is the final copy," I told Karen. "Please show it to your dad so he can look it over before the board meeting."

She flipped through it. "You write this?" she asked.

"Mostly."

"Lot of words," she said.

"Yeah. There are."

Before I left, Squeaky got up and whispered something in her ear. She bit her lip turned back to me, and asked, "You mind giving Squeaky a ride?"

"No problem," I said.

Squeaky gave her a kiss. He held her by the waist, pulled her toward him, then, hopped off the porch, and caught up with me.

"Hey, I appreciate it, man," he said.

I told him not to worry. I was glad to help out. Once outside, he pissed by the side of the driveway as I started the engine and turned the heater up. After he opened the door and sat and the heat blasted across him, I noticed a musty smell like mushrooms. His rump low in the seat, he said nothing. I put the Volvo in gear. I recognized the smell: it was semen. He scrunched down in the seat. He looked over the instrument panel of the car. I turned to see the red backup lights illuminating the narrow strip of gravel that curved down to the road.

"Cool car, man," he observed.

"I like it. It's safe and has a good repair record."

He nodded his head. We drove down the hollow, down along the dark curves in the road. Dust boiled up like a rolling fog.

I asked how he was doing. He sighed. "Hey, a good night man, really good, if you know what I mean."

I did know. I could smell it.

We drove in silence. His silence came, I imagined, from the afterglow of his pleasure; mine from worry about the next day and what, if anything, J.B. would say. I pulled into his driveway. He hopped out.

"You take care," I said.

He leaned over the door, "Hey, J.B., he's some riled up. Thought you should know."

"I do," I said. "Thanks."

Marie invited me to stay overnight at her place. She'd left the door open. I could use the side bedroom. I settled into the bed knowing I wouldn't sleep much. I spent hours going over the grant, mentally yellow-lining sections that I knew might cause controversy.

The next morning, Marie and I drove up to the folk school cabin. She told me Otrel couldn't make it; he was on the road. She'd warned me that she hadn't seen people as aggravated as this since the folk school burned down. She agreed to do what she could in the meeting, but advised me to hear them out before defending the grant.

A new wooden floor and three new windows had been installed in the log cabin. Folding chairs were set in a circle. We arrived early, I greeted Peggy and Bonnie when they arrived. They said a simple, "Hi," and sat down. The only one who greeted me with some enthusiasm was Cecil. He clapped his arms around me and whispered in my ear, "Don't worry." I tried to make small talk, asking about Jay and Bobby and the girls. But Peggy and Bonnie only offered polite, "They're fine." With a new shirt buttoned at the neck, new pants, and shoes shined, J.B. strutted into the room. He greeted everyone but me. He didn't look well. His eyes had deep circles under them. He had the hunched back of someone who spent hours under a car hood. He avoided me and sat in a chair opposite mine. After everyone had taken a seat, he asked Freda, who was the secretary, to read the minutes of the last meeting. She said that the board had reviewed a yellow and blue paper with a list of children with the title "mental health" or "mental retardation" on it. She held it up and shook it.

I wanted to contradict her, but I took Marie's advice and listened. Freda was furious. Her son's name was on it. Others had seen the list; no one was happy. The board denied the application and requested that whoever wrote the grant should explain why there was such a list.

Others shook their heads and looked in my direction. I assured them that I had, indeed, written the proposal. But no portion of it involved mental retardation. It was a child care proposal that required us to fill in all the forms. The listed families were those whose children would benefit from the child care program.

JB turned to me, "So you admit that *you* filled in the form?"

"I had to. It was required," I retorted. "But that was one page. Did you read the rest of the proposal?"

"As a matter of fact, I did," he said. He sat upright and turned to a page. "You talk about us as if we're some no good, ignorant people. Listen here." He flipped to another page. "You say we don't button our shirts." He lifted his hand to his neck to show me that, indeed, he *did* button his. "And you say we live in poverty." He flipped to another page. "And here you have statistics that *prove* we live in poverty." He looked up. "I don't like what you're saying about us. You make us sound like we're no good." He slapped the grant. "I think you're a two-faced liar. That's what I think. You're making a big salary so you can drive your fancy foreign car. And we get nothing. Nothing."

Marie looked at me and said in a low voice, "J.B., I think you need to—"

"Much respect to you, ma'am, but this ain't none of your business," J.B. said. He flapped the grant application in the palm of his hand like a preacher with a Bible. "This here's between Jason and the board."

"I'm a member of the board," Marie said.

"But you ain't in this grant like we are."

I asked if anyone else had read the new grant. No one had seen it except Bonnie. I'd passed out copies to each member and asked that they read it, mark pages that were problematic to them, and we reconvene the next day to revise the wording and make a final decision.

"I must tell you," I said, "that I had to write some things in the grant application in order to sell it to the feds. Most of you know me. You know how I respect you. I've changed some things already because Mr. Terry has brought up legitimate concerns. Language can be changed. No problem. Let's not make hasty decisions that will compromise our getting the grant."

Cecil, who'd been quiet most the meeting, spoke up. "I think that's a good idea. I respect Jason. I don't think that he'd do us harm. And, J.B., you ain't been round here much these last years, so I'd suggest you listen to this here man." He pointed to me. "He's done a lot for our kids and this community."

After the meeting, I went over to J.B.'s house and discussed the changes that I'd made. I let him know that if he wasn't happy with the language the words weren't cast in stone. Words could be changed. He told me he was real suspicious of government money. He had one of the better moonshining businesses in the hollow. The feds had arrested him. They found moonshine in his truck. He served time. He'd assaulted an officer and bragged that he knocked him good. He told me that any government program meant more government inspectors.

"In these parts, we don't want no one snooping around about things that are none of their business," he said.

It was clear that he would be a hard one to convince.

I talked at length with Marie about the language in the grant application. She thought, as J.B. said, it painted a picture of them as poor and helpless. When I described their clothing, it gave the impression of people who didn't care about their appearance. I mulled over her comments. and realized how powerful words could be. Thirty out of hundreds of words gave them the impression that I had no respect for them. I could do nothing about the words in the grant proposal. They were printed. They'd been read. I only hoped that the board could look past them, at what I wanted to do, and how much I was committed to them.

The Vote

The next morning, we met. Bonnie and Peggy were even less hospitable. They shook the grant application at me and said, "And we thought you were our friend!" I sat down next to Marie, who whispered, "Keep cool; let them talk."

The meeting began with the reading of the minutes of the last meeting. Then J.B. lambasted additional portions of the grant application. He read the portions that talked about "mental health workers," "a number of serious health problems," and statements such as "anxiety among women, fed by fears of children's health, school success, and misbehavior."

"This here is slander. It's saying we don't know how to raise our kids!" he shouted. He slammed the papers on the floor. "I don't know what the rest of you think, but I'm sick of outsiders coming here and thinking they know best. We know how to raise our kin. We don't need no mental health workers to tell us how to raise our kids."

I explained that, yes, it did sound bad, but it didn't reflect what I thought. I wrote it in order to sell the program, to make money available to the area. The money would be allocated to the community based on what they, the members of the board, decided. I'd written it. But it was just words, and words could be changed to suit them.

"If you don't believe it, mister, then why'd you write it?" J.B. said.

Peggy spoke up, "We are terribly disappointed in you, Jason." She looked sad and shook her head. Bonnie never looked up. Freda said that maybe it was time for the board to vote. Cecil remained silent, paging through the grant proposal and shaking his head.

It was moved and seconded that they vote to approve or deny the grant proposal.

I interrupted them. I had to make one more plea.

"Listen, everyone, you have the power to say yea or nay to the grant proposal. But you also have the power to rewrite it, to change the offensive language. I agree with you that the way it is written doesn't do you justice. So, let me work with you to change it. If you vote no, the door is closed. You cannot get the money. Look at what'll come into this community— $60,000.00. That's a lot of money and it goes to you and ..."

J.B. cut me off, "Bullshit. That money, much of it, goes to you, from what it says, and some director with a college degree. I don't see no one in the room with no college degree except you."

"Yes, that's part of the funding—I would like to work here and I do need a salary. But much of—"

"That's a big part of it," he said. "It'll pay your way and that lady who was up here last fall, the pretty one who was hanging all over you. Is that it?"

I clenched my fist and stood up. But as I looked around the room, at one face after another, I realized that it was over. Even Cecil wasn't looking at me. He was studying the grant proposal. Sure, I wanted Linda to work with me. I knew that she knew how to build a program. However, those were the faces of people who had lost their trust in me. I was just another outsider trying to make them into something they were not. And, even worse, I would make money on a grant based on their poverty. I sat back down, folded my hands in front of me and said quietly, "That's not true. I would work with you, and you as a board would hire from whoever applies. The federal government requires that you hire someone with a college education and with experience running a program."

J.B. said, "Huh," and laughed. "That's a good one."

Marie put her hand on my shoulder. "Let it go."

Greta moved that the board vote. When she asked for those who were favor of the grant proposal, Marie, Cecil, and I voted yes. When she asked who was opposed, everyone else raised their hands.

Once the grant proposal was voted down, Greta brought up what would happen to the folk school summer program. I told them that much of the monies in the grant would pick up costs for the folk school, staff and me. I also knew that the church's commitment to donate thousands of dollars was contingent on my getting the daycare grant. I wasn't sure I could carry on without the grant. I would check with Mr. Hook and see if there was enough money to run a summer program.

After the meeting disbanded, I went up to Bonnie, Peggy, Cecil, and told them that I had the utmost respect for them. I was sorry that it ended this way. They seemed confused. They said they were sorry, too. They hoped I'd stay.

"Can't you do the summer program?" Peggy asked.

"I hate to say it Peggy, but I need a job. I can't live on nothing," I said.

"Well, we'll feed you. Why don't you come up for supper? The kids would love to see you," she said.

I said I couldn't. I had finals.

"Do stay in touch," she said. "The kids will miss you."

"I'll miss them, too."

As Cecil left, he pulled me aside and said, "Reckon I'll not be seeing you in these parts."

He knew the score. He'd lived in Illinois, Ohio, and Michigan over the years. He knew how you had to have, as my dad said, the bottom line—a salary. I heaved a long sigh, looked back at the Folk Center, the plowed hillside, the hills beyond, and nodded my head. "This may end it for me. I'll see if I can make something happen, but it doesn't look promising."

He patted me on the back. "Come by. I'll give you something to take your mind off all this. I think you may need it."

He drove off in his black Lincoln. I chatted with Marie and admitted that I had no backup plan. She shook my hand and told me that she was here and to come by any time.

When I drove up Cecil's driveway, he was on the porch. He invited me up and we drank from a pint of moonshine. He showed me his pistol and revolver collection and rifles—twenty of them—and told me, as he had before, that, should there ever be an invasion I should hightail it right to the hollow.

He told me that he trusted me. "As for J.B., well, don't put a mind to him," he said. "He'd block anything good from happening there. He was always up to no good." As I left, he walked to the dump beside his yard, out past his eight-hundred-pound pigs. We stood there talking and looking over a ridge to the valley where the main road cut through the trees. I wondered what we were doing there when he said, "Wanted to give you a gift," and bent over, lifting up an old tire, and reached into a little chamber under it, to fetch for a fifth of moonshine.

"You take this and forget about today. You need to move on. I suspect that's what you'll do," he said and reached out his hand to shake mine. We stood there, hands clasped, for a moment. He stepped back and patted me on the shoulder again.

As I walked to the car, I said, "See you."

"Yep," he said as he headed up to the porch.

My chances at working in Cross Creek were over. I had alienated nearly everyone. Only days after I got back to Nashville, I informed Helen that the board had rejected the grant. Linda suggested that we try to get a grant for the Clearfork region and not keep it under the aegis of the folk school. I didn't want to write another proposal if it meant writing as I had about a people I respected because of who they were, not because of their poverty. I called Mr. Hook and told him about the grant. He extended his regrets and said he'd talk with the church council. Later in the week, he called back. I could tell by his voice that it wasn't good news. They rejected the funding plan. He told me to come by any time. I told him I would.

My father called and asked if I'd made any decisions about work. I lied to him that I was still exploring getting a daycare program started. He offered to set up some interview with some of his friends. His voice had a kind, sympathetic tone to it.

"It's what I did for your brother. It may help. You might be surprised and find something you like to do," he said. "You want me to see what I can do?"

"Go ahead," I said. He may have sensed my futility. "I'll let you know when I will be home."

"Outstanding," he said. "I think there are some real opportunities for you!"

When I hung up the phone, I stared out the window. The traffic moved steadily down the street. People going to work. People doing what they had to do to make a living. People like me. But somehow it didn't feel right. Not for me. Yet I didn't know what to do.

Exam preparation and writing my final thesis took up my time. I expected that I'd never hear from anyone in Cross Creek again. I was surprised to get a flood of letters from my friends in the hollow, particularly the kids. Of course, I wrote back.

A few days after I returned to Nashville, I wrote Otrel and told him what had happened. I wished he'd been at the board meeting. He might have turned it around. But he was on the road. I told him that I was devastated by how everyone seemed to turn on me and asked if he still supported me. I told him that, much as we had planned for him to teach guitar at the summer folk school and even though I had told him I had money, I didn't have it right now and might not have it ever. He wrote back a beautiful letter, one that he had worked hard on. He wanted me to realize that I had missed something that I should have known: that people did love me and wanted me to stay. Cross Creek was unlike anything I'd ever experienced before, and, most likely, would ever experience again. The people—Peggy, Bonnie, Cecil, and Otrel—wanted me to be part of their family, to be included in their lives. It was as if they were calling me home. I wasn't just a friend.

After I read his letter, my heart broke. He felt like family too, some integral part of who I was and, even if I could not afford to go back, I'd always feel that we belonged together.

This is what he wrote.

Dear Jason,

I will answer your letter I received the other day and I was glad to hear from you.

To let you no a little about my profile and to tell you I really like you as a friend. I am a friend to you, Jason, and I don't give a dam what you are that is your besness and I ant asking nobody for cherty and I talk to a lady in Knoxville and she informed me some informed some money is floating around somewhere or another and that we could make a comment and get money for facilities that is the way money progetes come off. So that way you and I and no one else on some bored has to spend any money. But I do not want to get down on my knees to beg any one because I don't have to fret we have a show date at the High school in November. By the way Erling was up the house the other day and jason, he says, is a friend I will say nothing but this I thin you are a fine boy and the family does to and watch and don't get into anything deep because this good old Unites States is good to ones it is free. We have our laws and we have our reading. We don't have to give nobody nothing unless we want to and for God Sacke lets keep it that way.

I ant got much education but I ant nobdy dam fool. Pleas do not quiston what I have said and I like you and I waont hav you feeling bad for nothing in this world so that bring us back to the music I like to play but I like to get paid of course to me it works just like another job.

Nobody in this world get something for nothing. Bill and Bobby caome to see me that other night to my family you is the best people we have every knone and don't say your arent coming to see Otreal, just say I am going home case when you are at my house its home case we like you like children. Jason I have a son about your age and he in VitNom and I would love something here worth it that he is dying against VitNon and I wont think that you would let me down and that is why I say you are my friend and we cant be friends in heavin if ther is sech place and sometimes I dout think ther is so I guss I am fetter find some thine but I don't mean to be ungodly but I would like to be able to pick my goalie and just go and play and sing and tell jokes and stories for always but I cant because have to make money so then you see why. But I wasn't asking you as you said in your letter for anything I am sorry you mis under stood the more money than you and I could get floating around some where now I know how to get it so good by and good luck come when you can and stay as long as you like.

Sined Otrel Hamton and Family

I wrote him back and thanked him for offering me a place to stay. In his heart, he would have taken me back just as, I was sure, when his son came back from Vietnam, he would welcome him in his home. When you have very little, it's strange how much you can provide and care for those in need. Peggy and Bonnie took me in, fixed me meals, gave me a bed to sleep in, and never gave it a second thought. They didn't want to know what school I had attended, what pedigree I had, what I planned to do with my life. They accepted me at face value and told me I was family.

Peggy's kids wrote me letters to come home and stay with them for the Fourth of July and that there was a bed waiting. Bobby talked about playing touch football and how I taught Milton, Eddie Terry, Rondel Hatfield and him to toss the ball right. He told me how, he fell asleep in class and the principal gave him five licks. And how Lois, his sister had a new car, a 1963 Chevrolet convertible, red with a black stripe, and how I could ride in it. And how after school he shot twelve squirrels with his new rifle which his mom would make into a good meal. And how he wondered if I saw Johnny Cash 'cause he liked "Ring of Fire." And how Erling came up to visit with O.J., a 6'2", 296 pound defensive end from Kansas State who kicked a soccer ball all the way across the road to the folk school cabin. And, he wondered too, if I had a girlfriend, and if I did, what she looked like: Does she have black hair? Is she tall but not too tall, about 5'8"? Skinny not fat; but not too skinny, around about 110 pounds? He told how Erling and his uncle Bobby walked around the folk school property, and Bobby asked where they were going to build the next cabin this summer, and how Erling said he would like to have one built by the spring so they could have water for the summer vacation, if he came up there. He wanted to know if I was coming up soon so I could help because he was having trouble with science. He was going rabbit hunting on Saturday night. They only shot one and cleaned it and put in the freezer so when I came in I could eat it. I would like rabbit.

He signed it, "Peace brother."

I wondered what Erling was doing in Cross Creek and whether he knew about the fiasco with the grant proposal. I wrote him, telling him the program was off, but got no reply.

Bobby's sister Lois wrote a surprising letter, given how, that first year, I'd insulted her belief in God. She told me about her new car; about how I'd helped her with her poetry; that she didn't want to kill herself any more but wondered if I ever did; then told about her new nephew; and then

You a sweet guy Jason what you said about being born when you met the

282

Lesters was really great, you're Beautiful Jason, you should always be so kind. It looks good on you. You know when I first met you I thought I wasn't going to dig you at all. You seemed so uptight like you were afraid. I thought you would be so snobbish, but you aren't. Maybe you were scared anyway you turned out to be a pretty nice guy. That's a compliment.

She was right. When I first arrived, I was frightened. I thought that I would never fit in. But I fell in love with them because they were genuine people. Lois talked about what was on her mind, not scripted to fit some polite formula of what you should or should not say. Lois talked about religion, about her wondering if God would accept her if she changed her religion from Baptist to Catholic. She wanted to know. I told her God was more interested in how caring a person was than what church the person was affiliated with.

As the letters kept coming, I realized that my two years at Cross Creek had changed me more than I'd changed anyone or anything in the hollow. I was part of their lives.

I wondered how often someone in Glen Brook bares their soul? I suspected, not often. Yet for those in Cross Creek, with no fancy clothes to hide behind, no elaborately decorated homes to blend into, no strict codes of propriety, they spoke from the heart and they listened when you said what concerned you.

In one last letter, Lois invited me to visit any time. She said that Peggy, her mom, said to tell me that she would really be glad if I could come and not to worry about how much I would eat. She added that Peggy had thought about the board meeting and regretted that she hadn't said something. The close of the letter said

I hope you can spend Xmas here also it would really be great. We could go sledding. Winter in the country is a real blast. You could almost lose your heart to the world if you wanted to.

I *had* lost my heart up there in the mountains. I wished I could find a way back. I wept as I read that line over and over. "You could almost lose your heart to the world if you wanted to." I wanted to. But how?

I figured that maybe Erling was staying with Marie if he was still up in Cross Creek. On a whim, I called Marie. I asked if Erling was there. He was. She told me how sorry she was that the grant had fallen through. She was checking on some other possibilities. She said people had calmed down and wanted me back. J.B. had gotten in a fight with Cecil, threatened him, and Cecil told him off. J.B. quit the board and left the next day for Chicago. No one had heard from him.

When Erling got on the phone, he asked if I was angry. I told him that I wasn't. But I was disappointed and discouraged. "That seems to be my nature," I told him. "I'm slow to hate the people who have wronged me."

"Not a bad trait," Erling said. "But it must be hard for you."

"Yes. It is."

"I wonder if I'm the only one who cares about the loss of the grant. Everyone seems to think it's no big deal."

"Oh, they *do* care," Erling said. "They're mad at J.B. now. I told them that the grant, by and large, was a good one. You may have added too much flowery language here and there. But it was good. And I let them know J.B. was way out of line."

"Thanks. But the grant deadline is gone, so it's dead."

"Too bad. You coming up for the summer?"

"No," I said. "I'd love to. But I need to find work."

"Hope you're not running back to dad," he said.

"Lay off, Erling."

"You're not, are you?"

"Not sure. I hope not. I really don't know what to do next. I want to get some distance from it before I make any decisions," I said.

There was a pause at the end of the line. "Jason," he said, "that distancing may not be the best thing to do. It comes from your middle-class world where everything is viewed at arm's length. I know you don't think much of religion, but I wonder when you will have a clear understanding that it's God who sustains us. You and I aren't the authors of compassion or concern, because we're dependent on this worldly hope. Remember: 'There are men who cannot be bought' which is to say that there are men who affirm God before they put their hope in others or in institutions. Maybe you need to step back and reconsider what your own faith is grounded in."

I thanked Erling for his advice but told him I didn't need God's help. I needed to wallow in defeat and let it settle in, before I moved on. Maybe this was the abyss he had spoken about years ago. If it was, I was certainly deep inside it and I didn't see any way out.

Before he hung up, he invited me again to the Joseph Campbell Folk School in North Carolina. I thanked him. Yet I had to come to terms with what my father had said: the almighty buck came first. I had to find a job. To be sure, the invitations from the hollow were appealing. I knew I had a home there. The option to return there to live, and find odd jobs was attractive. Yet the rejection still stung.

With the daycare project out of the picture and no other option except bumming a bed at Linda's apartment, staying in Nashville was no longer viable. I needed to shed my role as a student, take the professors' concepts and see what, if anything, applied to the real world. I'd already given up the notions about God being "greater than that which can be conceived." It didn't matter that I could analyze different theological arguments and explain the nature of religion and the imagination. What mattered now was a job.

One evening, while we were getting stoned, Linda asked me to show her some of my books that I'd stored at her house. I pulled out texts on systematic theology, sociology, and ethics. She paged through them.

"Do these make sense to you?" she asked. "They're so abstract."

"They do," I said.

She laughed. "I work with kids. They're concrete. They want to know if you love them, when the snack is served, and if you can soothe a cut."

"They may be better off that way," I said.

Linda nestled next to me. "I'm sorry the proposal didn't work out," she said. "You seem down. Is there anything I can do?"

"Yeah. Pass me the joint!"

Later, we went to bed together. Her hands sliding under my shirt and mine loosened her bra; one-piece of clothing after another dropped to the floor. She took my erection in her mouth; I nibbled on her breasts. Neither of us spoke. Our hands, our mouths did the talking. We made love twice. We held onto each other; the failed proposal, the months of work, the rising hopes, and the plans for being together all fell away in our long embrace. The next morning, a bit uneasy about our making love, I was quiet as I drank my coffee. If I didn't say anything, we could pretend it never happened. She sat across from me, dipping a doughnut in her coffee.

We drove to Helen's office. She asked me to tell her what happened. We wondered if the proposal could be modified and, perhaps, Linda could do something with it. Mostly, Helen wanted me to know that it was a good, solid proposal. She didn't want me to take the blame for what happened. In the end, Helen decided that the grant would have to be entirely rewritten for submission next year.

When we got back to Linda's apartment later in the afternoon, she offered me coffee and a bagel.

"Want to resubmit it?" she asked.

"No," I said.

She leaned over the table, pressing her hands in front of her.

"Can we talk about last night?" she asked.

"Sure," I said.

"Well, what happened?" she asked.

I sipped my coffee. The steam blocked my view of her. I set it down.

"Nothing," I said. "We made love."

"Huh," she said. "That's it?"

I smiled. "Guess so."

She furrowed her brow. "It was more than that to me. I mean, it blew my mind. When I am logical about it, I think, 'What blew your mind about that? When people go to bed, what happens happens.' Not that I didn't enjoy it very much. I guess it was just one of those things I never thought would happen, not between us. I remember how quiet we were this morning and I wonder if I freaked you out or something?"

"Well, I admit I was," I said. "I mean I didn't expect it. I told you about Ann. How mixed up I am about her. I still feel committed to Ann, so it freaked me out that I could just do it. And yet, what can I say?"

"You don't need to say anything. It was fine. I'm fine. We'll let it be," she said. She reached across the table and pressed her hand to mine.

"Thanks," I said.

Later that night, when I was curled up on her couch, she came into the room and asked if she could sit on the floor beside me and just talk.

"Something wrong?" I asked.

"I'm feeling very blue today. Really kind of deep purple like a bruise. Can't remember if I ever told you about colors: it's like one of my ways of understanding what's going on. Anyway, I'm purple. I got this thing about purple. It's not that it's royal. It's more that it's a mood, a feeling that that pulls me into it, so I'm surrounded by it and dwelling inside this purple haze."

"Are you stoned?" I asked.

She slapped my leg. "No, silly. Do you have a favorite color?"

"Blue, a deep ocean blue," I said. "I like the feel of it; it's watery and quiet."

"Nice," she said, putting her head on my leg.

We didn't want to admit it, but we both wanted to make love again. She became quiet and I did, too. Later, she slipped beside me on the couch. We made love again, this wordless drowning in flesh on flesh, the blue into purple, the purple into blue, that seemed to absolve all the loss each of us was feeling.

In the morning, Linda went to work. She had left a purple card with a note with one word, "Lovely." I sat at the kitchen table, feeling thankful for her, how easy it was with her. I pondered what I could do with my life. I couldn't return home. I had no job. I didn't want to go east to Ann. My education, much as I enjoyed the intellectual challenge, was useless. I had to give up academia and the world I'd found in Cross Creek. I had to find something else to do. But what?

I was used to being a student, thinking about one text for weeks, talking with others about its meaning, being totally absorbed in thought. Moving my attention to a regular job would be hard to do. Maybe I'd become like other people: I might use clichés, believe newsmen spoke the truth, subscribe to TV Guide, become enamored with a candidate, transform into a regular guy, a public figure, holding a respectful job and making a living. Maybe I'd have to go home, find a job there. That seemed the only option. But I dreaded it.

To me, the problem was that I had no idea what my new face would look like.

Avoidance

Don Beisswenger, my advisor, requested a meeting on the following Wednesday to help me plan for my future. He encouraged me to write down my positive attributes and accomplishments beforehand and suggested the arts.

That seemed unlikely to me. I knew no one in the arts. I wasn't an artist; I couldn't draw or paint. It was more likely that I'd have to work in a church. But I hated churches; most gave me the creeps. I was open to anything. I desperately needed work.

I never made the list Don requested. Instead, I made love with Linda, smoked dope, drank Jack Daniels on ice, and read Whitman. Time ground to a halt. I knew I should call my dad back and tell him when I'd return so he could set up the interviews. *Should, should, should* rattled in my head. I did nothing.

My lack of direction muddled me. When I had to be somewhere, it meant that I had to be something. But when I had no place to go and nothing to do, I could be anything. I could focus only on one thing: the moment.

I felt I should be anxious about being directionless. But becoming anxious and upset was difficult when I spent sweltering afternoons naked in an icy bathtub with my lover.

The weekend before I met with Beisswenger, I made one last excursion east. The heat became unbearable, so Linda and I drove to the Blue Ridge Mountains to find a waterfall in some hidden valley. It sounded like the one Erling had never found. We planned to camp out for the night, skinny dip in the stream, and make love on blankets under the stars.

On our drive to Boone, North Carolina, Linda told me about her two friends, both of whom starred in a production of the Daniel Boone story at an outdoor theater. One was a dancer. She wasn't sure I'd like him. He was a little immature. But the other, a woman, was a wonderful singer and very thoughtful. Linda grew up with her and was her best friend.

She described to me the best waterfall that she'd ever seen, a secret waterfall, one she used to go to as an undergraduate. She'd sit under it and bathe in its clear water. People skinny dipped there. It was like a little Eden.

Her old Ford roared across the state. Like a hound on a good scent, it wound down a highway to a country road, to a gravel road, to where North Carolina intersected with Tennessee and Virginia. Once in North Carolina, we drove down unpaved roads by furrowed fields to a muddy road with a bleached-out sign that said, faintly, "Waterfall."

The closer we came to her secret place, the more she talked about it. Most of the time no one cared if you skinny dipped. She figured we could sit around naked, get stoned, take walks, and make love. It would be our own haven. I liked the idea of one last fling before I applied for some job. She held my hand tightly and pulled me close to her.

"This will be so much fun. I've fantasized about doing this. But now it's real. I'm so glad I met you," she said, barely able to contain herself. She parked the car under a huge poplar. We trekked down a wooded path, mist hanging in the air. I could hear a low rumbling sound. Linda cried out, "Hear that? Not far ahead! It has a neat basin at the bottom, a little pool where we can hang out. Clear as glass. You'll love it!"

We walked for a mile, heading toward a deep roar that intensified the closer we came to it. The ground shook. When we came to a bluff, she took me by the arm.

"Close your eyes," she said. We stepped forward. She cried, "Shit!"

Instead of a stream and a basin, we were looking at huge falls. A torrent of water cascaded over a rock outcropping and splattered on the basin below. It sent up torrents of water that rose thirty feet high. It was impossible to hear. Her lips were saying, "Oh, my God" over and over.

We climbed down twenty feet to gaze at the middle of the falls. A five-foot thick column of water crashed by us. We held onto one another; the needle-sharp spray drenched us and chilled us to the bone. We couldn't get closer without risking our lives. I shivered and pointed up, signaling that I had to get out of there. She followed, looking back several times. We retreated to the car to warm off.

I held her while she wept over her dream being shattered.

"It's awful. What are we going to do?" she asked as if someone had died.

"Another time," I said. "Another summer."

We changed into dry clothes and considered getting a room at a local motel, but decided to drive to the outdoor theater where we had one of the staff cabins reserved.

—

Once we picked up the tickets her friend had left, we went to the cabins that her friend Robert told her were allotted actors for the summer. Robert, a tall redheaded dancer, greeted us and invited us to his cabin. His roommate, a lanky guy, jumped off his bed and offered it to us, saying he had to do some errands. We talked for an hour until Robert told us that he needed to get in costume.

"You will be surprised," he said. "You will not believe how macho I am." He lowered his voice. "I'm a fierce wilderness guy." He struck a pose with his arms flexed like a weightlifter.

The production, a musical, presented Daniel Boone as a great explorer and Indian fighter and as a family man, who wanted to do his best for his wife and children. In jeans and red suspenders, Robert joined a chorus of dancers. They were mountaineers in one scene, British soldiers in another, and Indians in another. In the final scene, they were pioneers heading west. Leaping, stalking, jumping, and pirouetting, he had amazing height to his jumps and an animated face. My eyes were riveted by him.

After the show, Robert invited us to a party. Linda's girlfriend, also a cast member, planned to be there, so we went. The party was held in a lounge inside one of the cabins. Cast members had gathered in a semi-circle. Robert sat beside his roommate on the floor. He looked at me and patted the floor next to him. Linda grabbed my arm and said, "I hope you don't mind but once Tracy comes, I'd like to spend some time with her. We haven't seen each other in years."

"Go right ahead," I said.

"You're a peach. Robert will take care of you. I already told him to watch out for you," she said, kissing me on the cheek.

At the party, the man playing Daniel Boone, a large stocky man, dominated the conversation. He was working on a Ph.D. in theater and aspired to be a director. We sat around him as he talked about his career to date. His girlfriend sat at his feet. He even called on people, asking questions about their lives and conferring his blessings. I wondered if everyone was as impressed with him as he was with himself. Linda nudged me and whispered, "Why doesn't someone tell him to shut up?"

Robert leaned over and whispered back, "His mother owns the theater."

The actor must have heard Robert because he pointedly asked Robert what he planned to do with his life.

Robert stood up, his drink in his hand, and answered, "I'm never going to grow up."

"You must be kidding," the Daniel Boone said.

"No, I'm not," Robert replied and jumped into the air, landing a foot from "Daniel." "Like Peter Pan, I'll be a child forever," and flapped his hands at the actor, who snorted, "You're such a fag!"

"Daniel" glared at Linda and me. We'd been laughing, delighted with Robert's performance.

"Grow up!" "Daniel" shouted.

Extending his arms and flapping them at "Daniel," Robert called out to us, "Come along Tinkerbell and Robin," and skittered out of the room on his tiptoes. Unable to stop laughing, we picked up our drinks and followed Robert. He'd gone to the refrigerator to get another beer. While we were there, Linda's friend arrived, apologizing for being late. "They want me to do a solo dance number. Had to rehearse."

After quick introductions, Linda told me that she would come back later and they left. Robert invited me to his room where we drank and talked. Despite his histrionic flair, he actually worked hard and planned to get his B.A. in the arts. He lounged on the bed; I sat in a wooden chair by the window. His roommate dashed in and leaned over the bed and whispered something in Robert's ear. Robert said, "How lovely," and kissed his friend on the lips and, feigning shyness, raised his eyebrows at me. When his roommate left, he asked seriously, "I hope you don't mind. We're—you know..."

I guessed the obvious, "Gay?"

"You have it, dearie," he said. "Would you like another beer?"

I said I would and asked what was going on with his roommate. As it turned out, he had a hot date with one of the leads. We drifted off to another room where two guys were in bed together, one lying on top of the other, completely clothed.

"I hope we're not disturbing you," Robert said to them.

"Oh, don't mind us. We're just rehearsing a scene," the man underneath said.

When we got back to his room, Robert told me to get on his bed. It was much more comfortable than the wooden chair. He would use his roommate's bed. Tired from the long day of driving, I dozed off and on as we talked some more. He wanted to find out what I did or planned to do with my life.

"Oh, dearie," he said. "You are just a sleepy-pie. Let me give you a massage. You can drift into la-la land," and, without asking permission, hopped on my bed, told me to take off my T-shirt and pressed me face down on the mattress. He clambered on top of me and began kneading my shoulders, pushing with the heel of his hand. I melted into his touch. After swooning for some time, just giving into him, he had me turn over and, sitting by my head, rubbed my face and cheek and neck. His crotch was nestled around my head and I could feel that he was aroused.

"You're a lovely boy," he said.

"So are you," I replied. "You touch like an angel."

"An angel?" he queried. "I'm more the satyr type."

I laughed and smiled up at his face. He leaned over and kissed me. With one move, he stretched beside me, his hand rubbing my chest and my legs. I put my hand on his cheek. He kissed me again. Before long, he slipped out of his pants, shirt and socks as quickly as if he were doing a costume change. He helped me out of my clothes. I surrendered to his hands.

We stripped off our underwear. He guided me to his lovely member, erect and proud. He held mine in his mouth. A ceiling fan swept air across us. I don't think either of us thought much about how it happened, but soon, moaning, we gave each other pleasure and fell asleep in each other's arms.

The door groaned. A light came on. I heard my name, "Jason." Disentangled from Robert's legs, I sat up. Linda stood a few feet from us, agape.

Shit, I thought and tried to wrestle myself out of Robert's arms. He awoke and turned around, sitting upright, looking at his friend Linda.

What could he say? I thought.

Not bothering to cover up, he stood up, walked right up to Linda, folded her in an embrace, and said, "Darling, no one owns anyone."

She wept; he patted her back. I scrambled to find my pants, underwear, shirt, socks, and shoes. He comforted her. "Hey. He's a lovely guy, your Jason. He's still a man. I only borrowed him. Look, here he is: dressed, ready to be with you. I bet he'll please you as much as he did me."

"Oh, Robert," she said, laughing. "You always know the exact wrong thing to say!"

I came over to them. He stepped back. I hugged her. She pulled back and stared at me.

"Do you know what's going on?"

"It's all right," I said. "I just drank a little too much."

"Is that all?" she asked.

"That's all," I replied.

"You think I'm going to believe that?"

"Believe what you want." I was aggravated that she'd become upset and equally perplexed how easily I'd fallen for Robert.

Robert stepped back from us and did a quick tap dance. "Liquor is the ruin of many a man," he said, waving his underwear over his head before he hopped into them, and twirled around us, arms extended.

"Robert, you can make light of anything," she said.

"It's the Peter Pan in me," he said, offering her a beer. She took it.

She turned to me. "You love me?" she asked.

"Of course."

"Okay," she said. I kissed her on the mouth.

The three of us sat on his bed, drinking.

At one point, he said, "You know we could do a threesome!"

Linda shook her head. "Not with you Robert. I'm not your type."

"You're right," he said. "But Jason here, he's a good little starter kit and you never can tell. It may be another first!"

She pushed him back on the bed and held him by the arms. "You know, you drive me crazy," she said.

"It's because I love you," he said.

"I know," she said and let him go. He kissed her on the cheek and flopped against the wall behind the bed.

"You two love birds need some sleep," he said.

We had a room of our own. I took her to bed. She held onto to me all night. In the morning, I made love to her. It was not the same as it had been with Robert. I felt more like a man giving the performance of his life. And I enjoyed it. But with Robert, it felt as if I were floating.

On the long drive back, we didn't talk as much as we usually did. I'd shattered some illusion of love that we'd fallen into since the daycare fell apart. Back in Nashville, we slept together for several nights. We made love. It was all right. She had to go back to work. She had a busy schedule. I knew that I needed to get a job. Maybe Wolfe was wrong. Maybe you had to go home again. That's where the jobs were. I didn't know what to do. I knew that I needed to get out of Nashville.

Unexpected

I aimed the Volvo east on Route 40, the same route I traveled to Cross Creek. It was the road that, had the whole enterprise not blown up in my face, I might have traveled again. This time, I was going further east: past Knoxville, past the Cumberland Mountains, where Tennessee, North Carolina and Virginia converge, along the Blue Ridge Parkway to the Cumberland Notch, where the whole eastern valley spreads out in West Virginia. I was headed to Nitrate, a town north of West Virginia's Capitol, Charleston, right along the Kanawha River.

Mr. Beisswenger had located a temporary summer job for me so I could sort out what I was going to do.

This turn of events came after I had returned to Nashville with Linda. The dorms had closed for the summer. Linda told me to find another place. She needed time to think. Mr. Beisswenger let me sleep at his house the night before the meeting.

He had a "United Nations family"—two of his own biological children, a boy and girl, both blonde; one Native American child, one African American, one Asian child, and one child from India. We ate dinner at a large picnic table in the kitchen. His wife, Margaret, managed the dinner crew: one set the table, one brought the serving bowls, one said grace, one cleared, one washed, and another dried. After dinner, we played board games—Scrabble for the older ones and Candyland for the younger ones.

The next morning, I met Mr. Beisswenger in his office. He sat across from me in a large arm chair. I sat on a paisley sofa. Posters graced his walls: Gandhi in his white khadi wrap; Dr. Martin Luther King, Jr. We chatted for several minutes. He told me to call him Don, wanting to make our meeting informal. I told him what had happened at the folk school.

"Too bad, too bad," he commiserated. "That would have been ideal for a guy like you."

"What do you mean?"

He pursed his lips and screwed them to one side. He took off his glasses and peered at them, rubbing one corner.

"Good question. Let me see how best to say this. You aren't like our typical graduates. They come here with a clear vocational goal: to be a minister, to serve the church or synagogue; or to go on to study and teach theology."

He laughed and leaned back in his chair, propping his feet up on an ottoman.

"Let's face it, your graduate thesis was unconventional: on atheism, a broadside against God and established religion, using Dietrich Bonhoeffer to be sure, but not exactly as he might have wanted to be used. You made a proposal about how to live your life, as he did, "in a world come of age," a world where God isn't necessary. It's not exactly your traditional thesis, given you've spent three years studying the New Testament, Old Testament, ethics and theology, working in a local church, studying pastoral counseling—all preparation to work in the church business directly or indirectly."

I was surprised that he remembered what I had written and interrupted him.

"Did you like my thesis?"

"I'm not sure that I liked it as much as I found it thought provoking but in a good way. It challenged many of the ways I see the world. That's not bad. But let's get back to your next move. You don't seem to fit the mold. You don't exactly seem like long-term ministerial material—at least not now." He furrowed his brow.

"That's true. I'm not the ministerial type," I said. "I never felt as if I fit the mold. I like to study theology. It interests me. But it felt as if everyone who came here wanted to do a job, to make a living. They weren't here to ask questions and to look at the deeper issues in their lives. I'm not interested in a job being some minister of God. That would make me sick. I want to get people to think, to ask questions. I certainly don't have the answers," I said.

"Exactly," he pointed his finger at me. "You don't conform. You'll not—at least not now—be happy in traditional jobs. You need to explore, to find work that will allow you to sink into the muck and slime, as Thoreau said, and find your own answers."

The leaves on the trees out his window rippled with a gust of wind. I studied them. Leaves swirled up and down like fingers at a typewriter. My mind wandered to the afternoons in the Cross Creek cabin where I'd sit and look out the back window at the dusty leaves of the cottonwoods and the small stream down the hillside. Those were peaceful days. I felt at home there.

I felt my legs rocking back and forth and cupped my hands between them as if holding onto something that was slipping away from me.

"Hey. You all right?" Don inquired.

"Sure, sure," I said absently.

"Jason," he asked, "are you aware of your restlessness?"

"I suppose so."

"Do you know what you want to do?"

"My dad wants me to come back to Chicago. He's willing to set up interviews."

"With whom?" Don asked.

"Some of his friends, presidents of big companies like Sears."

"You want to work there?"

"It's a job."

"Is that what you want to do?"

"I suppose. It's the only option I can see right now."

"You serious?"

"Not really. I'd rather be doing something else. I'd rather write. It's sad because I'm not too good at it. But I feel at peace when I do."

"You could find a job as a journalist, but—I am afraid you're right—you don't write like a journalist. In fact, you don't even write like a minister," he chuckled.

"What do I write like?"

"Well, I guess you write like a poet."

"A poet?"

"Yes, you think in metaphors. Erling told me that was one of the reasons he liked you: as he called it, 'the poetic nature of your soul.'"

"Erling never told me that."

"He told me. He said that you're a poet at heart. I think he's right. There's a certain restlessness in you," he said.

"Maybe that's what Erling was driving at," I said, remembering his advice to break loose.

"What'd he say?"

"He said that I should cut loose from my family. I should wander America as he does. But I just can't do that. I want to be able to make a living, to be on my own, and not be beholden to anyone. And, besides, traveling the country—what does that have to do with my finding work and having a career?"

Don rubbed his hands together, his cheeks puffed out, and then quickly expelled air.

"I'm not sure I want to say this. I'm not sure you're ready to hear it. I've never said this to anyone before and it's not exactly good advice. But here goes. What you do for work, Jason, is not very important. Of course—don't get me wrong—you must find work that you believe in and that nourishes you and does some good. But essentially, what you do for work will not be as important as your quest, delving into who you are and what makes the world tick, and writing it down, making sense of it."

It took me a moment to comprehend what he said, but it made sense. I had to find jobs that would allow me to explore and find new ways to see the world. But, even with that understanding, I was stuck: I needed work and needed it now!

I stood up and paced back and forth across the room. When I graduated from Divinity School, I knew that for the first time in my life, I had to make it on my own. I didn't want to go back to school, nor did I want to return to the Chicago area and rely on my father and his connections to get me a job. I had to do that on my own.

Don sensed my frustration. "What's wrong?"

"None of this helps me." I shoved my hands in my pockets and quickened my pacing. "Sure, I'd love to write. But right now, today, I *need* to make money. No one will hire me. I fucked up the one thing I cared about and worked to make happen. I destroyed it. It was mostly because of what I wrote. I need a job and no one is fucking—excuse me—going to hire me because, as you say, 'I want to explore and delve into things.'" I felt steel bands tighten against my skull. I burst out, "That's all bullshit. I'm sorry but that does me no good." I slammed my fist into my head. "Fuck. Fuck, Fuck."

"Stop it!" Don yelled. He grabbed my hands. "Sit down." I sat down for a few minutes, then stood up. He stood beside and continued to probe me about my writing.

"But that's who you are, isn't it?"

"What?"

"The delver and explorer," he said in a calm voice gaged to calm me down. I gazed into my palm which stung.

"Yes, yes, I suppose so," I said. I couldn't figure out what he was driving at.

"Take a seat. You're pacing like a caged lion. Sit down. Let's talk," he told me. I looked at the chair, which was as empty as I felt, went over to it, sat down, and realized that I was crying, tears streaming down my face. Soon enough, I was sobbing, convulsing like a little child.

Don came over to my side and patted me on the back. I felt like an idiot breaking down in front of him.

"There, there. I know it must feel awful to have lost the opportunity in Cross Creek. You loved those people. You loved what you did. They loved you. You know that in your heart."

"I messed up. I shouldn't have let J.B. have anything. He should have never seen the proposal. I should have withheld it and only showed the board a summary. He was a criminal. He screwed me. He screwed their future and I sat back and let it happen," I beat my fist against my forehead and cried out, "Damn. Damn. Damn. I'm such a fuck up!"

Don grabbed my hand and put his hand on my head and rubbed it. My skull felt as if it was going to crack open. "Come on. You don't have to be so hard on yourself. Sure, it could have gone differently. But, give yourself a break. You're new at this. You didn't know. You trusted everyone. That's not such a bad thing: trust. And now you know what we all come to know: trust is something you give in small or large doses, but not everyone is worthy of the gift."

I put my face in my hands and took several long breaths. He was right. The only problem was that I had let others down. I'd failed to see how words on the page are like the words in the Bible for some people. They can hurt as much as a punch in the gut. Marie had told me that the people missed me. But, even with all their wishes for me to come back, why did they vote down applying for the grant? Rather than being an opening up of life, adulthood felt like one door after another slammed in my face.

I heard a soft voice coming from what seemed like a long distance. "Let's leave that for now, Jason. You have to move on. I know it's hard. But you need to find a way. What do you want to do *now*?"

Don was seated across from me again.

"I don't know what I want to do. I don't want to be a minister. I don't want to teach. I can't go into business like my father wants me to do. I can't go to war; it's just impossible. I have more don't-knows than do-knows. I have no idea what to do."

"Jason, what you do is *not* the issue," he said. "Did you hear me? It doesn't matter what you do as much as it matters that you let each job—the work you do—inform your deeper work. You need to have a job. We all do. That's a given. The job in itself will never satisfy you. Do you see that?"

"I don't get it. Why is that? Why can't I just be like other people?"

He took the pipe off his desk, tamped down the tobacco with his thumb, then lit it, puffed on it, and stared out the window.

"You want to know why you're not like other people?"

For a moment, I wanted to say "no" because I thought that he'd sensed, as Will had, that I was different, not like other men. I didn't want someone else to tell me what I didn't want to know. But I also sensed that he knew something else I needed to hear.

"Yes," I said.

"You're different."

"Thanks!" I retorted cynically. "That *really* helps." Inside, I feared for sure that he had sensed that I was mixed up sexually. *How could he know?* I bit my lip.

"But you are!" he insisted.

I didn't want him to say what I feared most, my dreadful secret. *Why did he want to confront me with that?*

"What do you mean?" I pleaded, half-aware that I might be asking for more than I wanted to hear. "What makes me different?"

"You're an artist."

I was shocked, relieved, and flattered all at once. No one had every called me an artist. I'd never seen myself as one.

Confused, yes. Rebellious, yes. A fag, yes. Different, yes. But not an artist.

I had never created anything of any lasting worth—some drawings, several poems, lots of journal entries with my rambling thoughts, many pages filled with laments about my desires, resentments, and fears—but never any art.

I wanted to believe my ears and asked, "I'm an artist?"

"I believe so."

"So what does that mean?"

"You <u>must</u> pursue your art—whatever it will be—throughout your life. You have no choice. That's what's in you. And that means that, as I have said, don't worry about the work. It will come. You're personable. You're articulate. You're skilled. You're sensitive. Let's face it, you're also good looking and that never hurts in our society!"

We laughed, and he went on with his point.

"Find work and do it well, but keep your heart set on the larger calling which is your art."

"You're serious, aren't you?" I asked, disbelieving, yet wanting to hear more.

"Most certainly I am. Do you know what I mean by 'calling?'"

"Not exactly. I find the term weird. Whenever some guys said that 'God called me' I think they're deranged. I imagine God dialing their phone and saying, 'This is God. I'm calling you. Are you there, Jason.' 'Hang on, He's on another line...'"

Amused by my example, Don agreed that, indeed, the term sounded weird, but, as he went onto explain, "A calling at its best is not some voice from some fiery bush calling to us. It's more what's in our own nature—part of us we may not entirely understand but we must honor. It demands that we give ourselves over to it because we have no other choice. It requires that we delve into ourselves to find out what it means and where it is directing us."

He puffed several times on his pipe, tapped it in the ashtray, and put it down.

"I guess the only analogy that I can give is falling in love. I felt, when I saw Margaret for the first time, that I had no choice. And each time we have had a child, the moment I saw them, I fell in love again. They're my calling. This work is part of my calling too, but, if you pressed me, if you wanted to know what I must do, what nourishes my soul, it's being a husband and a father. Did I know that would be my calling when I was young? No. Did I fight against it as a young man? Yes. I was ambitious and competitive. I thought I should make big money. Be a professor. Write articles. Publish books. And move up the academic ranks. But, after I met Margaret and I started learning more about myself, I realized that family was my reason for being. As you may see from my work with students, creating family is what I do at work and at home too. For you, I think it will be the art."

He stopped and let what he said sink in and then continued.

"And, too, as you find your way with it, the relationships like with Erling and the people of Cross Creek will allow you to find your voice, a way to express yourself. You will eventually find a family of artists. Until then, from what I know about artists, it will be lonely. And you must find your own way. It's not easy. But one thing is for sure: if you deny the artist in you, you'll never be happy."

I wanted to ask him more questions, but he looked at his watch. I knew that he had another appointment. He moved to the side of his desk. His demeanor changed. He took on an official air.

"Let's get down to business. You need work and I think I have something that will tide you over." He picked up a piece of paper with a telephone number and a name. "Reverend Robert J. Highbottom, First Methodist Church. Nitrate, West Virginia."

"With a name like that, I'm not sure I can keep a straight face if I met him."

Don chuckled. "You'll manage. He's a person, after all. Despite the name, he's a Vanderbilt graduate, a respected minister and he is coming here with his family for a month in a post-graduate program we offer each summer. He needs someone to be an interim minister, take care of the church, do services while he is gone. They provide room and board and a good salary."

"Being a minister?" I exclaimed. "Being a fucking *minister*? No way!" I shoved the paper back to his desk.

Expressionless, he picked up the paper, "I wouldn't be so hasty." He pressed the paper back to me. "Jason. It's *only* a job. Work. Do you hear me? Work. It's not a life sentence. You'll not die. You did an internship at a church. You survived. It will get you on your way. Give him a call. I've told him about you."

As June bled into July, my money would run out. I had to make that call. It was a step. A job. I'd have to find some clear direction. This was like a stopover on a long flight across the country.

"You going to make that call?" he asked.

I didn't like the idea of being an interim minister, but it was an opportunity that I had to accept. I took the sheet of paper, folded it, and told him that I would think about it.

He squinted, "Think about it?"

I smiled, "All right, all right. I'll call him."

"There, you've got it. You're on your way. It's not a life-long commitment. It's a stepping stone. In time, you'll find another and another and so it goes," he said, grabbing me by the shoulder as we walked to the door. He shook my hand. "Keep in touch."

"I will," I said and headed to the apartment, which, I knew would be empty since Linda was at work. Over the past few weeks, the other guys had found jobs. I called Linda at work to tell her about the job. She said, "Hey, it's something, and something's better than nothing." It was true. I wrote letters to Erling and Ann. I wrote a longer letter to Marie and Peggy, and asked her to pass the word to the other members of the board that I had a job. After that, I had to write the most difficult letter—to my parents.

I wrote my parents to inform them that I'd not be coming home. My father had called to let me know that he had set up job interviews with several of his friends—Mr. Cain, chairman of the Board of Commonwealth Edison and Mr. Collins, president of Sears and Roebuck. He expected me to be home on time to do the interviews. I needed to spell out how the daycare program had fallen apart and what my plans were. But I also needed to let him know that I wasn't coming home.

Since my conversation with Don, I'd given some thought to what it meant to be an artist and at least how it clarified why I felt as I did. I knew I was most happy when I had a pen in my hand. What I hadn't clearly understood is how my choice to be an artist justified my breaking with my father and his hopes for my future. Rightfully, I should let him know what I was thinking. I knew that could be a problem. I wanted to be as matter-of-fact as possible. I knew that's what made most sense to him.

Dear Mom and Dad,

After considerable time, the ending has come. Government funds will not be allocated for the daycare and summer programs. The Cross Creek board withdrew its support. I knew this, to be honest, weeks ago.

I've spent time deciding upon a direction. Several options were open to me. Some demanded both a clarity and ambition that I don't have any more. I don't want to apply for an 8-5 job, to feel that I'm like everyone else just struggling to make money, or, as you say Dad, "contributing" to the GNP, or some variation on that general theme.

That wasn't a good beginning. I had to be more positive. I needed to state my position.

I have met with an advisor who helped me determine, given my education, my job options. I do appreciate, Dad, your offering to have me talk to your friends. Instead, I have accepted an interim minister's job for 8 weeks in Nitrate, West Virginia. There I hope I can write or work on my writing and get away from Nashville, (escape, really) from the failure of the Cross Creek projects. I can also get away from the ambition that controlled my earlier years—to be a big success and to make lots of money. Perhaps, to gain some insights into myself and who I am as an artist.

It isn't that I wish to deny your concern for my welfare or your concern that I be happy and successful. It's much more basic. I must be alone to determine the talents I have as an artist. e.e. cummings said there are three types of persons— artists, merchants and warriors. If you're an artist, then you must focus on your craft in order to be as creative as you can. If you're a warrior or merchant, you must compete against others or external challenges to show your mettle.

Each person must develop a set of skills and a reliable stock of knowledge to do his work. An artist is dependent on his own internal structure, and a shifting stock of knowledge that he must draw on in whatever art form he has chosen as his life work.

That is one way to say that my ambitions have more to do with my desire to be an artist than any desire to defy you. I have chosen a different career path.

But for you and me, Dad, the differences are more than a career path. It has to do with our beliefs about what is of value in this world. Once, after I wrote to you from college, the day after Dr. King's assassination, I said some things I believe about civil rights, not to argue with you, but to state my position. Afterward, my brother Jack called me to tell me that you were upset, and went on to inform me that you didn't particularly care what I thought. You were interested in what I did, who I dated, and how I planned to make a living. My thoughts I could keep to myself. I could accept that something was wrong with what I said, but I couldn't abide the option being given secondhand.

I put my pen down. What was I trying to do? Complain that Dad was the way he was? I had to take a different tack. Dwelling on the past would do no good unless I could explain why it bothered me.

I knew you wanted me to have freedom to do what I want, but that freedom had a price tag. If I dared to violate what you thought was right, I was cut off, left on my own. Back then, I followed my brother's advice and kept my mouth shut.

Later that summer, we talked, and you said, "Do what you like, son, but don't bother telling me what you think. Quite frankly, it upsets me. Your mother and I are set in our ways and have been as good as we can to you."

What you said was true. I felt, too, that I shouldn't communicate something about why I was doing what I did and what led me to go to Divinity School and to take poetry courses there. Literature and writing, although things you may value in your own way, are only secondary concerns to you. But for me, they are primary. You don't associate with writers; they aren't part of your life. Back when Jack was writing in college, he once told me tearfully that "Dad doesn't even care that I write short-stories. All he cares about is that I make a good living."

He was right, but, equally, I thought that he was wrong. How can one care about something that you know little about as a career? All the people you know are successful business people, who make a living selling products and making profits. You don't know any artists or writers. It seems in this country that the arts exist in their own world and big business exists in another. They might as well be on separate continents and speaking separate languages.

Years later, Jack chose working at Sears as a salesman, a career which pleased you. He has common ground with you. He's becoming, as you have told me, a good businessman, moving up the corporate ladder as a manager of a division. I'm pleased he's done what you wanted. He's become a success as you understand it.

On the other hand, I know I'm not going to please you because I want to write. A merchant's life isn't in the cards for me. Of course, I'll need to earn a living; I'll have to work hard. So I shall search for jobs that suit a writing life, which is, in a great sense, seeking a life where I can search for a form of expression. I do realize that all jobs are a form of expression, but few jobs demand that the end product of one's work and the profits of the work remain inside oneself, not in monetary satisfaction in external sales and profits.

How, then, do I find a common ground with you? I'm not sure. Maybe it's not for me to decide completely, nor for you. I must be certain that I can be respected for going down my own path....

I found that I couldn't go on. I was befuddled. What I felt stir inside me was an amorphous anger. Furiously, I scratched out a list to sort out what I was feeling:

Jason is in need of recasting
Jason will never please his dad
He isn't the dutiful son
He isn't a clean-cut American youth
He isn't happy with the world
He dislikes chatter and idle talk
He is a longhair most of the year and, no,
doesn't want to get a haircut while at home
He loves his mother and dad
but doesn't care to love someone who
expects him to act ways that are contrary
to what he wants, or needs or values
He doesn't need (ever) to keep up appearances that satisfy
their friends and members of the club...

I found that I could not make that list without second guessing myself, without taking my parents' point of view, without hearing "but all we've done for you" and "how can you say such things?" It was as if they had crawled inside my head and were speaking to me even though they were hundreds of miles away. I kept trying to anticipate what they would say:

Stating these things may sound petty. Why can't I do these things you ask— look as I should, dress as I should, think as I should (at least in public)? Isn't that a small thing to do for my parents who paid for my education, both undergraduate and graduate?

I reply, "Yes, it is." But I add, "What if you reverse the question and look at it from my point of view? Why can't you accept that I am different? Just because I think and feel differently from you does not mean that I'm asking you to think and feel differently than you already do. I only want you to acknowledge that I do. I don't even need to mention my ideas. I just don't want to feel as if you're always trying to keep me in my place.

Yes, I am your son. That's obvious. But how I'm to be and appear isn't under your control. How you come to accept me as I am is under your control, however. The point is that I don't want to wag my tail like our dog Tana because I appreciate all you have done. I just want to be myself and ...

Once again, I found myself writing in circles and threw my pencil across the room. It plinked against the wall and dropped to the couch. I folded up the letter, put it in my journal and left it for another day. For now, I would let them know by phone, a simple call to tell them where I was, where I was going, and what I was doing once I got there. I'd keep it simple.

My parents might not understand what I was about to do—to head off on another voyage to another strange land—any more than I did. But Don had given me a way to think about myself, and, although I hadn't figured out how to broach that with my dad, I had made a decision.

I'd hoped when I came to Vanderbilt to find a new home. I even thought I'd found one in Cross Creek. But I was still a wanderer. That was okay. I was going to stick with my decision not to go back to my parents' home. I would go wherever my next adventure would take me. I remembered what Mr. Hook said about painting, how it provided a refuge from having to make a living. I could also hear Erling, "Good lad," and saw him puffing on his pipe and nodding his head, "That's the way!" I never expected to be like him, to be going into the unknown, making up what to do next. I wanted to call him up and tell him, yes, I'd broken with my past, but I knew that I really hadn't done anything radical. I still hadn't confronted my dad. I had a long way to go to be truly independent. But I could see—and it made me smile—that squirrel in the oak outside my room sitting up, hands together, nodding, and saying, "You're getting the hang of it." I would have to find out what lay in store for me, piece together my fate, and take that next step.

I called Reverend Highbottom. He told me in a booming voice how much he'd heard about me. "Delighted," he said, "simply delighted to have a man of your character working with my church." He invited me to drive over and have dinner with his family. He told me that it was a perfect fit, the type of job that would meet my every expectation: to be an interim caretaker, to lead Sunday service, and work with the church youth. I took down the directions to his house and headed east.

As a former Poet Laureate of Portland, Maine, BRUCE P. SPANG has published a novel, *The Deception of the Thrust*, (2015). He wrote the libretto, *"Charlie!"*, a musical drama about the gay man murdered by three high school boys in Bangor. He's the author of seven books of poetry, including, *Not Just Anybody* (2016), *Boy at the Screen Door* (Moon Pie Press, 2015), *To the Promised Land Grocery* (Moon Pie Press, 2008), *I Have Walked Through Many Lives: Young Voices—Scarborough* (Moon Pie Press, 2009) *The Knot*, (Snow Drift Press, 2005), and *Tip End of Time* (Snow Drift Press, 2004).

He teaches writing at the Osher Lifelong Learning Institute at UNC in Asheville. He lives with his husband, Myles Rightmire, and their four dogs, five parakeets, and three fish in Chandler, NC.

This classic coming of age/quest novel will reward the reader. It ranges in time and place from a young man named Jason's privileged upbringing, to his time in college, to his experiences working and living among people in Appalachia living a hardscrabble life. As momentous events like the struggle for civil rights, the Vietnam War and the draft, and the terrible assassinations of those years unfold, Jason questions the very foundations of his life and struggles with his sexual and political identities. We care about Jason, who is a fully fleshed character. The writing is vivid and the characters are convincing. The historical backdrop is dramatic, but what captures our attention is the very personal story of this intelligent, thoughtful young man.

– Alice Persons, poet and publisher of Moon Pie Press